TOMORROW'S STEADFAST PRAYER

HISTORICAL CHRISTIAN ROMANCE

NAOMI RAWLINGS

TEXAS PROMISE BOOK 4

To my oldest son, Nathanael.

Last year, when I decided to dedicate this book to you, I jotted down a few sentences about hoping you do'd the right thing (like the characters in the novel) and wishing you a bright future, and that was the end.

Then COVID hit our family, and you got sick. Really sick. For months at a time. You couldn't go to school, and if you did drag yourself there, you could barely get work done. We sought doctors and doctors and more doctors. We traveled, then traveled more, then traveled even more. We paid for doctor after doctor with money we had, then with money we'd saved, and finally with money we didn't have at all.

Through everything, the traveling and sickness and lack of money, I watched you strive every day to do right. To get up and keep going and do the hard thing when everything about your life felt impossible and you just wanted to quit.

To be honest, I wanted to quit too.

And so this book is dedicated to you. Because it's about two people who do the right thing in an impossible situation, no matter what it costs them.

Just like you.

Thank you for being so strong.

Love, Mom

DESCRIPTION

The one thing she can't do is fall in love... at least not if she wants to save her sister.

Alejandra Loyola knows she's going to die. If having information about her uncle and cousin's illegal cattle rustling operation isn't enough to get her killed, then snitching on them to the law will surely mean her death—and she's snitched more than once. The only question is, will she be able to see her younger sister provided for before she dies?

When successful Austin lawyer Harrison Rutherford is called back to his home town of Twin Rivers, Texas, after his father falls ill, he finds himself inundated with the burdens of running a large shipping business. The one surprise waiting for him is Alejandra Loyola. The maid who works for him is quiet and sweet. Now if only she trusted him enough to tell him what leaves shadows under her eyes and a haunted look on her face...

But the longer Harrison stays in Twin Rivers, the more something seems amiss. Rustlers have been wreaking havoc on local ranchers for over a year, and Harrison is starting to wonder if the secrets Alejandra is carrying have more to do with his father and the rustlers than he wants to admit.

As the rustling ring become more dangerous, will Alejandra trust Harrison enough to tell him what she knows? Or will the rustlers prove powerful enough to destroy not just the ranches surrounding Twin Rivers, but any hope for a future between them?

From jagged mountains and green river valleys, to cattle ranches and vivid sunsets, Tomorrow's Steadfast Prayer offers a powerful story about love, faith, and doing the right no matter the cost.

PROLOGUE

Twin Rivers, Texas; November 1885

"What do you mean you couldn't get inside the camp?"

In the dimness of the empty guestroom, Alejandra Loyola could barely make out her step-cousin's face, but that didn't stop her from feeling the anger pouring from his gaze. "Leighton didn't invite me back. I can hardly just show up at a Ranger encampment for no reason."

"You should have flirted more."

"I did!"

She sensed more than saw Raul's sneer, and the heat of his breath brushed her face in the darkening room. "Obviously not enough. Maybe I need to send you to a cantina. A few days working on your back would teach you how to handle men better."

She stiffened, her mouth opening in shock as the full meaning of Raul's suggestion soaked into her. Then she drew in a breath and raised her chin. "You know full well your father wouldn't stand for that."

"Pity," Raul spat. "Just imagine all the information I'd have if he'd sent me a decent spy to work with."

"I'm not a spy."

He laughed. "Keep telling yourself that, *mi muñeca.*"

Raul slid something out of his pocket, and the dusky light filtering through the window gave her just a small glimpse of an envelope. "I suggest you find a way to get yourself inside that Ranger camp. If you don't, then you won't be seeing this."

She stared down at the letter, a cold sense of dread snaking through her. "Is that...?"

"From your sister? Yes."

She swallowed. When had Gabriella written? And how had Raul gotten his hands on the letter before she did?

He slid the missive back into his pocket. "Find a way to get inside that Ranger camp."

Her hand crept up to her throat. "What if they won't let me in?"

"Then you won't be getting any more letters from Gabriella."

"You're horrible!"

Raul laughed, the sound taunting in the darkness of the room. "No. I'm doing my job."

As though hearing his laughter from the other side of the wall, a chorus of jeers rose from the next room where Raul's men were finishing up a meal after returning from their most recent foray into Mexico.

Alejandra sniffled, trying to force her mind off Raul's latest trick. She'd find a way to get that letter in a day or two. "What are you planning in there?"

He shrugged. "Just another cattle run."

His words came out flippant, as though stealing thousands of cattle from hardworking ranchers on the Texas side of the border was only something to shrug about.

She had the sudden urge to grab her cousin's face and rake

her nails down his cheeks. "What if the Rangers catch you this time?"

"That's why I need you inside the camp. So we can be sure of what they know."

That's where her cousin was wrong. If she ever got into the Ranger camp, she'd do everything in her power to make sure the Rangers had the information they needed to catch Raul and his *desperados*.

But it was starting to seem like a hopeless cause. Despite being sent to town numerous times for the purpose of finding one of the two lieutenants and flirting with them, the Rangers didn't seem keen on letting anyone inside the camp that their captain didn't already know. In fact, Leighton, the lieutenant she'd been talking to, had been so proper and circumspect with her that she wondered if the captain allowed any fraternizing while his men were on assignment.

Either that, or she truly was terrible at attracting a man's attention.

"When is the next cattle run happening?" she asked. "How long do I have to get into the camp?"

Please, God, don't let him say tonight.

If something had been planned, hopefully she would have heard before now. That was one good thing about sharing information with Raul, it often meant he gave her information in return.

But if he ever found out what she did with that information...

She sucked in a breath. No. She couldn't think about that. Couldn't think about what would happen if she were discovered.

"We won't move for a few weeks yet," Raul said. "After the Americans celebrate their Thanksgiving. Want to make sure we get things right."

Good. That gave her plenty of time to do what came next.

And if she was really lucky—if she dared hope enough—maybe, just maybe, the Rangers and the sheriff would capture Raul on his next run.

"Now I want to see you around town with that lieutenant." Raul shoved his finger into her shoulder, hard enough she couldn't quite hide her wince. "Any time you have an afternoon off, I expect you to be with him. I want to make sure they have no information about our next raid."

She took a step away from him, dislodging his finger from the spot on her skin that was sure to bruise. "Do you ever get tired of this?"

"What?"

She swiped a strand of long black hair away from her face. "Stealing other people's cattle?"

Raul let out a short bark of laughter. "It makes my father richer, and in turn, me. Now you tell me, do you ever get tired of being separated from your sister?"

She looked down, even though the room was too dark for him to see her eyes. "You know I do."

"Then find a way inside the Ranger camp, or you won't be seeing this. Ever." He held the letter in front of her, the dim light from the window barely bright enough to illuminate the whiteness of the envelope.

Rather than look at it, she flung the door open and reached for the tray of soiled dishes sitting atop the dresser.

Tears stung her eyes as she fled from the room, though she couldn't quite say why. It was hardly the cruelest thing Raul had ever said to her.

But she was tired, so very tired of the life she was living. So very tired of being a pawn in her uncle and cousin's machinations, so very tired of missing her sister and wishing her mother and stepfather hadn't died, leaving her in her uncle's care.

Or maybe, she was just tired of living altogether.

Raul's laugh followed her down the corridor, then she

heard a door shut, probably because he'd gone into the room where his men were planning their next raid.

She didn't care. All she wanted was to return this tray to the kitchen, then find the comfort of her room.

"Hey there!"

A man appeared in front of her. She pulled back, but not quite soon enough to stop herself from running into him. The dishes on the tray rattled, and the entire thing would have fallen, but a hand reached out to hold the front of the tray. Then another hand settled on her shoulder, its touch warm and gentle.

"*Lo siento!*" She kept her gaze down as she spoke, staring at the place where the tray met the man's stomach. "I didn't see you there."

"It's all right."

At the sound of the deep, smooth voice, she glanced up to find none other than Harrison Rutherford—the son of Fort Ashton's owner—standing in front of her. "Mr. Rutherford, I... I didn't realize it was you."

He scanned her face with deep brown eyes that always seemed to see too much when they looked at her. "Have you been crying? What happened?"

"Nothing." And what a fool she must look, because even now, she could feel a tear streaking down her cheek. With her hands still holding the tray, she couldn't so much as swipe it away.

Laughter rose from behind her, and she looked over her shoulder to find the door where Raul had disappeared open a crack, a sliver of light spilling into the corridor.

"Who's in there?" Mr. Rutherford asked.

"Raul and his friends arrived this evening. I was told to bring them food."

"What did they do?" His voice turned soft, his eyes even more gentle than before.

She shook her head, causing a strand of hair to fall across her cheek that she couldn't brush away, just like the tear. "I already told you, nothing."

"It must have been something. Serving food shouldn't lead to you crying. Did they say something cruel?"

She couldn't quite manage to keep her chin from quivering, or another tear from spilling down her cheek.

Oh, why did she have to run into Harrison Rutherford, of all people? She almost wished she would have run into his father. He wouldn't have taken the time to even look at her, much less want to know why she was upset.

But the younger Mr. Rutherford was always trying to be nice. She'd met him the first day he'd come to town, nearly a month ago now. That time she'd actually dropped a tray of tea service after he'd startled her—and he'd given her money to replace the shattered dishes so she wouldn't have the cost taken out of her pay.

Now here he was again, asking questions, genuinely caring that something was wrong.

She wanted to say it was a ruse, that he was just being kind because he wanted something from her.

The trouble was, in the weeks he'd been at the fort, he'd not asked her for a single thing. He hadn't even told her to fetch him food from the kitchen, even though that was her main job.

Mr. Rutherford shifted in front of her, stroking his thumb over the side of his jaw for a moment before speaking. "Come to Austin with me."

She reared back, her breath hitching in her lungs. So he *did* want something from her. And just when she'd been about to believe he was kind and decent.

"I told you before, I'm not that kind of woman. You'd best look elsewhere for your entertainment." She should have known better than to let herself be softened by a few well-spoken words and a nice-looking smile.

"That's not what I meant." Mr. Rutherford released her shoulder and held his hands up. "Come to Austin and work in my house as a servant. I've need of another parlor maid, and you would do nicely."

"Oh..."

Go to Austin.

What would it be like to work for the younger Mr. Rutherford? To be far away from Raul and her uncle's scheming? *Bliss.* That's what it would be. Pure bliss.

Except... "I can't go to Austin, not even for a reason such as that."

"Why? You're not treated well here. You work constantly, yet you eat meals by yourself rather than with the staff, and Rooster and Raul have a singular hatred for you."

"You've observed all that?"

"I have."

She shrank back against the railing that lined the side of the corridor open to the courtyard below. Just how much did he know about her?

He sighed, the sound long and deep. "You need to leave this place, Alejandra. I'm concerned what might happen if you don't."

"I can't."

"Why not?"

"You already know."

He shook his head. "No, I don't."

She looked away from him, down into the courtyard where a few straggling travelers milled about in the growing darkness. "For the same reason I couldn't afford to pay for the broken dishes before. My sister."

"Gabriella." The name sounded soft on his lips. "She can come too."

Alejandra pressed her eyes shut. "If only it was as easy as

you say. But this is... we shouldn't... I can't talk about this. Now if you'll excuse me."

She opened her eyes, ready to dash down the corridor again, but Mr. Rutherford stepped in front of her.

"Here, take this." He reached into his pocket and pulled out his billfold, then peeled off several large bills.

"What... what are you doing?"

"Three-nineteen Enderfield Street. Can you remember that?"

"Why?"

"That's my address, and this is enough money for two tickets to Austin." He tucked the bills on the tray beneath the pitcher of water.

"Take it back. I'll not be joining you." But with both her hands holding the tray, she had no way to give the money back to him.

"It's already yours. Save it in case you find a way to come to Austin after all. And if the opportunity never presents itself, then take it with you when you finally get yourself free of this place. Use it to start again somewhere new." He stepped to the side. "Now you best take that to the kitchen."

She couldn't quite manage to tell him thank you as she moved around him, wasn't sure if she wanted to thank him or lecture him or call him names. She didn't allow herself to look over her shoulder at him, not even once.

But she could feel his eyes on her.

And she couldn't help but wonder, just what would it be like to go to Austin and work for a man as kind as Harrison Rutherford?

1

Austin, Texas; March 1886

What was a man's life worth?

Harrison Rutherford stared at the article in front of him, the coarseness of the newspaper it had been printed on almost like sand against the polished mahogany surface of his desk.

The headline from the center of the paper stared back at him in big, bold letters.

Jury Convicts Wade Tillerman.

It was only four words, and yet each time he read them, he felt as though a knife had been thrust into his chest.

But it wasn't his chest he should be worried about. It was Wade Tillerman's neck, which was set to swing from a noose in another week.

Harrison pushed his chair back from his desk and sank his head into his hands. Was there anything he could do?

File an appeal, sure. But on what grounds?

Ask for a stay of execution. But again, on what grounds?

The gossip rags that had circulated through Austin

throughout the two weeks of the trial were full of theories. That the judge had been paid off, that the witnesses were being bribed. That the jury was being blackmailed.

But he couldn't prove a lick of it. Which left him sitting alone in the office inside his house, staring at the bold words of the headline while Wade Tillerman was locked in a prison cell.

He had the sudden urge to grab the special edition of the paper—printed solely to spread news about the trial—and toss it into the fire. But that wouldn't erase the verdict the judge had delivered a few hours earlier.

Innocent men weren't supposed to be convicted for crimes they didn't commit.

Was it his fault? Had he done something wrong as Wade's lawyer?

Maybe if he would have found one more witness, or asked a few more questions when Mr. Crist or his son were on the stand...

The grandfather clock gonged the half hour, and Harrison jolted at the noise, then glared at it. It was a monstrously large and gaudy clock that had cost far too much money.

But it seemed every wealthy man in Austin had a grandfather clock in his study, and so Harrison had bought one.

And he'd put dark heavy drapes on the window, just like every other house had on his street, and ordered a gargantuan mahogany desk.

Again, like everyone else.

He'd tried his hardest to keep up appearances, and it had worked. For a young man fresh out of law school determined to prove he could make a name for himself without using a lick of his father's money, he'd done well for himself. Now, seven years later, he was in the position of having done work for just about anyone of importance in Austin, and he'd been invited to more highfalutin dinner parties and balls than he'd ever be able to attend.

Not too shabby for a man his father had claimed would fail without the family money.

Or at least, it hadn't seemed like he'd done too poorly for himself until today.

He looked around the office. Strange how he hadn't really hated the fancy furniture and expensive drapes before.

Maybe it was because none of the people he'd spent the past seven years ingratiating himself with were keen on talking to him anymore.

Turned out the Austin high society didn't take kindly to the lawyer who defended a servant accused of murdering one of their own—even if there was plenty of evidence indicating the servant was innocent.

And now that he'd lost the case, he'd be permanently snubbed.

Harrison tossed the newspaper aside before the urge to throw it in the fire became irresistible.

Right along with his law school diploma.

And his law license.

Somewhere in the house, a door closed with a rather loud thud, and footsteps beat a hurried path down the hallway, growing closer to his office. Then the door sprang open, banging into the bookshelf against the wall.

Harrison jumped to his feet. "Adeline."

She swished into the room in a flurry of lace and flounces, her pale blonde hair swept onto her head in a fancy updo that must have taken her maid hours to pin into place.

He came around the side of the desk to greet her. "To what do I owe—"

"I hope you're happy," she sniffed.

Willis, his butler, appeared in the doorway. "I'm sorry, sir. I wanted to ask if you were available, but Miss Wenthold slipped past me."

"That's quite all right." He held up a hand at the butler as

Adeline thrust the rolled-up newspaper that had been tucked beneath her arm at him.

"You've ruined everything between us." Adeline's perfectly pink lips turned down into a pout.

"I ruined..." His brows drew down and he unrolled the newspaper only to find it was the same as the one on his desk. "What are you talking about?"

"You, me, our relationship. I was hoping if you won the case, if you were somehow able to find the true murderer, you'd be hailed a hero." She fluttered her thick blond lashes at him, a sheen of moisture glistening in her crystal blue eyes. "But now that you lost, I refuse to be dragged down with you."

He rolled the paper back up and handed it to her. "I still think Wade Tillerman was innocent. Are you really more concerned about attending balls than the loss of an innocent man's life?"

"Can't you read? Wade Tillerman isn't innocent."

Harrison winced. "I know I lost, but that doesn't mean—"

"Oh, how could you!" Adeline stomped her slipper on the floor. It was ridiculously white for a shoe, and would likely be soiled the second she stepped outside.

"How could I what?" he gritted. "Lose? There's not a single lawyer I know of who wins every case he takes."

"Do this to me? I thought we were to be married!"

He blinked. "Ah, that was the general idea behind me calling on you, yes."

"Clearly, you aren't understanding the situation." Her pert little slipper stomped the rug again. "I'd already met with the seamstress to start planning my gown."

"You met with...?"

"But now I can never marry you! Even if it turns out Tillerman truly is innocent and you find the true killer, your reputation is sullied. And it's all such a pity." She looked around his office. "You have a rather nice house, and you're quite handsome too. I would have made you a fine wife."

"I never asked you to marry me." Was it just him, or was this conversation growing more ridiculous by the second?

She sniffed again, and a big crocodile tear slid from the corner of her eye down her perfectly sculpted cheekbone. "But you were going to ask, weren't you?"

That had been the plan. Eventually. It was the expected thing to do, after all. Adeline came from a high society family, and up until now, he'd thought she really would have made him a fine wife.

Or at least it would have appeared that way to everyone else.

A knock sounded on the open door, and Willis stepped inside. "Pardon the interruption, sir, but a telegram has arrived. I believe it's from Twin Rivers."

"Thank you." He took the sealed envelope and tucked it under his arm, then turned back to Adeline.

"Oh, go ahead and read it." Adeline raised her chin. The moisture in her eyes from a few minutes ago was now replaced with a look of hard determination. "I'm leaving anyway, and don't bother calling on me again."

She whirled on her heel and made a beeline for the door.

She was probably expecting him to chase after her, to beg her to let him back into her life, but as the door shut behind her, all he felt was the ache in his chest from the verdict against his client.

Harrison grabbed the letter opener from off his desk and used it to slice a thin cut along the top fold of the envelope.

A small slip of paper bearing only a handful of words floated to his desk.

But they were words that caused his life to change—for the second time in a single day.

2

Twin Rivers, Texas

She knew too much.

Everyone had their secrets, but as Alejandra Loyola stood over the still body of her boss, Mr. Bartholomew Rutherford, watching his lungs struggle for breath, she didn't wonder whether her secrets would end up killing her.

No, of that she was certain.

She only wondered whether she'd be able to see her sister provided for before she died.

Alejandra picked up the elaborate silver water pitcher and poured a bit of water into the equally elaborate basin, then dipped a cloth into it. The water wasn't very cool in the desert, but she wasn't sure what else to do for a patient who rarely woke and managed to be both incoherent and irate for the short times his eyes were open.

She wrung out the extra water, then took a few short steps to the bed.

Mr. Rutherford didn't so much as flinch when she placed it across his brow.

Just two weeks ago he'd been walking around, barking orders and acting like he owned the world. Now his face held a grayish tint, his eyes were sunken into his head, and he couldn't utter a single distinguishable word.

Alejandra looked at the tray sitting atop the ornately carved chest of drawers. The doctor had said to make sure he ate three times a day, but at breakfast he'd smacked the bowl of broth out of her hand, causing it to shatter against the fancy tile floor while the broth seeped into her shoes. Now it was an hour past lunch, and he still hadn't woken.

Was she supposed to wake him to eat?

A shout from outside drew her attention, and she stepped closer to the window. Cacti and shrubs dotted the rolling yellow hills that covered the landscape before dipping down into the green Rio Grande Valley. But that wasn't unusual for the desert. The unusual part was the steady stream of people trickling into and out of the massive adobe fort where she stood.

Fort Ashton was infamous along the Chihuahuan Trail. Towering above the desert, the massive hacienda was visible from miles around. Travelers came from far and wide to trade goods, seek lodging, and get a hot meal as they continued along the busy trail that ran from Chihuahua, Mexico, to San Antonio, Texas.

The three-story structure contained everything a person could want. The restaurant, trading post, kitchen, and servants' quarters were all on the first floor. Mr. Rutherford's living quarters and private guest rooms were on the second floor, and the hotel rooms were on the third floor, meaning the fort was always busy, and giving a worker like her little reason to leave the fort, ever.

And here she was tending its wealthy owner, who was too ill to notice his silver candlesticks or water pitcher, too sick to get any enjoyment from the intricate tapestries hanging from his walls or the ruby-studded gold pocket watch laying atop his chest of drawers.

"Alejandra."

She whirled at the familiar sound of her cousin's voice, her heart suddenly hammering against her ribs.

Dear Father, I thought he was supposed to be gone for another week.

She forced a smile to her lips and raised her gaze to meet Raul's hard, dark eyes. "I didn't realize you'd be back this soon."

Had something brought him back early? She tamped down the shudder that tried to steal up her spine.

He crossed to the bed, his lithe form and confident gait revealing the strength of his athletic body as he moved. "Have there been any changes with Rutherford?"

She shook her head. "He's the same as when you left." Which had been about a week and a half ago, only a few days after the apoplectic fit that had left Mr. Rutherford in his debilitating state.

"And you've been taking care of him the entire time?"

"I have."

"Good. What other news do you have?"

It was the same as always. Raul would be gone for days or weeks, then he'd return to the fort in a flurry, expecting her to update him on every last thing that had happened in his absence.

Alejandra glanced at her slumbering patient. "Do you want me to say it here?"

"I'm standing here, aren't I?" Angry lines creased Raul's brow.

"Ah, Mr. Rutherford, that is... Dr. Mullins said... well, he thinks apoplectic patients might be able to understand what's going on around them."

"The man can't speak a normal sentence."

"I know, but..."

A muscle pulsed at the side of Raul's jaw. "Just tell me what's been happening."

"Mr. Rutherford's son is coming. Fort Ashton received word from Austin shortly after you left. He's expected any day."

That was something she hadn't let herself think about too much. She could still recall the dark hair and caring eyes of the man she'd met last fall—eyes that were so much warmer than his father's.

Would Harrison Rutherford remember her?

"And Rutherford's son will be running the fort once he gets here?" Raul watched her carefully, his entire body coiled like a mountain lion ready to pounce.

"That's the plan, yes. I overheard Rooster say the younger Mr. Rutherford has something called power of attorney and will be in charge."

"I see." Raul whirled on his heel and stalked to the window, studying the landscape with a dark look. "Did you search the office while I was gone?"

"I did. Three times. But I didn't find anything. I think you and Felipe destroyed all of Rutherford's records the first time around, and I'm sure Rooster has been through the office too, looking for anything that might link Mr. Rutherford to everything. He's got just as much of an interest in keeping that hidden as we do."

"I still don't like it. What if we missed something?"

"I didn't miss anything." She'd been sneaking around that office for two years. She knew every nook and cranny of it, every odd and random place Bartholomew Rutherford might shove an errant paper. After the attack that had rendered him an invalid, she'd known right where he'd kept his ledger that had tracked the rustled cattle and had handed it over to Raul.

There was nothing in that office that would give Rutherford's rustling activities away to his son. Of that she was certain.

Raul pushed himself off the window. "You'd better be right."

She swallowed, not wanting to think about what he'd do to her if she was somehow wrong. Her cousin might not be able to kill her, but he had power enough to make her suffer in other ways.

"How have things been with Rooster running the fort?"

She grimaced as the image of Mr. Rutherford's burly right-hand man rose in her mind. "People like him even less than Mr. Rutherford. Two guards quit, and one kitchen maid."

If Raul was surprised by people quitting, he didn't say it. In fact, his face offered nothing about his thoughts other than the general anger he always seemed to carry with him. "What else?"

She shook her head. "It's been rather uneventful with Mr. Rutherford in the condition that he is."

"What about the Rangers?"

"They took two forays into Mexico, both brief. They didn't bring back any rustlers, if that's what you're wondering."

"Have any of them left Twin Rivers? Has Austin ordered at least some of them to go elsewhere since they aren't catching any rustlers?"

"Not that I can tell, but I'm only going by rumors. It's not as though I've been inside the encampment."

Raul sent her a hard glare. "I still wish we had a way to get you inside."

It wasn't like she hadn't tried, but the Ranger she'd been talking to last fall had taken a fancy to the general store owner's daughter around Christmas, and Alejandra's chances of getting into the camp had dwindled to nothing.

Right along with her chances of ever reading another letter from her sister.

She didn't know quite when Bartholomew Rutherford and her step-uncle had joined forces and started rustling cattle over the border and into Mexico. She only knew that Raul had been in Twin Rivers for over two years heading things up, and at this time last year, their operation was both large and undetected.

Once the sheriff of Twin Rivers had found out about the rustling, he'd called in the Rangers, and things had quickly gone downhill for her cousin.

"We need some kind of informant inside the Rangers, even if it's one of their own," Raul muttered.

Alejandra let out a short laugh. "Good luck with that."

He sent her another glare. "Lawmen can be flipped for the right price."

True, but the lawmen that worked for Cain Whitelaw? She couldn't see him tolerating a traitor in his midst. The women on the Mexican side of the Rio Grande said he was the best lawman they'd ever seen. That he had a special sense that allowed him to sniff out *desperados*. Even if she'd been able to get inside the camp like Raul wanted, she had a feeling Cain Whitelaw would have grown wise to what she was doing within a matter of days.

Unlike Bartholomew Rutherford.

She'd been reading his correspondence for two years and reporting every last bit of it back to Raul and her uncle, and the owner of Fort Ashton never had the slightest inkling what she was up to.

"Father won't like that the Rangers are still here." Raul started pacing in front of the window.

No, he wouldn't. "Perhaps you'll find a way to get cattle across the border without Ranger Whitelaw noticing."

Or maybe the Rangers would catch Raul himself the next time he stole cattle. But she'd been hoping for that very thing for over nine months, and it had yet to happen.

Raul had stopped pacing for a few moments in front of the window, but he turned abruptly and marched straight back to where she stood. "*Padre* gave me twelve weeks to get more cattle. He said to blaze another trail if I need to, but that I'm to bring him two thousand head. That's when he wants you to return to Mexico as well."

Her head jerked up. "Me?"

Raul stopped in front of her, his body large enough she had to fight the urge to take a step back from him. "He's made another match for you. I assume you'll be amenable this time around?"

"Never."

"What was that?"

Her back stiffened. The word had escaped before she could help it. She'd never be amenable to a match that benefited her uncle, but her cousin didn't need to know that.

"Oh, and I almost forgot, there's this." Raul pulled a letter from his pocket.

She instantly recognized the careful handwriting on the envelope and reached for it.

"Not so fast." He held the letter above his head, far too high for her to get it, but somehow close enough she had the insatiable urge to jump and try.

"Give it to me, Raul. Please. It's been months."

A chuckle rumbled from his chest. "Sometimes the only thing better than knowing you hate me is watching you force yourself to be nice to me."

"I searched the office for you three times, plus I gave you information about the Rangers. You have to let me read the letter. That was the deal."

Raul still held the letter suspended above her. "You didn't earn anything. You didn't give me any information about the Rangers I couldn't have figured out on my own, and you didn't find anything when you searched Rutherford's office."

"She's my sister!"

"Ah, yes." A cruel gleam flashed across his eyes. "And how long has it been since you've seen each other?"

Two years, three months, and twenty-six days. Alejandra

blinked away the pricking sensation at the backs of her eyes. "Too long."

"You have no one but yourself to blame for that."

She knew that, and yet, if she could go back in time two years, she wasn't sure she would change anything.

The door to Mr. Rutherford's room opened, and she froze, her hand poised above her head as she reached for the letter Raul still held out of reach.

Into the room stepped none other than Harrison Rutherford, all the way from Austin. He was covered in dust from head to toe, hadn't bothered to remove his hat, and stood just as tall and handsome as she remembered.

He looked at the bed where his father lay and took a step forward, but then his gaze landed on her and Raul, and eyes that had been soft with concern for his father narrowed at her cousin. "What's going on in here?"

XXX

ALEJANDRA WAS STILL at Fort Ashton.

Harrison was hoping he'd find otherwise upon his return, but as he entered his father's room, it was clear that little had changed, both for Alejandra and Raul.

As soon as he asked what was going on, Raul straightened, slipping the envelope he had been holding above his head into his pocket.

"Mr. Rutherford." Raul held out his hand to shake.

Harrison stepped forward and took it, though part of him would have rather not touched the scoundrel.

He'd been introduced to Raul Velez when he'd stayed at the fort in the fall but had never had a conversation with him. He'd just been told Raul conducted business for the fort on the Mexican side of the border.

The man hadn't stayed at Fort Ashton for more than a few days at a time, but when he'd been here...

Harrison's gaze swept to Alejandra. "Is there something you need from him?"

A dull pink crept onto her sun-bronzed cheeks. She glanced at him, then at Raul before bending her head. "Nothing. No."

"Was that a letter you were reaching for when I entered the room? It's not yours?"

"I..."

"Let me see it, Raul." He held out his hand.

Something hard flashed in Raul's eyes, but the Mexican yanked out the letter and slapped it into his palm.

Sure enough, the name Alejandra was scrawled across the outside of the envelope in swirling cursive. "Are you aware that it's a crime to open a letter that's not addressed to you?"

Raul's body tensed. "I was just the messenger."

"Who refused to deliver the letter?"

"She has it now," Raul spat, then turned for the door. "If you'll excuse me."

Harrison didn't excuse him, but that made little difference as Raul stormed out of the room.

Looked like he knew what his first act as head of Fort Ashton was going to be. He had no intention of keeping employees around if they were going to harass other workers.

"Is it true what you said...?" a soft voice asked from beside him, "about it being a crime to open another person's letter?"

He looked down to find Alejandra still there... and him still holding her letter.

He handed it to her. "Intentionally? Yes, it's illegal, a misdemeanor offense. Though I'm not sure that would deter Mr. Velez."

"Oh." She slanted a worried glance toward the door, and the

lines etched across her brow made him wonder if giving her the letter would end up causing her trouble with Raul.

But no, it couldn't, because he didn't intend to just fire Raul Velez, but also ban him from the property.

"Thank you for the letter." Alejandra slipped past him and stepped to the bed, where she replaced the cloth on his father's head with a fresh one. Her movements caused a whiff of flowers to swirl around him, a scent he remembered far too well from last fall.

Just like he remembered the constant fear in her eyes, and the way she could never quite bring herself to meet his gaze for more than a handful of seconds.

"What are you still doing here?" he asked, his voice somehow turning both deep and low.

"Tending your father."

That wasn't what he'd meant. He'd given her enough money to leave the fort twice over. So why was she still here, and in his father's room, no less?

He almost asked again, but she'd already wrung out the soiled rag in the basin and was now back at the bed giving him a description of his father's condition.

He stepped up beside her.

Only then, standing so close to the bed, did he realize how truly ill his father looked. When he'd first entered the room, it appeared as though his father had been doing little more than napping. But now he saw his father's skin was a deathly shade of gray, his body looked uncomfortably stiff, and the side of his face drooped. Cheekbones that were strong and pronounced last fall now protruded from skin that looked thin and frail, barely strong enough to cover the bone beneath it.

"What happened?" he whispered.

Alejandra looked at him, her brown eyes large in the light pouring through the window. "No one told you?"

"All I got was a telegram saying he'd suffered from apoplexy and was unconscious. I was thinking... hoping..."

What? That the unconsciousness would pass? It had been eight days since he'd gotten the telegram, six since he'd left Austin. His father could have recovered while he'd been traveling.

"Mr. Rutherford was in the trading post, negotiating a price with a traveler, when he suddenly clutched his head and fell over. The guards ran for the doctor, but when your father woke later that night, I'm told he was incoherent and irate. Unable to walk or move his left side."

"Were you there when it happened? In the trading post?"

She shook her head. "I was hired to work in the kitchen."

"You said he's woken up?"

"Usually every hour or so, but today he seems to be sleeping more."

"And when he does wake, he's not himself?"

"He can't talk. Or rather, no one understands what he's trying to say. And he can't move his left side, which also means he can't walk."

Harrison reached down and took his father's hand, cold and waxy against his own warm palm.

"I'm sorry," Alejandra whispered beside him.

He had no words for her in return, not when the man he was looking at seemed like little more than a shell.

"Do you want me to give you some time?" she asked. "With your father, that is?"

He drew in a breath, then shook his head. "No, thank you. At least not now. Perhaps I'll come back in a few hours."

She nodded as though she understood, but he wasn't sure she did.

He wasn't sure he himself understood everything—even though he was now the one in charge.

3

Harrison's boots clacked against the smooth tile floor of the corridor. Noise filtered up from the courtyard below, where people were talking or making their way to the dining room to eat. The trading post had already closed for the day, but many of the travelers staying the night would be at the post when the doors opened in the morning.

And he would be running things.

The thought made sweat slick his palms in the warm desert air. He wiped them on his trousers, then opened the door to his father's office.

He'd been told he would find Rooster, his father's righthand man, there. But he hadn't expected to find Raul and three other Mexicans in the room, along with two of his father's guards.

He stepped inside and met Raul's eyes. "Mr. Velez. You're fired."

The entire room froze. Every person grew still, as if moving so much as an inch would cause their ice-encrusted bodies to shatter.

"You... you can't do that," Rooster finally muttered.

Harrison's gaze snapped to Rooster, who was sitting behind

the large mahogany desk. The bulky, red-headed man had served his father for as long as he could remember, and he always looked as though he had a grudge against the world. Even now, something in his eyes made Harrison feel like a five-year-old boy who'd just gotten caught stealing an extra piece of cake from the kitchen.

"Do I, or do I not, have power of attorney for my father?"

Rooster's eyes narrowed into two thin slits. "You do."

"Then Mr. Velez is fired. I found him harassing one of the maids, and I will not tolerate any ill treatment of women while Fort Ashton is under my leadership."

"Harassing a woman?" One of the Mexican men looked at Raul. "He doesn't harass anyone except Alejandra, and she's his cousin."

Harrison stilled. His cousin? Of the handful of times he'd seen Raul and Alejandra together, he'd never have guessed they were related, not considering how Raul went out of his way to make her life miserable.

"Cousin or not, Alejandra is a woman and is employed here. Which means..." Harrison met Raul's dark gaze, enunciating each word so there could be no misunderstanding. "You're still fired. Guards, see to it that this man is escorted from Fort Ashton and doesn't return."

One of the two men standing beside the door took a step toward Raul.

"I'm going. I'm going." Raul held up his hands. "No need to touch me." He pivoted on his heel and marched toward the door, slamming it shut behind him just as he had done in Father's room.

"Follow him." Harrison jutted his chin toward one of the guards. "Make sure he leaves the fort and the other guards are notified that he's not to be allowed back in."

"You're being too rash. Raul procured Mexican wares for us to sell in Austin. I have a whole ledger filled with the goods he's brought us." Rooster turned in the chair and reached for a ledger on the bookshelf behind him. He tossed it onto the desk with a forceful thud. "Take a look if you don't believe me."

"Find someone else to bring us goods."

Rooster moved his angry gaze to the others in the room. "Felipe, you're in charge now."

A short man with a thatch of hair over his brow stepped forward. "Can I work with Raul outside the fort?"

"As long as Raul doesn't step foot onto my property," Harrison quipped. "But make no mistake, if I learn any of you are harassing women, I will cease all dealings with you. That doesn't just go for the women employed at Fort Ashton, but for all women on either side of the border. And that policy will be applied to the entire staff at Fort Ashton. Am I clear?"

Silence met him, the only sounds in the room the ticking of the clock and the occasional bit of conversation from outside floating up through the windows.

"Yes, sir," Rooster finally muttered, fiddling with the ledger he'd placed on the desk.

"*Sí,*" Felipe said.

The others soon followed suit, everyone murmuring some type of grudging agreement.

"Good. Now everyone except Rooster is dismissed. We have some business to discuss." Harrison raised his chin as the men filed past him and into the corridor, some of them casting angry glances his way.

He didn't care. Everyone knew his father was a hard man, but his father had always been far too permissive when it came to how men in his employ treated the women who worked at the fort. That was going to change, he wasn't about to apologize for it, and he didn't care how many men he needed to fire to prove it.

XXX

WITH MR. RUTHERFORD'S food tray balanced in her arms, Alejandra walked down the corridor toward the stairs. He hadn't woken once all day, and the tea, broth, and bread that was supposed to be his lunch now needed to be exchanged for a fresh tray in case he woke for dinner.

She sank her teeth into her bottom lip. Should she have tried waking him? Dr. Mullins had never told her to do such a thing, but a man couldn't survive long without sustenance.

Reaching the stairs, Alejandra used one hand to balance the tray against the wall, then used her free hand to turn the knob. She picked the tray back up as the door swung open, then jumped.

Felipe stood on the landing just inside the door.

"You scared me."

"Get in here." He reached out one hand to steady the tray. But his other hand clamped around her arm, and he dragged her into the stairwell. "What have you done?"

"Done...? N-nothing."

The stony look on Felipe's face said he didn't believe her.

"I... I've been in Mr. Rutherford's room all day. But he hasn't woken."

"You must have done something."

"I didn't."

"Then why did Rutherford's son kick Raul out of the fort?"

"Raul's been kicked out?"

Her voice must have sounded a tad too hopeful, because Felipe took a step nearer, his body looming over hers in a way that made her want to shrink back against the wall. "Let me ask you again, what did you do?"

"Nothing. Raul had a letter from Gabriella, but he was

refusing to give it to me. Mr. Rutherford's son walked in and made Raul give me the letter. That's all."

"Where's the letter now?"

"Does it matter? It's addressed to me."

"It does if that's what got him kicked out." Felipe leaned close enough the heat from his breath brushed her cheek. "With Raul banned, you're going to need to keep track of the younger Mr. Rutherford, be our eyes and ears. Raul has many questions about the younger Mr. Rutherford that need to be answered."

"I'm already your eyes and ears, remember?" She straightened and took a step forward, never mind how close it put her to Felipe. "Besides, is there something wrong with your ears? Your eyes?"

"He'll have correspondence of his own that needs to be read, and I saw him bring a satchel filled with papers into his office earlier. Raul wants to know what those papers say."

"My assignment was to intercept Mr. Rutherford's communications, not his son's. And if you haven't noticed, I'm quite busy tending the senior Mr. Rutherford."

Besides, the notion of reading the younger Mr. Rutherford's papers didn't sit well. If her uncle wanted to try swiping transportation contracts from under Mr. Rutherford's nose while Mr. Rutherford tried to expand his trading empire into the realm of cattle rustling, then the two of them were welcome to play games with each other all they liked.

She couldn't care less. Both were scheming, cruel men that deserved to be in prison.

But the younger Mr. Rutherford? He didn't deserve to be caught up in the deceit and treachery at Fort Ashton.

"You read his papers," she spat back at Felipe.

"Oh, sure, and if he catches me, I'll be tossed from the fort too." Felipe raked his eyes down her in a way that made her skin suddenly feel hot. "You have to be the one to do it. He won't suspect you."

"Maybe he should." The words slipped out before she could stop them.

Anger twisted Filipe's face, and he swung his arm into the tray. It crashed to the ground, causing the dishes to shatter against the tile floor, and broth and tea to splatter on the wall and her skirt.

"Look what you did!" She knelt to pick up the glass shards. "You're going to have to pay for this. Rooster gets angry whenever a maid breaks something."

"Me? No, *mi muñeca*. You'll be the one to pay."

"But I didn't—

"Tell me you won't obey again, and there'll be more than broken dishes to pay for."

She clamped her lips together as a thick lump formed in her throat. She wasn't going to pay for the ruined porcelain. Not this time. Not when she already needed to scrape together everything she could.

Almost as though Felipe had somehow summoned him, the door swung open behind her, and Rooster filled the doorway. He took in the situation with a single sweep of his gaze, then sneered down at her. "I see the cost for another set of porcelain needs to be deducted from your wages."

She sprang to her feet. "Felipe knocked it over, not me."

"Is that so?" Rooster moved his gaze between the two of them.

"She dropped it on her own," Felipe retorted. "You know how clumsy she is."

"He's lying."

Rooster narrowed his gaze at her. "Maybe you're the one that's lying so you can get out of paying for the porcelain."

"It was Felipe, and he did it intentionally."

"Who did what intentionally?" A controlled voice asked

from behind Rooster. A moment later, Mr. Rutherford's son appeared behind Rooster in the doorway. He glanced at the mess on the landing then looked between her and Felipe. "What caused the tray to fall?"

"She dropped it," Felipe said.

"Felipe knocked it out of my hand," she said at the same time.

The younger Mr. Rutherford rubbed the side of his temple, almost as though a headache was forming. "The fort will replace the porcelain without docking anyone's pay—this time. Alejandra, go find a broom to clean up the mess. Please don't try picking it up with your hands."

She swallowed. He remembered. The first time they'd met, it had been a situation very similar to this. Except dropping the tray had been her fault, and Mr. Rutherford hadn't been in a position to stop Rooster from docking her pay.

So he'd given her money to cover the cost of the broken dishes instead.

"There's a broom in the closet around the corner," she muttered. "I'll fetch it."

"Very good." Mr. Rutherford settled a hand on Felipe's shoulder. "Are you headed to dinner? I'll walk with you."

"I was going outside to find Raul."

"Very well. We best move so Alejandra can clean up this mess." He gestured toward the stairs, then waited for both Felipe and Rooster to precede him before starting down.

Thank you, Father, she breathed.

Mr. Rutherford was probably just being practical by getting everyone to move so she could thoroughly sweep the landing. He couldn't know that Felipe would have likely stayed there, threatening her with one thing or another until she agreed to read his documents.

Almost as though sensing her thoughts, Mr. Rutherford

turned at the next landing and looked back at her, then offered a small nod.

She sucked in a breath and found she couldn't pull her gaze away from him, even after he disappeared down the stairs.

Just what would life be like now that Harrison Rutherford, not his father, was running Fort Ashton?

4

Harrison leaned a shoulder against the window inside his father's office and stared out into the darkening desert. Cacti, yucca, and ocotillo greeted him, scrubby brown and dull green mixing with the rocky ground of the desert. The breeze drifted through the window, causing the thick drapes to rustle and brushing his face with a thin layer of desert dust.

He sighed. He probably should have left the reports and ledgers hours ago and gone next door to his father's room. He could get details from the evening nurse about his father's condition, hold his hand, maybe even pray over him.

But he couldn't bear to look at his father again. At least, not yet.

He could still remember the telegram he'd gotten in Austin, still recall the way the words had looked typed onto that tiny slip of paper. *Father suffered apoplectic attack. Unresponsive. Come home.*

The trouble was, he'd been completely unprepared for what he would find when he stepped into that room. How emaciated his father would be, the deathly gray shade of his skin, the way his lungs barely rose and fell in his chest as he drew in each fragile breath.

He'd taken the train to Midland, then headed south across the desert using the fastest possible route. Still, it took six days to travel from Austin to Twin Rivers, and he'd half expected to arrive and find his father fully recovered, running the fort as though nothing had happened.

Harrison shifted, leaning his shoulder against the side of the window as he stared out the familiar landscape. The subtle hills rolled until they dipped down into the Rio Grande valley in the distance. Beyond the river, the majestic Sierra Madres jutted up from the ground, spearing the sky above with a giant wall of rock.

It all looked the same as it had when he'd stood at this very window last November. In Austin summer brought dense, muggy heat, green trees, and blooming flowers; while winter brought bare trees and brown grass.

But the landscape of the desert never changed.

There was something peaceful about the constancy of it. Something calming.

Indeed, the landscape seemed like the only thing he could count on not to change.

Last time he'd stood in this spot, his father had not only been hale and hearty and running the fort with an iron fist, but Harrison had been a successful Austin lawyer.

A knock sounded on the office door, and he turned.

One of the guards poked his head inside and looked at the desk. "Mr. Rutherford?"

"Over here."

The guard drew his gaze to where he stood by the window. "I, ah, I just wanted to say I appreciate what you did earlier today, with Raul Velez, that is."

Harrison eyed the man. He looked vaguely familiar. Had he

been the guard who had escorted Raul out of the fort? "Thank you."

"Velez is nothing but trouble, sir. If it were up to me, I'd ban his other men from the fort too. They cause mischief with the guards, and they don't treat the womenfolk very kindly."

So he wasn't the only one at the fort that thought things needed to change. "What's your name?"

"Fordham, sir." The man stepped farther inside, and only then did Harrison notice he walked with a slight limp.

"How long have you been working here?"

"Only a few weeks. Got hired on right before your pa took ill. Before that I was a Ranger, until, well..." He gestured to one of his legs. "Took a bullet to the leg, and the doc wasn't sure if I'd recover. Can't be a very good Ranger if I have trouble walking."

"No, I don't suppose you can. Thank you for the insight, Fordham. If you see anything else unusual with the guards or Felipe or even Raul, please let me know."

The man nodded. "Yes, sir."

Fordham turned to leave, but before he reached the door, another knock sounded. Fordham pulled it open to reveal a second guard.

"Mr. Rutherford?" The guard peered around Fordham. "Sheriff Harding and Mr. Westin are here to see you. Are you able to take visitors?"

"Of course." Harrison made his way across the room while the guards left, not quite able to stop his lips from pulling into a smile as Wes and Daniel entered.

"Harrison, you rascal." Wes pulled him into a hug, then gave him a slap on the back. "You should have stopped by the ranch on your way in. Didn't know you were here until one of Daniel's deputies rode out."

"Yes, well..." Harrison rubbed the back of his neck. "Didn't quite have time for a visit."

Daniel's blue-eye gaze latched onto his from beneath the brim of his sheriff's hat. "Sorry to hear about your father."

"Me too."

"Is there anything we can do?" Wes asked.

If only there was some way for his friends to make things better. "Afraid not, but thanks for the offer."

"If that changes and you end up needing something, let us know," Daniel said, his eyes still assessing.

"I will." But what could he possibly need?

Besides an undertaker.

Harrison's shoulders slumped, and he turned and walked to his desk. Maybe sitting in the familiar leather of the chair would make this conversation a little more comfortable. Especially if his friends were going to keep looking at him like that. They already seemed to know too much, and he'd hardly given any details about his father.

"How long do you plan to stay in Twin Rivers?" This from Wes, who settled himself into one of the plush armchairs opposite the desk.

"Don't rightly know. For a while, I think." Five months ago when he'd been in Twin Rivers, he would have told his friends he was planning to leave as soon as possible, that he had a life in the city he needed to return to.

Now, assuming his father didn't miraculously recover, he needed to decide what to do with the fort, and that meant understanding what was required to run it first.

God, what does the future hold? What do You want from me here?

"How's Adeline?" Wes asked.

"She's... ah..." Harrison stuck a finger into his collar and ran it around the base of his neck. When had his shirt suddenly gotten so tight? "Things aren't going to work out between us."

"Really?" Wes's brow furrowed. "I thought it was already

decided. You said it'd be a perfectly convenient marriage for the both of you."

An image of Adeline rose in his mind, her white-blond hair and ocean blue eyes and delicate little face—all contorted into a mask of anger because he'd defended an innocent man without first stopping to ask if doing so might damage his standing in society.

"Catch those cattle rustlers yet?" he ground out. Hopefully that would get the conversation away from him and Adeline and anything else to do with Austin.

"No." Daniel scowled. "Didn't you see the Ranger encampment down by the river?"

"I didn't ride through town on my way in. Just came straight here."

When it became apparent just how widespread the rustling was last spring, the Rangers had been called in to deal with the rustlers, which had also brought their old friend Cain back to Twin Rivers as the captain. Unfortunately, it was taking Cain more time than everyone had hoped to deal with the situation.

"Cain says it shouldn't be that much longer before the outlaws are rounded up. Speaking for the ranchers in the area, it can't happen soon enough," Wes said. And he had every right to speak for other ranchers, since he owned one of the largest and most prestigious ranches in the state.

Though sitting together like this, with Wes slouched into an overstuffed chair, his arm hanging off his knee, a person would never be able to guess it. Sure, his hat was probably made out of some fancy leather imported from Europe, as were his trousers and vest. But he was first and foremost a friend. Always had been, and always would be.

"Had to bring on six more ranch hands just so that I have enough men to watch the cattle at night." Wes rubbed the back of his neck. "If I don't, the rustlers will find some hidden valley on my ranch and steal the cattle without us realizing it for days."

"It's been a while since anyone's lost cattle though." Daniel stood and helped himself to the pitcher of sweet tea sitting on the corner of the desk, then offered a glass to Wes. "We're still getting notes that tip us off to the rustlers, and they've become more accurate and consistent."

"The last time the rustlers tried taking cattle from me, Cain caught them just over the border." Wes took the glass of sweet tea from Daniel. "And all because of a note."

Harrison leaned back in his chair. "Any clue as to who's writing them?"

"Probably someone in Mexico." Daniel sat back down. "Cain and I have both tried tracking down anyone who might know things on this side of the border, but the leads never go anywhere."

"Well, I'm glad for the notes, whoever's leaving them."

"You and me both," Wes muttered. "That man deserves a special place in heaven for all the cattle he's saved."

Harrison reached out and emptied the last of the sweet tea into his own glass. "Hopefully you'll be able to thank him in person after the rustlers are caught."

"If Cain could just catch the leader, we'd be done," Daniel said.

Harrison took a sip of his own tea. "The notes don't help with that, huh?"

"Haven't so far." Daniel leaned forward. "But unfortunately, that's not my only problem."

"We had a bank robbery." Wes grimaced and scrubbed a hand over his face. "A real, true bank robbery."

Harrison set his glass of tea down so hard it thunked against his father's polished desk. "In Twin Rivers? When? How?"

"About a month ago." Daniel rubbed the side of his temple, almost as though thinking about it gave him a headache.

"Nothing was taken from the safe. The robbers showed up before the money from the till had been locked up. It was only about two hundred dollars, but it was enough to put the bank in a hard place, have people pulling their money out and saying they'd be better off hiding their money in their own houses."

"But now people are complaining about things going missing in their houses." Wes took a sip of tea.

Harrison raised his eyebrows. "Including the money that used to be in the bank?"

"You got it."

"You have any leads?"

Daniel shook his head. "Questioned a few people, but nothing came of it. I can't imagine anyone in town would do such a thing."

"Maybe it's done now." Wes set his empty sweet tea glass down on the desk. "Some vagabonds passing through."

Daniel nodded, then jabbed a thumb in Wes's direction. "He's right. Things have been quiet for a couple weeks. I wish I would have caught whoever was stealing, but I'm pretty sure he's moved on."

"What about things with the two of you?" Harrison crossed his arms over his chest and leaned back in his chair. "Did either of you end up losing money in the bank robbery? And how have your families been?"

Wes scowled. "Ellie's in labor."

"Right now?" Harrison nearly choked. "Why didn't you say anything?"

Wes just glared at him, and Harrison couldn't help but chuckle. "Your best friend's wife is about to have a baby. And you look like you want to kill someone."

The faint lines around Wes's mouth tightened.

"No reason to worry about Ellie though, right?" Daniel reached out and smacked Wes's arm. "Charlotte, the doc, and

Sam are all at Sam's place, but they brought the children to the A Bar W for the birthing."

"About the only place all of them will fit," Wes muttered, his lips still pressed into a firm line.

Daniel's face broke into a smile. "Keely and Anna Mae are there with the young'uns, but they kicked us out. Said I needed to find something for Wes here to do before he drove the women crazy and got the children worrying about Ellie."

"Learned you were here on the ride into town," Wes muttered.

So he was the distraction? Harrison laughed. "Ellie will be fine. No need to worry."

But even has he said the words, he couldn't help being a little concerned, simply for Wes's sake. Most men wouldn't give two thoughts to their friend's wife having a child, but Wes had lost his wife and daughter in childbirth two years ago, and he would carry the scars from that to his grave.

"I keep telling myself not to worry." Wes drew in a breath and raked his hand through his hair. "Keep telling myself that God's promised not to fail me or forsake me, even in hard times, even when things seem impossible. If something bad happens to Ellie, I'll have to trust that it's part of a bigger plan that I don't understand. But still... that doesn't make this easy."

No, he reckoned it didn't. Just like coming home and seeing his father hadn't been easy. Just like taking on—and losing—Wade Tillerman's case in Austin hadn't been easy.

But Wes had found a way to see God's faithfulness in his situation, even though pregnancy and childbirth would always bring back memories of the wife and baby he'd lost.

Harrison tilted his head back and looked up at the ceiling. Could he do the same?

5

A lejandra looked up from her sister's familiar handwriting and pressed the letter to her chest. She'd glanced at it quickly that afternoon, after the younger Mr. Rutherford had left the room, but she hadn't lingered too long lest she get in trouble for not working. Knowing her luck, Rooster would have walked into the room the second she pulled it out, then deducted a half day's pay from her salary for failing to carry out her duties.

But now the fort had settled down for the night. The kitchen had closed, guests were in their rooms, and Alejandra had changed into her nightclothes and spread her bedroll along the far wall of Mr. Rutherford's chamber.

A quick glance in his direction told her there had been no change in his condition—just like there had been no change for the entire day. Mr. Rutherford was still in his slumber, but there was something almost eerie about the way his chest barely rose and fell and his hands lay lifelessly at his sides.

But there was little she could do to change that, other than send for the doctor, who was attending a birth and unable to come to the fort.

Alejandra blew out a breath, then drew her gaze down to Gabriella's letter.

Dear Alejandra,

Thank you for your most recent letter. The nuns kept it for me to read when Tío Javier came on his last visit so I could share it with him.

The letter crinkled in her grip. Of course the nuns at Sisters of St. Mary's had done such a thing. Heaven forbid she be able to send a letter to her sister without their uncle reading it.

Just the thought of *Tío* Javier visiting Gabriella at her boarding school made her skin crawl. But their uncle would consider Gabriella too valuable for him to leave alone for any length of time.

Our uncle he seems happy with your activities in Twin Rivers, even though he's less than thrilled with Raul's progress.

Now tell me, how are you faring? Tío Javier is asking about you, and he remains ever concerned about the goings on there.

Of course he was. It was all part of his plan to control transportation routes in northern Mexico. Why partner with an *Americano* trader like Bartholomew Rutherford if *Tío* Javier could control the trade himself?

It was why she'd been sent to Twin Rivers and commanded to read all of Mr. Rutherford's correspondence, though she hadn't realized her uncle's true purposes at the time.

But really, must her sister keep bringing up their uncle? It was almost as though she could picture him standing over Gabriella's shoulder as she wrote...

Wait. Was that what their uncle had done? Had he dictated the letter and watched as Gabriella wrote it in her own hand?

And to think, she'd actually been excited when Raul had shown her the letter earlier.

Schooling here remains much the same. The nuns keep a close eye on me, at our uncle's bidding, of course. I am learning arithmetic and reading, becoming well versed in the English classics along with the Spanish ones. I'm told that it's important my English is impecca-ble. Señor *Montrose has enough business dealings in the United States that I need to be able to entertain* americano *businessmen and their wives right along with Mexican ones.*

Tìo Javier *tells me he's arranged a marriage for you to the owner of a silver mine. Unfortunately, it looks as though the marriage is set to take you west, far away from Chihuahua. He said it was neces-sary to place you far enough away from Chihuahua that no one would know of what occurred with my fiancé. He implores you to cooperate with the marriage arrangement this time, as do I.*

Alejandra drew in a breath. Did Gabriella mean it? Did her sister really want her to cooperate with the wedding? Or had that been written under *Tìo* Javier's orders too?

She shifted, the straw in the tick beneath her bottom suddenly hard. She wouldn't put it past *Tìo* Javier to travel to Chihuahua for the express purpose of having Gabriella write her a letter encouraging her to marry the man he'd picked.

If her betrothed owned a silver mine, then he'd need a rail-road to get the silver out of the mountains. And considering how her uncle was determined to control as much transporta-tion and trade in northern Mexico as he could, there would be some kind of business contract tangled up with the marriage agreement.

If she married the owner of a silver mine, she would want for nothing, at least on the outside.

But could she marry a man she didn't love, who might be just as cruel as her uncle or *Señor* Montrose?

She shook her head. No, of course she couldn't, because agreeing to marry him would mean abandoning Gabriella to marry *Señor* Montrose herself, and she couldn't leave her sister to a monster such as that, not ever.

I look forward to seeing you when you return to Mexico in a few more months. Tìo Javier *said I could leave Sisters of St. Mary's and spend the week before the wedding at* La Colina *with you. We'll*

*have one final chance to visit before you wed, and it will be just like
old times. I'm already looking forward to it.*

Sincerely,

Gabriella

Alejandra sucked in a breath, barely resisting the urge to
crumple the letter that made it sound as though Gabriella was
content to marry *Señor* Montrose, that Gabriella wanted her to
marry a man of her uncle's choosing as well.

But there, at the end of Gabriella's name was a small sketch
of a hawk.

Alejandra stared at the symbol she'd almost missed.
Gabriella had probably needed to make it tiny so their uncle
wouldn't grow suspicious.

Gabriella still wanted to escape. That's what the hawk
meant. The northern harrier was a brown hawk that went
north every summer. Just like they planned to do one day. The
two of them had talked about the bird in Mexico before they'd
been separated. Even then, they'd dreamed of leaving their
uncle and setting off on their own, though doing so when
they'd both been together had seemed far easier than now that
they were separated.

Alejandra reached for the bag she kept propped against the
wall by her tick and rummaged for her map of Mexico and
Texas.

Her hands glossed over a stack of handkerchiefs she'd been
embroidering to sell at the general store, one of which even had
a string of soaring hawks that edged the border, before she
found the roll of paper she sought.

She pulled the map out, then unrolled it and blinked down
at the familiar names—Austin, San Antonio, El Paso,
Chihuahua, Guadalajara, Mexico City.

If she squinted hard enough, she could make out Twin
Rivers, the small black dot where the Chihuahuan Trail crossed
from Mexico into Texas.

Only about three inches of space separated Twin Rivers from Chihuahua, Mexico, but those three inches were equal to almost 250 kilometers.

Her teeth sank into her bottom lip. If she only needed to worry about herself, she would have escaped Fort Ashton when Harrison Rutherford had given her that money last fall. But with Gabriella all the way down in Chihuahua...

Why, oh why had *Tìo* Javier put her in that boarding school? Why couldn't he have kept her at his hacienda instead?

But the thought of that made her shudder.

Gabriella would be closer at the hacienda, yes, but she would be with their uncle and Raul's older brother Enrico and the men who worked for them. At least Gabriella had a bit of protection at the boarding school.

Where she was being groomed to become a perfect wife for *Señor* Montrose.

An image of the fifty-year-old man rose in Alejandra's mind, and her stomach cramped. She could still remember the way he'd looked at her, still feel the gooseflesh that would always rise on her arms, the cold ball of lead that formed in her stomach.

Even now, two years after being sent to Twin Rivers, there were times when she wondered if what she'd done to get out of the betrothal had been worth it.

But all she had to do was remember the maid with the red streak across her cheek she'd found in tears after she'd spotted *Señor* Montrose leaving the servants' quarters. The maid had sworn she wasn't the only girl on the estate that he'd forced to his bed—or hit.

That's when Alejandra had devised her plan to wriggle out of the betrothal her uncle had set up.

But she hadn't realized just how much her actions would cost her.

Just like she hadn't realized her uncle would turn around and offer Gabriella to *Señor* Montrose in her stead.

Except this time instead of waiting for Gabriella to turn eighteen—as was the arrangement when Alejandra had been engaged—the wedding was set for the day after Gabriella turned sixteen.

That was supposed to mean Alejandra had six months and twenty-three days to get Gabriella and disappear with her.

But now her uncle wanted her back in Mexico in twelve weeks for her own wedding.

Alejandra bent closer to the map, her eyes following the trail from Twin Rivers to Chihuahua.

Supposedly, there was a woman just over the border in Mexico named Consuela Moreno. The rumor was she could help other women—ones who had just lost their husbands and needed work, ones who needed to leave violent men, ones who found themselves in difficult situations.

If Alejandra could find this woman, maybe she could pay to get Gabriella out of Mexico. It meant the two of them would be starting over with an uncomfortably small amount of money, but it seemed like her only choice.

The door to the room opened, and Alejandra jumped, a small squeak escaping from her mouth.

Mr. Rutherford—the younger one—stepped inside.

His eyes immediately found hers, and he frowned. "Alejandra? What are you doing in here?"

"I... ah..." She scrambled to her feet. "Just tending your father, is all."

"You sleep in here?" He ran his eyes along the wall with her bedroll.

"*Sì*, in case Mr. Rutherford needs something."

"There's not another nurse who watches him at night?"

She shook her head, causing a strand of hair to fall across her cheek. She swiped it away, but the action only made her realize that her hair was down. It wasn't that she usually wore it up, but a lot of Texan women claimed it was improper to leave their hair free, and standing in a room alone with the younger Mr. Rutherford, she suddenly felt conscious of each and every movement she made.

But maybe that had more to do with her nightgown than her hair?

Heat rose in her cheeks, and she turned and snatched her housecoat from the bedroll. The fabric was thin and flimsy, but it still seemed as though she should put it on.

"Just me," she muttered. "I'm the only one here."

If Mr. Rutherford was embarrassed by her flitting about, he didn't show it. Instead, he kept his clear brown gaze on her, his brow furrowed as though he was confused. "So you work in twenty-four-hour shifts? Will another maid replace you in the morning?"

"Um, no. That is, there are no other maids who help with your father. I'm the only one."

Silence fell between them, heavy in the ornate room with its thick tapestries and fancy bedposts.

"Your father isn't exactly a pleasant man to deal with when he wakes." She shifted from one foot to the other. "The two other maids who were helping with him quit last week."

"I see." Softness filled Mr. Rutherford's brown gaze, and even though he wasn't smiling, the subtle lines around his eyes and mouth somehow made him look kind.

The expression was so very different than the hard gazes Rooster and Raul usually gave her that she found herself wanting to stare at her feet. "I'm sorry about breaking the tea service earlier."

"Don't apologize for something that's not your fault. Felipe should be the one who's sorry."

She sucked in a breath. How did he know what had happened? She opened her mouth to ask, but another question popped out instead. "Did you really fire Raul because of me?"

His eyebrows rose. "It's more that I refuse to employ men who lack moral character. If I would have happened upon Rooster behaving that way with the cook, or Felipe harassing a parlor maid, I would have fired either of them on the spot."

"Oh." Part of her wanted to thank him. It was probably the expected thing to do. But wherever Raul was at the moment, he had to be furious with her—and she had a feeling she'd end up paying for it.

"I didn't know he was your cousin."

She moved to the chest of drawers, where Mr. Rutherford's dinner tray still sat untouched. "What does that have to do with anything?"

"It doesn't seem as though the two of you are on good terms."

"We're not."

He stood there, just staring at her as though he expected more. She busied her hands with cleaning up an imaginary dribble of broth. Maybe if she wasn't looking at him, she could wriggle out of giving him too much information. "Is there something more I can help you with, Mr. Rutherford?"

"I told you last fall, call me Harrison."

She wouldn't. It would be too scandalous for her as a maid to call him by his first name. "Is there something you need from your father's room?"

"No. Or rather, not anything you can help with. I just... came for some time with him." His voice grew soft, and she turned to find him staring at his father's bed. He'd taken a few steps closer to his father too. "I didn't realize you'd still be here. Actually, I have to admit, I didn't expect to find you here at all when I arrived. I thought you'd have left Fort Ashton months ago."

He studied her again, the soft glow of the lamp against his

face making her somehow aware of each and every movement he made. "How is your sister?"

Her throat grew thick. "I'd forgotten I told you about her."

"Her name is Gabriella, right?"

The lump in her throat grew even bigger, and all she could do was nod.

"Hey now, don't cry." He fished a handkerchief out of his breast pocket and covered the handful of steps that separated them. "Is she unwell? Is there something she needs? Something I can do to help her?"

She took the handkerchief and shook her head.

Why was Mr. Rutherford so kind to her? Why did he care so much about what she did or how her sister was or why she was at Fort Ashton in the first place?

Why had he given her that money last fall?

A million questions rose in her mind, though she didn't voice a single one of them.

But as she looked into his caring eyes and kind face, she couldn't stop herself from wanting to trust him—at least a little.

She only hoped it wouldn't get her into trouble.

6

Morning sunlight slanted though the window as Harrison sat in the familiar chair at the back of the trading post.

The table used for trading goods rested directly in front of him, and the scale sitting on the table near the wall was evenly weighted from what he could tell. The shelves behind the table sat empty, ready to hold whatever goods he'd procure.

His father had multiple freighters who spent their days traveling to and from Austin and San Antonio. At the end of the week, those shelves would be emptied and a freighter would be dispatched with a load of goods to be traded for a higher price in the city.

The room sat eerily silent now, but in a handful of minutes, it would be filled with activity, and he would be the one in charge of deciding what price to give for the traded goods.

Dear God, please be with me.

The truth was, he'd rather be in a courtroom packed with onlookers than sitting behind this table.

For as long as he could remember, there had always been a line out the door of the trading post at Fort Ashton, and always a cacophony of motion and busyness inside, even before the fort had belonged to his father.

Part of him still hated the fact the fort was his father's at all. His father had acquired it from Ben Ashton's widow through perfectly legal means...

But just because a man could legally take something didn't mean he should.

What would his father think of him now that he was running things? His father was just upstairs, only one floor above where he sat, but the man might as well be half a country away, considering his condition.

Harrison reached for the ledger sitting on the end of the table beside the scale. He smoothed the small bit of desert dust from the top, then opened it and ran his gaze down the dual columns, but he'd already known what he would find inside.

Fifteen cents for eight pottery plates.

Thirty cents for two hand-woven rugs.

Ten cents for a saddle blanket.

The prices were all ridiculously low. The plates would probably sell for twenty-five cents apiece in Austin, and the rugs would each sell for a dollar.

The door opened and Rooster poked his head inside. "Are you ready to open?"

Harrison drew in a breath. *Dear Father, You probably have some kind of plan in all of this, but I'll be hanged if I can tell what it is. Please be with me. I'm going to need an extra dose of grace today.*

He blew the breath out, then met Rooster's eyes across the room. "I am. Send in the first customers."

XXX

By the time he closed the trading post at noon, Rooster was glaring daggers at him. Still, Harrison couldn't help the skip in his step as he headed up the stairs for lunch, which he'd ordered to be brought to his father's room.

He knocked once on the door, then turned the handle and peeked his head inside. "Alejandra?"

"Come in." She was standing over his father, replacing the soiled rag that lay across his forehead with a fresh one.

"Has there been any change?" He stepped inside.

"None." Her brow pinched together with worried lines. "I've been trying to get some broth in him as he sleeps, but he doesn't seem inclined to swallow."

"Is there anything I can do to help?"

"You could try holding him in a sitting position. Do you think he'll be more likely to swallow then?"

"It's worth a—"

The door to the room burst open.

"What do you think you're doing down there!" Rooster barged inside. "You can't pay the Mexicans such a high price for their goods."

Harrison straightened. "Why not?"

"Because we won't make any money!" Rooster crossed his arms over his chest, the sleeves of his shirt cinched tight over his thick, corded muscles.

"I gave the travelers forty percent of the sale price for their goods. That leaves us earning thirty percent for transfer to Austin, and another thirty percent profit ratio for the store owners in Austin who purchase the goods."

"Your father only paid ten percent for the wares."

"I am not my father. I will not run things the way my father did." He narrowed his eyes. "Nor will I tolerate some of the behavior from employees that my father tolerated. Am I clear?"

"The only clear thing is that you're going to run this fort into the ground."

"What do you care, as long as I pay your salary?"

Rooster's lips flattened into a firm line. "What's going to happen when Mr. Rutherford takes back over the fort? You're going to get the Mexicans used to receiving forty percent. Do you know how long it's taken your father to work the price down to ten?"

Harrison slanted a glance at his father, who lay pale and still as death. "Rooster…"

"Don't." The man held up his hands, as though he already knew what Harrison would say. "Don't say it. I can see Mr. Rutherford there. I know he isn't well."

"Has Doc Mullins sent word about when he'll be here?" Alejandra stepped between the two of them. "I thought he was supposed to come yesterday."

"There's a baby," Rooster spat. "He'll be here when he's done attending the birth."

"The doctor's still at the Triple S?" Harrison raised his eyebrows. "Is there trouble with the delivery?"

Rooster shrugged. "I'm just repeating what the doc's wife said when I sent Dugs into town for him this morning."

Harrison rubbed the back of his neck. He'd known Ellie was in labor last night, but was it normal for a woman's labor to last eighteen hours? He hadn't been sent news of the birth, but that had only caused him to think the babe had been born without issue.

"Send Dugs to the A Bar W to see if there is any news about Ellie or her baby," he said.

Rooster's lips flattened. "He's got other tasks he's been assigned."

Harrison only crossed his arms over his chest. "It's my friend's wife giving birth. Have a little compassion."

"Fine, but you still need to reconsider how much you pay—"

"It's my trading post."

Rooster's big, muscular shoulders drew taut. "You won't have much of a post if your guards all up and quit."

That would cause a problem for a few weeks, especially considering how many travelers passed through the fort each day, but he'd be able to hire new men given time. "Something tells me I'd be able to manage. But if you have a problem with how I'm running things, you can leave at any time."

It shouldn't have been possible for Rooster's jaw to grow harder, yet it seemed to turn to stone before his eyes. Then Rooster turned and stormed out the door, slamming it so hard Harrison couldn't stop himself from wincing.

"Sorry you had to witness that." He looked over at Alejandra, who had sidled to the far side of the room and was busying herself with a broom and dustpan.

"It's hardly the worst I've seen of him. But I must admit you have a knack for setting him off."

He smirked. "I've been setting Rooster off since he was in short pants."

"I suppose you're a bit braver than me." She coaxed the dust into a small pile, then bent to whisk it into a dustpan. "I learned long ago it's not to my advantage to have men mad at me."

She spoke the words nonchalantly, as though they were nothing of importance, but something inside his chest tightened.

"Just how did you learn that lesson?" His words were soft against the stillness of the room.

Noise drifted up from the hubbub and commotion outside the fort, and a breeze toyed with the drapes at the window.

Alejandra only ducked her head, causing a cascade of loose black hair to cover the side of her face as she dumped the dust into the waste bin.

That hair was going to be the death of him. Did she ever wear it up? Probably not, few Mexican women did. Growing up on the border, he'd learned to think nothing of it.

But now, standing in a room alone with her, all he could see was how the long strands draped her shoulders and the back of her serving uniform like a beautiful blanket, how the light from the window glinted off the glossy dark strands.

All he could think of was how those same dark tresses had reflected the light from the lamp last night. And how vulnerability had lurked behind her eyes then, just like it did now.

"Alejandra." Harrison took a step closer to her, her name whisper soft on his lips. "What makes you so afraid of men?"

Her eyes came up to meet his, wide and soft. "I... I don't know."

Didn't know, or wouldn't tell him?

He'd wager money on the latter.

She licked her lips and took a step away from him. "Thank you, though, for standing up to Rooster. It's nice to see. And thank you for giving the travelers a fair price. I like the change."

"I like it too."

A strand of hair had fallen against her cheek, and it was all he could do not to tuck it behind her ear and stare in to the deep brown of her eyes.

He'd seen thousands of eyes like hers before, the same shade of brown, set into bronze skin with long black hair. The features were common among Mexican women. And yet somehow her eyes were more lovely, more vibrant, more spellbinding, her hair more silky and glossy.

He took a step back and cleared his throat.

What had they been talking about?

The price he was paying for goods. Right. "You should have seen the look on the first man's face this morning when I offered him forty cents for his saddle blanket. And right after him, I gave the man who brought half a dozen pottery plates fifty cents for the lot, not ten cents. He was elated."

"That's wonderful." She offered him a smile.

A real, true smile.

Her eyes lit up, her cheeks curved beneath her eyes, and she grinned so big the smile took up the entire bottom half of her face.

And now he was right back to staring. At her hair, her eyes, her lips.

She was beautiful...

And troubled.

And hurting.

He forced his gaze away from her. She'd obviously been hurt by a man—or men—before, which meant the last thing she needed was another man ogling her.

But was there a way he could help her?

Maybe if he spent enough time with her, if she grew to trust him, she would tell him what was wrong, where her family was, why she was even at Fort Ashton.

And then he could set things right.

Yes, that's what he'd do. He would spend his lunches with her, and perhaps time at the end of the day like they had last night. And he would earn her trust.

And the part of him that enjoyed spending time with her? That liked seeing her tentative smiles and cascading hair and deep brown eyes?

He shifted. Probably best not to think about that too much. "I need to get back downstairs."

"But your tray." Alejandra jutted her chin toward the lunch sitting atop the chest of drawers. "You haven't eaten."

He walked to the food and grabbed half the ham sandwich and a handful of grapes. "I only have time for a few bites. If you haven't eaten yet, you can finish the rest." He stuffed a trio of grapes into his mouth.

"But ah, the grapes and the pie, that is..." She twisted her hands together, then gestured to the far side of the room. "That food is meant for you. My lunch is over there."

A smaller tray sat atop a stool near where her bedding had

been rolled up in the corner. The food on it was meager, some sort of soup and a roll. "Eat mine then. Please. That's not going to provide the nourishment you need to take care of my father."

XXX

ALEJANDRA SWALLOWED, her throat tight as she stared at the tray of food. The younger Mr. Rutherford clearly didn't understand how the kitchen worked at Fort Ashton. The help didn't get grapes or pie, only paying customers. And that didn't take into account that Rooster would be furious if he learned she'd eaten more food than she was supposed to.

But that was only if he found out...

Mr. Rutherford shoved the final bite of sandwich into his mouth, then stepped to his father's side and reached out to take his hand. The older Mr. Rutherford didn't move, but the younger man still stood there for a moment, his shoulders slumped and his head bent.

Then he straightened and headed for the door. He didn't speak as he left, but his sigh reverberated through the room. Part of her wanted to follow him, to smile and tell him that his father was just going through a rough spell. That Mr. Rutherford would recover soon. That he shouldn't lose hope.

But she wasn't foolish enough to ply him with false platitudes.

"Well, well, look what you're eating for lunch these days."

At the sound of the voice behind her, Alejandra whirled around.

Raul leaned against the second doorway into the room, the one that was close to her bedroll, his arms and feet crossed as if he hadn't a care in the world.

She scowled. "You're not supposed to be here."

"Unfortunately for you, the only person who cares about that is Rutherford, and none of the guards are going to snitch on me." Raul pushed himself off the wall and walked to the dresser.

She realized where he was headed a second before he reached the tray.

"Hey, that's mine!" She leapt at him, but not before he swiped both the sandwich and the grapes.

"Your lunch is over there." He pointed toward the paltry tray of bread and broth sitting beside her bedroll.

She was getting tired of eating the same food every day, of going to bed hungry each night and waking hungry each morning. "Eating a few bites of real food won't hurt anything."

"It will if Rooster finds out, or have you forgotten you're relegated to eating broth and bread?" He smiled at her, but there was nothing kind about the curve of his lips.

"Only because you broke that serving bowl and then blamed me." But even if she could travel back in time and face Rooster over the shards of that cursed broken bowl again, she'd still ask for her food to be garnished rather than her wages.

At least that way she'd have more money for getting Gabriella out of Mexico.

Alejandra stepped forward and reached for one of the grapes in his hand.

He backed away before she could snatch anything. "It was your fault. If you wouldn't have been arguing with me, I would have had no reason to throw it at you."

"You're horrible, do you know that?"

He popped one of the grapes into his mouth and grinned.

She moved to grab the piece of pie before he swiped that too, but Raul shifted in front of her, blocking her path to the dresser.

Her hands involuntarily gripped the sides of her skirt, her

fists forming tight balls. But she forced herself to draw in a breath, long and deep. She had to calm down. Grapes and pie weren't worth fighting her cousin for.

Or rather, that's what she tried to tell herself, but she could almost taste the sweet moistness of the grapes as she watched him pop another one into his mouth, almost taste the savory flavor of the ham from his sandwich and the sugary filling of the dried cherry pie.

"I see you've attracted Rutherford's attention." Raul tossed the last bite of the sandwich into his mouth. "That's going to come in handy."

"I haven't attracted anyone's attention. Mr. Rutherford was here visiting his father, that's all."

Raul tilted his head to the side, studying her. "I think not."

She turned and grabbed the broom from its resting place against the wall, never mind that she'd just swept the floor.

She'd have to be more careful around Mr. Rutherford from now on, make excuses to go to the kitchen or privy or something when he came to visit his father. She couldn't afford for Raul to get any ideas.

"It'll be easier to know what Rutherford is up to this way. You'll be able to tell us if he finds something he shouldn't in that office."

"He won't find anything. All his father's secrets have been destroyed."

"You hope. But if he does find something..." Raul tapped his fingers together. "I've already hired men in Austin to look into his business dealings. I'm sure he's got a secret or two buried there that we can use against him."

"Use against him for what?"

"Just how long do you think we can run a rustling operation under his nose, especially seeing how we use three-quarters of his guards each time we go on a raid? He's bound to notice something is amiss."

Her corset suddenly seemed to grow tight, the boning digging into her sides. "The younger Mr. Rutherford isn't like his father. You won't find anything you can use to blackmail him."

Raul let out an evil little chuckle. "Won't I? Everyone has secrets, Alejandra. Even you. Now tell me, what did you discover last night when you read the papers in his satchel?"

"I already told Felipe. I'm not reading Mr. Rutherford's private correspondence. It's just that, private."

"You will if I tell you to." Raul stepped directly in front of her, never mind he scattered the small bit of dust she'd managed to sweep. "Just like you're going to use some of your feminine charms on him round about ten o'clock tonight and keep him distracted so that he doesn't realize ten of his guards are gone."

Feminine charms? She had no feminine charms, but even if she did, she certainly wouldn't use them the way Raul insinuated.

Wait. Had he said ten o'clock? *Tonight?* "What's going on at ten o'clock?"

Raul raised an eyebrow. "Isn't it obvious? I was going to wait a couple days, make sure the plans were foolproof, but I've only got twelve weeks to get the cattle, remember? It'll be a big run too. It has to be."

Alejandra swallowed the bitterness in her mouth and forced away any thoughts of how Raul might expect her to distract Mr. Rutherford. If her cousin was moving tonight, then she only had one chance to get information from him.

"You didn't waste much time." She worked to keep her voice even as she went back to her sweeping. If she could just appear calm, like she was only casually interested in the information, he'd think nothing of giving it to her.

"I assume you're headed to the A Bar W. Again." Since Raul was still in town, the cattle must be coming from somewhere in the county. Stealing from north of here meant he'd be gone for several days. "Don't you think they've hired enough extra hands to keep an eye on the herd by now?"

"There's a mountain pass on the far east end of their property. No one watches it."

"I see."

Mountain pass. East end of the A Bar W. Ten p.m. She repeated the information in her head twice over, just so she didn't mix something up.

"Keep Rutherford distracted and read his files. I need to bring him in on the rustling, but not until I can be certain he has no choice but to go along with it. The sooner that happens, the easier this will be."

Bile rose in her throat. Harrison Rutherford didn't deserve to be spied on.

But what if she was wrong? What if Mr. Rutherford wasn't as kind and honest as he seemed, and he had a secret big enough and ugly enough Raul could force him into his smuggling ring?

Wouldn't it be better to know now?

She swallowed, then glanced at Raul, who was still watching her. "All right, I'll keep Mr. Rutherford occupied tonight."

She had no choice, no matter how much she detested his games. Because unlike Mr. Rutherford, he had plenty of information he could use against her if she didn't comply.

7

Two dollars. That's how much it had cost Alejandra to get Mariposa to leave her post in the kitchen and sit with Mr. Rutherford. Four days' pay, just so she could have a half hour away from the fort. She wouldn't be concerned if she didn't need the money, but she had no idea how much it would cost to get Gabriella out of Mexico.

Oh, how had her life come to this? How had all her scraping and saving and hard work boiled down to choosing between her sister or the local ranchers?

Alejandra pulled the shawl up higher over her head as she made her way down O'Reilly Street. She passed the bank and general store, the haberdasher's, barber shop, and livery. People meandered into the road and horses clomped on the packed dirt, some pulling wagons and some not. During the hot months of summer, travelers along the Chihuahuan Trail dwindled to a slow trickle, but the early March temperatures lent both the trail and the town of Twin Rivers to bustling activity.

Hopefully it was enough activity that she wouldn't be noticed as she made her way to the sheriff's office.

Her feet already knew the path, and she'd long ago memorized the lines of buildings that made up Twin Rivers. After all, she'd traveled this stretch of road enough over the past year that she could make the walk in her sleep.

But never before had she traveled it in the middle of the day.

Would someone notice her? Would someone figure out what she was up to?

Please, God, no. Protect me. She uttered the prayer without thinking, then pressed her eyes shut. She wasn't quite sure why she bothered to pray, not after the past two years, and yet, she couldn't stop herself.

Hope deferred maketh the heart sick. Her stepfather had shared that verse with her after her mother died, but before his own passing.

He'd been so different from her mother in that regard, talking to God freely, as though they were friends, while her mother had gone to the priest to confess her sins. Her stepfather hadn't prayed to *Santa Muerte*—the Saint of the Dead—either. He'd met missionaries in western Mexico who helped him find a different way of worshiping God. And he'd once told her that leaving the religion his parents and brother practiced help him to step away from that part of his family too, which had been good.

Now, looking back on everything she'd come to know about Javier Velez, she had no doubt why her stepfather had wanted to get away from that part of the family. The two of them had been partners once, many years ago, but the Juan Velez she remembered had wanted nothing to do with Javier.

No, the Juan Velez she remembered had told her to hope in God, no matter what trials crossed her path. She'd clung to that verse about hope in those early days of mourning her mother, then again when her stepfather passed. It had become something of a habit for her, a pattern.

So even now, after two years of being separated from her sister and living at Fort Ashton, she couldn't stop herself from believing God would hear her and help.

If she stopped believing that, she'd have nothing.

No hope.

No light.

No reason to keep going.

Besides, God had answered her prayers over the years. And God had certainly helped her. He'd given her just about everything she asked for—except seeing Gabriella.

Except escaping Raul and his father.

Still, that didn't mean she'd stop counting the little things. They mattered. Today mattered. What she was about to do mattered.

She glanced up at the cloudless blue sky. *Please, God, let me slip the note under the door unnoticed.*

Her first hope was that the town would be busy enough no one would be at the sheriff's office. If a fight had broken out at the saloon or court was in session, the office could be empty.

But before she even reached the steps, she could hear voices coming from behind the closed door.

She glanced around. Across the street, a mother took the hand of her child and led him into the courthouse, and a wagon with a team of oxen rolled slowly down the road. No one seemed be paying her any attention.

And why would they? Entering the sheriff's office in the middle of the day was a normal enough activity. No one watching her would know that she'd only ever made this trip early in the morning, before dawn lit the sky and there was anyone around to see her.

But what if slipping a note under the door and then running off drew the attention of someone across the street?

She drew in a breath, then forced it out.

There was no help for it. She had to deliver this note, or Mr. Westin would lose more cattle.

She climbed the porch steps, suddenly wishing for her light, airy Mexican clothes that would allow her to move freely rather than the heavy fabric and constricting corset of her serving uniform. Hopefully no one was standing just inside the door. Hopefully no one would notice the note. Hopefully no one on the street would remember the woman with her shawl pulled over her head.

She swallowed, then wiped her hands on her skirt before slipping the envelope with the scrap of paper inside it from her pocket. It had the exact information Raul had given her written inside.

Mountain pass. East end of the A Bar W. 10:00 p.m.

She bent and slid it under the door, then scampered off the porch and around the side of the sheriff's office.

The door creaked open as she ducked around the side of the building, the sound overly loud in her ears.

Had she gotten around the building in time?

It didn't matter. There was nothing left for her to do but run.

And run she did. Through the small space that separated the sheriff's office from the candy shop and into the back alley that ran parallel with O'Reilly Street. The stiffness of her corset prevented her from drawing deep breaths, and her heavy skirts and petticoat tangled about her legs. But she did her best to race past the back of the livery and haberdasher's and barbershop, her heart thundering in her chest as she raced all the way back to the servants' entrance to Fort Ashton. Shoving the key Raul had given her into the locked door, she scampered up the stairs, then tried to slow herself to a walk as she headed down the corridor lest she draw any unnecessary attention.

She paused outside the door to Mr. Rutherford's room and

drew in a final, calming breath before pushing the door open and stepping inside.

Then she froze.

Mariposa wasn't in the room, but the younger Mr. Rutherford, Dr. Mullins, and Rooster all stood gathered around the bed.

Rooster turned to look over his shoulder, then narrowed his eyes at her. "Where were you? Why was no one here when Mr. Rutherford woke?"

"He's awake?" She tried to see around the men to the bed.

Rooster's glower only darkened.

"I had to step out." She licked her suddenly dry lips. "But Mariposa..."

The lout. She'd given the woman her money, and she hadn't even stayed in the room!

"Where were you?" Harrison asked.

"I... ah... the... the privy."

Dear God, forgive me for lying... and please, help me not to get caught. It wouldn't be hard to figure out her lie, especially since she'd told Mariposa that she was leaving the fort and running into town.

XXX

She was hiding something—again.

Harrison rubbed the back of his neck. Her face was flushed, and her chest heaved as though she'd been running.

He didn't know a single person who ran back from the privy.

Why did everything with Alejandra feel like it was a secret?

And why did those secrets only make her seem fragile and vulnerable?

With most women, if secrets were involved, he would feel a bit betrayed, or at least like he couldn't trust the woman. But the situation seemed the exact opposite with Alejandra. He almost felt inclined to trust her because she was so secretive.

But his father was of bigger concern. He forced his gaze off the delightfully pink shade of her cheeks and back onto Dr. Mullins. "You said to use the vial on the right to wake Father, but the one on the left should calm him if he panics?"

"Yes, exactly." The doctor gestured to the two blue-tinted bottles that sat atop the headboard. "Come here, Alejandra, so you understand which is which."

She approached the bed, then came to a stop between him and the doctor, causing a whiff of flowers and sunshine to ripple around him. Privy? Indeed.

"Should I wake him to eat every few hours?" she asked the doctor. "Is all the sleeping he did yesterday bad?"

The doctor frowned as he studied his patient. "Not necessarily, no. Most doctors believe the brain needs rest to heal. It could be that the extra sleep is a good sign, especially if he's not waking as agitated as he was a week ago."

The doctor bent down and gripped his father's hand. "Mr. Rutherford, blink if you can understand me."

His father's milky blue eyes blinked.

"Do you feel as though you can try sitting up in bed? Blink once for yes, twice for no."

He blinked once.

"Very well." The doctor moved to the head of the bed and readjusted some pillows, while Alejandra guided him into a sitting position.

His father's movements seemed jerky and unnatural, but both Alejandra and the doc muttered words of praise. The doc even pointed out how he had some use of his left arm.

Rooster, on the other hand, looked like he wanted to start tearing the bed apart.

"What's wrong?" he asked the burly man.

"I just... it's that..." Rooster scratched the back of his head, and if Harrison wasn't mistaken, the man might have even blinked back a glint of moisture from his eyes.

Dr. Mullins and Alejandra continued their conversation in quiet tones, discussing what should be given for food, how often Father should be woken or bathed, and other things pertaining to his care.

"Will Mr. Rutherford get better?" Rooster finally blurted, a muscle pulsing at the side of his jaw. "I mean, he can't talk. He can't get up. Yesterday he didn't even wake up on his own."

"But now he's awake and about to eat," the doctor said, glancing over his shoulder to where Alejandra now stood with a bowl of broth.

Judging by the way Father had already opened his mouth for the first spoonful, he didn't object to the food.

"So you think he can still get stronger?"

Harrison couldn't blame Rooster for asking. The same questions were banging around in his own head.

"Let's step over here, shall we?" The doctor gestured to the far side of the room, near the second door and Alejandra's bedroll.

Harrison followed the two men to the corner.

"I can't make any promises about Mr. Rutherford's recovery." The doctor removed his glasses, causing a small tuft of gray hair to stick out above his ear. "With apoplexy, patients can sometimes recover fully, but the brain can also end up permanently damaged."

The doctor breathed on his glasses, then rubbed the lenses with the bottom of his shirt. "The good news is that Mr. Rutherford is now understanding some of what's going on around him, and he wasn't on my last visit. I'm aware having him sleep for thirty hours straight can be a bit frightening, but the best thing his brain needs to recover is rest. Having him sleep for so long isn't a bad thing as long as he gets adequate nourishment. I'd say we're making progress."

"How long?" Harrison couldn't quite keep the rasp out of his voice. "How long until we know whether he'll recover?"

The doctor shrugged. "Can't say. Could be your father lives like this for years."

He shouldn't be able to feel his face turn pale, but Harrison swore every last bit of warmth drained from it.

Rooster's own white face didn't look much better.

The doctor positioned his glasses back on his head, then reached out and laid a hand on his shoulders. "I really am sorry, son."

"Thank you," he croaked. "But... ah... I best head downstairs now." He'd left a line of people waiting at the trading post when the doctor had arrived.

"And I best be going too," the doctor answered. "Sorry it took me so long to get here though."

"That's okay, I'm just glad to hear all is well with Ellie and her baby." The doctor had brought news of the birth with him when he'd arrived.

"Indeed." Doc Mullins nodded. "It's a sweet girl they've got. Madeline Elise."

Harrison couldn't help the smile that crept across his face. "Madeline, you say? That's a good name."

And he couldn't think of a better man to be a father than his childhood friend, Sam Owens.

"I'll show you out," Rooster said to the doctor.

But when Rooster pulled the door open, a trio of women stood just outside, one about to knock on the polished wood.

Harrison instantly recognized the portly woman with silver-streaked hair standing behind the two younger ones, and a smile split his face.

"Mr. Rutherford." The kitchen maid—Mariposa, if he remembered correctly—curtsied, her smile as wide and bright as the desert landscape. "These two women arrived for you. They said they'd been sent for."

Behind him, Alejandra let out a huff of breath.

"Excuse us," the doctor said.

Mariposa stepped back so that the doctor and Rooster could exit.

"Yes, yes, come inside." Harrison gestured them into the room, then waited beside the door for Consuela to pass. The second she stepped inside, he opened his arms and wrapped her in a full-body hug. "When I sent word to your sister's shop this morning, I didn't expect you to arrive."

"It's good to see you, Harrison," her accent-laded words were muffled against his chest.

Consuela had been the housekeeper at the A Bar W for as long as he could remember. After Wes's ma had died, she'd become something of a surrogate mother—and not just for Wes, but for him and Sam and Cain, who had all grown up without mothers.

"It's been too long." He gave her another squeeze before letting her go.

"*Si.* Though you'd see more of me if you would stick around town."

"That does put a damper on things, doesn't it? Now if you would have stayed working at the A Bar W, I'd have..."

She made a slashing motion with her hand. "We do not bring that up. I am happy where I am, in Mexico."

The way she said Mexico, with an h rather than an x sound in the middle, only reminded him of how different their worlds were.

"You are missed. Please know that."

She smiled. "*Gracias.*"

"Alejandra." Harrison looked at the bed, where Alejandra

stood. She'd shifted his father into a restful position, and it looked as though his eyes were drifting shut. "I have people for you to meet."

She set his father's empty broth bowl on the tray and came toward them. "*Hola*, Mariposa."

Mariposa's cheeks turned pink. Then she reached into her pocket and handed Alejandra something. "This, ah... this belongs to you."

"*Gracias.*"

But whatever it was that Mariposa gave Alejandra, it didn't cause her to smile. In fact, she only seemed to stare harder at the other woman.

Harrison stepped between them and cleared his throat. "Ah, Alejandra, this is Consuela. Her sister runs the weaving shop across the river."

Alejandra's eyes grew wide for a fraction of a second before she blinked the emotion away. "You're Consuela? Consuela Moreno?"

The woman tilted her head to the side. "*Si*, and you are?"

"Alejandra Loyola."

"It's nice to meet you, Alejandra. I have heard your name before, with you being just across the river from my sister."

"I've heard your name too." Alejandra shifted from one foot to the other. She looked as though she had more to say, but no words came out.

Consuela seemed to sense her discomfort too, because she reached out and rested a hand on Alejandra's shoulder, stopping the fidgeting. "You should come visit me sometime, no? Over at the weaving shop? I am staying with my sister for a few weeks."

She nodded. "*Gracias.*"

"And now for the reason I sent word to your sister." Harrison turned toward the young woman Consuela had brought with her. She didn't look very old to be working for him, but that likely meant her situation was dire. "Who have you brought me?"

"This is Hermine." Consuela smiled at the girl. "Her sister works at the weaving shop, but Hermine is old enough to work now, and there are no more looms available."

"I see. How old are you, Hermine?"

The girl stepped forward, her black hair falling about her shoulders. She wasn't particularly pretty, with a long, oval-shaped face and pointy chin, but she had a youthful bounce to her step and seemed eager enough to please him. "Sixteen, sir."

"And you know English?"

"Yes."

"Are you good at caring for others?"

"Yes, I have four younger brothers at home but no mother. I help tend them."

"Well then, it sounds as though you'll be perfect for the job. I'll have you work with Alejandra for a few days. She'll show you how to properly care for my father and see to his needs."

"You're hiring another maid?" Mariposa blurted.

"And I'm supposed to train her to... to help *me*?" Alejandra's voice squeaked over the word *me*, and her brow furrowed as though she was confused by the notion someone would help her.

"Do you not think you can train Hermine?" He raised an eyebrow at her.

"I can, but..." She bit her bottom lip.

"When was the last time you had an evening off? Before my father fell ill, was it not?"

She ducked her head. "*Sí.*"

"But now you are working around the clock, twenty-four hours a day, eating and sleeping in this very room, and not even able to find time to use the privy without being accused of abandoning your post."

"I... I suppose." She kept her head bent, her eyes trained on the floor.

"I am hiring another worker. I'm quite confident Hermine will work out, but if she doesn't then I'll find someone else. It does my father no good to be cared for by a nurse who's too exhausted to adequately do her job, and it does me no good to lose a decent and reliable employee because she works herself into the ground. Am I clear?"

She raised her head to finally look at him. "Perfectly, sir."

"I'll leave the two of you to get started then. If all goes well —and I anticipate it will—I'll put you on a rotating schedule so you can each have time off."

Hermine stepped forward. "I will work hard, *Señor* Rutherford. You will not need to hire another *persona*."

"I'm glad to hear it." He couldn't quite tell what Alejandra was thinking, but at least Hermine was happy about the arrangement. He turned to Consuela. "I don't suppose I can talk you into staying for dinner in a few hours?"

She offered him a small smile. "Not today, I'm afraid."

"Tomorrow then?"

"Tomorrow should work." She inclined her head to the side, then gave a slight nod. "Now I best be off."

"Me too." He could only imagine how late he'd need to keep the trading post open to get through all the travelers waiting for him.

But if working late meant his father would get better care, then it was well worth the sacrifice.

The trouble was, he was almost as happy about Alejandra getting time off as he was about his father's care improving. Had he ever been so concerned about a single employee before?

Sure, he could make a speech about how getting adequate rest meant Alejandra would be able to work harder, or about how he intended to see that all his workers were well provided for.

But his feelings went deeper than that.

And he wasn't quite sure why.

8

D *istract Harrison.* Raul's words played in her mind as Alejandra made her way toward Mr. Rutherford's office, where a thin stream of lamplight shone from under the door.

The hour wasn't terribly late, but the courtyard below was mostly empty, as was the corridor of the hotel on the floor above her. Travelers were always eager to be up with the sun and headed on their journey at the first sign of daybreak, so most of the fort settled down around sundown. Either that, or they were in town at the saloon, cavorting and playing cards.

Alejandra slowed as she neared the door and wiped her palms on her skirt.

The younger Mr. Rutherford had always treated her kindly, so why were her palms sweaty? Why was her heart racing?

Oh, these nights were always the worst. She couldn't sleep, not a wink. All she could think about was whether the note she'd passed to the sheriff would end up being correct. Whether the Rangers would stake out the right spot, whether Raul had changed plans at the last minute and not bothered to say anything.

There was so much that could go wrong. The ranchers in this part of Texas had already lost far too many cattle to her uncle. And while a cattle company like the A Bar W was big enough that losing some stock wouldn't hurt it, smaller ranches like the Triple S or the Circle M could end up going bankrupt.

It was too much to stomach.

The truth was, maybe she needed a distraction tonight as much as Mr. Rutherford did—even if she refused to distract him in the way Raul wanted.

She'd simply check on him, make sure he was comfortable working, then keep an eye on the light under his office door. She'd stay up late enough to make sure he went straight to bed after he was done working, so he wouldn't notice just how many guards were gone.

Yes, that was what she'd do. Then she wouldn't have to worry about exactly how she was supposed to distract Mr. Rutherford for an interminable amount of time.

She knocked on the office door, then waited until she heard the familiar rumble of his voice calling her inside.

She turned the knob and stepped through the doorway. "Forgive me for the intrusion, Mr. Rutherford. I was headed downstairs to get a fresh pot of tea in case your *padre* wakes in the night. Would you like something from the kitchen?"

His brow furrowed, and a scowl crept across his handsome face. "You could have gone to bed early and sent Hermine down for the tea. The point in hiring another nurse was to give you a rest, not have you pick up extra kitchen maid duties."

"I... um..."

He sighed. "I'm sorry. I shouldn't be so short with you. I've been stuck at this desk for too long, and I'm sure you're trying to help. It's just... never mind."

He stood and came around the desk, then gestured to the small sofa that faced the window. "Take a seat over there. Turns out I have a half pot of tea that's not terribly old, and some left-over pie."

"Pie?" She couldn't help the way the word escaped like a dreamy whisper. Was he really going to give her pie? And this time Raul wasn't around to swipe it from her.

As though already anticipating the sweet taste of the dessert, her stomach let out a loud growl.

He raised an eyebrow. "I take it the pie from lunch agreed with you."

Her face heated. Why did her stomach have to betray her in front of her boss?

"Take a seat." He tilted his head toward the small sofa, then picked up the tray that held both tea service and pie from his desk. "That's twice now you've called me Mr. Rutherford. I'll make a deal with you. I'll share some of my pie—if you promise to start calling me Harrison."

She stiffened. "It's not proper. I work for you."

"It's plenty proper." He made his way to the sofa with the tray. "You don't hear Rooster calling me Mr. Rutherford, do you?"

"Rooster is different."

"Why is that?"

She huffed. "Something tells me you're smart enough to figure it out."

Mr. Rutherford set the tray down on the low table in front of the sofa, then slid a large slice of pie onto a plate.

"This pecan pie is one of my favorites. But I mean it—no pie if you keep calling me Mr. Rutherford." A faint smile curved the corners of his mouth.

He only made the offer in jest, she was sure. He couldn't know that it had been a month and a half since she'd had any real food to speak of. "All right. I'll call you Harrison, but only in private. I'm not going to call you by your first name with others around."

He grinned at her and handed over the pie with a fork. "You have yourself a deal, Alejandra."

The first taste of the pie was heavenly. The only problem was, the flavors that filled her mouth were so good she didn't want to chew, she just wanted to sit there and let the taste soak into her tongue.

Mr. Rutherford settled himself beside her with his own piece of pie.

She had the urge to stiffen, but she drew in a breath and forced herself to relax. There was nothing inappropriate about sitting on a sofa with a man while eating a piece of pie.

Just like there had been nothing inappropriate last night when he'd stopped by his *padre's* room.

But also like last night, the air around them felt entirely too intimate. A glance out the window told her darkness had descended on the desert. The light of the moon cut a silvery swath across the cacti and shrubs, and the breeze was just strong enough to sweep through the window and brush her face as she ate.

"Did you need to use the elixir to wake my father for dinner? How did he do?"

Right. Nothing unusual about sitting here, especially not if Mr. Rutherford was more focused on his father than her. "Yes. He was calmer when he woke this time. Not as angry or riled up as he has been."

"And how is Hermine? I take it she has things under control if you're headed off to the kitchen."

"She's with Mr. Rutherford now, but I think she's going to be a good choice for a nurse. She fed your father dinner entirely by herself. All I did was watch."

"I'm happy to hear it, but you're doing an excellent job caring for him too, Alejandra."

Something about the moment, about the sound of her name on his tongue made the breath stop in her lungs, then shutter out in a long whoosh. Did he realize how close they were sitting? That the edge of her skirt brushed his trousers, that the heat from his shoulder was radiating into hers?

She drew in another breath, then forced her gaze away from the handsome man with perfectly shaped lips and wavy brown hair and chiseled cheekbones.

"So tell me," he said, his voice as gentle as the breeze kissing her face, "how is your sister?"

She nearly choked. "W-w-what?"

"Your sister? Didn't you get a letter from her yesterday?"

Oh, that. Of course it was an innocent question. Of course he couldn't know what was truly going on with her and Gabriella and their uncle.

"She's... well." As well as could be expected, at least.

"Where is she?"

Alejandra swallowed, the sweet pie suddenly turning sour in her mouth. It was another ordinary question. But how did she answer it without drawing suspicion?

"Somewhere in Mexico?" Harrison prodded. "You clearly miss her."

"I do miss her. A lot. And she's... she's in Chihuahua." There. That wasn't so bad. Chihuahua was a big enough city. She could tell people where her sister was without revealing everything about their situation.

"Why aren't you there too, with your family?"

Or not. She blew out a breath, long and slow, then slanted a glance at Harrison. He watched her intently, waiting for a response. And something told her if she didn't give him some sort of answer, he'd only keep digging.

"My family isn't in Chihuahua, just my sister. She's at a boarding school."

"Really?" He repositioned himself on the couch, slanting himself so he automatically faced her. "Where do your parents live? Do you have siblings besides your sister?"

"I... ah... my parents are dead. My father died before I was born, and my mother when I was seven, only two years after Gabriella was born. She got remarried to Gabriella's father. His name was Juan, and he raised us alone for five years before he died too. We both went to live with my uncle then."

"This uncle is Raul's father?"

"*Sí.*"

Harrison slid his plate onto the table. "I assume your uncle is rather wealthy if he can afford to send your sister to boarding school."

She gave a single nod, then trained her eyes on her empty plate, almost able to guess the next words that would come out of Harrison's mouth.

"Yet you ended up working here as a servant. You must have found your uncle's house rather distasteful."

Was it possible to feel a person's gaze on you?

It shouldn't be. Alejandra kept her own face down, her eyes staring blankly at the dirty dish in her lap. And yet she could swear she felt the heat of the questions swirling in his eyes, the intense curiosity that she'd not be able to satisfy, because she could never tell him everything.

"You have no idea," she finally muttered.

She didn't expect him to hear the words, but he must have picked up on them, because he reached out and rested his hand over hers on her lap. "I'm sorry you've had a hard time of things with your uncle."

She swallowed back the sudden thickness in her throat. "*Gracias.*"

"Is there anything I can do to help? Other than make sure Raul actually hands over the letters from your sister, that is?"

She pulled her hand away from his. "I'm afraid not, but it's kind of you to offer."

Very kind. In fact, it was the biggest kindness anyone had shown her since she'd arrived in Twin Rivers.

It almost made her want to lean over and rest her head on Harrison's shoulder, to feel his arms wrap around her. Though he wasn't stocky of frame, something told her his arms would be strong and solid. The kind of arms she'd be able to lean on not just tonight, but tomorrow and the day after that, and the day after that.

But what would he think of her if he knew the truth? That she'd been reading all of his father's communications for two years? That now she was supposed to start reading his, just like she was supposed to read through every last paper stuffed into the satchel leaning against the side of his desk? That tomorrow Felipe or Raul or someone else would ask her how many of his papers she'd read and then want her to account for every last detail of their conversation?

That she could go to the law at any time and give them enough information to bring down the rustlers, but doing so would mean her own death and doom her sister to a marriage that just might be worse than death?

So instead of leaning her head on Harrison's shoulder, she stood and gathered the empty dishes onto the tray. "I best get down to the kitchen and make that tea for your father."

"Thank you for sharing the pie with me, Alejandra."

She stilled at the sound of her name on his tongue once again, but only for a moment. Then she pursed her lips and ignored the warm sensation spiraling through her as she strode toward the door.

9

"Rutherford knows something."

Alejandra's eyes sprang open, her heart thudding against her chest as she tried to find the speaker in the dark room.

"Tell me what you learned last night." A hand fisted in the fabric of her nightgown and hauled her up until hot breath brushed against her face.

"Raul?" She blinked against the darkness. What time was it?

"I said, tell me what Rutherford knows."

She glanced across the room, where she could just make out the silhouette of Mr. Rutherford's bed in the dim moonlight that trickled through the window. Hermine was downstairs in the room that the two of them were now sharing, getting a full night's sleep.

"I... he doesn't know anything. He's mad, remember?"

"Not that Rutherford. The son." Raul gave her a small shake, his hand still fisted in the fabric of her nightdress. "The Rangers ambushed us tonight. Rutherford must have learned about our raid and told his friends."

She sucked in a breath then let it out in a long rush. Her

note had worked. *Thank you, Father.*

"Well? What did you learn from him? What does he know?" Frustration edged Raul's voice, which grew a bit louder each time he spoke.

She pulled away from Raul's grip and shifted backward on her tick. "Mr. Rutherford doesn't know anything. How could he? He's barely been here for two days."

"He must have found something in his father's office. The office you said you searched."

She stiffened. "I searched that office three times over. The Rangers might have been tipped off about your raid, but they certainly didn't get any tips from Harrison Rutherford. He was clueless as to any goings on earlier."

"You spent time with him?" A bit of the tension drained from Raul's voice, though it was still too dark to make out more than his vague shadow.

"Over an hour, just the two of us in his office. He didn't act the least bit nervous, didn't even glance at the clock or pay attention to the time. All he did was ask about my family, how I ended up in Twin Rivers from Chihuahua."

Raul snorted. "That must have been an interesting story."

"I made it as boring as possible."

"What did the papers in his satchel say?"

She swallowed. "I... I didn't have a chance to read them. He stayed up late working, and after a while, there was little reason for me to linger in his office." Or rather, she'd wanted to escape his office before she grew closer to him, but she wasn't about to admit such a thing.

"Then go read them now while he's sleeping."

"Now?" Sweat beaded along her hairline, and not because the room was overly hot. "I don't... that is..."

Did she have the option to refuse? Especially considering she'd spent the past two years reading anything and everything of Harrison's father's that she could get her hands on?

But Harrison Rutherford was a good man who was nothing like his father. He didn't deserve to have his correspondence read behind his back.

She feigned a yawn. "I feel as though I've just gone to bed. Perhaps I'll read the papers tomorrow."

"You'll read them now," Raul growled. "Sneak into his office and grab his bag, then bring it back here. No one will think twice about a lamp shining from beneath the door. They'll assume you're tending the older Mr. Rutherford."

"The papers he brought with him from Austin aren't going to tell you how the Rangers found out about your raid."

"I lost two men tonight. Two!" Raul nearly shouted the word. "Shot dead only a handful of feet from where I was. What if they would have shot me too? Then where would we be?"

Free. Like Gabriella's hawk.

Free to go where she wanted, when she wanted, without someone always looking over her shoulder. Free to earn money as she pleased without wondering if one day she'd walk into the storage room where she'd hidden her savings behind a stack of flour barrels to find Raul had taken her money.

Free to find a way to get Gabriella out of Mexico.

Was it terrible of her to wish that her cousin had been shot? To wish him dead so she could have her freedom?

She shifted on the tick, a sickening feeling cramping her gut. There was a time where she'd never have thought such a thing about another person, but now?

A hand wrapped around her elbow in the darkness, then jerked her forward until she could feel the heat from Raul's body. "Harrison Rutherford is a loose end that I have no control over. That needs to change. Now. Go to his office and find me something I can use against him."

No. Her tongue ached with the desire to say it, but she held the word in.

Resisting Raul was pointless. She couldn't risk angering him to the point he'd send her back to Mexico, where she'd have no money and be under the constant watchfulness of her uncle and his guards.

Besides, she was already doing everything she could to get him captured and removed from her life.

But what if Harrison Rutherford was hiding something? What if he was less honorable than he seemed? He had seemed so kind and caring earlier, offering her pie, telling her to call him by his first name, offering her a seat on his comfortable sofa.

But what if it was a ruse?

The sooner she found out, the better.

XXX

"Are you sure you won't take them?" The farmer with sun bronzed skin who sat across the table in the trading post frowned at Harrison. "They are beautiful hogs. The best. Two of them are outside the window. See?"

Harrison shifted, using the invitation to turn toward the window and inhale a whiff of fresh air. He'd only been back from lunch for an hour, but the room was packed with warm bodies, the stench of sweat mixing with the smell of spices and leather and wool.

Honestly, he didn't know how his father had sat at this table day after day in the stifling heat. And to think, he'd even opened the trading post an hour late that day, seeing how the entire town and fort had been agog about two rustlers being shot just south of the border last night, when Cain and his men had apprehended a couple hundred cattle stolen from the A Bar W.

Harrison scanned the desert outside the fort, his gaze stopping on a portly woman he assumed was the farmer's wife. She waved at him then pointed to two hogs.

Harrison smiled at her and turned back to the farmer. "I'm sorry, but we don't transport livestock."

Especially not in the quantities the farmer was expecting. If one or two hogs were going to San Antonio, they might be able to accompany the next caravan. But thirty-five of them?

"But *Señor*—"

Harrison held up his hand. "If you want to take them to San Antonio, you will need to drive them there yourself."

"I brought them *here*, all the way from—"

"Mr. Rutherford, sir."

Harrison looked up to find one of his father's guards plowing through the maze of packed bodies.

"There's been a bit of a disturbance. You're needed in the courtyard."

Harrison pushed to his feet with a bit too much enthusiasm. "Excuse me. I'll be back in a few minutes."

A collective groan rose up from the men filling the room. News of him paying more for goods hadn't taken long to spread. It seemed as though half the town of Ojinaga had shown up today, everyone trying to trade a handful of odds and ends so that they could verify for themselves that Fort Ashton was indeed paying more for wares.

"I've been waiting three hours," one man called out.

"I've been here for two!"

"I know. I know." Harrison raised his hands. "I'll be back as soon as possible, and I will keep the doors to the post open late tonight. Everyone in line now will be seen before I have my dinner. I swear to it."

More muttering rose from the crowd as he threaded

through the throng of people, but Harrison didn't let that stop him.

Once he reached the back of the room, he turned to the guard. "See to it that no one new is allowed in this line. If others want to trade, they will need to wait until tomorrow."

"Yes, Mr. Rutherford. The sheriff is this way."

The sheriff? That's what the disturbance was?

As soon as Harrison stepped into the sunshine of the court-yard, he spotted both Daniel and their friend Cain, who was captain of the Ranger unit camped by the river. They were surrounded by maybe a dozen people, including a spitting mad Rooster.

"Sheriff," Harrison said as he approached. "Captain Whitelaw. I hear your mission was a success last night."

"Not as successful as I'd hoped." Cain sauntered toward him, his long blond hair tumbling over his shoulders. "I wish we would have been able to capture a couple of the men. Then maybe we would have more information about their leader. The two we shot ended up dying before we could move them to Doc Mullins's."

"At least you prevented Wes from losing more cattle."

"That we did." Cain gave a firm nod, then shoved a piece of paper at him. "But now we've got ourselves another problem. Did you see a man who looks like this pass through the trading post yesterday?"

Harrison studied the sketch. The face staring back at him was clearly Mexican, but so many people went through the fort that it was impossible to remember a single face. It was the same as when he'd gone searching for Hernando, his cook's missing son, last fall.

"I really can't tell you. I'm sorry."

"We think he tried trading a pair of silver candlesticks and picture frame, if that helps."

"Oh, yes, I remember now. Or better, I remember the

candlesticks and picture frame. The man wasn't happy with the price I would give. He was the only person all day who refused to trade with me."

"And the man in the sketch is the one who had the candlesticks?" Cain's alert, hazel-colored eyes seemed to be taking in everything going on in the fort around him, not just the conversation they were having.

Harrison closed his eyes and tried to recall the interaction from yesterday. "Yes, I really think I saw him—"

"Do we need to send for your father's lawyer?" Rooster's voice cut through his memory.

Harrison blinked at the guard. "Mr. Adams? What would we need him for?"

Cain snatched the paper away from him. "No need for lawyers just yet. We're only looking for information."

Rooster came up beside them, his bulky arms and tightly coiled muscles making him look almost overweight compared to Cain's lithe, sleek form. "Mr. Rutherford Sr. doesn't give information to the law without Mr. Adams present."

Harrison sighed. "I'm a lawyer too, remember?"

The guard scowled. "That doesn't mean you should be your own defense."

Harrison rubbed his temple. "I don't think I'm defending myself." He turned to Cain. "Am I? Have I been accused of something I'm unaware of?"

Daniel stepped into their group, apparently done speaking with the woman who'd been beside him for five minutes or better. "The man in that sketch was found dead this morning, about five miles outside of town. His saddlebags contained no valuables, but judging by the food and clothes he had, he looked as though he was headed on a long journey. We came here to see if he had passed through the fort."

"Which he did," Harrison added.

Rooster harumphed beside him.

Daniel dipped his head. "I've had three different people tell me he tried to trade candlesticks and a picture frame. Evidently, he was quite boisterous about not getting a deal in his favor and deciding to go to San Antonio himself."

"And then he ended up dead," Harrison muttered.

"Exactly."

Harrison shook his head. "Like I told Cain, I remember him being displeased with the price I offered for the candlesticks, but I don't have my father's eye and had no way of telling if they were real silver. I had no idea ill had befallen him until just now. But feel free to ask around the fort, and I'm happy to answer any other questions you might have."

"We didn't find candlesticks or a picture frame on him," Cain drawled. "Nor did we find a horse, though there were tracks near his body. Could be a simple robbery gone bad."

Rooster snapped his fingers. "It was probably bandits. Heard they gave a group of travelers trouble north of here a few weeks ago."

Daniel frowned. "What travelers? And what kind of trouble? This is the first I've heard of it."

Rooster went on to explain how bandits had robbed a group of travelers near where the railroad was being laid in Alpine a few weeks ago.

Harrison listened for a bit, then excused himself. But even as he went back and took his place behind the table inside the trading post, he couldn't wipe the image of the man with the candlesticks from his mind. Nor could he stop himself from wondering, if he would have traded the man for that silver yesterday, would he still be alive?

XXX

"Something doesn't sit right about that body." Daniel repositioned the hat on his head to better block the sun as he stared out over the desert. Here they'd just had success in stopping more rustlers last night, but that triumph hadn't even lasted a day now that a dead body had turned up.

"I agree about the body," Cain said from beside him, his lanky gait covering the path back to Twin Rivers at nearly double the pace Daniel normally walked. "Can't put my finger on what the problem is though."

"Me neither." Daniel sighed. "Reckon the guard might be right. It could have been bandits."

"Wasn't no bandits harassing travelers north of here two weeks ago."

"How do you know?"

Cain shrugged, his shoulders moving up and down in that lackadaisical way he had. "Would have heard."

"We did hear. Just a few minutes ago."

"That was made up."

Daniel studied the Ranger who walked beside him as though he hadn't a care in the world. He and Cain had never been much of friends. Sure, they'd grown up together, and they'd each shared friendships with Harrison, Wes, and Sam, which meant they'd spent a good bit of time running roughshod over the desert together. But the two of them had always fought more than they'd gotten along...

And that had been before Pa had lost his leg to a band of outlaws while Cain had been tasked with guarding the town.

Still, Cain Whitelaw was a force to be reckoned with. Daniel didn't wonder why the man had been promoted to a Ranger captain and now led his own group of thirty men. If he was a betting man, he'd put his money on Cain being right about Rooster making up the story of bandits near Alpine. The man had a way of sensing these things.

The truth was, Cain was more outlaw than lawman. In fact,

that's what people who saw him always thought. There was something about the long blond hair that Cain didn't ever bother pulling back into a queue, the dusty brown overcoat he always wore, the carefree way he carried himself, and the razor-tipped sarcasm that rolled off his tongue that made people naturally assume he was on the wrong side of the law.

And maybe that was what made Cain so good at his job. He didn't just look like an outlaw—he thought like one too.

"I'll send my deputies out to canvas the town," Daniel said. "See if someone else might remember the traveler. Should probably send Abe up to Alpine to have a chat with the sheriff there too. Just to rule out Rooster's story about the bandits."

Cain swiped a blade of desert grass from the side of the trail, then peeled back the outer shoot before sticking the stalk in his mouth. "Don't bother. The only people you need to question are at the fort."

Daniel slanted Cain a glance but didn't waste breath asking how Cain knew that too. "You want to know what worries me the most about all this?"

Cain quirked an eyebrow.

"How the body was found. If the Cunningham boys wouldn't have made that bet with the Miller boys about there being a hidden stream north of the Chihuahuan Trail, no one would have stumbled on the body. I mean, whoever put the bullet in that traveler's chest did a pretty fine job of hiding him out in the middle of nowhere."

Cain scratched the side of his head and looked to the north, in the general direction of where the body had been found. "Hadn't thought of that. Been a while since I've been through that stretch of desert. You know it better than I do."

"Just think about it. If the Millers and Cunninghams wouldn't have been over a mile off the trail searching the desert, what would have happened to the body?"

"It would have decayed long before it had been found or identified."

"Exactly. The man likely has a family back in Mexico, but the only reason I have to get the Mexican law involved and track down the family is because his body was found and I can prove he was murdered. If the body hadn't been found..."

"His family would have been waiting for his return for months, only to have him never come back," Cain finished.

"And we would have never heard of it, especially not with the family being on the other side of the border. We wouldn't even know to search for a body."

Cain's face darkened beneath the shade of his hat. "That makes me like this even less."

"It makes me wonder if there might be more bodies out there somewhere. Remember last fall Harrison had a cook with a son that went missing somewhere along this stretch of trail. The last time he was seen was at Fort Ashton, then he just up and disappeared."

"I think Marshal Redding was working with him on that. Think there was another person or two they were looking for, but the case went cold." Cain rubbed the side of his head beneath his hat brim.

"That just makes me wonder, maybe we need to search the desert for more bodies."

They reached the edge of O'Reilly Street, the main road that ran through town. Cain waited for a wagon to pass, then started walking down the well-trodden road. "*You* need to search the desert, you mean. My men are here to catch the rustlers, remember?"

"Right," Daniel gritted. "That's what I meant. Me and my men."

Cain whacked him in the shoulder, a grin spreading across his face. "I was teasing. Relax a little. As long as I'm not using the men to look for rustlers, you can have whomever you want for your search. If you want me to help coordinate it too, I can, but something tells me you'll do a fine job."

Daniel felt his shoulders relax as he climbed the steps to his office. "Thanks. And thanks for coming with me today."

Cain had just happened to be inside when the Cunningham boys had burst through the door before lunch, stammering about how they'd found a body. He'd offered to ride out with him to take a look so he didn't have to call in an extra deputy.

"You have to let me know which is better. The rosemary or the cheddar."

"Huh?" Daniel finished opening the door to his office and blinked, letting his eyes adjust to the dimness of the room after being in the sun.

"The bread." His sister shoved two pieces of bread in his face, then pushed a strand of long brown hair over her shoulder. "I can't decide which to try selling at the general store."

Abe, who had the distinction of being the longest serving deputy in Twin Rivers County, sat behind the small desk shoved against the far wall of the room. "The cheese is better. Tell her."

A third familiar voice said, "I think she should offer both."

Daniel blinked again, then moved his eyes in the direction of his wife's voice, only to find her sitting behind his desk, a hand resting atop the growing mound in her stomach.

"Hey, darlin'. Didn't realize you were coming to town today." His boots clomped against the wood plank flooring as he crossed his office, then bent to give Charlotte a peck on the cheek.

She smiled up at him, the look on her face so wide and pure he had an unquenchable urge to lower his lips and kiss her—and not chastely.

"I wasn't planning to come." Her breath brushed against his cheek as she spoke. "Not with Anna Mae scheduled to come over and try some bread recipes. But when we had an argument over which kind she should bake to sell at the general store, we decided to come here for a second opinion."

"I'll give you an opinion," Cain offered.

"Thank you!" Anna Mae handed him the two pieces of bread Daniel hadn't taken earlier, then whirled, her wide Mexican skirt swishing behind her as she made a beeline for the table at the back of the office where the bread was set out. "You still need to try some, Daniel."

She cut a piece of bread from each loaf, spread a dollop of butter across them, and brought them to his desk. "Here you go."

Daniel took a bite of the first one. Subtle hints of rosemary filled his mouth, the taste of the herb a gentle compliment to the texture of the bread. "This one is delicious, but..."

He took a bite of the cheese bread, and another set of flavors exploded on his tongue, the chewy goodness of baked cheese adding both flavor and extra texture to the loaf.

He groaned, his mouth still half filled with food. "I'm not sure I can decide."

"That's what I said." Charlotte tore off a piece of the rosemary bread on the desk. "It's impossible to pick."

"Not for me," Cain answered around his own mouthful of food. "It's the rosemary, hands down."

"No, it ain't." Abe slapped his hand on the desk. "It's the cheese."

"Maybe you could try combining them and make a rosemary cheese bread." Charlotte tore off another bit of bread from the piece he'd set on the desk.

"Not sure I'd be able to pick if you gave me a third choice." Cain patted his flat belly.

"You could take a couple loaves down to the Rangers," Charlotte suggested. "I'm sure they'd help you decide which one's better."

Cains straightened. "You don't need to come down to the camp. We can decide right here. I like the rosemary."

Daniel sent his wife a scowl. Cain was right. The last place Anna Mae needed to be was in a camp full of single men. With her long brown hair, delicately sculpted face, and dark eyes, she was too beautiful for her own good. And now that his parents had up and moved to Houston, he was the one responsible for keeping her in check.

"That's a good idea, Charlie." Anna Mae planted her hands on her hips and studied the bread on the table. "I should test the bread on the Rangers."

"Or you could take some to the Owens," Daniel suggested. "I'm sure they wouldn't mind some extra food with Ellie just giving birth and all."

Anna Mae humphed. "That's not going to work."

Charlotte snickered, then pulled her hand up to cover her mouth, but the gesture came a moment too late.

"What's going on at the Owens's?" Daniel gave his wife a little nudge.

"Anna Mae got herself kicked out." The hand that covered her mouth wasn't quite able to hide her smile.

Daniel narrowed his eyes at his sister. "What'd you do?"

Anna Mae crossed her arms over her chest. "How am I supposed to know? All I can tell you is Sam said if we did any more hovering, he'd have us arrested for trespassing. The man's a tyrant."

Charlotte cleared her throat, a grin still plastered across her face. "Actually, to be clear, he said I was welcome back, but that if Anna Mae did any more hovering, he'd have her arrested."

"Now that's something I've got a hankering to see," Cain drawled, a half-smile raising one corner of his mouth. "Daniel locking his sister up."

Anna Mae shot a death glare at Cain. "You'd get some kind of twisted pleasure out of that, wouldn't you?"

"Not worth it." Daniel held his hands up in a gesture of innocence, even though he could see Anna Mae being just bullish enough that she'd need to be threatened with a night in jail. "If I lock her up, I'll spend the next fifty years of my life paying for it. Sorry, Cain. Blood before water an' all."

Cain's lips twisted up in a taunting grin, and he studied Anna Mae as though he was envisioning her behind a cell door, just for the fun of it. "Let me know if you change your mind, Sheriff. That'd be a hoot to watch."

"Now you listen here..." Anna Mae stepped forward and jabbed a finger into Cain's chest. "If you think for one moment that—"

"If Sam sent you home, I take it Ellie is doing well?" Daniel came around the side of his desk, closer to Anna Mae in case he needed to haul his firebrand of a sister off Cain.

But his question broke Anna Mae's glare, and she took a step away from Cain. "More than fine. She's up and around, baking biscuits and cutting vegetables for dinner."

"Ellie's right natural with the babe," Charlotte added, then settled a hand on her own stomach, a wistful look on her face. "I expect she'll have a whole heap of young'uns with Sam."

"Shouldn't come as a surprise seeing how she's got eight younger siblings," Cain muttered.

Anna Mae shoved another strand of hair behind her shoulder. "All I can say is, I hope one day I'm as good with a babe as Ellie is."

Cain's face turned suddenly pale, and a look Daniel couldn't quite name crossed it.

Cain must have sensed his gaze, because he looked up, and their eyes met, but Daniel still didn't have a clue what the odd look meant.

"Did you decide which loaf of bread is better?" Cain jutted his head toward the extra piece of rosemary bread on the desk. "Otherwise, I can take the loaves to my men and let y'all know the verdict. No need for Anna Mae to come down to the camp though."

"Oh, that's perfect!" Anna Mae clapped her hands together, then made a beeline toward the table, where she busied herself putting the loaves into the sack on the table. "Now I can test my doughnuts on the men tomorrow instead of waiting until Sunday."

Cain scowled. "You don't need to test the doughnuts on the men."

"Sure I do. They give me the quickest answers."

Daniel rubbed his temple. How could his sister be so clueless when it came to men and the ruckus she caused at that camp? "Anna Mae..."

"I'll come into town and get them," Cain snapped. "I already said there was no need for you to come down to the river."

She frowned. "Why? Your men like my visits."

"Do I really need to spell it out for you?"

"Spell what out?"

Charlotte snickered, then gave her head a small shake.

"You distract my men," Cain mumbled, his ears turning red. "I can't have you down there, because whenever you arrive, they forget what they're supposed to be doing and feel entitled to a break."

Anna Mae straightened. "And what's wrong with the men having a break? Maybe you work them too hard."

Cain crossed his arms over his chest. "That's not the point. You're not allowed at the camp anymore."

"You're being an oaf."

"I'm being sane. And a good captain. Now you heard me. No more visits." Cain snatched the sack of bread out of Anna Mae's hand and whirled toward the door, leaving Anna Mae to scowl at his back.

"I'm a grown woman, Cain Ramos Whitelaw. I can—"

Thud! The door slammed shut.

"—Go anywhere I please," Anna Mae muttered, then stomped her foot, her glare hot enough to burn a hole through the wood of the door.

Daniel sighed. "Anna Mae, how many times have I told you to stay away from the Rangers? Don't get upset because Cain's saying it too."

"The men like what I bake. Besides, you should see the trail food they eat if I don't bring them anything. All pork and beans, I swear. You can't tell me there's something wrong with baking them bread or doughnuts."

"There's nothing wrong with baking them bread or doughnuts." Daniel rubbed the back of his neck. "Just do it how Cain said. Let him know you have food, and he'll come pick it up. Or I can take it down to the river."

"It's not the same."

"And it's not proper for you to be in a camp filled with men. There's only one kind of woman that visits camps like that, and it's not a lady." Didn't his sister notice the way half the Rangers drooled over her?

She could have a husband twelve times over if she wanted one.

And yet, not a one of the Rangers seemed like the type of man who could make his sister happy.

Not a one person in town seemed like the type of man who could make his sister happy.

To be honest, not a one person he'd ever met seemed like that type of man.

And it was a problem. She was too pretty, too friendly, too energetic. Men fell in love with her everywhere she went, and even though she was old enough to get married, she seemed years away from settling down.

He didn't have the first clue what to do about it—other than to ban her from the Ranger camp.

10

"What have you found out?"

Alejandra jumped, then put a hand to her chest, her heart suddenly hammering against her ribs as Raul stepped out from the behind the door of the stairway.

Good thing she'd only been carrying soiled sheets from Mr. Rutherford's bed when she'd opened the door. If she'd been holding a tray, every dish would have shattered.

"You can't sneak up on me like that. You'll scare a year off my life."

"I asked what you found out, and be fast about it. I don't have much time." Raul looked over his shoulder and down the empty stairwell. "One of the guards almost spotted me sneaking in."

"I thought you said the guards would let you come and go as you pleased, never mind what Mr. Rutherford said."

"Most of them," he gritted. "Not that Fordham fellow or his friends. They've taken a disliking to me."

"I wonder why." She meant to speak the words to herself, but they emerged a little louder than she intended.

Raul's lips pressed into a hard line, and he reached out and fisted his hand in her hair.

She yelped and dropped the bedclothes. "Stop. You're hurting me."

He only dragged her closer. "I want to know what those papers in Rutherford's satchel said, and you're going to tell me. Now."

"N-n-nothing."

His grip tightened, and she sucked in a breath, then winced against the pain. "I told you to read those papers last week, and you still haven't done it?"

"I did it, I promise. The papers just didn't say anything of use. I would have sent word to you if they had."

The words were out before she had time to think about them.

Would she have turned over information Raul could use against Harrison? She wasn't sure, not really. But it hadn't mattered, because there had been nothing to pass on.

Raul's fist tightened yet again, and she reached up and clamped her hand around his wrist, trying to stop him from pulling harder. "Please stop. That hurts, and I'm telling you the truth. There was nothing helpful in that satchel."

He released her hair, then shoved her backward, barely giving her enough time to clamp a hand over the screaming section of her scalp before she hit the wall.

"What was in the satchel then?" He loomed over her, his eyes hot.

She licked her lips. "Lawyer papers. Court documents. Lists of legal fees. Briefings. Mr. Rutherford works for men like your father. Everything in the bag was some kind of business contract or sale or legal fee. There was the negotiation of the sale of a warehouse at an astronomical price and a lease for land where they want to put in a new railroad station."

Raul's eyes narrowed, and a muscle pulsed at the side of his jaw.

She pressed herself harder against the wall and swallowed. "I swear to you, Raul, everything in that satchel was so legal it was almost painful to read. If the younger Mr. Rutherford is involved in anything underhanded, he certainly doesn't have evidence of it in that bag."

"What about his mail? Is there anything we can use in that?"

She shook her head. "He hasn't gotten any mail. He's only been here a week, and I don't think the post has caught up with him yet."

Raul's lips twisted into a sneer. "Keep watching. If anything turns up..."

"I'll let you know."

Raul searched her face for a moment longer, then spun away from her. "Maybe my informants in Austin will find something in his office."

Her stomach turned sour. That was the second time he'd mentioned hiring men in Austin to search Harrison's things. Why couldn't her cousin leave the poor man alone?

"What about the senior Rutherford's mail?" he snapped. "I know he's had communication I need to see."

"I pulled out the relevant letters. There was one about a contract to transport pottery from Chihuahua to San Antonio."

"Where is it?"

"In the top drawer of my nightstand. Do you want me to meet you outside with the letters later tonight or give them to Felipe?"

"No. I'll get them on my own."

She stilled. "But they're in the room I share with Hermine."

"I'll be able to sneak in there easier than I was able to get here."

The thought made her cold. It was true Raul would sneak

into her room from time to time, but usually because she was there. She didn't want him nosing around by himself.

Not that she had anything he'd care about besides her money, and she was too smart to hide that in her room where he could easily find it. But still, the thought of him being there, touching her bed, sifting through the second drawer in her nightstand—the one that held her underthings—made a shutter ripple through her.

"When's your next raid?" she blurted, half without thinking. Was it too much to ask God to allow Raul to be caught during it? She wasn't sure how much more of this she could take.

Raul narrowed his eyes. "Why do you care?"

She swallowed, then shook her head. Teach her to speak without thinking first. "No reason. I was just wondering if you needed me to distract Mr. Rutherford sometime soon."

"I'm hoping to do something next week, but I want to stay quiet about it. Can't risk losing any more men, or I won't have enough left to make cattle runs."

"Of course."

She offered Raul a tight smile. But he didn't smile in return, just turned and disappeared down the stairs, intent on searching her room.

11

"Please, God, let the raft be on this side of the river."
Alejandra whispered the words into the night as she ducked into the clump of shrubs on the bank of the Rio Grande. Raul usually kept the raft hidden here, but since he'd been banned from the fort, she had no way of knowing what side of the border both he and the raft would be on.

She'd tried crossing the border two weeks ago, right after Hermine had come to the fort, but the raft had been gone, and she hadn't left early enough to give herself time to walk to one of the shallow river crossings. Then last week she'd gotten word Consuela had been gone, so there was no point in making the trip.

Now Consuela was supposedly back at her sister's weaving shop, and Alejandra had left the fort right at midnight, hoping that if the raft wasn't there, she'd at least have time to walk to one of the crossing points. She couldn't afford to wait much longer, not when the calendar flipped ever closer to the time she was supposed to return to Mexico.

Please, God, let the raft be here. Let me be able to meet with Consuela.

Alejandra thumped through the brambles, trying to see the ground with the thin sliver of moonlight filtering down through the brush. Did she have the right spot? Maybe she needed to head a bit upriver?

Or maybe the raft wasn't here at all. Last night the Rangers had foiled yet another of Raul's raids, thanks again to a note she'd left for the sheriff. The fort had been alive with the news when she'd awoken that morning, but she'd not seen Raul or Felipe all day. Rooster and the other guards who went on the raids had all been at the fort, acting as though nothing had happened. That meant her cousin was probably somewhere in Mexico, lying low, and it would be a week or two before he'd—

Thunk!

Her foot connected with something hard, and she sucked in a breath, then clamped her hand over her mouth so no one could hear her silent cry of pain.

At least she'd found the raft. She slanted her gaze toward the sky, a wide expanse of black with an intricate tapestry of stars. *Thank you, Father. I think?*

She sucked another breath in through her nose, then tried her best to ignore the pain in her foot as she picked up the oar from the center of the raft and gave the simple wooden platform a shove into the river. She waited for the last minute to step aboard, which allowed her to keep her feet dry as she glided silently into the middle of the river.

She paddled quietly, letting the river current take her at an angle. She had to admit, Raul had picked a good place to hide a raft. In the two years since she'd come to Twin Rivers, no one save Raul and his men had ever found it. It was just far enough west of town that no one bothered to cross the river here, and the shrubs were thick enough on both sides of the river that it could be easily concealed.

By the time the raft reached the opposite shore, the throbbing in her foot had turned into a dull ache. Hopefully it would continue to lessen, even though she had a two mile walk or better. She pulled her shawl over her head and set off. This part of the trip was familiar. She'd used this raft to visit Ojinaga before, sometimes even under Raul's direction. But the house of the weaving shop manager was located east of town on the river, and she was less familiar with that stretch of desert.

By the time she arrived at the small house situated beside the large adobe factory, she guessed it to be about two in the morning. That gave her an hour to conduct her business, and two hours to get back to the fort undetected.

Dear Father, please don't let anything go wrong.

She raised her hand and knocked softly on the door.

Silence greeted her.

She knocked again, harder this time. The sound echoed over the desert, but what else was she to do?

A moment later, a dim lantern flickered in one of the windows. She heaved out a breath as the door opened a crack.

"Who's there?"

"Alejandra Loyola. I am looking for Consuela Moreno. She said I should visit sometime."

"Alejandra, *sí*? Come in, come in."

The door opened to reveal none other than Consuela standing there with the lantern.

"I'm sorry to come in the night. But it's hard for me to get away during the day." Alejandra stepped inside.

"You are hardly the first woman to seek me out at this time. Let's sit in the kitchen. You look as though you could use a bit of tea." Consuela closed the door, then bustled down the narrow hallway to the kitchen at the back of the house. She gestured to one of the chairs at the table. "I have heard of you before, living in Twin Rivers and working for that horrible

Rutherford. Is it a job at the weaving factory that you'd like, or do you want to leave Twin Rivers altogether?"

Alejandra looked around the small kitchen with its hutch, handful of cupboards, and stove. This was what it was like to visit the infamous Consuela Moreno? She got led into a homey kitchen and offered tea before discussing business? Even in the middle of the night?

"I want to leave." Alejandra settled herself into the chair.

"You are friendly with Raul Velez, yes?" Venom filled Consuela's voice as she spoke Raul's name. "That would make it impossible to stay in Twin Rivers."

"We're not friends."

Consuela pumped water into the tea kettle, then set it on the stove. "That is not what the women say."

"We're cousins. His father is the brother of my late stepfather."

Consuela stilled, their eyes meeting across the kitchen. "That will make getting you out of Twin Rivers more difficult. Do you want to resettle in America or Mexico?"

"America, but..." She licked her lips, then blew out a breath. "I don't need your help leaving. I need your help getting my sister out of Mexico before I go."

"You have a sister?" Consuela reached onto the shelf above the stove for a tin of tea leaves.

"At Sisters of St. Mary's Boarding School in Chihuahua. Her name is Gabriella."

The plump woman turned away from the stove, where the kettle was hissing and gurgling as it warmed. "How is it that you are a maid at Fort Ashton, but your parents are sending your sister to boarding school?"

"It is my uncle's doing. My parents are dead, and I'm afraid the rest is a rather long story. Let's just say that I'd have left Twin Rivers long ago if not for my sister. She isn't safe, and I need to take her with me."

"A boarding school where girls aren't safe?" Consuela's brow furrowed as she poured hot water over the tea leaves. "I've not heard of this."

"It's not the school that's unsafe. It's my uncle."

"Ah, Raul's father, yes?" She moved to the small cabinet on the wall and took a pencil and paper from the drawer. "Where does your uncle live?"

"His estate is outside Juan Aldama, about thirty-five kilometers from Chihuahua."

"And his name?" Consuela leaned over the table and began writing.

It felt heavy on her tongue, but Alejandra forced herself to speak it. "Javier Velez."

The pencil thudded against the counter. "Javier Velez? As in, the former governor of Chihuahua? Owner of *La Colina* Cattle Ranch?"

Alejandra swallowed. "That would be him, yes."

"You expect me to kidnap the daughter of such a powerful man?"

"Niece. Gabriella is his niece. And it's not kidnapping if she goes willingly."

Consuela tossed her pencil onto the table, the steeping tea on the table long forgotten, even though the scent of poleo and mint filled the room. "Niece, daughter, it makes little difference. I help grown women flee difficult situations, sometimes with their children, yes, but it's not the same. I cannot take a child away from her guardian, and especially not from a family like the Velezes. Every constable in northern Mexico would come after me."

"Not if they didn't know you did it."

"I cannot."

Alejandra reached into the pocket of her skirt and pulled out a stack of bills. "I can pay."

Consuela's nostrils flared. "I do not take money from women in need. I find them work or give them money."

"Then help me. Please. My uncle, he's not a nice man."

"I'm aware."

Something about the way Consuela said it, about the hard edge in her voice, made Alejandra wonder if she'd helped women escape from her uncle before. "Then you know Gabriella needs to be rescued."

"And what happens once I bring her to you? Surely you don't expect her to work at Fort Ashton without your uncle finding out."

"We disappear. I have money hidden, plans made. I would have taken her away already, but I can't get to Gabriella with Raul at Fort Ashton watching everything I do. My uncle would know within hours of my disappearing, and he'd assume I'd be heading straight for Gabriella. He'd be right."

The older woman's dark brown eyes gave nothing away as she studied her. "What is it that you do at Fort Ashton?"

"I am Mr. Rutherford's nurse. But before he fell ill, I was a kitchen maid."

"That's not what I meant. Yes, you have jobs that you work, but if your uncle wanted you to play servant, why not give you a position in his own house?"

She looked down at the scarred table. "He sent me away when I fell out of favor with him."

"There is more to the story."

The chair suddenly felt hard beneath her bottom, and she shifted awkwardly. "It's not a story I can share. But none of this changes that Gabriella is in danger. If you don't help, I will have to try myself."

She scoffed. "You just said your cousin would catch you within hours of leaving Fort Ashton, that everyone knows how badly you wish for your sister."

"They do." She cast her eyes back down at the table. She

wished she could have kept that from Raul and her uncle, wished she could have somehow hidden her love for her sister. But doing so had been impossible, especially after her uncle decided to separate them. "I won't be able to live with myself if I don't try to get my sister. If you can't help, I will go to Chihuahua on my own."

"You'll end up dead."

Death was something she already risked each time she slid a note under the sheriff's door.

The room was silent around them, the air still with the dead of night, while scents of the tea grew to fill the kitchen. Consuela took a few bills from the stack on the table, then slid the rest of the money back across the rough wood. "I suspect this endeavor will cost more than usual. There will no doubt be guards or workers at the school to bribe."

"So you'll help?" She blew out a breath, her chest feeling suddenly light.

"I will go to Chihuahua and see what I can learn about this Sisters of St. Mary Boarding School. I will see if it's possible to take your sister and disappear without leaving a trail, but I won't risk getting caught. If the job is too dangerous, I will refuse it."

"Thank you," she muttered, a lump rising in her throat.

Consuela reached across the table and took her hand. "I'm sorry for you and your sister, that you've had to live with your uncle. He has a reputation."

"There's no reason for you to apologize. It's not your fault."

The older woman sighed, her shoulders sagging with the rush of air. "If there is one thing I could change about this world, I would give everyone the same opportunities. Life doesn't deal them out fairly. Some women have it harder than others."

Alejandra thought of the women she saw every so often at Fort Ashton. The ones with husbands who smiled when they led them to their guest rooms at night and scooted the chair out for their wives at dinner. The ones who looked at their husbands with adoring eyes—and received the same look in return.

"I learned long ago that little about life is fair," she muttered.

Consuela patted her hand. "I will try my hardest for your sister... for you."

"And I will pray your efforts are enough to bring Gabriella to me."

Because if they weren't, she didn't want to think about what she'd have to do next.

XXX

HE COULDN'T SLEEP. Again.

Harrison stood at the window of his father's office and swallowed a gulp of the scalding coffee he just had brought up from the kitchen. He should probably be at his desk, looking over the bank statements and earnings reports from Fort Ashton. Yesterday he'd discovered a discrepancy between the amount of money deposited into his father's bank account in January and the amount of money his father appeared to have made from Fort Ashton. His father had an additional seventeen hundred dollars that Harrison couldn't explain.

The thought of it had kept him up half the night and driven him from his bed at far too early an hour. But dawn was breaking over the desert, and he couldn't stop himself from watching the first rays of pink and orange creep over the sky no more than he could stop himself from drawing breath.

The view had always soothed him, even as a young boy

with little to do other than avoid his father's harsh lectures, he'd always loved sunrise on the...

Wait. Was that a traveler coming toward the fort? He frowned. It was awful early for people to be milling about. If the person heading toward Fort Ashton had come from Mexico, he would have had to cross the Rio Grande in the dark.

Not he. She.

Harrison studied the figure, whom he could now tell wore a skirt. Was it Alejandra?

He wasn't sure how he knew. She looked no different than any other woman would with a long, dark cape that covered her clothing and a hood pulled low over her head. Perhaps it was the way she bent her head toward the ground, as though too afraid to look up at her surroundings. Or the way her shoulders were hunched forward, as though she carried the weight of the world on them.

He sighed and set down his coffee, watching as she grew ever closer.

She wouldn't come through the main entrance of the fort. That had a guard posted by it at all hours, even when the gate was closed. But there was a small, locked entrance on the southwestern side of the building. He'd bet his finest saddle she had a key.

He strode out the door, his long gait eating up the tile beneath his boots as he rushed down the corridor. He took the stairs two at a time, then darted across the center of the courtyard. He had just enough time to lean against the wall where the small entrance hall met the wider corridor. He crossed one foot over the other and his arms over his chest, acting as casual as he could manage.

A moment later, the key turned in the lock, causing a low scratching sound as the ancient gears worked to open the door. Alejandra stepped inside with her hood still pulled over her face, then closed the door behind her and locked it.

He opened his mouth to speak, then clamped it shut. Part of him wanted to blister her ears with a lecture. To demand she tell him where she'd been and why, and interrogate her about why she felt the need to be out and about in the middle of the night, especially with rustlers running roughshod over the countryside.

But pushing her never got anywhere, and yelling would only serve to awaken the guests and draw attention to the fact Alejandra hadn't been in the fort.

Dear God, what do I say? How do I get her to trust me?

It had been three weeks since he'd arrived, and several times a week, he and Alejandra shared pie and conversation in the evening before bed. He'd be lying if he said he didn't look forward to those times, but she always seemed to keep the conversation centered on small, mundane things and directed away from herself.

She still hadn't noticed him standing there, not with the way her head was bent toward the ground, so he spoke first. "Lovely morning to be out for a stroll, wouldn't you say?"

She startled, her gaze shooting up to his as she pressed a hand to her chest. "Harrison, you scared me."

She pulled the hood back from her face, revealing a head full of glossy black hair that was quite mussed.

He had the sudden urge to ask her to brush it, here and now, just so he could watch.

Which could only mean there was something wrong with him. Maybe he'd eaten bad meat at dinner last night, or he'd added a bit of whiskey to his coffee that morning and somehow forgotten about it. Either way, there had to be something off, because what man wanted to watch a woman brush her hair?

But the feeling didn't go away as she stepped closer and looked at him with those wide eyes that were somehow both vulnerable yet filled with secrets.

"Were you looking for me? Is it something with your father? I thought Hermine was capable, but perhaps I—"

"My father and Hermine are fine. It's you I'm worried about."

"Me?" Her brows drew down, causing faint lines to wrinkle the usually smooth skin of her forehead. "Whatever for?"

"Why don't you tell me? What were you doing outside the fort—and don't tell me you were going to the privy again. No one puts on a dark cape for that. Besides, I saw you from my window, and you weren't coming from the direction of the outhouses."

She sighed. "Mr. Rutherford—"

"Harrison."

"Harrison. I... please don't ask questions of me... I just... I had a visit to make. I made it, and I promise not to let it interfere with my work."

"I don't see how that's possible, since I know you were in my father's room until at least eleven last night. Tell me, did you sleep at all?"

She stiffened. "Did you? If you knew I was awake at eleven, and you saw me coming back to the fort just now, you must not have slept either."

"I at least laid down in bed and tried."

"I'll work Hermine's shift tomorrow to make up for my tiredness today, and if I break any dishes, you can deduct an additional ten percent from my pay."

His jaw involuntarily clamped shut, and he sucked in a breath through his nose. Was she trying to be infuriating? "This is not about you breaking dishes or being tired at work. I'm concerned about you, Alejandra. You, as a person who needs rest and sleep. You, as someone under my employ, who therefore falls under my scope of responsibility. And I'm concerned about where you were. Alone in the night, completely by yourself. It simply isn't safe."

"And yet, you're not insisting I tell you everything about where I was or what I was doing?"

Harrison raised an eyebrow. "You asked me not to question you, remember? Unless... unless you want to tell me?"

Their gazes locked, and her mouth clamped shut.

"Of course you don't," he muttered. "You don't answer half the questions I ask, always acting like you're a Pinkerton agent with knowledge of some big state secret."

"My life, it's not simple, not cut and dry, black and white the way yours is. Please understand."

"I'll try. But I want you to come to me next time." He reached out and took her hand where it dangled at her side. "I'll go with you. I won't ask any questions of you. I don't even need to talk to you on the way. But please, please don't do whatever you just did by yourself again, it's not safe."

"I was in Mexico, visiting... our mutual friend."

"Consuela?"

Panic lit her eyes, as though she couldn't believe she'd just told him where she'd gone. "Please don't tell anyone. Promise you won't."

"I won't." Though he didn't have the first clue why visiting Consuela would be a secret, or why she'd gone in the dead of night. "When she said you should visit sometime, I'm sure she would have been happy to entertain you for lunch."

"It's not that simple."

He raked a hand through his hair. "It never is with you."

"No, but..." Her throat muscles worked overly hard as she swallowed. "Thank you."

And then she was in his arms, all five foot, six inches of her. Her arms wrapped around him, squeezing him tight, and her head settled against his chest.

He stroked a hand over the tangled tresses falling down her back. She felt good pressed against him, almost as though she belonged there, with their breaths mingling each time one of them exhaled and the warmth of her body seeping into his.

He cinched her closer to him, his one arm settling against the middle of her back while his other hand delved deeper into her silky mess of hair. "What are you thanking me for?"

"For being here. For not making me tell you where I was."

His breath stirred the soft wisps of hair on her forehead. "You told me anyway."

"Yes, but you didn't make me. You didn't storm down here demanding to know where I'd been or why. You listened. And offered to go with me, to keep me safe. And I just... thank you."

He pulled back just far enough to look fully into her face. "Anytime."

Her breath brushed against his chin, soft and warm, and her eyes stared straight into his. "Why are you so kind to me?"

He swallowed. Standing there, in the early morning light, with her face turned up to his, it was all he could do not to lower his lips to hers and taste her sweetness.

"Because you deserve better than the life you have at Fort Ashton, than being separated from your sister, working all hours of the day and night, and enduring snide comments from Rooster and Felipe. So if I'm the one person in here that can be kind, then I count it as an opportunity from God."

And he didn't intend to waste it.

12

A lejandra let herself into her room, her chest heaving as she sucked air into her lungs. How many times had she used the servants' entrance to the fort? She'd never once had anyone notice her, and yet today of all days, Harrison Rutherford had been there waiting.

But she couldn't be upset about it, not given the way he'd wrapped his strong arms around her and held her against the solid, steady beating of his heart. Not given the way he'd offered to go with her next time she forayed into Mexico, just so he could protect her from outlaws.

Not given the way his words from a few minutes ago still floated through her head. *You deserve better than the life you have at Fort Ashton, than being separated from your sister... so if I'm the one person in here that can be kind, I count it an opportunity from God.*

"Where have you been?"

She whirled around, her foot slipping on the loose tile in the floor that always seemed to be tripping her.

"Raul?" Her heart hammered against her ribs as she made out her cousin's shadowed form in the corner. "Get out."

Raul stepped forward, allowing the faint pink light from the window to brush the side of his hard face. "Not until you answer my questions."

"You're not allowed to be here, and Harrison Rutherford is awake. If I scream, he'll hear."

"The younger Rutherford is awake, is he?" Raul stroked a hand over his jaw, his smile turning feral. "I see."

A sickening sensation cramped her stomach. "You see nothing. I wasn't in his bed!"

"No? Then where were you?"

She swallowed. Why had she just denied being in Harrison's bed? Now her cousin would have nothing but questions for her, whereas before... No. She wouldn't let herself think that, wouldn't even entertain the notion of letting Raul believe she was willing to play the harlot.

"My whereabouts are none of your concern."

He crossed the room to her in half a second and raised his hand. She didn't have time to block the swing before his open palm connected with her face. The slapping sound of flesh meeting flesh echoed through the room, and her cheek burned with the impact.

"Someone has been tipping the Rangers off. Surely you heard that they confiscated my cattle two nights ago. My men and I barely escaped, and you know I can't afford to lose any other workers. So where were you? It had better be making yourself useful in Rutherford's bed."

"I was in Mexico. Check the raft if you don't believe me. I'm sure you'll find its position slightly different than how you last left it."

"Then how do you know Rutherford is awake?" Raul loomed over her, his body large and hulking.

"He saw me coming into the fort, had the same questions for me as you do, though he was much more polite in his asking."

"What were you doing on the other side of the river?"

She threw up her hands. "I am tied here, night and day, away from Gabriella and my friends in Juan Aldama. Who have I to talk to or visit with at Fort Ashton?"

"You were visiting friends? In the middle of the night?" He took a step back from her but kept his eyes narrowed. "I don't believe you."

"When else would I go? I've not had a day off in weeks."

"I still don't believe you."

"Fine." She shrugged, trying to act as though she didn't care, as though he didn't have the power to ruin her. "Don't believe me then."

"That's the second time this month the Rangers have been waiting for me," Raul snarled. "Someone is snitching on me."

"Maybe Mr. Westin has hired enough extra hands that they spotted what you were about before you had the cattle over the border."

"No. The Rangers were lying in wait in Mexico, an ambush set up in the perfect place where the trail narrows into a canyon. They knew what trail we'd be on beforehand." His hard eyes met hers. "Now tell me what you know. How did the Rangers learn I'd be on that trail?"

"What? Me? You—you think I know s-something?" Her heart pounded against her chest. Raul was angry each time his cattle were caught, but he'd never before questioned her about it. Never before expected her to know something about how he'd been discovered. He didn't suspect her... did he?

"I want you inside that Ranger camp."

She flung her hands up. "I'm bound to Mr. Rutherford's bedside, remember? That was your doing. Your idea. You wanted to make sure I still had access to all of Mr. Rutherford's mail. You asked me to go through his office and make sure every trace of the rustling was gone. You even asked me to find out if he had any extra funds from your most recent run that he hadn't deposited in the bank and someone might find. Now you want me to sidle up to one of the Rangers? And this after you told me to spend the last three weeks getting close to Harrison? I can't very well charm him and a Ranger at the same time. It's too small of a town. Everyone would see me flirting with two men and then neither would be willing to talk to me."

"The run from a few weeks ago was planned hastily. I'm prepared to say someone could have made a mistake and let something slip that tipped off the Rangers. But the one from two nights ago? The one we'd been planning for over two weeks? No one should have known about it." Raul jabbed a finger into her shoulder. "Yet those blasted Rangers knew where I was going to be. How?"

"Maybe they have spies in Mexico." Alejandra licked her lips. "I bet the Rangers are paying for information about you."

A sneer crept over her cousin's face. "They do. And I pay them more to give the Rangers the wrong information and report back to me."

"Maybe some of them are playing both sides, or not everyone is reporting to you."

"I told *you* my plans, remember?"

Blood roared in her ears. "You... you think I told the sheriff?"

His dark eyes turned into two thin slits. "Not the sheriff, the Rangers."

Her heart rate only increased. The Rangers. Right. Cain Whitelaw was the most obvious person to be tipped off, not Sheriff Harding. "I've never spoken to Ranger Whitelaw, not once. And how would I have told him what you were doing when I can't leave Mr. Rutherford's bedside?"

A muscle pulsed at the side of his jaw. "I don't know, but there's no question in my mind someone is acting as an informant."

This was it. He was going to figure out what she'd been

about, and then he'd drag her off into the desert and put a bullet in her chest.

She squeezed her eyes shut. *Oh dear Father, give me the words to say. Help me direct his attention away from me.*

"And you automatically think I'm the one who betrayed you?" She laughed. It sounded a bit maniacal and tinny to her ears, but hopefully the noise would cover the pounding of her heart, because she swore it had to be loud enough for Raul to hear. "Then look at your men. If you think there's a rat, start with the people who actually go on the cattle drives. Maybe it's Felipe."

"Felipe would never betray me."

"Maybe he's trying to get you caught so that your father will put him in charge of the rustling." She wasn't sure what was worse, lying and not feeling any guilt about it, or how easily she infused false sympathy into her voice.

"That's ridiculous," Raul spat.

But she could see the idea take root inside his head.

Now she just needed to keep the suspicion directed away from herself long enough for Consuela to bring Gabriella to Twin Rivers.

XXX

An opportunity from God.

Was that really what he'd said when Alejandra had asked why he was so kind to her? It sounded so pious, so spiritual...

So detached.

Harrison swung up into the saddle of his horse and nudged Toronto across the busy coral toward the gate.

He should have kissed her. He should have told her he had

feelings for her. He should have told her he'd find a way to reunite her with her sister and offered to marry her.

Wait.

Marry her?

He was getting ahead of himself. He didn't even know her that well.

But he knew she was a hard worker. Knew she was loyal. Knew she didn't have a mouth that blabbed other people's business all around the fort like Mariposa or some of the restaurant staff.

And he knew she was beautiful.

Still, after the disaster he'd almost gotten himself into with Adeline, he wasn't about to rush looking for a wife.

"Headed out, Mr. Rutherford?" the guard at the gate asked.

"I am. Rooster is running the trading post for the afternoon. I won't be back until after dinner."

"Enjoy your time away."

Harrison smiled. He intended to enjoy himself, yes, but he also wanted to get information. Why would Alejandra need to see Consuela so badly she'd leave the fort in the dead of night? Finding out meant paying a visit to Wes at the A Bar W.

Harrison dug his heels into Toronto's side, letting the horse have his head for the half mile that separated Fort Ashton from Twin Rivers. Once in town, he slowed the beast to accommodate the wagons and passersby, then tipped his hat at Daniel, who was standing on the porch of his office—with Wes.

Harrison steered Toronto toward his friends.

"Howdy, boys." He swung off his horse and tied him to the hitching post before climbing the steps. "Was just headed out to see you, Wes."

Wes clapped him on the back. "How are things at the fort?"

"Too busy." He hoped he didn't end up regretting his decision to leave for a few hours. Rooster had said he could manage the trading post, but he was half expecting to return and find the guard had paid the Mexicans an abominably low price in his absence. He'd told Rooster to follow the new prices and that he'd be checking the ledger after he returned, but he couldn't say whether his instruction would do much good.

"Glad you found time to get away." Wes leaned a shoulder against one of the posts holding up the roof of the porch. "Haven't seen much of you since you got to town."

It was true. He usually spent most of his time in Twin Rivers visiting with the friends who had been more of a family to him growing up than his father. But this time...

Harrison shook his head. Probably best to just ask Wes his questions and get back to the fort. "Did you know Consuela's in Ojinaga?"

Wes poked his tongue into the side of his cheek. "I know she stays with her sister from time to time. Wasn't aware she was there right now."

"Ever think of offering her old job back?"

"I tried. She's not interested. Has something else she's been doing."

Harrison leaned against the porch railing, trying to look casual and relaxed. "And what is that?"

Wes glanced at Daniel, who'd stopped smiling at some point and was now looking at him with his stoic lawman face.

"Reckon it's not any of my business," Wes drawled. "Or yours."

Harrison looked between his two friends. "Don't suppose you have any notion why one of my maids would sneak across the river in the dead of night to visit her then?"

Daniel straightened. "Who was it?"

"Oh no." Harrison crossed his arms over his chest. "Not until one of you tells me why my maid would visit Consuela in the first place, and it's obvious you both know."

Though it wasn't obvious why they were being so secretive about it.

Wes rubbed the side of his jaw. "Consuela's been... helping women."

"How?"

"The same way she did at the A Bar W when she helped her sister open the weaving shop. She's finding jobs for widows with young children."

"My maid isn't a widow, and her needs are perfectly well met at Fort Ashton." Harrison pushed himself off the porch railing and took a step closer to Wes. "What aren't you telling me?"

"Um... any chance your maid might want to leave Fort Ashton? Because sometimes Consuela helps women... ah, get away from difficult circumstances."

"What kind of difficult circumstances?" Harrison kept his gaze pinned on Wes and tried his best to ignore Daniel, who had his lips clamped tighter than a sprung beaver trap.

"Do you remember the baby at our house last fall? His mother was one of Cain's informants, and Consuela helped her escape after the rustlers got a little too close."

"Enough." Daniel stepped between them. "This is part of an ongoing criminal investigation, Wes. You can't just share information with whomever you please."

"Harrison's been our friend for as long as either of us can remember, and you think he's going to go track down the rustlers and let them know about Hortencia?" Wes's eyebrows rose until they disappeared beneath his hat brim. "Even if he did, I'd wager they figured it out after she up and disappeared."

Daniel crossed his arms over his chest, and the man was large enough for it to look ten times more intimidating than when Harrison did it. "They don't know how she disappeared, and they weren't aware of what she was doing the entire time she passed information to Cain. Nor do you know the status of his current informants."

Harrison squared his shoulders. "My maid isn't an informant. It would be impossible. She's stuck at the fort day in and day out. There's no way she'd have knowledge of any rustling activity."

Daniel whipped his icy blue-eyed gaze back his direction. "So maybe her sister is the informant, or her mother, her father, her brother. My point is, the more people who know what Consuela is up to, the more danger it could bring to the women she helps."

Women she helps.

Like Alejandra's sister.

As soon as the words left Daniel's mouth, everything clicked.

Alejandra wouldn't need Consuela to leave Twin Rivers, not with the money he'd given her last fall. But she wasn't going to go anywhere without Gabriella.

Did that mean she was hoping Consuela could bring her sister to her?

It fit perfectly.

"That's why it's imperative Cain and I talk to this maid." Daniel pulled a small notepad and a pencil stub from his pocket. "Now who is she?"

Wait. What? He blinked at his friend. "You're not talking to her. I just said she's got nothing to do with the rustlers."

"She might know something you're unaware of."

"She doesn't." The mere thought of Alejandra knowing anything about the rustlers made a chill travel down his spine. The outlaws hadn't been afraid to kill men, and there was little to indicate they'd suddenly grow a conscience when it came to women.

And here he was, letting his imagination run away with him again. Alejandra could have nothing to do with the cattle rustlers. It simply wasn't possible. "She probably snuck out in the middle of the night because it's been far too long since she had any time off, and she didn't have time to visit Consuela during the day."

Hadn't Alejandra told him that very thing earlier? But Hermine had been working for him for several weeks now and was doing a fine job with his father. He would see to it Alejandra got a day off tomorrow.

"Just tell me who she is." Daniel's voice held a determined edge. "I'd like to have that talk all the same."

Harrison shook his head. "It won't work, but I best be getting back to the fort. Thanks for the information."

He tipped his hat at his friends and started down the stairs.

"Wait," Daniel called after him.

But Harrison was already swinging onto Toronto. "See you at church tomorrow," he called over his shoulder, then nudged his horse into a trot.

Harrison readjusted his hat to better shield him from the glare of the afternoon sun, not quite able to stop the memories of Alejandra that filled his mind, like the look in her eyes as her arms had wrapped around him that morning. Or her soft words as she'd thanked him for offering to help her without demanding to know more about the situation.

Getting more involved with Alejandra Loyola just might be the most illogical thing he'd ever done—but he didn't have the heart to pull away from her.

13

Alejandra suppressed a shudder as she stepped out of the servants' entrance and started toward town.

Her skirt moved freely about her ankles, allowing her to take much longer strides than when she came to town in her servant's uniform, and the wind from the desert rippled through her shirt, letting her skin breathe in the morning heat. Growing up as a *Tejano* near the border between Mexico and Texas, she understood much of what Texan women did, but she'd never understand how they dressed. The desert was too hot for high necklines and thick fabrics and stifling corsets. Yet that was the uniform the senior Mr. Rutherford insisted all female workers at Fort Ashton wear, and that was the clothing most of the women around town stuffed themselves into.

But today she wore clothes that she'd brought from home. A long green skirt and airy shirt that moved when she walked rather than fought against her.

Dong. Dong. Dong.

Up ahead, the church bells chimed the ten o'clock hour.

She'd left the fort just late enough to slip into the back of the church after the service had already started. Now all she had to do was get up during the pastor's final prayer and leave a minute or so early if she wanted to avoid curious gazes and questions.

Heaven knew she'd had enough of those lately.

Raul had sneaked into her room again that morning, this time asking question after question about Felipe, wanting to know if she'd noticed anything unusual about him, if she'd ever seen him talking to the Rangers or holding a private meeting with Rooster.

Then he'd asked for a word-by-word account of her conversation with Harrison from the previous night. Fortunately, her time with Harrison had been short. He'd seemed quite distracted with his paperwork and hadn't been inclined to talk.

But she'd never seen Raul so paranoid before. Now that he'd decided there was a spy, her cousin seemed determined to pay close attention to everyone.

She wrapped her arms around her middle, even though the air was warm. "Oh dear God, please let Consuela bring Gabriella to Twin Rivers quickly."

But if Gabriella arrived and they left Twin Rivers, who would inform the sheriff of the next cattle raid?

Alejandra swallowed as she made her way past the livery and haberdasher's. Once she knew she'd be able to escape Twin Rivers and get her and Gabriella somewhere safe, she'd have to leave a final note for the sheriff, telling him everything so that the Rangers could...

What?

Go into Mexico and bring her uncle back to Texas to face trial for his rustling operation?

Common criminals were caught and brought to one side of the border or the other to face charges all the time. But the former governor of a state?

Her uncle just might be too powerful to face the consequences, even if caught.

The piano played the opening to "Amazing Grace" as she tiptoed up the wooden steps of the church and slid into the back pew, humming the familiar words to the song under her breath.

Alejandra had memories of her stepfather pulling her close and bidding her to sing this very song with him as her mother lay ill. The Protestant hymn seemed to bring her peace, never mind that her mother was Catholic.

She hummed the words in her mind along with the congregation, but when they reached the third verse, Alejandra couldn't quite stop tears from misting her eyes.

Through many dangers, toils, and snares,
I have already come.
'Tis grace that brought me safe thus far,
And grace shall lead me home.

If only the grace that the song spoke of had brought her mother through her illness, then she might not ever have learned the evil *Tío* Javier was capable of. None of them had back in those days.

The song ended, and the preacher went to the pulpit and opened his Bible.

A Bible lay in the middle of the pew. She wasn't sure if it had been left there on accident or if it was there for visitors like her, who hadn't been to church in so long they wouldn't think to bring a Bible.

Either way, she grabbed it and opened to the passage in 1 Peter 3.

"Let's start in verse twelve." The preacher wasn't a large man, but he had a voice that filled the church to the rafters. And while she'd never had a conversation with him herself, he had a reputation for being kind and well liked among the people of Twin Rivers. "'For the eyes of the Lord are over the righteous, and his ears are open unto their prayers: but the face of the Lord is against them that do evil. And who is he that will harm you, if ye be followers of that which is good? But and if ye suffer for righteousness' sake, happy are ye: and be not afraid of their terror, neither be troubled."

The pastor looked up from the pulpit, his kind eyes scanning the congregation. "Today, we're going to talk about a rather unpleasant subject. Suffering."

Alejandra winced. Couldn't the man preach on being kind to your neighbor or making moral choices?

"I know some of you have suffered recently. There was a bank robbery a couple months ago, some things have gone missing around town, and ranchers are living in fear of waking up one morning to find their cattle gone. But the Bible promises, 'The face of the Lord is against them that do evil.'"

Alejandra sank back into the pew. Oh, why had she picked today, of all days, to come to church? It was almost as though the preacher knew about Raul's actions—and that she was aware of most things her cousin did.

"But I also want to say, the situation could be worse. When Peter wrote this book of the Bible, Christians in the Roman Empire were suffering immense persecution." Preacher Russell went on to describe the various dangers that Christians had found themselves in during Peter's day, saying that Peter himself had been martyred for his faith, as had all of the other apostles save John. In some instances, Christians had even been fed to lions or burned alive. Wealthy people who became Christians were sometimes in danger of losing their grand houses and other riches.

"I know Twin Rivers has been going through a rough time," the preacher continued. "But none of us are being targeted by the State of Texas because we came to church on Sunday, as was the case for the believers in First Century Rome. The Bible says not to be afraid of the terror, neither be troubled."

Alejandra shifted in the pew. She wasn't being targeted

because she went to church, but with Raul suspecting a spy in his midst, she had to admit she was more than a little afraid.

"Let's look down at verse seventeen," the preacher said.

She drew her gaze warily back down to the Bible in her lap.

"'For it is better, if the will of God be so, that ye suffer for well doing than for evil doing. For Christ also hath once suffered for sins, the just for the unjust, that he might bring us to God, being put to death in the flesh, but quickened by the Spirit.'"

The preacher went on to talk about Christ's suffering, and how He had paid the steepest price of anyone who had ever lived, and how it wasn't as though the passage promised no suffering for those who did right. In fact, it almost seemed to promise times of trial and trouble, but Christians needed to cling to God's promises during those times.

"Just remember this," the pastor said, his voice still resonating loud and strong throughout the small church. "If you are suffering right now, it will not last forever. As Christians, we always have hope that shines eternal in heaven, and this also gives us hope for the future here on earth. Revelation twenty-one, verse number four says, 'And God shall wipe away all tears from their eyes; and there shall be no more death, neither sorrow, nor crying, neither shall there be any more pain: for the former things are passed away.'"

Did the Bible really say that? Alejandra turned to Revelation 21. Sure enough, the Bible promised God would wipe away tears, and that there would be no more pain or suffering.

But not here on earth. In heaven.

"Maybe you've lost cattle over the past year, maybe you've lost jewelry, or friends who have moved away because of the crime plaguing Twin Rivers. Maybe a loved one has passed or your body is growing feeble with age. Whatever your situation, please understand that your hope is not gone. There will come a day when God shall wipe the tears from your eyes. Until that day comes, your job is to do right and be faithful, regardless of the suffering you might endure."

An ache filled Alejandra's chest. The pastor said to do right and be faithful, but what if passing the sheriff more notes led to her getting caught? Did that mean God had even more suffering in store for her on earth? For Gabriella too?

Please, God, at least let me see Gabriella be free of our uncle before I die. Lead my sister somewhere safe and protect her. And protect Consuela too, don't allow her to be harmed because she agreed to help me.

The pastor said a few more things, then bowed his head to close the service in prayer.

Alejandra stood, her heart beating quickly as she slipped out of the pew along the side of the church—and not because she was sneaking out.

She kept her head down, careful not to disturb anyone in the pew in front of her. The trouble was, she only took one step toward the back of the church before running smack into a man standing in the side aisle.

She slowly raised her gaze. Harrison.

His eyes weren't closed in prayer but were watching her, questions running through them.

Why was he standing at the back of the church, not sitting in a pew? And just how long had he been there?

Had he been watching her without her knowing?

She swallowed, then tried to step around him, but he reached out, took her arm, and bent his head close to her ear. "Don't be in such a hurry. There's a picnic after the service."

"I need to get back to the fort. Your father—"

"Surely you can spare another hour."

The prayer ended, and the church filled with activity. People were standing in the pews, talking to neighbors and gathering belongings.

"Is the problem Hermine?" Harrison stepped into the pew

she'd just vacated, making room for the people filling the aisle and headed toward the door.

Alejandra followed him into the empty space.

"If you're supposed to relieve her at noon, I'll see to it she's well compensated for the extra time she stays with Father." He extended his arm to her. "Now come, there are some friends I'd like you to meet."

"I..." She looked at his arm, extended so very politely. There was a part of her that wanted to reach out and take it. He was just being gentlemanly, after all.

But would Raul find out?

Definitely.

And he would expect her to report every word that she overheard at the picnic.

Her stomach churned.

"Is something wrong?" Harrison dipped his head closer to hers, allowing her to hear him clearly despite the chattering and chaos around them. "Do you not want to go?"

"Harrison, there you are." A beautiful woman with glossy black hair and an angelically chiseled face bustled down the row. "I was worried you hadn't come."

Harrison turned, a smile brightening his face. "Anna Mae, this is Alejandra. She works at Fort Ashton. I was trying to convince her to come for the picnic so I could introduce her to you and the others."

"Of course she's staying for the picnic, aren't you, dear?" The woman came up and hugged her.

Of all things. Hugged her. A complete stranger.

Alejandra stiffened and tried to pull back, but the woman kept right on talking, her arms clamped around her back as though they were long lost friends who hadn't seen each other for a decade.

"There's all kinds of food. I tried a new dish with potatoes and cheese and a bit of cream mixed in. I think it's delicious, but my brother, Daniel, has declared cheese and potatoes don't go together and refuses to try it. You'll have to taste it and let me know what you think. And do you like pie? I got Keely to order pecans in special to the general store, just so I could make some pecan pies today."

Anna Mae pulled back from the hug but kept one arm around her shoulders as she prodded Alejandra out of the row and toward the church door.

Harrison gave her a lopsided half smile over Anna Mae's head and followed behind them.

Anna Mae kept talking the entire time it took them to make their way to the churchyard where people were spreading blankets on the ground. She kept her arm wrapped around Alejandra's shoulders too, and for some reason Alejandra couldn't quite explain, she didn't want to pull away.

The touch felt good.

Like coming home after a long journey.

Or maybe like being folded in her mother's arms and sung a lullaby before bed.

Anna Mae led her around the churchyard, introducing her to more people than she could count. They finally settled at a group of blankets with people Harrison introduced as his closest friends.

First was Wes and his wife Keely, who had curly red hair and freckles and a smile that kept climbing onto her face. They owned the A Bar W, which would have made her squirm, but Anna Mae didn't give her any time to think about Wes and Keely before she introduced her to Wes's sister, Charlotte, who had hair the color of caramel and was married to the town sheriff.

Finally, there was another married couple, Ellie and Sam. Ellie had red hair and freckles, much like Keely, but her hair wasn't curly. She and Sam owned the Triple S Ranch, and they had a tiny baby and a heap of older young'uns who darted all over the picnic area.

With so many new people about, part of her wanted to be nervous, but Alejandra couldn't quite stop herself from relaxing into the friendly chatter and teasing.

For the first time since her stepfather died, it almost felt like she belonged somewhere.

14

Harrison had tried to put distance between them last night when Alejandra had come to his office to see if he needed anything from the kitchen. He'd acted distracted with his paperwork, which wasn't exactly honest. He'd been distracted, all right, but because of Alejandra.

It seemed that not talking to her only caused him to think about her more—to the point of not getting a blasted thing done and not being able to fall asleep until the wee hours of the morning.

And then she'd shown up at church, looking beautiful with her hair down and wearing a wide-collared shirt that scooped around her neck and a skirt so light it shifted with the breeze.

It was the first time he'd seen her in anything other than her serving uniform or nightdress, and she looked beautiful.

When he'd walked into church and saw her sitting at the back, soaking in each word the preacher said, every thought of keeping her at arm's length had fled his mind. Here she was, in need of a friend, in need of help, and trying to make the best of her situation. It was almost as though God wouldn't let him avoid her, even if he wanted to.

Harrison watched her across the picnic blanket as she took little Madeline into her arms and hugged the babe to her chest. He didn't think he'd ever seen such a genuine smile on her face.

Ellie said something near her ear that he couldn't quite make out, but Alejandra's smile only widened.

On the other side of the churchyard, the womenfolk finished setting food out on the tables, and a line for the meal formed almost instantly, but no one from their group moved.

"Hey, Ellie."

Ellie's oldest brother—Martin, if he remembered correctly —came up to her.

"Do you mind if I..." His words trailed off as he spotted Alejandra holding his tiny niece. "Who's this?"

"Alejandra," Ellie said, tucking a strand of red hair behind her ear. "She works at Fort Ashton."

"You live here? Not just passing through?" Martin took off his hat and offered Alejandra a lopsided smile. "Pleased to meet ya."

"I... ah, thank you."

"Have you been to the food table yet? I'd be happy to carry your plate."

Harrison pushed himself to his feet. "I'm accompanying her to the food table, Martin."

Alejandra's bronzed cheeks turned the slightest shade of pink. "Yes, I was going to eat with Mr.—Harrison. Thank you for the offer though."

The boy looked between the two of them. "Is that... are you two courting?"

"¿Qué?" Alejandra's hand stilled where it had been rubbing Madeline's back. "No!"

"Well then, can I escort you to the food table instead of Harrison?"

"No. I mean, sí... I mean..." She glanced at him, a panicked look in her eyes.

"Alejandra isn't in a position to be courted, Martin, not by me, and not by you or anyone else. If you're looking to escort a woman to supper, it seems like Gertie Cunningham is in need of a companion." Harrison jutted his chin to where Gertie stood with her parents and younger siblings.

The young man twisted his lips together, his gaze moving from Gertie to Alejandra and back to Gertie again. "All right, I guess I'll take Gertie."

His shoulders slumped as he trudged off in Gertie's direction.

"*Gracias.*" Alejandra sidled up beside him. "I didn't realize, that is... why would he think...?"

Because you're young and beautiful and all alone. Harrison cleared his throat rather than spout the first thought that popped into his brain. "Martin's at the age where a boy starts noticing women."

"Pretty sure he's past that age." Sam elbowed Wes. "Wes here had all but proposed to Abigail by the time he was eighteen."

Wes gave Sam a shove. "Stow it."

"What can I say?" Sam shrugged. "Boy's like me. Wants a family somethin' fierce, and he's good enough around the ranch I told him I'd build him a house, hire him on full time if he's in need of his own place."

"Can we go back to the part where you said Alejandra can't court anyone?" Anna Mae frowned at Alejandra. "Are you betrothed to someone back in Mexico—or is it just Harrison and Martin you want nothing to do with?"

"I... ah..." Alejandra shifted awkwardly on her feet and clasped the babe tighter to her chest. "I don't have feelings for anyone in Mexico, no."

"Well, if it's Harrison and Martin you want nothing to do with, we can always introduce you to Cain," Keely said. "He's in need of a good wife."

Harrison choked. "Don't even think of it."

"I agree. Alejandra here looks far too nice to put up with the likes of Cain." Sam winked in Alejandra's direction.

"Y'all talking about me?" a laidback voice drawled.

Harrison turned to see Cain and Daniel approaching the blanket. Cain wore his usual half smile, but Daniel's face was drawn into a mask of serious lines.

"Honey, what's wrong?" Charlotte pushed herself up from the blanket and went toward him. "Is it the rustlers again?"

The sheriff wrapped his wife in a hug. "Someone stole money from Mr. Granger's house last night."

"Another robbery?" Charlotte's brow furrowed. "I thought whoever was robbing people had moved on."

Daniel filled her in on details about the robbery, but Harrison didn't quite catch them all because Alejandra took a step closer to him, causing the flowery scent of her skin to float around him.

"You're friends with the sheriff and Ranger captain?"

"We grew up together. Why?"

"I just... didn't know, is all." She gave Cain a long look, then handed Madeline back to Ellie. "I need to get back to the fort."

"Not without eating first." He took her hand and tucked it into his arm. "And as I told Martin, I'll take you."

"I'll join you too." Anna Mae grabbed Alejandra's other arm and started toward the food line. "The roasted pork smells delicious, doesn't it?"

Anna Mae sucked Alejandra back into a conversation as they filled their plates and returned to the blanket. After she finished her food, Alejandra ended up holding Madeline again, rocking and cooing to the babe as she drifted off to sleep.

The womenfolk stayed deep in conversation, laughing and smiling and including Alejandra in their group as though she'd been friends with them for decades. It was the most he'd ever seen Alejandra smile.

Someone slapped him on the shoulder, and he turned to find Sam grinning at him.

"And here you told Martin you're not courting her."

Harrison scowled. "I'm not. She's a maid at Fort Ashton and nothing more."

"That's why he can't stop looking at her." Wes popped a bite of cookie into his mouth. "Because they ain't courting yet, and he's worried someone else is going to come and steal her away."

"That's not... never mind." Harrison pursed his lips and scooted over so his back was to Alejandra. "There. Now I'm not looking at her. Happy?"

The trouble was, sitting with his back to her only made him wonder what she was doing.

Wes grinned and slipped his billfold from his pocket, then peeled off two dollars. "I wager he'll get married after Independence Day but before Thanksgiving. You want to counter, Sam?"

"With the way he's looking at her?" Sam released a chuckle. "Boy howdy, you're gonna lose some money. They'll be married before the beginning of July, no doubt."

"You're both going to lose," Harrison growled, "because there isn't going to be a wedding."

"Sure there isn't." Sam loosed another guffaw, then nodded toward something behind him. "Looks like your future wife is getting ready to leave. Figured you should know, just in case you want to walk the lady you're 'not courting' home."

Harrison turned to see the women had all stood, and Alejandra was handing Madeline back to Ellie, saying that she'd stayed too long.

Harrison pushed to his feet. "I'll walk you back."

"Oh." She looked over at Sam and Wes, who were grinning like buffoons at the two of them. "Don't leave your friends on account of me."

"It's not on account of you, I promise. I don't like to work on

Sundays, but I have a pile of paperwork waiting for me back in the office. Still trying to get caught up on all the aspects of the fort I'm now in charge of."

She took his extended arm. "I suppose it makes sense to walk together."

"My thoughts exactly." Walking her back to the fort was the gentlemanly thing to do. There wasn't anything romantic or courting-like about it, never mind Wes and Sam's taunting grins.

"You seemed like you enjoyed yourself today," he said as they started off across the churchyard.

She smiled up at him. "I did. Thank you for talking me into staying."

"I'm glad you were finally able to get a day off. It's nice to see you relax for a bit, and wear something other than a serving uniform."

She gave a small shudder. "Those uniforms are wretched. There's no room for your skin to breathe."

"Are those birds on your shirt? Did you embroider them?"

She reached up and fingered one of the threaded patterns just below the drawstring on her neckline. "They're hawks, yes."

Not all Mexican women embroidered their clothes, but the ones who did usually stitched flowers or vines along their necklines and sleeves. "I'm not sure I've ever seen a hawk on a shirt before."

Alejandra's face flushed. "It's a northern harrier, actually."

He raised his eyebrows.

"They... fly north. Every spring. They leave Mexico and they just... fly away."

"I see."

And he did. That bit of information, the fact she'd stitched a bird that flew wherever it willed along her neckline, told him more about her than an hour's worth of conversation in his office.

The pink in her cheeks slowly turned to a deeper shade of red as he watched her.

He knew he stared far longer than was appropriate, especially considering they stood in the middle of the street where anyone could see them, and yet he couldn't seem to pull his gaze away.

Finally, she looked down. "We best continue on to the fort."

"Right, yes." He offered his arm again, and she took it.

But the silence felt heavy between them, and it was all he could do not to keep looking at the string of hawks edging her shirt. "I... um... I'm glad you had fun today. With the women, that is. I overheard Anna Mae and Ellie offer for you to visit them sometime. I believe your next day off is Thursday? You should go see them."

Her hand stiffened. "Oh no, I couldn't."

"Sure you could. They enjoyed talking with you."

"They were probably just being polite."

He held in a sigh as he led her past the sheriff's office and toward the livery. Why was it hard for her to believe that women her age might genuinely enjoy her company? "I suppose if you won't go visit them, I'll have to invite them all to Fort Ashton for a meal."

"So I can serve your friends?"

He stopped walking, never mind that they were right in the middle of the road. "So you can come to the dinner and enjoy spending time with some women your own age."

"Oh." She pulled her hand from his arm.

"I'm sorry," he muttered, though he couldn't quite stop his jaw from clenching together. "That came out a little too harsh. I just don't understand..."

He clamped his lips together. He could try asking why she thought so poorly of herself, but would he get an answer?

If he had to guess, Alejandra didn't think there was anything unusual about how her cousin and Rooster treated her, about being always asked to serve others and give of herself without ever getting a bit of rest or having anyone show kindness back to her.

And he didn't know how to change that. He was trying to treat her better, to show what decent behavior was, yet his actions only seemed to make her uncomfortable.

But getting upset around Alejandra wasn't going to solve anything, so he offered her his arm again. "We better continue back to the fort."

She settled her slender hand against his forearm, her skirt brushing against his legs as they started walking once more. "I must admit, your friends seem wonderful. You're truly blessed to have such people in your life."

"Yes, I suppose I am." Though he hadn't realized just how blessed until meeting Alejandra, who had no one she could rely on.

"And I think Anna Mae is the most beautiful woman I've ever seen."

"She truly is lovely, isn't she?"

"You should marry her."

"I beg your pardon?" He stopped walking again, for the third time in only a few minutes.

She blinked up at him. "Don't you want a wife?"

"Ah... yes? No? Maybe someday." He sighed and cast a glance up at the sky, where a hawk happened to be soaring. "I grew up without a mother, and my father always managed things well enough. Guess I've never been of the opinion that I needed to marry to be happy."

"And you've never met a woman who convinced you that you'd never be happy without her in your life?"

Well, there had been Adeline, but their relationship had felt like an obligation, not something that brought him joy. "Not really, no."

"Then it's decided." She gave her head a firm nod. "You need to pay a call on Anna Mae."

"I never agreed to such a thing."

Alejandra started walking. "She seems like the type of woman to enjoy a picnic, maybe a horseback ride."

"Bet she'd enjoy doing those things with you more than she would with me."

Alejandra's brow furrowed. "You think so?"

"I do."

"Let's make a deal. I'll visit Anna Mae on my day off, if you take her on a picnic first."

"Alejandra. I have no desire to—"

"So that's a no?"

He pressed his lips together. Was she really going to make him take Anna Mae on a picnic before she paid a call on her new friend?

Alejandra was just stubborn enough he didn't want to risk saying no. "Fine. I'll invite Anna Mae on a picnic."

"Good. She's beautiful. I'm sure the two of you will fall in love *pronto*."

"What? No. That's not what Anna Mae and I will be doing. I mean, she's lovely, yes, but there's more to loving a woman than beauty."

Besides, if I'm going to spend time with a woman, I don't want it to be Anna Mae. I want it to be you.

Where had that thought come from? He enjoyed Alejandra's company, true. But that didn't mean he intended to court her. He was only spending time with her because she needed help.

He wasn't doing anything for Alejandra that he wouldn't do for Ellie or Charlotte or Anna Mae.

So why did it feel different when he was with her?

And why couldn't he get the sudden desire to take her on a picnic out of his mind?

15

"You had a conversation with the Ranger captain yesterday."

Alejandra jerked awake, her eyes flying open at the sound of the accusing voice in her room. "Raul."

"What did he say to you?"

She blinked in the direction of her cousin's voice, although her room was too dark to make out more than a shadow beside her bed. "What?"

She started to sit up, but as the covers slipped from her shoulders, she became keenly aware her thin, worn nightdress was the only thing covering her from Raul's eyes...

And just as aware that she and Raul were only step cousins —not related by blood.

She clutched the covers tightly to her chest and scrambled back into a seated position.

"Well," Raul snapped. "What did he say?"

She blinked again, trying to clear the fogginess of sleep from her brain. "Who? When?"

Raul leaned close, his warm breath grazing her chin. "Don't you toy with me."

"If you want better answers, maybe try approaching me at a normal hour of the day, not sneaking into my room like a criminal."

"The Ranger captain. You had a conversation with him yesterday, at the church picnic."

She rubbed her head, trying to think back. "I was introduced to both Captain Whitelaw and the sheriff yesterday. I said hello but not much more, as it was time to line up for food. After I got back from the food table, both lawmen were gone."

"Did they say anything was wrong?"

"The sheriff said a man in town had been robbed the night before. Mr. Granger. That was all I heard. The sheriff and Captain Whitelaw had their own conversation for most of the time they were at the picnic."

"What were they talking about?"

She shrugged. "How should I know?"

Raul leaned close. "Your job is to get information."

"My job is to read Mr. Rutherford's mail and nothing more."

"I want whatever information is most useful. If the Ranger or sheriff are around, then learn as much as you can from them. Whatever they say is bound to be more useful than anything Rutherford says.

"Sorry. You seem to have left out those instructions before," she gritted. "Now is there something else you need, or will you leave me alone so I can dress for the day and go check on the senior Mr. Rutherford?"

"What did the younger Rutherford say at the picnic?"

She rolled her eyes. "That the weather was nice, that he thinks Hermine is working out well helping with his father, that he doesn't enjoy being trapped in that cramped trading post for hours on end every day."

"Anything about the rustlers?"

"No."

"What about his friend, Westin? You ate lunch with the big rancher."

"He talked with the smaller rancher about acquiring a new bull this fall and using it to breed both herds."

"Useless. All of it's useless." Raul gave a sharp shake of his head, and though it was too dark to see his glower, she could feel the heat radiating from his gaze. "What about the women? Did you strike up a friendship with them?"

A hard ball of dread formed in her stomach. He wasn't going to ask her to spy on Anna Mae or Charlotte, was he?

"You should find a way to spend time with them again," he went on, never mind that she hadn't answered his first question. "Maybe they'll invite you to the A Bar W and give you a tour. Bet Westin has some useful papers in his office. I'd like to know how many cowhands he employs and get my hands on a map of his property. The ranch is so vast, it's hard to figure out all the places he might be hiding cattle."

"I'll see what I can do." Her voice shook with the lie, but Raul didn't seem to notice. Instead, he left the side of her bed and started toward the door.

"I'm taking my men north for a few weeks. Hopefully I'll have better luck with my cattle raids up there. Keep your eyes and ears open while I'm away, and read any and all letters you can get your hands on—that goes for both Harrison and his father."

The door clicked shut softly behind him.

Alejandra dragged in a breath, then pressed a hand to her mouth lest the sob building in her chest break free.

Spy on the Ranger and the sheriff. Spy on Harrison. Spy on women who were trying to be her friends.

The list never ended.

For the first time since her stepfather had died, she actually felt as though she might belong somewhere yesterday, as though she might be able to be happy again.

But not when she was expected to turn around and betray the first people who had treated her decently in years.

XXX

CAIN YAWNED and rubbed a hand over his face, trying to blink the grit out of his eyes, but that didn't seem to help as he swung off Maverick and stumbled toward his tent. His informant in Mexico had been wrong about the rustlers moving Saturday night, and when he'd gone back to check on the man last night, he'd disappeared.

Was there another dead body hidden somewhere on the vast Mexican desert? His gut told him yes, even if the thought made him want to howl.

Here he was with a mission to save lives and uphold the law for a living, but all he did while trying to catch the rustlers was get men killed.

Or put women in so much danger they had to flee.

He shook his head. Since Hortencia had left, the only reliable informant he had was the person who slipped Daniel notes. Not only did he not have the first clue who the man was, but he also didn't know what side of the border he lived on, or how he always seemed to have such accurate information.

Could it be one of the rustlers? Cain pulled on his lower lip. That would explain why the information was always good, but not why the man was passing it along. If a rustler wanted to be done, why not just sneak off in the night and disappear into the wide-open spaces of the Southwest?

"Don't worry, Captain, we'll find Ernesto. He was probably just away for a night."

Cain looked over at Tony, the young Ranger he'd taken with him into Mexico last night.

"Hope you're right, but I fear otherwise." Cain stifled a yawn, then slapped the boy on the shoulder. "Going to get some sleep. Maybe I'll be able to make better sense of things when I wake."

But before he could take so much as a step toward his tent, laughter erupted from the direction of the firepit. A lot of laughter.

Cain scowled. Were Cooper and Zeke fighting again? The men would be emptying chamber pots and scrubbing dishes for a week.

He strode around a tent and walked toward the noise. More laughter echoed through the camp as he rounded another cluster of tents.

Then a familiar voice floated through the air.

A familiar, *female* voice.

"Anna Mae," he growled as he strode around the final tent separating him from the fire pit.

Sure enough, she stood near the fire with a pan of some sort of pastry in her hands. The men filled the benches around the pit, hanging on her every word—even the men who'd been assigned morning chores.

She turned and smiled at him, the look on her face so bright and beautiful that he could see half his men fall in love with her right then and there.

He didn't smile back. In fact, he'd wager he was the only man in the blasted camp not smiling, which made his scowl deepen. "I need a word with you."

"All right." She took her spatula and wriggled it under one of the pastries, then handed it to Johns. "Let me give out the rest of these, and then we can—"

"Now. I need a word with you now." He scanned his men, watching the smiles drop from their faces as they looked back at him. "The rest of you best get back to your chores, or we'll run extra drills this afternoon."

"Is something wrong?" Anna Mae swept toward him, her sunny smile replaced with a look of concern. "Don't tell me the rustlers struck again."

"Is something wrong?" he repeated in an attempt to calm himself, but somehow hearing the question again only made him angrier. "I told you not to come here. Yet here you are, traipsing out to camp when I'm gone."

She stopped close enough that the flowery scent of her perfume filled the air around them.

"I tried to send you a note that I'd have doughnuts for the men this morning, but you weren't at camp. What was I supposed to do? Let the food go to waste because you were off galivanting around the desert?"

She'd brought doughnuts? He looked down at the pan she held, and his stomach growled. They looked delicious—not that he was about to admit it. "I should arrest you for disturbing the peace."

"Arrest me?" She blinked up at him, her eyes wide and unassuming. "I'm not doing anything illegal."

"Not illegal, just... nonsensical." Cain sighed. Could she really be too naïve to notice the effect she had on his men?

When they'd first arrived in Twin Rivers nine months ago, he hadn't thought anything about Anna Mae bringing his men treats. She was beautiful, yes, but she certainly wasn't the first person to cook for them when they rode into a town.

Trouble was, they'd been here for nine months, and Anna Mae wasn't just a good baker, she was a beautiful woman. A beautiful, single woman.

He hadn't been joking earlier about half his men falling in love with her. He didn't want to even try guessing how many marriage proposals she'd gotten. Last week alone he'd broken up three different fights over which man was going to call on Anna Mae next.

Even now, he could hear loud voices coming from the direction of the fire in what was sure to be the newest argument about Anna Mae.

"You can't come here anymore."

She frowned, her pan of donuts still balanced in her hands. "The men like my food."

"Not as much as they like arguing over you."

"What's that supposed to mean?"

The voices from the fire grew louder, and he shoved a hand in that direction. "You hear that?"

"Sounds like a couple of your Rangers are having a disagreement."

"Do you know what they're disagreeing about?"

She shrugged.

"Who's going to court you first."

"That's ridiculous. I'm not going to court any of them. I've already told them so."

"Well, obviously, it didn't get through their thick heads, because I guarantee that's why they're arguing."

"Really?" She looked back over her shoulder, but he'd moved her far enough away from the fire that a tent blocked the view of the argument. "I didn't mean to cause problems for you, Cain, truly I didn't. I just..." She licked her lips.

Lips that were far too red and full.

And was that a shimmer of tears in her eyes?

Oh, hang it all. She wasn't going to cry, was she? What was he supposed to do with a crying female?

"Let's finish this discussion in my tent." He turned and threaded his way through the camp. Maybe if he pretended not to notice the crying, her tears would go away.

"I guess I didn't understand when you told me not to bring

bread the other day," she said as he held his tent flap open for her.

He rolled up the flap and tied it open before entering, just so there would be no question about his conduct toward Anna Mae while they were inside together.

But would Anna Mae have thought of such a thing on her own?

He knew the answer, and it made him want to tear a hole in something.

"I know you are trying new recipes to sell at the general store." Her parents had moved at Christmas, and now she was on her own, renting a room from Wes at the A Bar W and making ends meet by selling her baking. "If you have something new that you want the men to try, just have your brother bring it, all right?"

"Okay. Although I have to say, I'll miss the men."

He raised an eyebrow. "Any one of them in particular that you'd miss seeing?"

She grew quiet, her eyes finding a random spot on the canvas for her to stare at without seeming to see anything.

He didn't think Anna Mae had shown signs of being sweet on one of his men, but maybe he'd missed something.

She sucked in a breath and drew her gaze back to his face. "Actually, I...

Her lips clamped shut.

So there was someone. That was probably for the best. He'd let Daniel know and leave the rest to her brother to figure out.

"I should go." She crossed his tent to the table where she'd set her doughnuts. "The fried apple won over the cinnamon yeast rings, in case you were wondering."

"I wasn't."

The words came out a bit terser than he'd planned, but she only smiled at him, completely unphased by his crankiness as she worked the spatula around one of the few remaining pastries. "Do you want me to leave you one? It's going to get your hands sticky though, just a warning."

She held the spatula toward him, and he couldn't stop himself from taking the treat and biting into it. Yeasty goodness filled his mouth.

"See? I knew you would like it."

He grunted.

She turned to pick up the pan, but her hands moved to the open sketchbook lying next to where she'd set the doughnuts. "Is this the man who was murdered?"

"Sure is, but that's not his best likeness." Cain shoved another bite of the fried apple goodness into his mouth, then reached around her and grabbed the sheet of paper sitting on the table. "This is the one I've been showing people."

She glanced at the paper, then moved her eyes back to the notebook. "You draw the most beautiful faces."

The bite of doughnut stuck in his throat, and he had to force himself to swallow. "Lifelike. The faces are lifelike. For work. I don't draw beautiful things."

"What about landscapes? Do you still draw those?"

He stilled, the final bite of doughnut paused halfway to his mouth. "How had she remembered his landscapes? He hadn't drawn those in years. "Only if I need to remember an area, like I'm plotting an ambush or some such. As I said, everything I draw is for work. See, here's the area where we found the dead body."

He shoved the last bit of food into his mouth, then handed her the other drawing that had been sitting on the table.

She scanned the page. "Can't say I know the spot, and I'm pretty familiar with the desert around here."

"Your brother said the same."

He held out his hand for the sketchbook, but rather than hand it to him, she flipped back a page. The drawing he'd done of Preacher Russell stared back at her. She turned the page again to a drawing of her brother.

"Just for work, huh?" Her eyes sought his. "Tell me, are my brother and the preacher suspects in the murder?"

"You know they're not." He could feel heat climbing up the back of his neck, singeing his ears. He had an almost irresistible urge to snatch the notebook away from her. It was private, after all, not something he'd ever intended for others to see.

But Anna Mae was smiling as she flipped through each page, her eyes dancing as though she could literally see the people on the paper come to life.

She paused at a page near the back of the notebook, then tilted her head to the side, studying it. "This is Alejandra. Harrison's friend from yesterday."

"Yes."

"Had you met her before?"

"I've seen her around town a few times. Took an interest in one of my lieutenants for a bit, but he had eyes for the oldest Cunningham girl."

"Did you draw her because she's beautiful then? Because you wanted to remember how pretty she is?"

She's not as beautiful as you.

Cain clapped his hand to the back of his neck. Where had that thought come from? And worse, what had possessed him to almost say it? "No."

"Then why?"

He shrugged. "Can't rightly say. There was something about her yesterday, and I never can tell when a sketch might come in handy. It's always best if I draw it right away, while the person or landscape is still fresh in my mind."

Anna Mae ran her eyes over the page again. "She looks like she's hiding something, like she has secrets—at least in this sketch. But yesterday, she didn't seem secretive, she seemed... afraid. I think she needs a friend."

"Can't think of a better person to be her friend than you."

Anna Mae flipped a few more pages back in the notebook. Then she suddenly stopped, the rosy hue draining from her cheeks.

Cain took a step closer to see what she was looking at.

Herself.

He felt all the heat from his face plumet to his toes, and he reached for the notebook. "You best get back to town."

But she didn't release it. "This... this is me?"

There was no way it could be anyone but her, not with the cascading black hair and happy eyes and delicate facial structure. "I said it's time to go."

"But why would you draw a sketch of me?"

"Same reason I draw sketches of everyone else. Sometimes it's work, sometimes I'm bored." And sometimes he couldn't sleep at night and needed his brain to calm down.

Though drawing Anna Mae certainly didn't help him sleep. If anything, it only guaranteed a night where she haunted his dreams. Only guaranteed that he'd wake up in the morning thinking about a captivating woman with mesmerizing dark eyes and a smile bright enough to light up a room at midnight.

"But this... it... it makes me look... beautiful."

"You are." The words were out before he had time to stop them.

"You think I'm beautiful?"

He groaned. "Everyone thinks you're beautiful. It's why my men can't stop fighting about you."

She set the notebook down, and he found himself blowing out a breath. At least now she wouldn't—

His thoughts slammed to a halt as she took a step closer to him, her deep brown eyes latched onto his in a way he couldn't look away from. "I didn't ask about your men. I asked about you. Do you think I'm beautiful?"

He licked his lips—when had they gotten so dry?—and

forced words through the sudden lump in his throat. "I... ah... I think you're my friend's sister, and I need to watch out for you. That's what I think."

"You didn't answer the question."

"And I don't intend to. I'm only going to be in town for a few more weeks."

"Why would that matter—unless you do think I'm beautiful?" She took another step nearer. "Unless you're attracted to me and don't want to admit it."

She was standing close to him now. So close that her flowery scent twined around him and the heat of her breath grazed his chin. So close that if he bent his head a few inches, his lips would brush against hers.

He stared down into her soft brown eyes, his breath hitching in his chest. Then he backed away. He was the illegitimate son of a reckless lawman and a cantina girl, named Cain because his father considered him a curse—just like Cain in the Bible.

He didn't have any business thinking about Anna Mae Harding in a romantic way, let alone kissing her.

"I don't understand." She gave a little huff. "Why won't you say whether you think I'm beautiful?"

"Because you want to get married one day." His voice came out low and raspy. "You want to settle down and have a passel of young'uns, and I'm not the type to stay in one place for more than a few weeks, let alone speak vows and raise a family."

And he wasn't the type to stand around his tent talking about feelings either. He grabbed the doughnut pan off the table and headed outside, leaving Anna Mae to trail him into the sunshine.

"Bryant," he hollered. "Anna Mae here needs an escort back to town."

The Ranger had been checking shoes on the horses, but as

his gaze landed on Anna Mae, his face lit up. He released the leg of the horse he'd been inspecting and scampered over.

Bryant Lindley was a good man. A bit on the young side, but he came from a solid family down near Brownsville. The man didn't leave a trail of broken hearts in his wake or visit brothels when they rode into a new town, and he never got into fistfights, not even over Anna Mae.

If he could see Anna Mae settling down with one of his men, it would be Bryant.

Bryant exchanged a few pleasantries with Anna Mae, and the two of them started across camp.

But as he watched the two of them go, Cain swore he could still smell the flowery scent of her perfume surrounding him, could still hear the soft intake of her breath when she'd flipped to that sketch of herself.

And he knew exactly what he'd be dreaming about as soon as he lay down.

16

Harrison eyed the stack of envelopes sitting on the desk, then dragged a hand through his hair. The paperwork at Fort Ashton seemed endless. No matter how many hours he spent behind his father's desk, he could never quite manage to keep up with everything. And now an entire stack of new mail had arrived for him to go through.

He reached for the envelopes and shuffled through them. They were all addressed to his father, except...

He blinked down at the two envelopes that held his own name. It was the first time any mail had come for him at Fort Ashton. Both envelopes had been forwarded from his address in Austin, and both looked rather important.

He grabbed the letter opener and slit the envelope from the U.S. Senator's office first.

Dear Mr. Rutherford...

He scanned the letter, then threw it down onto the desk, his stomach twisting. This had to be some kind of joke. A cruel prank someone in Austin decided to pull after the Tillerman verdict.

He picked up the second envelope and yanked it open, only

to find a similar letter, this one claiming to come from the Federal Judiciary instead of a sitting U.S. Senator.

Both letters claimed to offer him a vacant seat as a federal judge in San Antonio—and both letters also claimed his actions in the Tillerman case had led to his consideration for the position.

He crumpled the letter from the "judiciary" in his hand. A sick, twisted joke. No one got awarded a federal judgeship after losing a case as prominent as Wade Tillerman's.

Knock. Knock. Knock.

Harrison straightened at the knock on the door, then opened the closest desk drawer and shoved the letters into it. He'd burn them later.

The door opened to reveal Daniel and Cain.

"Looks like you're having fun in here." Daniel stepped into the room and jutted his chin toward the pile of papers on the desk.

"Thought it would be better than spending most of my day in the trading post. I was wrong." Harrison scrubbed a hand over his face, trying to rein in the string of twisted emotions those two letters had unleashed, then looked down at the ledger in front of him.

It only served to remind him of another problem he couldn't solve—the extra money his father had in the bank.

He'd discovered more than just the deposit in January that he couldn't explain. There was no rhyme or reason to the timing of when they appeared. Sometimes the bank accounts balanced perfectly for several months, and other times there was a series of unexplained deposits separated only by a week or two.

He couldn't figure out where a lick of it came from.

"Figured we'd stop by, see how things are going," Cain drawled.

Harrison held in a groan. Barely. "I'm letting Fordham run

the trading post this morning. Gave Rooster a chance on Saturday, but he's still convinced he needs to pay the Mexicans an appallingly low price for their wares. So far, it seems like Fordham is doing better."

"Fordham?" Daniel settled into one of the wingback chairs opposite the desk. "Don't know much about him. He hasn't been working here all that long, has he?"

"No, and I think that's why I like him. He was hired on just before my father fell ill. Former Ranger, but he got injured and walks with a limp and needed a job."

Cain straightened. "A former Ranger, you say? What's his full name?"

"I believe his first name is Clint."

"Clint Fordham." Cain gave a small shake of his head. "Never heard of him. Was probably stationed west of here, maybe in El Paso."

Harrison sat back in his chair. "I've got to say, he seems like too decent of a man to want to work here for long, but I'll take him for as long as I can get him."

"Maybe he'll want to stay as long as you're running the fort." Daniel swiped the apple sitting on the corner of his desk and took a bite.

"Maybe. It certainly won't hurt to have a man I can half trust on my payroll."

"The second I can't trust one of my men, I fire him. Figure life is too short to waste it on untrustworthy sorts." Cain hooked a thumb in his belt loop and leaned against the wall. "So, the woman who went to see Consuela last week, is she here?"

Harrison jerked his gaze to Daniel. "I said you couldn't speak with her, and here you are telling Cain about her?"

"Cain said he needs to know why she went to visit Consuela." Daniel spoke around a bite of apple.

"Not even I know for certain."

"It won't be a long conversation. Just call her into the office. You can be here the entire time we question her." Daniel took another bite of apple.

"No."

"Why are you so protective of her?" Cain tilted his head to the side, studying him in a way that made him suddenly want to fidget.

"I'm not."

"Liar," Daniel quipped.

A soft knock sounded at the door, and Alejandra poked her head inside.

His jaw clenched. Why, oh why, had she picked now to interrupt?

"Harrison, I need to... oh..." Her eyes moved from Daniel to Cain to him. "I'm sorry, I didn't realize you had company."

"It's all right. Give me a minute to finish up here and I'll come meet you in Father's room."

"Yes, sir." She gave a quick dip of her head, then started to close the door.

"Wait a minute." Cain pushed himself off the wall. "Come inside. I have a few questions for you."

Alejandra cast a nervous glance his direction but opened the door just far enough for her to slip into the room.

"Have you ever paid a visit to a woman named Consuela Moreno?" Cain asked.

She whirled toward the desk, her face draining of color. "You told them where I went?"

"No." Harrison pushed himself to a standing position. "Cain was guessing."

She clamped her jaw tight and glared at Cain, which only caused a lopsided smile to tilt his lips. "Harrison's telling you true, darlin'. He never said you visited her."

"He must have said something, otherwise you wouldn't be here asking questions."

"I asked Wes a few questions about Consuela on Saturday." Harrison came around the side of the desk and went to where Alejandra stood. "Daniel happened to be there, but had I any idea my conversation with Wes would lead to an interrogation, I wouldn't have asked in the first place."

"You still haven't said why you visited Consuela," Cain drawled.

"Because she invited me. Ask Mr. Rutherford if you don't believe me. He was there when she extended the invitation."

"If it were nothing more than a social call, you wouldn't have gone at night, and you'd be more willing to answer our questions."

Emotions flashed in her eyes; hurt, rage, and desperation all rolled into one heated glare. Then she raised her chin and squared her shoulders. "If you'll excuse me, I left Mr. Rutherford's father unattended and need to check on him."

She swept toward the door, then slammed it shut behind her.

"Four weeks." Harrison pointed a finger at Cain. "Four weeks of sneaking her pie and drawing her out and trying to get her to talk to me, and you ruin it in the span of ten minutes."

"Why do you care?" Cain crossed his arms over his chest. "If I were to go downstairs and talk to your cook or a scullery maid, would you object?"

"Are you daft?" He threw up his hands. "She needs help, but she's been hurt before and doesn't trust easy. I don't know how to help her—unless I get her to trust me enough to tell me what's wrong, and you just walked back all the progress I've made."

"I like her." Daniel bit off another piece of apple.

"You're married," Harrison snapped.

Daniel laughed. "I didn't mean it like that."

"Simmer down, lover boy." Cain slapped a hand on his

shoulder, a laidback grin creeping across his face. "I doubt the sheriff is moving in on your woman."

"She's not my woman."

"Sure she isn't." Cain sent him a wink.

A wink. As if he was some schoolboy about to be rewarded a peppermint stick for obeying.

"Reminds me of a frightened mouse." Daniel tossed his apple core into the rubbish bin. "But there's something strong about her too. Like she's got a spine of steel, but she's not sure when she's supposed to show it."

Harrison crossed his arms. "Is there anything else you two ruffians want, or can I show you out?"

"Look out, Cain." Daniel pushed himself out of his chair and stood. "You just got him in trouble with his lady, and now he ain't too happy."

Cain shrugged. "Probably for the best. He's better off without a lady—or don't you remember that pact? Harrison's not allowed to get married either."

Harrison thumped his chest. "Turned thirty in January. The pact is dead to me."

Daniel smiled at Cain. "Looks like you're the last one left who's under thirty. Think we can get you married off by October?"

"There is no earthly chance. Not by October, and not ever."

Harrison slapped Cain on the shoulder. "I don't know. Kind of wonder what you'd look like with all that long hair shaved."

"Respectable," Daniel muttered. "That's what he'd look like. Less like an outlaw and more like a lawman."

Cain removed his cowboy hat and ran a hand over the long, wavy hair that came to a stop in the middle of his back. "You two have about as much chance of shaving my head as the Rio Grande does of freezing in July."

Harrison opened the door and stepped out into the corridor. "That just makes me want to try all the harder to find you a—"

"Someone get the sheriff!" A shout came from the courtyard below. "We found the murderer!"

The murderer? Harrison strode to the railing and peered down to find Rooster and two other guards dragging a man across the courtyard.

"I'll fetch the sheriff," someone called, and two men started for the corral.

"No need," Harrison shouted at the quickly growing crowd. "The sheriff is already here, as is Captain Whitelaw."

He gestured toward where his two friends had come to look over the railing, then turned and started for the stairs.

He was the first one to reach the courtyard, though Cain's long gait quickly overtook his as the Ranger rushed toward the man being held captive.

But the person being held by the two guards looked a whole lot more like a boy than a man—a rather familiar boy.

Martin Owens.

Daniel raced past, his eyes hard and jaw determined, but Harrison slowed to a stop.

Martin Owens a murderer? The eighteen-year-old who had escorted Gertie Cunningham to the food line at the church picnic yesterday?

Harrison didn't need to hear the rushed explanation Rooster was giving to not believe a word of it.

"It wasn't me, Sheriff. I swear." Martin tried to pull away from one of the guards, but the guard only tightened his grip on the boy. "These men grabbed me and started accusing me of things I didn't do."

"Then explain why I found this on you." Rooster handed a sack to Cain, who quickly opened it and pulled out a silver candlestick—one that looked exactly like the candlestick he'd refused to pay the murdered traveler for. "We caught him trying to steal a horse and escape town."

"I wasn't trying to steal anything." Martin tried twisting away from the guard again. "I found the horse, saddle and all, and was bringing it back to town. The bag was tied to the horse. I swear it!"

"He wasn't headed toward town when we found him," one of the guards said—Griggs, if Harrison recalled.

"They're lying!" Martin was shouting now. "I was riding a horse that wasn't mine, it's true. But I was headed straight for Twin Rivers to get you, Sheriff. I found the horse out past Hidden Canyon. The sack with the candlestick was in the saddle bag, but there wasn't a camp or anything to make me think the owner was around. The horse was wandering, and I knew you were looking for a silver candlestick, so I was bringing both of them to you. I swear it."

"The horse belongs to Mr. Rutherford," Rooster shot back, his eyes trained on Daniel. "Griggs rode it into town this morning, then put it out to pasture with the others. Martin here must have sneaked into the pasture and stole it."

"No!" Martin wailed.

"Enough." Daniel held his hands up. "Martin, I hope you understand that this situation looks suspicious and needs to be investigated, even if what you're saying is true."

"It is." The boy swallowed. "But I understand."

"He's lying through his teeth," Griggs said. "I saw him sneaking out where we pasture the horses after I got back from town. Must have killed that traveler too."

"What reason did Martin here have to kill the traveler?" Harrison took a few steps deeper into the crowd.

"The silver candlesticks," Rooster sneered. "Everyone knows he lives on the poor ranch outside of town. They got so many young'uns, I'm betting they're always in need of money."

"We get by just fine," Martin snarled right back at Rooster.

"Like Mr. Rutherford said, I got no reason to kill anyone, and even if I did, do you think I'd leave town? My entire family is here."

"How do we know his family isn't already gone?" Rooster crossed his arms over his chest. "There might even be proof of the murder in their house."

"You're lying again." Martin straightened. "My family is still here. Pa and Leroy are both riding the fence. They gave me trouble about begging off so I could take Gertie on a picnic. That's why I was out by Closed Canyon. I was looking for a good spot. The sheriff here can search the house if he wants, the barn too. You won't find anything tying me to that murder."

Harrison winced. Chances were, Daniel wouldn't find anything incriminating if he searched the Triple S. And it was clear Martin believed that to be the case. But the lawyer in him wanted to advise Martin to make Daniel get a warrant first, especially since there wasn't a substantial enough motive to explain why Martin would commit a crime so grave he could end up swinging from a noose.

He didn't believe for a second Martin would risk his life and the reputation of his family for a pair of silver candlesticks.

"All right." The firmness of Daniel's voice resonated through the crowd. "Thank you for the information, guards. Captain Whitelaw and I will take Mr. Owens here out to the Triple S, search it, and decide whether Mr. Owens needs to be charged with any crimes based on our findings."

Harrison blew out a breath. He was probably getting himself all worried for nothing. Daniel was clearly searching for a reason not to arrest Martin, otherwise he'd be handcuffing the boy and locking him in a jail cell while he searched the ranch.

Once Daniel was away from the accusatory glares of his guards and the search turned up nothing, he'd release Martin and say this whole thing had been a misunderstanding.

Besides, Harrison would bet his saddle that with a family as large as the Owenses, Martin would have an alibi for when the murder had been committed.

But as he watched Daniel and Cain lead Martin out of the fort, he couldn't help feeling like something was wrong.

And that feeling had a lot more to do with the guards who worked for him than it did with Martin Owens.

XXX

THERE WERE times when Daniel loved being a lawman. Seeing justice served to outlaws while order and peace were preserved for law-abiding citizens gave him a sense of satisfaction and contentment.

But watching his men dig through haystacks and search crates inside the Owens's barn was just about the hardest thing he'd ever done.

"Are you sure this is necessary?" Sam gritted from where he stood next to Daniel. Every single member of the Owens family had come to watch the search, and seeing how Ellie had eight siblings plus a babe of her own, that meant there were thirteen people crammed inside the entrance to the lean-to style barn.

"Hold on to your britches," Daniel muttered. "When nothing is found, I'll be able to write this up as a misunderstanding, no charges filed and no harm done."

Sam looked at him with hard eyes, never mind the twentysome years of friendship between them. "Or you could have just said the whole thing was ridiculous in the first place and not even bothered coming out here."

"And how would that look? I can't give the appearance that

I'm letting someone get away with murder just because I'm friends with his father."

"You're not letting him get away with murder. He never committed it in the first place," Sam growled.

"Simmer down, Sam." This from Cain, who stood with a hand on Martin's shoulder, watching as two of his men searched the barn along with the two deputies Daniel had assigned to the task. "Daniel didn't even arrest him. See? No handcuffs. Facing an accusation like this has a way of raising a man's hackles, to be sure. But it's best to let us run an investigation and clear his name."

"We're almost done." Daniel lifted the bandana from his neck and dabbed at his brow, where beads of sweat were forming—and not because of the spring heat. "Give me five more minutes, then I'll release Martin and you can get back to your day."

"You think we'll be able to work after this?" Sam's eyes blazed. "What if you up and decide to search the house next?"

"Just the barn, Sam. That's all we need to look at."

"Listen to your friends, love." Ellie left where she'd been standing with the children and sidled up to Sam. "They're just doing their job. Besides, if one of our horses went missing, and someone showed up with it at Fort Ashton, wouldn't you want Daniel to investigate?"

Sam looked down at his wife. "I suppose."

"I hate to say it, Sam, but you're acting angry enough I'd be suspicious if I didn't know you," Cain drawled. "It's the ones who get all antsy when I do a search who usually end up guilty."

"No one here is guilty of anything!" Sam threw up his hands, his voice loud enough it resonated against the ceiling beams and then bounced back down. "And I say having my son accused of something he didn't do and my barn searched is plenty of reason to get angry!"

Bryce and both of Cain's Rangers climbed down from the hayloft on the far side of the barn. "We're done, Sheriff. Didn't find anything that might link Martin to that horse."

"Of course you didn't," Martin snapped. "Because I'd never seen the horse before this afternoon."

"Did anyone search those sacks of feed?" Daniel nodded to the three sacks sitting just inside the door.

Abe came out of one of the horse stalls, and the men all looked at each other.

Bryce shrugged. "Don't think so."

"Search them, and then we'll be done." It was a ridiculously obvious place to look. No one would hide a candlestick right inside the door to a barn. But like Cain said, Daniel didn't want to risk one of the guards from Fort Ashton coming back and accusing him of releasing Martin because of his relationship with Sam.

"Sheriff? I... ah, I got something here." Bryce looked over his shoulder, the tips of his ears read.

Daniel left where he'd been standing beside Sam, but he hadn't quite reached Bryce by the time his deputy pulled a shiny candlestick out of the sack.

He stopped, and a sickening sensation twisted his gut.

It couldn't be right. It couldn't be a matching candlestick. There was no way Martin had killed that traveler.

But he didn't need to move any closer to know the silver object matched the candlestick Cain had pulled out of the disputed horse's saddlebag an hour earlier.

"I didn't put that there!" Martin shouted from behind him. "It wasn't me! I've never even seen a candlestick like that before today!"

Daniel's heart felt as though a dozen lead weights had been strapped to it. He unlocked the handcuffs from his belt loop and turned toward Martin.

"Nothing but an accusation, huh? This was all just to clear

his name?" Sam sounded ready to explode, and Daniel couldn't blame him.

"I don't understand." Ellie looked between Sam and Martin. "What... what does this mean?"

Daniel glanced at Ellie, then away, his heart plummeting into his stomach. "Martin Owens, you're under arrest for the murder of John Doe."

"But he didn't do it. None of us have seen that candlestick before." This from Leroy, Martin's brother who was only a year younger than him.

"He was with us all night when that traveler was killed." Sam stepped between him and Martin. "You'll never be able to place him at the scene of the crime."

"Couldn't someone have put the candlestick in the barn?" Leroy looked at him, his eyes round and large. "It was right inside the door and we've been out working all day. Someone could have sneaked it in here."

They could have, yes. In fact, Daniel would bet his entire house and every last penny he had stashed in the bank that's exactly what had happened. "That's not up to me to determine, Leroy. It'll be up to a court of law."

He stepped around Sam, whose glare was hot enough it just might burn down the barn.

Cain had already pulled both of Martin's hands behind his back, and the metallic clink of the handcuffs snapping into place resonated through the barn with the force of a firing shotgun.

"Bryce, take him out to the horse, please."

Worry filled the young man's eyes, but he didn't say so much as a word as Bryce led him away.

Daniel turned to Sam and Ellie. "I know Martin didn't—"

"That's enough." Cain clamped a hand down on his shoulder, his grip heavy. "You're the sheriff in a murder investigation. Whatever you're thinking, you can't say it. Now let's go."

"Yes, go. And don't bother coming back." Sam crossed his arms over his chest.

"Sam, don't. I promise—"

"Don't promise him nothing." Cain's grip on his shoulder grew tighter. "Not unless you're willing to risk having Martin acquitted and then the case tossed out on appeal due to bias."

Daniel clamped his jaw shut. No. He wouldn't risk that, but the notion of riding off the Triple S without saying so much as a word to Sam or Ellie made his chest ache somethin' fierce.

How was Cain managing?

He glanced over his shoulder, but Cain looked as hard as granite. There was no kindness, no hint of a smile, nothing that indicated a heart might beat beneath the hard muscle and bone of his chest.

Was he going to have to become as hard as Cain to see this murder investigation through?

He wasn't sure he had it in him.

17

He was back to being a lawyer. Harrison stared out the window at the morning landscape of yellow rock, cacti, and towering, craggy mountains. How had the one thing he'd wanted to avoid, to never do again in his life, fallen into his lap?

And with one of his friend's sons, no less.

He took a sip of coffee, but the strong brew didn't stop the worry from swirling through his mind. Hopefully things would turn out differently than they had for Wade Tillerman.

But if he failed? If Martin Owens ended up hanging from a noose?

He nearly dropped his coffee.

He'd never be able to forgive himself if what happened to Wade ended up happening to Martin.

And yet, when Daniel had come to him last night and told him they'd found a matching candlestick in the Triple S barn, Harrison couldn't make himself turn down the case.

He could still recall Daniel's words as his friend had stood in this very room, still feel the full implication resonating through him.

"I want to tell you something as a friend, not as a sheriff," Daniel said, his voice gruff.

"Go on." Harrison set his papers down and looked straight at his friend.

"Martin didn't kill that traveler."

"We're agreed on that." Though as a lawman, Daniel shouldn't be saying such things—not unless he wanted to find them used against him at trial.

"Someone planted that candlestick in the barn."

Harrison straightened. "What makes you think that?"

Daniel only shook his head. "I don't know. My gut. A sense. Nothing that can be proved in court."

"I'll need a written report of the search. Did Cain sketch where the candlestick was found? How far away was it from an opening to the barn? Do we know if any of the Owens family was in and around the barn in the hours preceding your search? Just how hard would it have been for someone to sneak the candlestick in there?"

"You're missing the point."

Harrison leaned back in his chair. "How? If I'm going to argue the candlestick was planted—"

"Then your best bet is to figure out which one of your men planted it, because I'd bet my bank account that while Rooster and those other guards were stirring up a scene here, someone else snuck off to the Owens's place."

"But why? What motive would they have to...?"

Daniel sent him a stare so hard his words trailed off.

Harrison raked a hand through his hair, letting the information he had swirl through his mind. He'd known something was off in the courtyard earlier, but he'd come straight back up to his office afterward. He was still trying to figure out why there was too much money in his father's bank accounts. Eventually he'd planned to weed through the men his father had hired and figure out who was trustworthy enough to keep on and who he needed to let go.

Harrison met Daniel's eyes. "You think my guards murdered that traveler."

Daniel crossed his arms over his chest. "It's the most obvious explanation. And for some reason Martin Owens seemed like the best man to frame for it."

"But we have no motive for the murder, especially with the candlesticks reappearing. That means we can clearly rule out a robbery gone wrong."

"I don't have all the answers, but if I were you, I'd hire some new guards."

Harrison raked his hand through his hair. "Half my problem is I have too many of them. I can't keep track of where they all are or what they're doing at any given moment. I certainly don't need more."

"I'm not talking about normal guards." Daniel braced his hands on the desk. "I'm talking about men I pick. I want to bring in two men who temporarily pose as guards but who can pay attention to what the men your father hired are up to.

"But I have to admit, all this makes me wonder..." Daniel pushed off the desk and started pacing. "Whatever happened with the men you were searching for last fall? The ones who disappeared on the trail. Did you find them?"

"No. We never found any men, nor did we find evidence of foul play. It was like they just up and disappeared. I believe the marshals left the case open, but it's gone cold." And his housekeeper back in Austin still nursed a broken heart over her missing son.

"What if the traveler we found wasn't the first man to be killed on the trail? What if he was just the first person to have his body found?"

A sickening sensation twisted Harrison's stomach. "I'm starting to think there's more going on here than we've been aware of."

"Me too." Steel edged Daniel's voice. "Which means we need some evidence. If I find you men to pose as guards, can you afford to hire them?"

"*Absolutely.*"

"*Good. I'll have people here by the end of the week.*"

The end of the week seemed like too long to wait, especially with Martin behind bars. Harrison sighed, then sucked a breath of warm desert air into his lungs. He needed to go to the jail this morning and visit the boy.

No, the man. Martin had turned eighteen two weeks ago. If only he were still a boy, then maybe he'd be able to avoid hanging as the penalty for murder in the event of a guilty verdict. But not with Martin being a legal adult.

Dear God. Please send someone else to take this case.

The prayer was a bit ridiculous, considering Twin Rivers didn't even have a judge or prosecutor, let alone a defense attorney.

But at the same time, it was the only thing he could manage to pray for.

If he were a better man, he'd be reminding himself of God's faithfulness right about now, telling himself that God might have a plan for him with Martin's case, even though he'd failed Wade Tillerman.

But where was the plan?

He couldn't see it. All he saw was another case he was going to lose...

And this time he wouldn't be letting down a family of strangers—he'd be letting down a friend he'd known for over two decades.

A knock sounded on the door, and he looked up, half expecting Alejandra to poke her head into the room and give him some kind of update on his father.

But Hermine was the one who opened the door. "I'm sorry to disturb you, Mr. Rutherford, sir, but do you remember how you told me to report on anything unusual I saw regarding Alejandra?"

Harrison set his coffee cup down on the windowsill. "Go on."

"Well, sir..." Hermine shifted from side to side, her hands twisting nervously in front of her. "Have you noticed what she eats?"

He couldn't say he had. "What about it?"

"She doesn't get sandwiches or stew like the rest of us."

He blinked. Was she right? Now that he thought about it, he'd never really seen her with vittles beyond broth and bread, much like what his father ate. "What else?"

"It's odd, really. When the two of us are working in your father's room together, Mariposa will bring up two trays, one for me and one for her. The food is different between the trays, but Alejandra never asks for any of my food or questions why her tray barely has anything on it. She just attacks the food as though she's half starved, and then goes on as though nothing unusual happened."

"Is she working this morning?"

"Yes, sir, my shift just ended, and this is my free day."

"What time is breakfast usually brought up?"

"Eight-thirty."

"Wait in my office for a bit, and then I'll have you go next door and relieve Alejandra for a few hours this morning. I'll see to it that you're compensated for working on your day off."

Harrison didn't wait for her to answer as he flung the door to his office open and strode down the corridor.

No food.

Was his staff really giving Alejandra no food? But now that he thought about it, he'd never seen her with a sandwich, never seen her with grapes or eggs or stew. And he'd certainly never seen her with pie except when he gave it to her in his office.

And she acted far too appreciative of it.

He took the stairs two at a time, pausing long enough at the bottom to tell one of the guards in the courtyard to find

Rooster. Then he burst through the large wooden doors to the kitchen. Breakfast was in the process of being plated, half of it already laid out on a trio of large wooden tables.

Harrison surveyed the first table. "Is this the staff breakfast?"

Each plate had been laid out with two poached eggs, two pieces of buttered toast, and a dollop of jam.

"Yes, sir." Mrs. Aguilar left her place by the stove to come stand beside him.

Her daughter, Mariposa, who stood next to the stove with a clean plate in her hand, had stopped to watch him, as had the two other kitchen workers in the room.

"Is there a problem with the food?" the portly cook asked, concern lining her face. "Your father always said I could serve the staff eggs two days a week, and porridge the other days, but if you want me to only do porridge because the eggs are too costly, I can..."

He held up his hand, stopping the explanation, and then pointed to the table that held plates laden with scrambled eggs, a single slice of bacon, and a modest spoonful of fried potatoes. "This is for the restaurant guests, I assume?"

"Yes, sir."

"And those plates over there are mine and Rooster's?" He pointed to plates at the end of the table that held three pieces of bacon and heaping piles of both eggs and potatoes.

"Yes, sir."

"And who are those plates for?" He held his hand in the direction of two plates sitting at the very end of the staff table. Both held broth and bread, though one plate at least had butter and a dollop of jam for the bread. Not so for the other.

"One is for your father. The other is for Alejandra."

He raised his eyebrows. Up until this point, he'd had no reason to complain about *Señora* Aguilar's cooking. She always provided prompt, filling meals. They weren't as fancy as the meals his chef in Austin had prepared, but considering how many people *Señora* Aguilar cooked for, he thought she did a splendid job.

"And why, pray tell, does Alejandra's plate seem to be missing eggs, a second piece of bread, and butter and jam?"

The woman looked between him and the plate, her face losing a bit of its color despite the heat of the kitchen. "Because she only gets broth and bread, sir. Rooster's orders."

"Just how long ago did Rooster tell you to only give Alejandra broth and bread?"

The woman shifted from one foot to the other. "Before your father fell ill. Maybe six weeks ago?"

"Six weeks." It was all he could do not to curse. Here he'd thought Alejandra was eager to share pie with him at the end of the day because she enjoyed being around him, but in reality, the poor girl was just starved.

"Do you know why Rooster told you to withhold food?" He worked to keep his voice even. To not reach out and slam his fist into the table or grip *Señora* Aguilar's pudgy shoulders until bruises formed.

"She asked for it, sir. She broke a bowl, and Rooster was going to dock her pay, but then she asked if she could have her food garnished instead."

Harrison sucked in a breath through his nose, though the action did little to calm the blood boiling in his veins. What person would ask to be starved to death rather than get paid?

"A broken bowl?" he forced himself to ask. "How often does Alejandra break dishes?"

"Not so often as the serving girls or guests at the restaurant. We've got tile floors. A little slip, and dishes get shattered. Sometimes a whole tray of them go at once. That's why we order in these cheap white plates. We have crates and crates of them in storage. But Alejandra serves the guards and Mr. Rutherford, so she's always got the fancy dishes." The cook pointed back at his plate. "See there? How your plate has the blue edging? Good china, that is. Mr. Rutherford always insisted on the best, but when the fancy pieces get broken, Rooster wants the worker's pay docked so a replacement can be ordered."

"But Alejandra is the only worker assigned to serve my father and the guards, correct?"

"Used to be that way, before she started nursing your father. Now Mariposa does some of it, but Rooster forgave her for the plate that got shattered."

"So Alejandra is the only person who has to pay when a dish gets broken?"

The cook scratched the side of her head, her brows creasing for a moment before she shrugged. "*Sí*, but she's got more fancy dishes than anyone else."

"She wasn't the one to break the bowl, Mr. Rutherford. She just got blamed for it."

He turned at that and looked at Mariposa, who still stood by the stove, though she'd gone back to plating food. "Explain."

"It was Raul, sir. He broke it and said it was her fault."

"And you know this how?"

"I saw it. I was bringing a separate tray of drinks up to the parlor. Raul got angry and threw the bowl at her. Barely missed her shoulder, but claimed that if Alejandra wouldn't have made him so mad, he wouldn't have had cause to throw the bowl."

"I see," Harrison gritted through clenched teeth.

The door to the kitchen swung open, and Rooster entered. "You asked for me?"

He took a step toward the hulking guard, straightening himself to his full height, which was only a couple inches shorter than Rooster. "If you ever, for any reason, attempt to starve an employee again, I will fire you on the spot. Do you understand?"

Rooster glanced at the tables laden with food, his eyes coming to rest on Alejandra's plate. "Mr. Rutherford, sir, I—"

"Come see me in my office in an hour. I would deal with you now, but I've got a half-starved employee who I need to ensure gets fed first."

Harrison turned back to the cook. "*Señora* Aguilar, I want a feast brought up to my office. Eggs, bacon, potatoes, muffins, pastries, fruit. If it's breakfast fare and we have it somewhere in this kitchen, I want it in my office. Do you understand?"

"*Sì, señor.*"

"And make sure Alejandra gets served the same thing as me for the rest of the week. Same portions, same food, same everything. I don't want there to be a single difference between our plates."

"*Sì, señor.*"

"After this week, Alejandra is to go back to receiving the normal rations that all other workers get. And if anyone, for any reason, ever tells you to diminish someone's food again, I want to know immediately. Am I understood?"

The woman nodded again, then used her apron to reach up and wipe at the sweat forming along her hairline. "*Sì, señor.*"

"Good. I'll be waiting in my office." Harrison turned on his heel and strode from the room.

18

Alejandra knocked softly on the door to Harrison's office, then poked her head inside. "Hermine said you wanted to see me?"

"Come in and close the door." Harrison stood from where he'd been sitting behind his desk.

His desk that was covered in a mountain of food.

She took a step inside and closed the door as instructed, trying to ignore the scents of potatoes and eggs and bacon wafting through the room.

A small growl rumbled through her stomach, and she winced. Mariposa had been slow to bring up breakfast today, which meant she still hadn't eaten her bread and broth.

"I had a special breakfast brought up this morning." Harrison picked up one of the two plates sitting at the edge of his desk and held it out to her. "Take what you'd like. Ladies first."

"But..." She bit the side of her lip. If Rooster found out about this, he'd ration her food for another month, and here she was only a few weeks away from having her normal portions returned.

"Is there a problem?" Harrison asked.

"I... that is..." She reached out and took the plate from him, but only stared at the food.

"Please eat, Alejandra. Every time I see you, you're slurping broth like my father or nibbling on bread. This is my way of ensuring you get a full meal—since I can't trust the kitchen to provide you with one, or you to tell me when you're being denied food."

Her gaze shot up to his. "You found out."

"You should have told me you weren't eating."

She clenched the empty plate in her hands. "I was eating."

"You and I both know broth and bread isn't enough sustenance for a healthy person." His voice sounded rough, almost as though he was angry. "Hang it all, Alejandra. The bread on your plate this morning didn't even have butter on it!"

She worked to blink back the hotness pricking her eyes. "A bowl got broken, and I couldn't afford to have my wages docked, so I asked for the food to be taken away instead. I thought it would just be for a few weeks. Turns out the fort spends less money on feeding the staff than I thought."

He blew out a breath, then tugged the plate from her hands. "How many eggs do you want?"

"A spoonful, please."

"And do you want bacon?"

She nodded.

He worked his way down the desk, asking how much of each dish she wanted. His actions were brisk and his voice rough. Yet he didn't lecture her when she told him to skip something, didn't complain that she had too little food on her plate. He simply dished up what she said, then brought the plate to the low table by the sofa, where they usually shared their evening pie.

She sank into the comfortable cushions while Harrison returned to the desk for his own plate.

"If there's something you want more of, you are welcome to have seconds. Or thirds, or fourths. If we run out up here, I'll have more brought up from the kitchen." He sat down beside her.

"This will be plenty." She took her first bite and let the rich flavors fill her tongue.

The truth was, she'd gone without for so long that she wasn't even sure she'd be able to finish the food on her plate, and her plate was far from full.

She took a second bite, then a third, suddenly too hungry to bother talking. When her food was nearly gone, she glanced up to find Harrison watching her while his own plate remained untouched. "Aren't you going to eat too?"

"Not feeling very hungry this morning."

She set her fork down. "Are you angry with me?"

He gave his head a small shake, and when he looked at her, she wasn't sure what to do with the emotion in his eyes. In fact, she couldn't even name it. Worry? Kindness? Concern?

She'd spent the past eight years of her life since her stepfather died surrounded by men who always made it known when they were angry—and they weren't kind about it. But Harrison didn't seem angry, he seemed...?

Despondent, maybe? Ambivalent? But he clearly wasn't ambivalent about the amount of food she'd been consuming, otherwise he wouldn't have ordered a feast brought to his office.

"Why didn't you tell me?" he finally said, his voice holding an unusual tremor as he spoke.

"I..."

"You had to know I would have stepped in as soon as I found out about the food."

Oh... He wasn't angry.

He was hurt.

And she'd been the one to hurt him.

She drew in a breath, suddenly unsure of what to say. "I don't suppose I thought about it overmuch. I just made sure to thank you for the pie, because I really appreciated it."

"Come here." He set his plate down on the table, then reached for her, gathering her close. Her head instinctively found the crook of his shoulder and his arms wrapped around back.

She sat there for a moment, his warmth surrounding her while his heartbeat thumped against her side, and the feeling of safety soaked into her.

Because for the first time in years, that's what she felt —safe.

"Why don't you tell me when something troubles you?" he whispered into her hair. "Why don't you give me a chance to fix things?"

"Because you can't. And if I were to tell you everything..." How did she start? If she confessed what her uncle and Raul had been up to, he'd send for the sheriff.

"How do you know I can't help with your troubles when you haven't told me what they are?" Harrison's voice was soft against her head, his breath causing her hair to ruffle.

"I... I just..." She sighed, then shifted so that she could look up at him.

It was a mistake. His eyes were warm and sincere, the lines wrinkling his brow so full of concern that it was all she could do to press her lips together and keep her story inside.

Would he send for the sheriff if she told him everything?

Or what if, instead of calling in the law, he offered to help her?

"Explain the money to me," he urged. "Why are you so insistent on saving money that you starve yourself?"

Oh. That's what he wanted to know? Not her secrets. Not about the rustlers. Not about how she'd been reading his father's mail for over two years.

"Please, Alejandra." He nuzzled his nose into her hair. "Answer me. I don't want any more secrets between us."

She sighed. There would always be secrets between them, and there wasn't anything she could do to change that. But right now, in a small way, she could give him a bit of the information he wanted. "So I can leave."

"I gave you enough money to leave last fall. Do you need more?" His hold tightened around her. "Or is it that you don't have a place to go? Tell me what I can do to get you away from your uncle."

"You can't, because he still has my sister."

And there it was, the bald truth of it. She could do nothing more than pass notes to the sheriff and hope Raul got caught until she knew Gabriella was safe.

The weight of it settled around her, a dark cloak that felt heavier than the laden down wagons traders used on the trail.

"How does Gabriella feel about your uncle? Does she like the boarding school where he has her?"

"She hates my uncle, much like I do. And as for the boarding school, I don't know. In the last six months, Raul has only given me that one letter from her, and I'm pretty sure my uncle was standing over her shoulder, dictating every word she wrote."

"So the question becomes, how do we get her out of Mexico? But I have a hunch you've already seen to that."

She stiffened. "You know why I went to visit Consuela?"

"It was a logical guess, but even if Consuela is happy to help for little pay, I don't imagine getting your sister out of Mexico will be cheap."

"If she brings me Gabriella, I won't complain."

"And after Gabriella arrives?" Harrison asked. "I'm assuming Raul can't know."

She blew out a breath, her gaze finding the vast desert beyond the window. "After Gabriella arrives, you'll wake up one day, and I'll be gone. I'm sorry I can't tell you when, and I doubt I'll be able to warn you before it happens, but at least you'll know why I've disappeared."

"Where will you go?"

She shook her head.

"Is that to be a secret too?" His body grew tense beside her. "I can't send you a letter, even if it's mailed from Austin? Or... or come find you one day, just to see how you're faring?"

She pushed away from him and straightened. "I can't tell you because I don't know. I'll go far away and north, somewhere so far *Tío* Javier and Raul won't be able to find me."

He was silent for a moment, only the sounds of his breath and the ticking of the wall clock filling the room. Then his arms came around her again, and he pulled her back into the solid warmth of his chest. "I'll miss you."

She gave her head a small shake. "No. You'll have plenty of maids to replace me. Did you know Rooster is turning away workers? News has traveled through Ojinaga. Fort Ashton is a good place to work now that you're in charge."

"No. Suppose that's what happens when I leave the hiring up to Rooster though." Harrison's voice was just hard enough she guessed that Rooster wouldn't be doing much hiring in the future.

"But I'm afraid you missed my point, Alejandra." He spoke her name in that soft way he had. "I said I'd miss you... as a person."

"Oh." Their gazes met, and she suddenly couldn't swallow, couldn't breathe, couldn't do anything but stare into his rich brown eyes.

He took a strand of her long, silky hair and swiped it behind her ear, his breath brushing her cheek.

"You shouldn't," she rasped.

"I beg your pardon?"

"Miss me. After I'm gone. You shouldn't."

He swallowed, and he was so close she could almost hear the sound. "But I will."

A lump formed in her throat, and her neck muscles grew so tight she couldn't speak. Because she'd miss him too.

And she didn't want to think about what that meant.

19

"I didn't do it." Martin Owens's voice echoed through the jailhouse.

Harrison studied his notepad where he was recording everything the boy said while Martin sat on the other side of the locked cell door.

"I don't know how that candlestick got in the barn. All I can say is that I wasn't the one who put it there."

"And where were you the night the murder was committed?" Harrison forced his gaze onto Martin, though that was the last place he wanted to look, not with the anguish that creased every line of the boy's face or the way he couldn't stop his hands from shaking.

But he needed to watch Martin's facial expressions. They could give much about a man away—especially if that man were to take the witness stand during a trial.

And Harrison had to know what the jury would see in Martin's face when he recounted these things.

"I was at home with my family, just like any other night," the boy answered sharply. His body had gone stiff at the insinuation he would have been anywhere else. "You can ask them if you don't believe me."

"I will." Harrison closed his notebook, then pushed himself to a standing position. "That's enough questions for one day. I'll review my notes and then return if I think of something else to ask."

Martin stood. "Is that enough to free me with? I can answer more questions if it helps—as many as it takes."

"We've been at this for almost two hours. I think I have everything I need, but if—"

"Why is this happening to me?" Martin gripped his cell bars, his knuckles turning white with the fruitless effort to shake them. "Who did this? And why did they pick me?"

Harrison's stomach churned. Not because he hadn't expected the question, but because it sounded far too similar to the last time he'd been asked that very question by an innocent man locked behind bars.

"I aim to find out."

"Ellie's worried sick, and she don't need that with a new baby to care for. And Sam needs me back at the ranch. Leroy ain't half as good at helping with the cattle as I am. Sam says it all the time. You gotta get me outta here, Mr. Rutherford. Please say you can get me out."

The boy's words ended on a desperate plea, and Harrison was afraid to look at him for fear he'd find tears streaking Martin's face.

"Everyone's worried, but the best way to get you out of this is to take things nice and slow." He glanced down at his notes. "How about you walk me through how you found the horse again, just to be sure I didn't miss anything."

He'd already asked the question four different ways, but it was also the best place to poke holes in the guards' stories.

"I told you, that horse wasn't something that escaped out of the paddock. I found it grazing west of Closed Canyon. Sure, its reins had come untethered, but it seemed awfully familiar with the terrain, like it knew just where it was and was used to being in the area."

Harrison rubbed a hand over his jaw. If he could make the jury think that the horse had been found wandering loose and Martin had been doing a good deed by trying to take it to the sheriff, the rest of the case against Martin fell apart. He could then argue that the rider of the horse had seen Martin and known the sheriff would soon have the candlestick linking the owner to the murder, and then the owner had ridden to the Triple S to hide the other candlestick in an effort to frame Martin.

But did that mean one of his guards was a murderer?

The thought sent a chill down his spine. And yet, if that were the case, none of that explained why other guards would cover for the murderer by bringing Martin to the fort and claiming the horse he'd found had been stolen.

Harrison asked Martin a couple more questions, then closed his notebook for a second time and hightailed it out of the jailhouse. A gust of wind ripped at his hat when he stepped outside, but it wasn't enough to soothe the itch that had grown between his shoulder blades.

Nor did it erase his memories of Wade Tillerman. He could still see the dark shadows of Wade's jail cell, still hear the sounds of the others behind bars as he questioned the man who claimed he hadn't killed his boss's wife.

By this point, Wade Tillerman had been hanged and buried six feet under. Harrison had filed for an appeal before he left for Twin Rivers, of course, simply because it was the only thing he could do to spare the man's life. But he hadn't heard anything from the lawyer he'd handed the case to, which only left him to conclude that Wade Tillerman was dead, and his widowed mother and fifteen-year-old sister were both mourning his loss and struggling to make ends meet given the lack of Wade's income.

"Well, well, if it isn't the infamous lawyer set to restore justice to Twin Rivers."

Harrison looked up to find Cain standing smack dab in front of him, his long blond hair blowing in the wind. "What do you want?"

"You come from the jail?" Cain looked past him toward the sheriff's office. "How'd your interview with Martin go?"

"I didn't have any magical epiphany that will make Daniel release him and drop charges, if that's what you're asking."

Cain tilted his head to the side. "Bothers you to see an innocent person locked up, does it?"

Harrison's jaw clenched. "What kind of man do you think I am?"

"An honest and honorable one."

"Then you shouldn't be surprised I'm upset."

Cain shrugged. "You need any help, let me know. Already had a look around the area where Martin claims to have found that horse, but it didn't turn up anything of use."

"Daniel said the same thing." He scrubbed a hand over his face. He shouldn't be taking his bad mood out on Cain, but this business with Martin was just so heavy.

"Don't get too impatient." Cain slapped him on the shoulder. "Something will turn up, and when it does, Daniel isn't going to act like the police back in Austin. He doesn't have a wealthy family pressuring him to keep everything he uncovers secret. He'll give you the information you need to clear Martin's name."

Harrison almost opened his mouth to ask how Cain knew the police in Austin had been so standoffish about sharing information in the Tillerman case, but the Texas Rangers were headquartered there, and Cain kept abreast of the goings on in the state capitol, so he would know all about Wade Tillerman.

"Maybe you're right. I need to keep in mind that Daniel doesn't want Martin behind bars any more than I do." Harrison looked around the busy street. "I have another question for you though. Is there somewhere we can talk?"

"I was on my way back to camp. Walk with me."

They walked in silence for a few minutes, waiting for a wagon to pass and sidestepping a Mexican woman with a string of five children headed into the general store.

It wasn't until they were clear of the town and traipsing through the long grass that grew near the river that there was enough privacy to ask Cain his question.

"Let's say I wanted to bring someone to Texas from Mexico, someone who's under eighteen."

Cain stopped walking. "You lookin' to add kidnapping to your list of skills?"

"I'm speaking hypothetically."

"Sure you are."

"Just tell me, what's my likelihood of getting extradited to Mexico?"

"If you don't get caught and manage to get far enough away from the border? Nonexistent."

"What if the girl's guardian is powerful?"

Cain plucked a blade of grass and stuck the stalk into his mouth, his eyes surveying the river and camp in the distance. "How powerful?"

"I don't know. A lot of money and resources. Maybe someone like Wes?"

"Depends. Just how committed would this man be to finding you? Let's flip this around and say someone kidnaps one of Wes's cowhands. In most cases, if a cowhand gets dragged a hundred miles from the border, there ain't no chance of anyone from Texas finding him. But Wes could use his money to hire an army of men to go looking south of the border. If he was willing to pay enough and wait long enough, that cowhand would eventually resurface."

"If someone kidnapped Keely, he'd spend every penny he had to get her back," Harrison muttered.

"And he'd succeed, I have no doubt. Another thing to keep in mind, even with all his money, he'd be privately funding his search. He doesn't have enough diplomatic power to pressure the Mexican government into tracking a man down. That's the real thing you want to avoid. Don't toy with someone who can wield pressure on either the state or federal government. If extradition papers get issued for you, you'd have every bounty hunter in America after your sorry hide."

Harrison shook his head. "I don't think the situation would come to that."

"So what's this about?" Cain twisted the stalk of grass lazily between his fingers, but there was nothing lazy about the sharp look in his eyes. "I don't need to tell you that you could end up disbarred for this kind of thing. But worse would be getting caught and dragged back to Mexico. The last place you want to find yourself is in a Mexican prison. And the last thing I want to do is find a way to break you out."

Harrison grinned. "You'd come break me out?"

"I'm a lawman, not an outlaw," Cain drawled, his voice even drier than usual.

Maybe so, but that was just about the kindest thing Cain had ever said to him, and he couldn't stop a warm sensation from filling his chest. "The law isn't always able to stop evil from happening. In fact, sometimes evil can happen, and there's no law against it. What's a man to do then?"

"What's right. Hang the law. A real man'll do what's right."

"Exactly."

Cain thumped him on the shoulder, then started walking again. "You got any plans to cross that border, you come talk to me first. It'd be easier on both of us if I help you get whoever it is you're after rather than having the lot of you caught somewhere in Mexico."

"Consuela's already working on the problem.

Cain's step hitched. "This has something to do with your woman then."

"She's not my woman."

"Sure, she isn't."

Harrison repositioned his hat on his head. "She's not mine now, and she never will be. Because once her sister gets here, she won't be able to stay in Twin Rivers. It's as you said. Given her uncle's resources, it won't be easy for either of them to disappear. So don't tell me she's my woman."

Just saying the words aloud made him feel raw.

Had he admitted something like that in front of Wes and Daniel and Sam, they all would have let loose with hoots and taunted him about falling for a woman. But Cain didn't acknowledge the emotion of the statement, just kept right on walking into camp. "Like I said, you need to go into Mexico, let me know."

"I'm hoping Consuela can handle things."

"This is Alejandra's sister, you say?" Cain turned his direction. "At least now I know your woman's not involved with the rustlers."

Harrison stiffened. "I already told Daniel she wasn't involved with the rustlers."

"I know, but Consuela's helped more than one of my informants, so it made me wonder..." Cain frowned, his voice trailing off as he stared at the path between the tents.

Harrison followed his gaze to find Anna Mae weaving her way through the camp.

"What are you doing here?" Cain snapped, stalking toward her.

Good grief. Why did Cain sound so angry? She was probably just bringing food to the Rangers.

"Howdy, Anna Mae," Harrison said as he came up to her, only to realize he'd cut off something Cain had been saying to her in a low voice.

He looked between the two of them. Cain—his unflappable friend who never gave away a hint of emotion—stood with fists clenched and shoulders tight, a small muscle pulsing at the corner of his jaw.

And Anna Mae had a smug little smile on her face.

"Is something wrong?"

"Not at all." Anna Mae turned to him, her smile turning genuinely sweet. "In fact, I'm glad I found you. I'm so happy to hear you're taking Martin's case. That poor boy! Now as for my brother..."

Her hands clenched into fists, and her eyes suddenly looked ready to shoot fire. "I still can't believe Daniel arrested Martin. I already told Daniel I'm not saying a word to him until he frees that poor boy."

Harrison rubbed the back of his neck. "Not sure he had much choice about locking Martin up, considering the evidence against him."

"Everyone has a choice."

"I'll do my best to make sure Martin gets acquitted," he tried to assure her.

"Can I help with the case?" Anna Mae took a step closer to him, causing the hem of her skirt to brush his trousers. "I'm good at talking to people. I could ask around town and see if anyone saw something suspicious. Or maybe Charlotte and I can go back to the place in the desert where the body was found. Charlotte knows the desert better than anyone. She might be able to—"

"You are *not* going to where the body was found," Cain gritted. "So help me, woman, there's a murderer roaming around. The last thing anyone needs is for you and Charlotte to be his next victims."

Anna Mae planted her hands on her hips. "I'm not going to see that boy hang, Cain Ramos Whitelaw, nor will I let you stop me from trying to clear his name."

"Ah, actually, it's my job to make sure he doesn't hang." Harrison stepped between Cain and Anna Mae, but that didn't stop Anna Mae from glaring daggers over his shoulder. "I appreciate your offer to help, but these kind of things take time. The judge isn't scheduled to be in town for six more weeks. I'm sure I'll be able to use your help somewhere in there, but first I need to familiarize myself with the case."

Anna Mae rocked back on her heels, a bit of the tenseness draining from her body. "You mean it?"

"Of course. You're more familiar with the people in town than I am, and I'm sure that can be of help. But I also meant what I said about this process taking time. Freeing Martin is going to require patience."

"I'm terrible at patience." Anna Mae crossed her arms over her chest and gave a little huff. "'It's a virtue,' Pa always said, but it's not a virtue I have any hope of attaining."

"Well, I have something you can do in the meantime. I'd actually... ah..." He rubbed the back of his neck, which suddenly felt hot. "I'd like to take you on a picnic."

"You... me...? Oh." She blinked at him. "But I thought... that is, don't you and Alejandra...?"

"I'm trying to convince her to visit you on her day off. She needs a good friend or two, but she feels like she'd be a bother, plus she thinks I need to find a wife, so I struck a deal with her on Sunday. If I take you on a picnic, she'll visit you. Her next day off is Thursday, and I was hoping you and her could do something then, so do you have time for a picnic today or tomorrow?"

"Wait." Anna Mae held up her hand. "Don't you have feelings for Alejandra?"

The heat from the back of his neck spread to his ears. "Don't reckon that's any of your business."

"Well, if she thinks you need to find a wife, and you have feelings for her, why aren't you asking her on a picnic instead?"

"It's complicated."

"I don't see what's so complicated about it. You say, 'Alejandra, will you go on a picnic with me?'"

"And she'd say no." Why were they talking about this? He'd invited Anna Mae on the picnic, not Alejandra.

"Then maybe you need to do a better job of convincing her of those feelings you were wearing all over your sleeve at church on Sunday."

"What do you think I'm trying to do?" he gritted.

She rolled her eyes. "Not that, if you're asking me on a picnic instead of her."

He shoved a hand into his hair, knocking his hat askew. "I should have known this would be too complicated."

"It's not complicated. All you do is say, 'Alejandra, will you go on a picnic with me?'"

"And I already told you that isn't going to work!" He repositioned his crooked hat. "Never mind, I'll take Gertie Cunningham on a picnic. That's bound to be easier than this."

"So it doesn't matter whether you take me or Gertie? Any ol' woman will do?" Anna Mae stomped her foot on the dusty ground, her eyes skewering into him.

Confound it. How many questions was she going to ask? He didn't begin to understand how Daniel and Charlotte put up with her. And Cain was standing here voluntarily!

Though to be fair, Cain had been laughing for most of their conversation.

"Look..." Harrison blew out a breath, then sent a quick prayer up to God for patience. "I don't know how else to say this, so I'll try telling you again. Alejandra's in a hard place, and she needs a friend a heap more than she does a suitor. You could make friends with a scorpion if you set your mind to it. So if I take you on a picnic, can you please come to the fort on Thursday and take Alejandra to visit Keely or Ellie or something?"

"Yes," Cain answered for her. "She will."

Anna Mae turned her glare in Cain's direction. "You have no right to—"

"You've got a friend who needs help, and you're a decent person, so you'll help him. And when you're spending time with Alejandra, you won't needle her with fifteen thousand questions about Harrison either."

"But..."

"Just do it, Anna Mae," Cain growled.

She huffed out a breath, then tilted her head and looked at Harrison. "I can needle him on the picnic, right?"

Cain grinned. "Oh, you can ask him questions until the cows come home."

"Thanks," Harrison muttered.

Cain tipped his hat at his friend. "Anytime. Now how about you go on that picnic this afternoon and meander down to where Martin was found 'stealing' that horse? See if you find anything unusual."

"Oh." He blinked at Cain. "That's a good idea."

"So I can't go searching the desert by myself, but you'll let me go with him?" Anna Mae jabbed a thumb his direction.

"Don't be daft." Cain plucked one of the grass stalks from his shirt pocket and stuck it in his mouth.

"You realize if I go on a picnic with him, half the town will think Harrison and I are courting, and—"

"No one would know if you met down by the river at the boulders west of town."

Anna Mae tilted her head to the side, and Harrison could see the ideas forming behind her eyes. "I suppose. I have some baking I need to do this morning, but maybe we could do an early dinner? We could meet at the boulders at three?"

"That's perfect. I should be able to break away from the fort by then."

"Just be careful," Cain said. "My men and I have already searched the area once and didn't find anything suspicious, but I figure someone more familiar with the desert might get a little farther, especially if she's real slow at meandering through the area, making it look like she's enjoying some time with her sweetheart."

"Reckon so. Now I best get back to the fort. Anna Mae, do you need an escort back to town?" Harrison offered Anna Mae his arm, but she shook her head. "I need to talk to Cain."

"I'll see you in a few hours then."

XXX

CAIN WATCHED Harrison weave his way through the maze of tents that made up the Ranger encampment. As soon as his friend was out of earshot, he turned to Anna Mae. "Could have sworn I told you not to come back here just last week."

She gave her head a haughty little toss. "No, you told me not to bring your men anymore food, which I didn't."

It was all he could do not to curse. His men had been looking her direction ever since she'd arrived, though none of them had actually been fool enough to stop working and approach while he and Harrison were both present. But give it another minute or two, and his men would suddenly start interrupting him with inane questions, then manage to invite Anna Mae on another picnic or ten.

"Let's go to my tent." He turned and stalked away, slowing his gait just long enough for her to catch up. "Next time you need to see me, send a note. I'll meet you at your brother's office."

"I'm not setting foot in that office until Martin has been freed."

"Your brother's only doing his job. Three men accused Martin of horse thievery and then that candlestick showed up in the Triple S barn."

"But not the picture frame that was with it."

"No, not the picture frame. That's still missing." Cain held the flap open for her, then tied it to the side of the tent before stepping inside. "Now what did you want to see me for? And it had better not be your brother."

Her eyes flashed. "He could release Martin on bail."

"That's a judge's job, and there ain't no judge around to set bail. Besides, judges usually don't allow bail for murder charges."

"It's just wrong!" She threw up her hands and paced from one side to the other in a series of quick, dainty steps.

He should have realized she'd come to visit this morning. If she wasn't talking to her brother, she'd need to vent her anger somewhere. He'd send any other woman who came to him for such a reason packing, but he just couldn't make himself turn Anna Mae away.

And it made no sense. She had enough emotions for ten women bottled up inside that petite little body of hers, and he didn't do emotions.

Especially not female ones.

"If Daniel did anything other than lock Martin up, he'd have half the town calling for his removal as sheriff on account of playing favorites." Cain took a swig of water from the canteen sitting on the table. "Your brother can't go soft on a person just because he's friends with the person's pa. He took an oath against such things when he got sworn in as sheriff."

She stopped pacing long enough to look at him. "Do you think Martin murdered that man?"

"No."

"Then why don't you do something?"

"I did. I told your brother to get Harrison involved. He's the best shot Martin has."

She narrowed her eyes. "Unless we find who really killed that traveler."

He pointed a finger at her. "That's not your job."

"Then whose job is it?"

"Daniel's. Harrison's. Maybe mine, though Rangers usually don't get themselves tangled up in local murder investigations."

She pressed her lips together, and he could almost see her scheming up ways she might help clear Martin's name.

Confound it. Why did the woman have to be so all-fired insistent on getting herself into trouble? "I just told Harrison to take you on a picnic out that direction so you can snoop around. That's the best I'm going to offer. And whatever snooping you do, it can't be by yourself. I want to make extra certain you understand that."

"I understand," she muttered.

"Good. Now it's time for you to go. Let me call Bryant to walk you back."

"Wait, I haven't had a chance to ask you to Easter yet."

He paused, his feet only a few steps from the entrance to the tent. "Excuse me?"

"Easter. It's in two weeks. We're going to church, and then we're going to the A Bar W afterwards for dinner. I came out here to invite you, but as soon as I saw Harrison, I got distracted by my oaf of a brother." She stepped toward him and rested her hands on his arm. "Will you come? Easter dinner isn't something to eat on a wooden bench around a firepit."

He stared down into her face, the delicate lines and angles, the smooth, creamy skin, the sincere brown eyes. How long had it been since someone had invited him to a dinner? Like he belonged. Like she wanted him there and would notice if he didn't come. Like he was part of a... a...

A family.

Confounded woman.

He swallowed the lump that had risen in his throat and used his driest, most disinterested voice when he finally drawled, "Reckon God would strike me right dead if I stepped foot inside Preacher Russell's church."

The comment would have been enough to scare anyone else off, but Anna Mae only tilted her head to the side and narrowed her eyes at him. "Why? What have you done?"

"Reckon you aren't my priest neither."

"And I reckon you aren't Catholic and wouldn't know the first thing to do with a priest." She dropped her hands from his arm.

And hang it all, but the spot on his arm where her hands had just been suddenly felt cold.

"And we both know God's not going to strike you dead for going to church. Heaven knows you were inside that building enough while you lived with Preacher Russell."

He froze, every muscle of his body suddenly refusing to move. In fact, he could almost swear his blood stopped moving through his veins, that his heart stopped beating for a full half a minute.

How long had it been since anyone brought that up?

He hadn't lived with the preacher for very long, only for the two years after his ma passed and before his pa showed up and offered him a job with the Rangers.

But it was long enough to remember the cozy nights by the fire, the way Miss Emmaline would rest a hand on his shoulder and smile at him, or Preacher Russell would scoot a chair up to the table after dinner and help him with his literature essay.

Part of him would never forget how nice it felt to be seated around their small kitchen table eating a meal of shepherd's pie —no matter how badly he wanted to.

Cain swallowed again, because that stupid lump had climbed right back into his throat. "A lot of time has passed between then and now. Thanks for thinking of me, but I'll forego Easter service."

"What about dinner?" Her voice was quiet against the noise from the camp outside. "Will you at least come to that?"

He sighed. Why was she so determined to include him? Didn't she understand that he wasn't part of Twin Rivers and her group of friends? That he'd chosen to leave that part of his life behind a decade earlier?

But as he met Anna Mae's eyes and saw the hopeful look on her face, he didn't quite have the heart to tell her no.

20

Alejandra paused at the door to Harrison's office. It was cracked just enough for her to spot him at his desk, studiously working away beneath the gentle lamplight, his dark hair cast in shadows while his chiseled jaw looked far too serious.

She rapped softly at the door, then stepped inside. "Do you need anything from the kitchen?"

It was the same question she asked him every night, but somewhere along the line, it had gone from being a matter of practicality to an exchange she looked forward to.

She stepped farther into the office, then stopped. There, next to his desk, were two crates of papers. She'd known some of Harrison's belongings had arrived from Austin earlier. It had taken the guards almost an hour of going up and down the stairs to move everything that had arrived.

But she hadn't realized his papers had been with the furniture and other possessions.

"I don't need anything from the kitchen, no." Harrison smiled at her, then jutted the end of his pencil at the twin pieces of pie sitting on a tray with tea service. "But I need someone to share this pie with me."

She pulled her gaze away from the crates of papers Raul would demand she read as soon as he returned. "You don't have to offer me pie anymore. I promise I'm getting my fill at meals."

"You'd better be."

She gave her head a small shake. "You should have seen the plates Mariposa brought me for lunch and dinner. It was enough to feed five grown men."

"And yet, I'm still convinced that if you don't help me eat this pie, you might wither away to nothingness during the night." He stood and came around the front of the desk, then picked up the tray and carried it to the table by the sofa.

She sank into the soft cushions and let him hand her a plate. "How was your picnic with Anna Mae?"

He shook his head as he poured her a cup of tea. "Annoying."

"Really? But she's so lovely. I assumed—"

"What? That if I took her on a picnic, I'd fall madly in love with her?" A grimace pinched his lips. "Each time I find myself looking at her, thinking that she just might be one of the prettiest women I've ever met, she opens that wretched mouth of hers, and once she starts talking, there's no hope for it."

Alejandra giggled. "I like all her talking."

"You're allowed to like it. You're a woman." Harrison sat beside her on the sofa. "It was all I could do not to strangle her. She argued about which direction we should go, where we should take our horses next, how long the picnic should last, and that was all within the first fifteen minutes. In the end, all I could do was pray God blesses whoever ends up marrying her with an extra dose of patience. The poor sap's going to need it."

She burst out laughing, the urge so deep and uncontrollable she had to set her pie down lest she dump it on her lap.

"I'm sorry," she finally managed. "Truly I am. I thought I was doing you a favor by prodding the two of you on a picnic. I had no idea it would make you miserable. That wasn't my intention."

"Truth is, Alejandra, there might be a woman I want to take on a picnic, but it isn't Anna Mae."

Oh, dear heavens. The way he was looking at her took every last bit of laughter from her mind and caused her hands to dampen.

"I... um..." She looked down, the faded stain on her apron suddenly interesting. "I heard about what you're doing for Martin Owens. I'm glad you took his case."

If she wanted to wipe the romantic look from Harrison's face, she'd found a way to do it.

His expression turned instantly dark, and he stared out into the dusky desert before answering. "Don't get your hopes up about Martin. I don't want you or anyone else to end up disappointed."

"But everyone's saying—"

"Don't want to know what everyone's saying. The evidence is stacked against Martin, and even if I manage to uncover something promising, court cases, judges, and juries, can all be unpredictable. A lawyer can think he has an ironclad case and still end up losing."

"I don't think you'll lose." She reached out and rested a hand on his arm, but his jaw only tightened.

"I wish I had the same confidence that you do."

"Of course, I have confidence in you." She stroked her fingers lightly up and down the tense muscles of his arm. "Why wouldn't you have confidence in yourself?"

XXX

HARRISON SHOOK HIS HEAD. Alejandra looked at him with such hope, such assurance, that he could barely force himself to meet her gaze.

"My last case in Austin... it didn't go well."

Somehow it felt like he was confessing a crime, even though he still couldn't see how he'd done anything wrong. He reached for his cup of tea, gulping down half the liquid in a single swallow.

"What happened?" The soft stroking motion of Alejandra's fingers moved up to settle on his shoulder.

He hadn't spoken of it, not once. But sitting with her in the stillness of the room, watching as night slowly descended over the desert, he couldn't keep the story in.

"I defended a man from a murder he didn't commit, and I lost."

Her hand pressed against his shoulder, the warmth of her skin seeping through his shirt. "Even though he was innocent?"

"The family of the murder victim, they're rich and powerful. They own railroads that run all over Texas and Oklahoma. When Rosalind Crist was found strangled to death in her bedroom, the newspapers carried headlines for days."

"And you ended up defending the man who was accused of her murder?"

He nodded. "The police charged one of the livery drivers that worked for the Crists. How and why they chose him, I'll never know. The evidence the prosecution presented was so weak they could have charged any servant in the house." He let out a sharp, bitter laugh. "Sometimes I wonder if they decided to charge Mr. Tillerman by writing the names of all the servants on slips of paper, dumping them into a hat, and then pulling one out."

"So he came to you for help?"

He could still remember the day Mr. Tillerman's mother had arrived in his office, her worn and faded gown a stark contrast to the polished floors, plush furniture, and smartly dressed secretaries surrounding her. He'd recognized her last name instantly, and when she said she was trying to find a lawyer for her son, he told her the court would supply a public defender.

She said they'd tried that and their first two meetings had gone dreadfully, that the defender wanted Mr. Tillerman to plead guilty and accept life in prison in exchange for hanging.

Harrison hadn't been able to stop himself from taking the file of papers she'd offered and looking through them that night. When he realized just how flimsy the evidence against Mr. Tillerman had been, he'd taken the case.

"Could a liveryman afford your legal services?" Alejandra asked.

"I took the case for free." His voice emerged rough, as though he'd just swallowed a handful of desert rock. "The evidence clearing Mr. Tillerman was cut and dry. I couldn't have asked for a prettier defense case."

"So how was it that you lost?" Alejandra's hand started moving again, this time up and down his back.

"I still can't explain it, not really." But the story poured from his lips anyway. He told Alejandra how he'd presented his evidence in court. How the prosecution had two witnesses that placed Tillerman inside the house at the time of the murder, but he'd had over a dozen men testifying Tillerman had been at the saloon while the murder was committed, after which he'd gone home to where he lived with his ma and younger sister.

He'd eviscerated the prosecution's attempt to establish a motive for Wade Tillerman to kill Rosalind Crist. And he'd even found a couple servants willing to testify that Mrs. Crist had been heard arguing with both her husband and oldest son the evening of the murder.

It had seemed like an easy case, something a first-year law student could handle.

But his invitations to soirees and dinner parties and balls had ended almost immediately upon taking it, and Adeline had shown up at his house in tears, asking how he could dare to defend the person who had killed her mother's friend.

Yet the reaction among the working class had been the opposite. Mr. Tillerman was framed almost immediately in the press as a victim, the target of a rich family who was using their wealth to hide the true circumstances of their matriarch's death.

And Harrison had been hailed as a hero for defending him.

"Did you feel like a hero?" Alejandra moved her hand from his back, causing a sudden coldness to appear where her skin had just been.

"I... no. I don't think so. I was reeling more than anything. I never imagined defending Mr. Tillerman would get turned into some kind of war between the upper and working class. I never imagined that it would cost me the legal practice I'd spent so long building in Austin. I lost clients I'd had for years."

"That must have been hard."

"I felt like I didn't belong anywhere. I couldn't walk into the gentleman's club where I was a member without getting snubbed, and yet I didn't feel as though I belonged in a saloon across the street from a factory either. The trial only lasted for two weeks, but it was the longest two weeks of my life."

"What happened at the end? You still haven't said."

Harrison pressed his eyes shut and recalled the day of closing arguments, the heat of the courtroom from too many bodies being crammed inside, the stench of sweat from the workers, the ringing of the judge's gavel as it banged against the bench.

The prosecution had arrived in court that morning claiming new evidence in the case had been discovered and wanting to either call or recall half a dozen witnesses to the stand, every one of which discredited his client.

Some of the witnesses Harrison had never seen before. Others were servants who had already testified but suddenly changed their stories. The most damning testimonies were from two of the liverymen who worked with Mr. Tillerman. They'd originally testified that he'd left the house after bringing Mr. Crist home from work on the day of the murder, but that morning they both changed their stories to say that Mr. Tillerman stayed in the livery, lurking around until after dark, when they both saw him go into the house.

When Harrison asked why they had originally said Mr. Tillerman left the Crist residence by six o'clock on Thursday night, they both claimed they'd mixed the defendant up with another liveryman.

Closing arguments had turned into a dog and pony show, and the papers had all printed special editions immediately after the jury broke off for deliberation.

"We lost," he finally told Alejandra, his voice shaky. "And the only reason I can think of is witness tampering, that maybe the true murderer paid witnesses to testify against my client. The Crist family certainly had enough money to do so."

But even if he suspected one of the Crist men killed Rosalind, he had no way of narrowing down which one. The police hadn't given him access to any information that might help him point an accusatory finger at another person, not even their interviews with the Crists.

"I still don't understand it," he rasped. "Even with the new witnesses, how could the jury have found Wade guilty beyond all reasonable doubt? Everyone had reasonable doubt about Wade's guilt. Do you know how many people stopped me in the street and thanked me for representing Wade against the powerful Crist family?"

"I can imagine it was a lot, especially if the newspapers covered the trial as heavily as you say."

"Multiple times a day."

A couple of the more salacious papers had even run articles claiming Crist himself had killed his wife and was paying off witnesses to ensure another man hanged for his crime.

Of course, the articles hadn't had a lick of evidence to back up what they were saying. He knew. He'd visited the offices of several publications trying to track down who their sources were. In each instance, the "sources" were rumors reporters had overheard being murmured in saloons and boarding houses and not anything he could use in court.

But the jury had issued a guilty verdict nonetheless, and Wade Tillerman, the only son of a poor widow and the only brother of an equally poor sister, had been sentenced to death by hanging.

If he closed his eyes and thought hard enough, he could still hear the fateful sound of the judge's voice booming through the courtroom, sentencing Wade to death.

"I feel guilty, like... like it was in my power to stop Wade from hanging, and I failed."

"You didn't fail." Alejandra rested her hand atop his, which were clasped together tightly over his knees. "You did the best you could. It sounds to me like justice is what failed, or at least the system."

"I can't help but wonder what will become of Wade's family now. He was their main source of income and..." His words choked off, the lump in his throat suddenly too big for him to speak.

"You started calling him Wade," Alejandra said softly. "When your story began it was Mr. Tillerman."

"The papers all called him Mr. Tillerman, of course, and last names are used for all official court proceedings and documents, but you're right. Somewhere in the midst of everything, Mr. Tillerman became more to me than a name on a piece of paper. He became Wade, a living man with worries and fears, hopes and dreams. Did you know he only planned to work for

Crist for another year before he'd have enough money to buy a farm outside of Austin and propose to his sweetheart?"

"That sounds like a nice dream."

He shook his head. "A good lawyer never gets emotionally involved with a case, and yet, I wasn't able to stop it... just like now I can't stop myself from being emotionally involved with Martin's case."

He pushed himself off the sofa, the blood rushing far too swiftly in his veins for him to sit still. "If I couldn't clear Wade's name, then how am I supposed to clear Martin's? This case is going to be a lot harder. There are three men placing Martin with that stolen horse, and a candlestick was found in the Owens's barn."

"Maybe God means for you to defend him anyway, even if the results aren't guaranteed."

He whirled toward her. "Why do you say that?"

Her shoulders rose and fell in a shrug. "Because maybe... maybe this is the path God has for you. Maybe God knows you're the best man for the job, and so He brought the case to you."

He threw his hands up. "How can I be the best man for the job when I've failed so horribly?"

"You were trying your best with Mr. Tillerman, weren't you?"

"Absolutely."

"Then what happened to him isn't your fault. Isn't there a Bible verse somewhere about God loving the just?"

"Psalm 37:28 says, 'For the LORD loves the just and will not forsake his faithful ones. Wrongdoers will be completely destroyed; the offspring of the wicked will perish.'" It was the first one that came to mind. Miss Emmaline had made him and Cain and the others memorize it for school after they hid a lizard in her desk.

"There you have it. I think you need to rest in the fact that you did what you could for Mr. Tillerman, and you'll do what you can for Martin, and leave it up to God to 'not forsake his faithful ones.'"

He sighed. She had a point, but... "That's easier said than done."

"Perhaps, but don't you think God could prevent Wade Tillerman from being hanged if He wanted?"

"That only makes it worse." He stalked to the window and stared out over the darkening desert. "Wade never should have been convicted when he was innocent, but God didn't just allow that to happen, He also allowed the judge to sentence him to death. Perhaps this shows just how weak my faith is, but I can't understand why God would do such a thing."

She pushed herself off the sofa and came to stand by him. "Stephen in the Bible was innocent, and God allowed him to be put to death."

He blew out a breath as the familiar story swirled through his mind. He hadn't thought of it quite like that. "I suppose there was some good that came of Stephen's death, like Paul eventually becoming a Christian."

"That's my point. God might have had something more going on with the Tillerman case than you can understand. But now that it's done and over, you can't let your frustration over what happened in the past hurt your desire to defend Martin. He needs the best lawyer in Texas."

He looked down at her, at the smooth planes of her face and gentle curve of her neck and glossy darkness of her hair. "And you think that's me?"

She gave a firm nod. "*Sí.*"

A small smile pulled at the corners of his mouth. "You have an awful lot of faith in me, considering you've yet to see me work as a lawyer."

"Oh, well... I..." She glanced at his desk, and a strange look crept over her face. Then she swallowed and looked down.

"You're right. But given how hard you're working on Martin's case, I have no doubt you'll win. Now I best be going."

She stepped away from him, then turned and fled, her head down even though her curtain of hair didn't quite hide the rosiness in her checks.

He blinked at the door as she pulled it shut with a bit more force than necessary.

What had he done to scare her off in the middle of a conversation?

XXX

HARRISON STARED up at the ceiling above his bed, the light from the full moon outside just bright enough to cast a pattern of silvery shadows across his ceiling.

Another sleepless night. How many had he had since returning to Twin Rivers? At first thoughts of his father had kept him up, but now that Father was slowly improving, it was the image of a woman with long black hair and vulnerable eyes that filled his mind.

Except those eyes hadn't been wide and vulnerable earlier. They'd been filled with concern—for him.

Maybe this is the path God has for you. Maybe God knows you're the best man for the job, and so He brought the case to you.

Harrison thrust the covers aside and stood, heading onto the balcony where the desert breeze ruffled his hair.

Was she right? Was defending Martin God's plan for his life right now, and he'd somehow missed it?

Is this what You want for me, God? I thought I was following Your plan in Austin, but what if I wasn't? What if what's happening in Twin Rivers is part of Your plan instead?

Had God brought him here, not because of his father or because he needed to escape wild newspaper stories in Austin, but because someone needed to defend Martin?

And here he was wallowing in so much guilt over the Tillerman verdict that he couldn't see what God had placed in front of him.

He still wasn't comfortable with the idea of Wade Tillerman dying, not when he was innocent, but yet, he had to admit that could have been part of God's plan too. Just like it had been part of His plan for Stephen to die in the Bible.

Just like it had been part of God's plan for Wes's first wife to die.

Just like it was part of God's plan for him to come back to Twin Rivers.

He scratched the side of his head. It was the first time he'd let his thoughts wander that direction. Yes, he'd come back to Twin Rivers after getting that telegram, but out of duty, not because he'd stopped to ask God what He'd wanted.

He'd started looking through the records at the fort out of duty, not because it might be what God wanted.

He'd even agreed to take Martin's case out of duty, not because he'd stopped to ask what God wanted.

Alejandra was the only part of his time in Twin Rivers that hadn't felt like duty. The only part he'd consulted God over, because she so obviously needed help, and he was lost as to how he should give it.

But tonight she had been the one to help him see how blinded he'd been, to point out that he couldn't let things that happened in the past get in the way of the future God had for him.

And what was the future God had?

He knew defending Martin was part of it, but what about the rest?

Was it to remain here in Twin Rivers running the fort and offering legal services when needed?

And if that's what his future looked like, would Alejandra somehow get to be a part of it?

A breath of wind rippled the curtains around his window, and he tilted his face up toward the sky. *I'm listening now, God. Please show me what You have next.*

21

"Look at how easily you sat up today." Alejandra beamed at Mr. Rutherford, who'd done most of the work sitting up for lunch.

The right side of the older man's mouth curved into a half smile. "I... good."

Or at least she thought that's what he said. It was still hard to understand him, but she could usually make out a word or two.

"Would you like some mashed potatoes and gravy for lunch?"

"Yes."

She gave him another smile. In the weeks since his apoplectic attack, he'd slowly started to improve. He still couldn't move his left side very much, which meant he couldn't walk, but he had a little better control of his muscles, and he could talk through the right side of his mouth. Doc Mullins was hopeful the paralysis on the left side of his body would continue to lessen, and that he'd eventually be able to walk again.

She spooned a bite of mashed potatoes into his mouth,

which he swallowed eagerly. "I was thinking maybe you could go outside today. Just for a half hour or so, to feel some sunshine. A wheelchair arrived for you, and—"

"No." His eyes turned hard.

"But don't you—?"

"No."

Her shoulders sank. "The doc thinks it would do you some good to get out of this room. Is there somewhere you'd like to go?"

"Sleep."

"Maybe after your nap—"

"No."

He might only be able to speak a word or two at a time, but those words were becoming terser and his eyes harder with each suggestion that she made.

"All right." She spooned the last bite of potatoes into his mouth. "Would you like to sleep now, or do you want me to read to you?"

They'd been making their way through a copy of *Little Men*, though she couldn't really say whether Mr. Rutherford enjoyed the novel.

"Sleep." Mr. Rutherford pulled one of the pillows out from behind his back and shifted himself farther beneath his quilt.

"Very well." She moved all but one of the pillows out from behind him and was drawing the drapes on the window when the door opened and Harrison stepped in.

"Father, I..." He stopped, taking in his father's still form and the eyes that were already half closed in slumber.

"Did I miss lunch?" He pulled out his pocket watch and glanced at it.

"We ate a little early. Your father said he was hungry."

"He's still talking then?" Harrison stepped to the bed and studied his father, who'd drifted off to sleep in a matter of seconds.

"And moving more, yes. He nearly sat up by himself."

Harrison gave a brief nod. "I'm happy to hear it." He sent her a small smile, but she glanced away.

It had been three days since he'd told her about Wade Tillerman.

Three days since she'd told him he needed to try his best in Martin's case and trust God with whatever happened.

Three days since she'd spotted those boxes of files sitting on the floor beside his desk.

She'd not gone into his office since.

He'd given no indication he thought her behavior odd, and he hadn't come to seek her out either. But now, standing in the same room, she could barely look at him.

Harrison was doing everything he could to bring justice to the world and see right done.

And what was she doing?

Spying on his father. And as soon as Raul returned, he'd insist she spy on him too. Insist she read every one of those papers, even though she knew what she would find.

Honesty. Integrity. Kindness.

She could think of no better words to describe Harrison Rutherford.

If only she held to similar principles in her own life. If only she could claim she was as honest with Harrison as he was with her. Or as kind. As generous.

"I should take your father's tray to the kitchen," she mumbled, avoiding looking at him as she picked the tray up from the bedside table.

"I'd like to talk to you first." He held the door open. "Let's go to my office."

Her feet rooted to the floor. She didn't want to go in there, not with those crates sitting beside his desk to taunt her. She couldn't even look at them without feeling guilty. "Harrison..."

He raised an eyebrow at her.

Did he understand how hard it was for her to look at him and not blurt out everything about her uncle and Raul and the spying?

Somehow she'd grown too close to him and started to trust him too much. Somehow she'd begun to... to... to...

What?

Fall in love with him?

She couldn't let herself love him, not when she'd be leaving as soon as Consuela returned with Gabriella.

Either that, or leaving to get Gabriella herself. Because if Consuela stayed gone for much longer—

"Are you all right?" Harrison took a step toward her, concern lacing his face.

"Fine," she blurted, then picked up the tray and hurried through the open door. At least she wouldn't be tempted to hug him if she was holding something.

She went to the railing and looked down over the busy courtyard below.

Harrison closed the door to his father's room, then came up beside her. He didn't say anything about her not going into his office, but his eyes held so many questions that she started to wonder whether standing by the railing where others could see them was actually better than going into his office where she couldn't avoid looking at those crates.

"After our conversation the other night, I did some thinking and praying, and I decided that you were right. I was placing too much guilt on myself for what happened to Wade Tillerman, and I think that was affecting how I was approaching Martin's case. He deserves the best from me."

"I'm glad what I said was helpful."

"I also decided that God wants me to make some changes to my legal practice."

Her gaze shot up to his.

"You see, up until now, I was focused on... well, on proving my father wrong. On getting the most prominent clients I could in Austin and making a name for myself. It's not that I didn't help people along the way, like Wade Tillerman or the occasional worker who came to me with a problem. But helping people like that wasn't my goal. My goal was..." He shook his head. "You know that verse in the Bible about laying up for yourself treasures on earth, verses storing treasures in heaven? Let's just say I became a little too focused on earning those earthly treasures and lost sight of my heavenly ones. But I'm going to change that. I don't know if God wants me going back to Austin and resuming my practice there, but if that's where God leads, I'll be changing who the bulk of my clients are and focusing on using my legal knowledge to help those who need it most."

"Like Martin and Wade."

"Like Martin and Wade."

Her throat almost felt too tight for her to speak. And it was a good thing she'd come to the railing after all, because if they'd been alone in his office, there was no way she'd be able to resist stepping into his arms, feeling the warmth of his embrace, and listening to the beat of his heart beneath her ear. "I... I think that's very honorable of you, Harrison. I have no doubt that whatever happens next, you'll do your very best to help those who need it. Just as you've done with me. You're... you're a good man."

Too good, really.

He offered her a sheepish smile, the tips of his ears suddenly a bit red. "I'm afraid I'm not nearly as good as you think I am. But that leads me to another question. Have you received word from Consuela or Gabriella?"

She looked away. "No."

"How long has it been since Consuela left? Two weeks?"

"Three."

"Do you want me to hire men in Mexico to check on her?"

He would do that for her? Of course he would. Because he didn't know how to be anything other than helpful and kind.

Even though she didn't deserve it.

Her chest felt suddenly hollow, as though the warmth that had occupied it just a moment ago had been chiseled out, leaving only a cold, empty space behind.

"Thank you for the offer, but I'm worried that hiring men would only alert my uncle to what's going on. He has informants everywhere."

He leaned forward. "I don't want you going into Mexico after your sister by yourself."

She shifted from one foot to the other, her eyes focusing on a random traveler below. How had he known she'd been toying with that very idea?

"Promise me, Alejandra, please."

She sighed. "Raul is gone on business for my uncle. This is the perfect time for me to slip away from Twin Rivers without him knowing."

"When is he set to return?"

She shook her head. "Anytime."

"Let's wait another week, then if there's still been no word from Consuela..."

"What? You'll go into Mexico with me?"

He pulled on his lip. "I'll see what Cain thinks is the best way to get Gabriella out."

"It's too much, Harrison. You don't need to do that for me. You don't need to try to... to take on my problems as your own."

"I know I don't *need* to. But maybe I *want* to."

He was being too kind again, making it almost impossible for her not to fling herself into his arms. She took a step back from him instead, making the distance between them circumspect and formal enough that anyone below would think he was talking to her as an employer to his servant.

Which was good. Just like it was good that they hadn't

shared any more pie in his office or heartfelt conversations. Because no matter when Consuela returned or whether Gabriella was with her, one thing was certain.

She would need to leave Twin Rivers and Harrison behind.

And she couldn't afford to get any more attached to him than she already was.

22

"Fishing? You really brought me here to go fishing?" Alejandra looked around at the idyllic setting. A decent-sized stream flowed beneath the shade of cottonwood trees, and tall green grass grew right up next to the sandy bank. A series of craggy bluffs ran along one side of the field dotted with desert grass and cacti, adding a beautiful backdrop to the picturesque scene.

All in all, it was the perfect day and the perfect place for a picnic. But that didn't explain why there were half a dozen fishing poles lying beneath a large cottonwood tree next to the blanket and picnic hamper. Nor did it explain why Charlotte and Ellie were busy tying flies to the ends of their fishing lines while Keely held Madeline.

"Of course I brought you here to go fishing." Anna Mae looked at her as though she'd gone daft. "I told you as much when we left Fort Ashton."

"I thought you were joking." What was she supposed to do with a fishing pole?

"Why would we be joking?" Charlotte called from where she'd waded into the stream in her bare feet. "It's great fun!"

"It's a man's sport."

"Why should they get to have all the fun?" Ellie blew a little kiss at the baby, then waded into the stream beside Charlotte.

"You don't have to fish if you don't want to," Keely patted the spot on the blanket beside her. "Fishing isn't my favorite, but it's still nice to visit with friends."

"You have to at least let me show you how to cast." Anna Mae grabbed her arm and dragged her over to the fishing poles. "No sitting on the blanket until you try. Now pick a fly. I recommend one of the blue or brown ones if you want to catch something, but you can choose any one you want."

Alejandra stared down into the wooden box that displayed a host of hooks tied with colorful thread that resembled insects, then bent down to grab a silvery blue one. "Don't expect me to catch anything."

"The stream is filled with fish this time of year. Here, let me show you how to tie it." Anna Mae took the fly from her hand and attached it to the pole, then went through the motions of showing her how to cast.

Charlotte hollered from the river as she pulled her first fish out of the water, and Ellie rushed to help her net it.

Alejandra felt a smile creep across her face as she headed out into the water and cast her rod once, then twice, then a third time. The top of the pole wobbled with each movement that she made, but she had to admit there was something relaxing about standing barefoot in the cool stream, moving her arm with the weight of the rod and watching her fly arc out.

This was the second time she'd visited with the women on her day off, and she couldn't be more grateful Harrison had prodded her into it, especially now that she and Harrison weren't talking very much.

It wasn't that they were fighting, but gone were the nightly conversations in his office or the kind smiles he'd been so quick to give her around the fort.

And it was for the best. She knew it was.

Now if only she could get herself to stop missing him.

And really, how ridiculous was she being? Who missed someone that they saw every day? It made no sense.

"So tell us, how are things at Fort Ashton?" Ellie waded back into the water after tying the fish she'd just caught to a string beside Charlotte's near the bank.

"Good." Alejandra cast a fly out onto the water, but she didn't get the cast quite right, and it landed only a few feet from where she stood. "The elder Mr. Rutherford is improving. He's staying awake for several hours at a time now, though he still can't really talk."

"That's why things are good, because Bartholomew Rutherford is recovering?" Anna Mae gave an exaggerated shudder. "That man's so cruel I don't even like thinking of him."

"Have things changed much with Harrison running the fort?" Charlotte sent her fly out over the water in a perfect arc.

Alejandra thought of the full plates of food she'd been getting for the past two weeks, ever since Harrison discovered she hadn't been eating. "Yes. I don't know how to describe it except to say everything's just better with him there."

"Look at that smile," Anna Mae teased. "It wouldn't have anything to do with thinking about Harrison, would it?"

She nearly dropped her fishing pole. "No, no. Harrison and I are... I mean, Mr. Rutherford is... we're hardly talking at the moment, to be honest."

Ellie raised an eyebrow at her. "Then why is your face turning red?"

Was her face red? She reached up to feel the side of her cheek. "Not because of Harrison. It's just hot out here."

"Uh huh." Charlotte sent her fly back over the water with another perfect arc. Dratted woman. "If that's the case, then you won't mind telling us what's been happening between you two."

"There's nothing to tell! Well, other than that he's nicer than his father."

"And that's why you're blushing?" Anna Mae's lips tilted in a knowing smile. "Because he's not a tyrannical brute?"

"You three are impossible." She reeled her line in. Had she actually thought fishing was relaxing? "Harrison and I are friends and nothing more. You're imagining things that aren't there."

"Are you sure?" There was an unmistakable softness to Charlotte's voice, even though she worked to reel in another fish. "I used to think that way about Daniel, but there was more between us. There always had been, really. I just didn't want to admit it."

Alejandra shook her head. "I'm sure. In fact, I won't be in town much longer. I have commitments back in Mexico."

"You're going back to Mexico?" Anna Mae paused her rod mid-cast, causing both the fly and the line to plunk unceremoniously into the river. "For how long?"

"My uncle has a man for me to marry there." She hoped it was a lie, at least the part about going back to Mexico, but there was no question about whether she'd be gone from Twin Rivers in a few more weeks, and it was best to just let everyone think she'd returned home.

"You're marrying someone who's not Harrison?" Charlotte turned to her, and the fish she'd been trying to reel in took off down the river, stretching the line taut across the water. "Oh, fiddlesticks."

Charlotte worked to draw the fish back in, but the silvery little trout seemed determined to free itself.

"Do you want to marry this man?" Keely asked from where she was dipping Madeline's toes in the water near the bank.

"I..."

"You don't look excited about it," Ellie said.

"Yeah, what if you don't go back to Mexico and marry this

brute?" This from Anna Mae, whose brows were furrowed together with a thunderous look.

"I never said he was a brute." But he would be. Her uncle didn't know how to pick any other kind of man.

"If you marry Harrison, your uncle won't be able to force you to marry another person." Anna Mae gave a firm nod of her head. "Yes, that's exactly what you should do. Ladies, we need to plan a wedding on the quick."

"Wait. What? No. I can't just up and marry Harrison. You don't understand the kind of man my uncle is." Oh, why had she said anything about Mexico? Maybe it would have been better to just up and disappear one night without trying to tell her friends why she'd left.

Besides, if she married Harrison, she wouldn't put it past *Tío* Javier to kill him just so she' be free to marry again.

"What if you didn't have to go back to Mexico?" Ellie reeled in her fishing line, then turned to her rather than making another cast. "Let's pretend for a minute that if you wanted, you could stay in Twin Rivers and marry Harrison. Is that what you'd choose to do?"

Heat pricked the backs of her eyes, and she quickly blinked it away before the other women could notice. "I... I don't know."

None of this was even worth thinking about in the first place, because she'd always have Gabriella to consider.

Not that she was about to tell her new friends about her sister. Harrison knowing was already one person too many. "There can't be anything between Harrison and me. I never thought there could be, so I haven't spent too much time dreaming of the impossible."

She'd be a disaster if she let herself do that, if she dwelt on all the things she couldn't have. So she just tried to focus on the good things God had put into her life, on the hope He gave her every day.

Except each day that passed without Gabriella arriving in

Twin Rivers made that hope seem farther and farther away.

"I'm sorry." Charlotte reeled in her broken line, the fish she'd lost having taken off with her fly. "When I saw the two of you together at the picnic, I thought sure Harrison had finally found himself a woman. He tried courting in Austin, you know, but none of the women he was interested in were ever a good fit."

"He did?" Alejandra straightened. "How do you know?"

"My sister Mariah lives there. With Wes and Harrison being such good friends, she often included Harrison's latest doings in her letters."

"Oh." She hadn't known that. What did Mariah think of Mr. Tillerman's court case? Had she written anything to Charlotte?

If so, Charlotte must not feel inclined to talk about it, because she pulled another fly from her pocket and busied herself tying it onto the end of her line.

Alejandra cleared her throat. "Truthfully, I was thinking perhaps Anna Mae and Harrison might—"

A peal of laughter cut off her words, and she looked around to find all four women giggling.

"Harrison can't stand me," Anna Mae gasped. "I drive the man crazy."

"It's not because she tries to," Charlotte added. "It's always an accident, I swear, but it's the funniest thing to watch."

Anna Mae tossed a strand of hair over her shoulder. "Oh goodness, every time I'm around him, I can see his temper slowly start to boil, and just because I ask him questions! Who gets mad about questions?"

Alejandra snorted. "Someone who likes calm and quiet. Though I have to say, Harrison did mention praying God gives whoever marries you an extra dose of patience after he returned from that picnic the two of you went on."

The women fell into another fit of laughter, and this time Alejandra found herself joining in.

She'd miss her friends when she was gone, but hopefully she and Gabriella would be able to share times like this after they escaped.

At some point during the laughter, Madeline started to cry. Keely tried dipping her toes back in the water, then bouncing her, but the babe only wailed louder.

"I think she's hungry," Keely said.

"It's just as well. I'm hungry too." Anna Mae sloshed her way back to shore. "Let's take a break and eat."

Charlotte finished reeling in yet another fish as the rest of them clambered out of the river and made their way to the blanket. Madeline calmed the second Ellie took her and started unbuttoning the top of her dress, and the rest of them settled in with shaved ham sandwiches, dried apples, and cookies.

"Even if you have to go back to Mexico soon, you're still coming to Easter, right?" Keely took a bite of her sandwich. Her hair was a bit wet from the river, and it framed her face in a curly halo of red.

Alejandra broke off a small piece of her own sandwich. "I don't know. Mr. Rutherford is steadily improving, which is good, but it also means he needs a little more attention than when he slept all day."

"But you have to come to Easter." Anna Mae swiped a handful of dried apples from the tin in the middle of the blanket. "We'll all be at church together, and then we'll go out to the ranch."

Alejandra looked at Charlotte. "Are you going?"

It was no secret that things were tense between Daniel and the Owenses, although no one would have guessed it if they'd seen Ellie and Charlotte fishing together a few minutes ago.

Now an awkward tension settled around them, and Alejandra shifted uncomfortably in the quietness. "I'm sorry. I shouldn't have asked."

"It's all right." Charlotte looked down and fiddled with

something on the blanket. "Daniel is working on Easter so that his deputies can spend the day with their families."

"I hate this," Anna Mae pronounced. "It's just so stupid."

"My brother's in jail awaiting trial for a crime he didn't commit," Ellie snapped, the fury in her tone contrasting sharply with the sight of Madeline nursing. "That's not stupid, it's wrong and unfair and horrible."

"Yes, but Harrison will get him freed," Anna Mae retorted.

Alejandra looked up at her. "What makes you so certain?"

"Daniel and Cain and Wes all say he's the best lawyer they've ever known, and he's been working on the case something fierce. He's at the jail visiting with Martin every day."

"You're right that he's working hard. Half the time when I stop by Harrison's office to see if he needs something from the kitchen, he's looking at notes for Martin's case." Though it didn't seem as though Anna Mae or any of the other women knew about the case he'd lost in Austin.

"I wish he'd never been charged in the first place." Charlotte wrapped her arms around herself in a lonely sort of hug. "I feel like I can't be friends with Ellie, like she hates me—and she'd have good reason to. But then, Daniel and Cain are both insistent that Daniel is only doing his job, and at this point, there would just be trouble if he up and dropped charges against Martin, and..." She drew in a breath, her eyes misting with tears. "It's all just so horrible."

"I don't blame you for any of this, dear," Ellie reached over and settled a hand on Charlotte's leg.

"But you blame my husband."

Ellie's shoulders straightened. "I blame whoever put that candlestick in our barn."

Alejandra blew out a breath. "The more I think of it, the more I'm certain it was one of the guards from Fort Ashton. It had to be."

Ellie's gaze snapped to hers. "What makes you say that?"

"How it happened. I mean, three guards dragged Martin into the fort claiming he'd stolen that horse. So if three guards already knew about it, why not four or five? There are enough of them that one could slip away undetected for an hour and ride out to the Triple S."

"You can't say anything." Charlotte leaned forward, lowering her voice to all but a whisper. "But Daniel thinks whoever killed the traveler is the one who planted the candlestick."

"It's the only thing that makes sense," Anna Mae muttered. "Why else put that candlestick in Ellie's barn?"

"But if what Alejandra said is true, does that mean someone who works at Fort Ashton murdered the traveler?" Charlotte looked directly at her.

"And does that mean that other guards at the fort know about it and are covering for him?" Ellie's eyes met hers across the blanket.

A quick glance at Anna Mae and Keely told Alejandra that the other's woman's eyes were on her too—as though she somehow had answers.

But she didn't. "I wish I could say why. Truly, I do."

But she didn't have a clue, unless…

Unless the horse didn't really belong to Mr. Rutherford, and Rooster and Griggs had lied to cover for the horse's true owner. One of the rustlers?

With the candlesticks showing up, it was the most likely reason for the traveler to be killed. Not because someone was trying to rob him, but because he'd somehow gotten too close to the rustlers.

But her friends wouldn't know that rustlers could be involved.

And they certainly wouldn't know that she was privy to more information about the rustlers than anyone else.

The trouble was, how would the traveler have stumbled

upon the rustlers in the first place? Raul was careful to keep his activities well away from the busy Chihuahuan Trail. If the traveler had been on his way to Austin, there was no way he would have run into Raul or any of his men.

"I'm sorry." She apologized for the second time, then shook her head. "I really don't know. I was just trying to make sense of things, but the more I think about it, the more confused I find myself."

"You and me both." Anna Mae popped a dried apple into her mouth.

"Thank you for trying." Ellie raised Madeline to her shoulder for a burp. "I just keep praying that truth will prevail. That Martin's name will be cleared and the true murderer will be arrested. And that in the meantime, I'll have the strength to trust God."

Alejandra blinked. "You're trying to trust God... even with, well, everything?"

"Yes, why wouldn't I be?"

"I don't know. I guess I just... It seems like your situation is extra difficult, that's all."

"It sounds like your situation is difficult too." Ellie gently tugged a strand of red hair away from Madeline's clenched fist. "You're being forced to go back to Mexico and marry a man you don't have any feelings for."

They didn't know the half of it. She was trying to put her hope in God, but the longer she went without hearing from Consuela, the harder it was.

"Remember what the preacher said a few Sundays ago?" Keely took a sip of water from her canteen. "He preached on suffering for righteousness. He said that if you suffer for righteousness, you should be happy. He said not to be afraid."

But the face of the Lord is against them that do evil. And who is he that will harm you, if ye be followers of that which is good? But and if ye suffer for righteousness' sake, happy are ye: and be not afraid of their terror, neither be troubled. She'd read that verse over and over since hearing that sermon.

"That passage the preacher used, it said something about God's ears being open to the prayers of the righteous too," Charlotte added. "Everyone knows Martin is righteous, God included. No one in your family did anything wrong, so I have to believe God will make things right."

Ellie offered a small smile. "Maybe I need to go home and read that passage."

The other women all gave Ellie encouraging nods, but Alejandra stared down at the blanket. She had no doubt that passage of scripture would work for Ellie's family.

But would it work for her?

She was trying to be righteous. She was trying to pass information about the rustling on to the law, and she'd decided not to read any of Harrison's papers. But she wasn't innocent the way Ellie's family was. She knew who the rustlers were, could walk into the sheriff's office and tell him every last thing he wanted to know that afternoon.

Doing so would mean jeopardizing Gabriella, but what if God wanted her to confess things anyway? What if God refused to help her and Gabriella because of the secrets she was keeping, and they both ended up in Mexico married to terrible men?

"Hey, are you all right?" Anna Mae leaned over and rested a hand on her shoulder.

"Yes, I'm fine. But I'll... ah... I'll keep an eye out for anything unusual at the fort. See if I can spend a little more time with the guards and figure out something that could be useful. The sooner we can see Martin out of that jail cell, the better."

Ellie reached out and patted her hand. "Thank you, Alejandra. That would mean the world to me."

Alejandra forced herself to smile back, even though nothing on the inside felt like smiling.

23

He couldn't prove the horse that Martin had supposedly stolen had come from Fort Ashton.

Daniel scooted the list of Bartholomew Rutherford's livestock closer to where he sat hunched over his kitchen table and read it for what felt like the fifteenth time that day.

The list said Rutherford owned three bay-colored quarter horses, but when he'd gone back to Fort Ashton to count the livestock after arresting Martin, there had been four horses matching that description in the pasture. When he'd asked Rooster about it, Rooster had said the extra bay belonged to Griggs, one of the guards who'd accused Martin of horse theft.

Daniel might have normally been suspicious, but the number of black quarter horses in the pasture and stable hadn't matched Rutherford's livestock list either. And there'd been an extra appaloosa too.

Considering all the workers and travelers at Fort Ashton, he wasn't sure the list of the livestock Bartholomew Rutherford owned would ever exactly match what was in the stables and pasture.

That there'd been an extra bay quarter horse gave legitimacy to Martin's claim he'd found the horse wandering the desert.

But if the horse had truly been extra, then had Rooster lied to him about who the horse belonged to?

That only drove him back to his suspicion that one of the guards at Fort Ashton had killed the traveler. But he still had no motive for the murder, especially since both candlesticks had been recovered and the only valuable thing the traveler had that was still missing was the silver portrait frame.

The extra guards Harrison had hired hadn't been able to figure out much about Rooster or the men he was closest with either. They reported it felt like there were two groups of guards at the fort: Rooster and his men, then Fordham and a couple stray guards who weren't part of Rooster's clan. And getting information out of Rooster's clan was proving futile.

Daniel leaned back and stared at the papers in front of him. It was almost as though the deeper he got into the investigation, the less things made sense.

Like why one candlestick would turn up in the Owens's barn but the other in the saddlebag, and all while the portrait frame was still missing?

Why hadn't the killer taken both candlesticks and the frame at the time of the murder? If the horse would have tried to take off with one candlestick while the killer held the other and the frame, wouldn't he have stopped it?

Daniel shifted, causing the wooden chair to creak beneath him. He didn't think Martin had anything to do with that traveler's death, but even if he did, it wouldn't lead to the candlesticks turning up in two different places. The first thing Martin—or anyone whose goal was to rob another person—would have stolen was the horse. It was more valuable than a pair of candlesticks and a portrait frame.

And Martin would have made sure the horse was either

tethered or he was holding the beast's reins before he shot the traveler lest the horse was gun shy.

Then, if Martin were truly the killer, he would have taken the horse back to the Triple S, searched the saddlebags there, and removed all valuables at that time.

Didn't the fact the horse had been roaming around with a candlestick in its saddlebag three weeks after the murder prove stealing hadn't been the murderer's motive?

But if not stealing, then what?

And how did the killer know to plant the candlestick in Martin's barn?

Had framing Martin for the murder been the true killer's intent all along? Had Martin somehow gotten himself tangled up in a situation that had given him enemies?

It was worth asking Martin about in the morning.

The wall clock chimed the half hour, and Daniel leaned back, stretching his arms out over the chair. The sun was beginning to set, causing the light slanting through the windows to cast the kitchen in an orange glow, yet Charlotte still hadn't returned home.

He'd known she'd be gone fishing with the womenfolk for the better part of the afternoon, but he'd certainly expected her to arrive before supper. Maybe she'd gone to dinner at the A Bar W with Anna Mae? Or she might have been invited out to Sam and Ellie's.

At least the womenfolk were still talking, even if Sam wouldn't so much as look at him at church.

Or on the street.

Or in the general store.

Or anywhere else their paths crossed.

Daniel sighed. Was it just him being hopeful, or did all his evidence indicate the candlestick had been planted in the Owens's barn?

Would a judge and jury be convinced when the documentation he had was presented?

Daniel scratched the side of his head. This was almost as frustrating as the bank robbers, who'd appeared and then disappeared without a trace. He considered himself a fairly decent lawman, but that didn't mean he could track ghosts across the desert.

The door to the house opened, and he jumped, then turned to watch as Charlotte stepped inside. "You're home from the sheriff's office early."

"I wanted some quiet, and perhaps a bit of extra time with my wife. Thought you'd be back sooner."

A soft smile tilted the corners of her mouth, and she came over and rubbed his shoulders. The bulge in her stomach pressed into his back in a way that sent warmth straight to his heart. "You might not have gotten extra time with me, but did the quiet at least help?"

"I saw Sam in the general store today. I didn't realize he was there, or I would have waited until he came out." He wasn't sure why he said it, especially when she hadn't asked about Sam, but it was the first thing that tumbled out of his mouth. "I want this done and over. I want my friend back."

"Come here." Charlotte's hands left his shoulders, and she tugged on his arm. "Let's sit on the sofa."

He let her pull him out of the chair and lead him to the sofa, where soft cushions enfolded him. Charlotte curled up next to his side, the bump in her midsection snuggled between them. Her hair tickled the bottom of his chin, and he inhaled the scents of sunshine and river and... fish.

"Where are your fish? Are we having them for dinner?"

"We are. I'll bring them in after a bit. First, tell me what Sam did when he saw you."

Daniel pressed his eyes shut. "Nothing. He just... nothing."

It shouldn't hurt so much. But when a man lost twenty years of friendship in the space of a day, how could it not hurt?

Charlotte slid her hand up his shoulder to toy with the wisps of hair at the back of his neck. "Doing nothing's better than shouting at you."

"Is it? You should have seen the look in his eyes. His whole life, all that man has wanted is a family. Growing up, I tried to step in and be something of a brother to him. So did Wes. And heaven knows the two of you were so close I half expected you to marry. Now that he's finally got himself a family, I'm putting his oldest son behind bars."

"You're doing what you have to."

"Am I? Because I feel like this is splitting me in two. My sister won't talk to me, we weren't invited to Easter, and..."

Charlotte reached up and laid a finger over his lips. "Stop, Daniel. This isn't going to solve anything."

"Neither is investigating the traveler's death, evidently." It seemed like all he'd been doing lately, yet he had nothing concrete enough that would allow him to drop charges with a clean conscience.

"We were just talking about this at the creek."

He blinked. "You were? Even with Ellie there?"

"'But and if ye suffer for righteousness' sake, happy are ye: and be not afraid of their terror, neither be troubled.'"

He sighed. He remembered the preacher using that verse in a sermon a few weeks back, but... "How is that supposed to help me clear Martin's name?"

"You're doing right, Daniel. You're upholding the law, even though the costs are high. So don't be scared of the suffering. God promises to hold you up and support you."

He groaned. "Maybe I don't want to be supported. Maybe I just want Martin to be free."

"You realize this is part of why I fell in love with you? Why I married you?" She leaned her head against the crook of his shoulder and settled a slender hand on his chest. "You have a sense of justice and right, and you're unwilling to let it go, even when things are hard."

"I don't know that things have ever been quite this hard before. If only Pa were still here. He might know what to do."

"Your heavenly Father is here. He can show you."

He drew in a breath. "Maybe I need to try relying on Him a little more."

"I'll pray He gives you clarity."

Daniel twisted his lips and turned to glance at the table. "I want to interview Martin again tomorrow, then I think I need to head back to Fort Ashton and try questioning some of the guards and workers again." It would be the third time he'd done interviews, but he had a better idea of what to ask this time around.

"Even if you don't find a way to drop the charges against Martin, I'll still love you."

He drew his wife close and closed his eyes. He and Sam might not be talking, but at least God had given him a woman who was willing to stand beside him, even when things were difficult. "I know, and I love you too."

XXX

H<small>E SHOULDN'T HAVE COME</small>.

Cain looked around the table filled with people he'd known for as long as he could remember. Harrison, Sam, and Wes were all there for Easter dinner, as were Anna Mae, Keely, Ellie, and Alejandra. Ellie's siblings had all come too, and they filled the far end of the table with excitable, incessant chatter, while Sam and Wes talked about the price of cattle and a ranch in

Montana they wanted to buy a bull from. The womenfolk huddled together in the middle of the table, laughing and talking as though they'd been friends for decades, never mind that Ellie and Keely hadn't even been in Twin Rivers a year ago.

Cain shifted uncomfortably in his chair. He was the only one who didn't seem to belong.

It wasn't that the A Bar W was too fancy. He'd been in fancy places plenty of times before. And it wasn't that the A Bar W was unfamiliar. After all, he'd grown up playing in the Westins' guest rooms and terrorizing the ranch hands.

Across the table Alejandra bounced Madeline on her knee and exclaimed she'd gotten bigger since the picnic a few weeks ago, but the babe didn't look a lick different to him. No babe ever did. Truth be told, he'd never understood how women could tell one babe from another.

Everyone at the table was so all-fired comfortable with each other, so happy. He listened as Sam, Wes, and Harrison started talking about the new ranch going in up by Midford, and Anna Mae asked about the babe's sleeping habits. There was a rhythm to the conversations, a natural flow that didn't involve him.

"Where's your brother?" he asked Anna Mae, who was seated beside him.

If Daniel was here, they could at least talk about the rustling activity—or lack thereof.

It must have been the wrong question, because the table suddenly fell silent and all eyes moved to him.

Anna Mae stiffened in her chair, then raised her chin. "How should I know? I already told you I'm not talking to him."

He quirked an eyebrow. "It's been two weeks since Martin was charged, and you still haven't talked to him?"

"Why would anyone here talk to him?" Sam growled. "He's accusing my son of a murder he didn't commit."

"Because he had to. That blasted candlestick was found in

your barn, or have you forgotten?" Cain folded his arms over his chest and sent a scowl right back at Sam.

"Only because someone put it there," the oldest Owens boy after Martin snapped—was his name Leroy or Levi? Or maybe Leslie?

"I, ah, talked to Daniel about Easter." Wes rubbed the back of his neck, then took a sip of water. "We thought it best that he have dinner elsewhere this year."

"He and Charlotte came for dinner on Thursday." Keely tucked a strand of curly red hair behind her ear and offered him a wan smile. "We had a nice visit."

"And us womenfolk got together on Tuesday," Anna Mae added. "Charlotte was there."

Cain glanced at Harrison, who was diagonally from him. "What do you think about all this? Tell them they're being ridiculous, that Daniel's only doing his job and doesn't deserve to be shut out."

Harrison winced. "Actually, while I think Martin's innocent, until it can be proven in a court of law, it's best if the Hardings don't fraternize with the Owenses."

Right. Cain sat back in his chair. Legally, it made sense for Daniel and Sam not to have any contact. But seeing Wes sitting there without either his sister or his best friend, and Anna Mae forcing a smile to her face and pretending as though she didn't miss her brother a lick, it made something inside him hurt.

The Hardings, the Westins, and Sam had always been inseparable, a family in their own right. Sure, he'd walked away from Twin Rivers, but he'd always know that Sam and Wes and Daniel were all in the town where they'd grown up, raising families and being friends and supporting each other no matter what life dealt them.

Cain had never had trouble standing on the side, watching from a distance, and claiming he didn't belong.

But hang it all, Sam and Daniel and Wes belonged together,

and Anna Mae deserved to have her brother and best friend in her life.

"Anna Mae, how are your baked goods selling at the general store?" Ellie asked. "I've been so busy with Madeline that I haven't had a chance to come into town and buy something, but I plan too soon."

Anna Mae's smile turned genuine. "I can't keep my cheese and rosemary bread on the shelf. Mr. Cunningham says he sells out within an hour of me bringing in a batch. My apple dumplings are quite the same. Next Mr. Cunningham wants me to make some meat pies. He thinks he can sell them to travelers on the trail who don't want to take the time to stop by Fort Ashton and eat at the restaurant."

"Sounds like an excellent idea," Harrison said. "Maybe you could set up a booth to sell your food closer to the trail. You'd get a lot of business."

"Not unless someone tends it with her," Cain growled.

Everyone looked at him as though he'd suddenly sprouted a horn from his forehead.

Did no one at this table have a lick of common sense? Did they not understand that dangerous men could cross the border into Texas just as easily as honest ones? "The trail isn't the kind of place a single woman like Anna Mae should loiter."

"Maybe I can pay Henry and Christopher to man the booth for me." Anna Mae looked down the table to where the two Owens boys sat. "Would you two like a job over the summer?"

"That's a great idea." Keely served herself a second helping of potatoes. "I wouldn't mind helping a couple days a week either."

The conversation continued around him, moving from Anna Mae's job to plans for the Independence Day Festival in July. Wes claimed he wasn't having a house party as big as the one his father had hosted every June, but he hadn't been able to get out of inviting a few business acquaintances and their families for three weeks.

At some point the group moved from the dinner table to the parlor, where talk continued about who would win the prize for best prickly pear jam at the festival, and whether Anna Mae would trounce everyone in the shooting competition for the sixth straight year.

It seemed as though they could talk forever, all of them smiling, all of them completely comfortable.

Cain stood against the wall and watched, not quite able to scratch the spot between his shoulder blades that had started itching. What would it feel like to belong to a group like this? What would it feel like to settle down in Twin Rivers and spend his evenings with friends, his years watching his friends' young'uns grow into men and women?

Maybe even have a few young'uns of his own.

Cain shoved himself off the wall. What was he thinking? He'd gone mad, clearly. He was the illegitimate son of a vagabond turned Ranger and a Mexican prostitute. Men like him didn't have families.

He stalked out the fancy, etched-glass French doors that led from Wes's ornate parlor onto the terrace. He needed a bit of air, that was all. Air and space to clear away the tomfoolery that had filled his mind.

But the terrace wasn't empty. A lone feminine form stood by the railing, looking up at the southern wall of the Hacienda.

"What are you doing?" he barked, the words emerging a little rougher than he intended.

Alejandra jumped, then looked his direction, her hands nervously fiddling with the sides of her skirt. "Ranger Whitelaw, I didn't realize you were out here."

"That doesn't explain what you're doing."

Harrison seemed to grow more besotted by the day, but

there was something about Alejandra Loyola that made the hairs on the back of his neck prickle.

Why would she be standing outside instead of enjoying the chatter with everyone else? Instead of helping herself to a second piece of pie like the other women?

He looked over his shoulder at where she'd been staring when he'd stepped outside. Why had she been looking at the wall so intently?

Harrison claimed she had a sister in Mexico that needed help, but what if the story was made up? What if being invited here for Easter gave her the perfect chance to steal from the A Bar W?

Had Harrison seen any proof that this sister of hers existed?

"Well?" Cain came to a stop in front of her. "I asked what you're doing. Trying to figure out where Wes and Keely's bedroom is so you can slip up there undetected? Maybe take a valuable little souvenir back to Fort Ashton with you?"

She jerked back. "I should slap you for such a comment."

"A comment that you didn't deny."

"You really think that's why I'm out here?" Her eyes flashed. "To steal from the only people I call friends? And to think, everyone inside that room actually likes you, though I don't know why."

He didn't know why either. And she still hadn't denied trying to steal anything.

"If you must know, I'm out here because they all know each other a bit too well. It can be overwhelming. But I never would have thought someone could take me coming out here to catch my breath and turn it into me doing something illegal."

The stiffness drained from his shoulders. He was a brute. An utter, complete brute. Here she was, out here for the same reasons as him, and he'd automatically assumed the worst. "I'm s—"

"Alejandra?" Harrison stepped onto the terrace. "There you are. Is everything all right?"

"Oh, everything's just fine," she said dryly. "Except for the fact your friend thinks I'm out here trying to plot which room of the house to rob."

Harrison stalked forward. "Did you say that? Seriously, Cain? Do you see evil in every person you come across?"

Cain stepped back, inwardly wincing. It was as he'd thought. He didn't belong, and he never would. Too many years growing up with a mother who only wanted to use him and a father who didn't want to acknowledge he existed. Too many years on the trail with nowhere to call home. Too many years trying to think like an outlaw in order to catch them.

Too many years of not having family and friends for him to be a part of them.

"Reckon I was mistaken. Sorry. I was just leaving." He turned and hopped over the stone railing before Harrison could say more, stalking toward the paddock where Maverick was tethered.

XXX

"You've been quiet this evening," Harrison's voice floated over the desert as his horse trotted down the worn trail that led from the A Bar W into Twin Rivers.

"I'm just enjoying the night," Alejandra said from where her horse walked beside Harrison's. It was a beautiful night, truly. The moon was a low, bright ball of light hanging over the desert, and the air was just the right temperature to be neither hot nor cold.

"I hope you're not letting what Cain said bother you."

The sigh that emerged from her mouth was a bit louder than she intended.

"Sometimes he forgets to see the good in people. He... he had a rough upbringing."

"I'm not that upset about it." She couldn't be, not when her cousin had commanded her to sneak into Wes's office and snoop around if she ever gained access to the A Bar W.

She hadn't, of course. Now that she'd come to know Wes and Keely, she couldn't bring herself to betray them. But Cain's comment about her robbing Wes's room had been a little closer to the truth than she wanted to admit.

She was sick of the snooping and sneaking. She'd even avoided reading Mr. Rutherford's mail a few times, and she'd been doing that for two years. The whole notion of pretending she was an innocent maid was starting to make her feel ill. But she didn't know how to get herself out of the situation.

She'd always planned to stop snooping when Consuela arrived with Gabriella and the two of them disappeared together, but she wasn't sure she could wait that long.

Should she tell Harrison everything she was involved in right now? What she knew about the rustlers?

She slanted a glance at Harrison, then pressed her lips together.

No, she couldn't risk it. But she could write everything down so that there was some kind of record of what had been going on in Twin Rivers.

If Raul returned and figured out just how badly she'd fallen for Harrison, he might force her back to Mexico, and then Harrison and Daniel and Cain would never learn the full story of what was happening. They deserved that much.

She'd stay up late to write the letter tonight, and then she'd come up with a place Harrison was sure to find it if she disappeared, but that Raul would never think to search. That meant she couldn't put it anywhere in her room. But maybe somewhere in his father's room. By the bedroll she slept on when she had nursing duty, perhaps?

"Did you enjoy yourself?"

She looked over at Harrison, only to realize they were almost through Twin Rivers and would be to the fort shortly.

"I did," she answered. *Right up until I didn't.* "The food was wonderful. And your friends... they're really something special."

"You're special too, Alejandra." Harrison's voice was soft against the night, and she couldn't stop herself from slanting a glance his direction.

He was being too kind again, because if he knew the truth about her, he wouldn't say she was special. He'd say she was the most wretched, deceitful person to ever live.

"Thank you," she finally mumbled.

They rode in silence for a few more minutes, the fort growing ever larger on the horizon. When they reached the gate, Harrison only needed to tip his hat to the guard, and he opened it.

The corral was mostly quiet as they crossed, with only a few late travelers inside. Harrison guided Toronto over to the far side, where a stable jutted out from the wall surrounding the fort.

He swung off the horse, then raised his hands toward her. "Let me help you down."

She was fully capable of dismounting on her own, but she leaned toward him anyway.

His hands closed around her waist, and the warmth from his skin easily seeped through the thin fabric of the Mexican shirtwaist she was wearing. He lifted her just enough for her to free her leg from the opposite side of the horse, then swept her down, their bodies brushing as he slid her to the ground.

He held her there for a moment, his hands still on her waist while he looked down at her, their faces so close that his breath brushed her cheekbones each time he exhaled.

"I feel like we're drifting apart," he whispered. "Like you're becoming something of a stranger to me, even though we see each other every day and sleep under the same roof."

She drew in a breath, long and hard. "We have to be strangers, Harrison. I'm leaving."

And yet, she did nothing to move away from him or cause his hands to drop from where they were growing quite comfortable against her waist.

They'd settled into an odd sort of half friendship. Going to church that morning and then dinner that afternoon was the most time they'd spent together all week, and she'd been with womenfolk for most of that, not Harrison.

"I'm leaving, remember?" And she had no intention of letting Raul use her against Harrison for the short time she had left in Twin Rivers.

He gave his head a small shake. "How could I forget? All you do is remind me."

She looked up into his eyes, soft and large beneath the dim lights in the corral. "Things are better this way."

Even though she said the words, she wasn't sure she believed them. Because there was a part of her that missed Harrison. Missed him asking how her day had been or whether she'd gotten enough rest, missed him asking if she'd gotten another letter from Gabriella or what her favorite thing about the desert was.

Missed the kindness in his gaze, and even—maybe—the comfort of his arms. Not that he'd held her enough she should miss anything about it. Only that one day after he'd discovered she hadn't been getting enough food.

It made no sense for her to miss something that had only happened one time.

Did it?

"I'm not sure anything is better like this, but if it's what you want, then..." His hands dropped from her sides. "...then I'll respect it."

"Thank you," she mumbled.

The trouble was, she really didn't feel like thanking him. She felt like throwing herself into his arms and telling him every last thing about Raul and his father.

But the moment she did that, he'd stop looking at her with tenderness or asking her to share pie with him.

The moment she did that, everything would change, and not just for her, but for Gabriella too.

The few moments they'd shared—the ones she cherished the most—were nothing more than a ruse. Not one of them would have happened if Harrison knew the truth about her.

24

He was losing her.

Harrison watched Alejandra walk away from him without so much as a "goodnight."

How had she gone from the woman who would sit for an hour and talk with him every night to muttering a few sentences a day to him with her eyes cast down the entire time?

How had she gone from the woman who would have chatted with him the entire trip back from Fort Ashton to the one who held herself reserved and aloof?

Was it something he'd said? Something he'd done?

He reached up absently to stroke Toronto's nose. It had changed that night he'd told her about Wade Tillerman. He'd thought doing so would bring them closer together, but it had somehow driven them apart.

Now he couldn't say so much as three sentences to her without her reminding him she was leaving.

As though she had no choice in the matter.

As though there was no way to possibly thwart her uncle.

Harrison heaved in a breath. What if they married? Then what would her uncle be able to do to Alejandra? He certainly wouldn't be able to force her to leave Twin Rivers and go back to Mexico.

He could offer to marry her, but it was almost as though Alejandra didn't want to fight for him, almost like if her uncle up and died and had no way to dictate her life any longer, she would still choose to walk away from him.

And it hurt.

He'd known all along she had secrets, but for the first time, it was starting to feel like the secrets between them were too big to overcome.

XXX

"WELL, well, aren't you sleeping peacefully?"

Alejandra woke with a jolt, then looked around the room to find a familiar form by her bedside.

Not Consuela. For a second she'd hoped...

But no, Raul was the one who stood there, his eyes burning in the dim light of early dawn.

She pushed herself up to a sitting position and yawned. It seemed as though she'd just closed her eyes, but...

The letter.

She glanced at the nightstand, where her letter and pencil still sat. She'd folded the letter in half, but nothing more. It had been so late by the time she'd finished, that she hadn't bothered to find an envelope or warm any wax to seal it. If Raul picked up the paper, he'd find everything about *Tío* Javier and the joint rustling operation and the trade war he'd started with Bartholomew Rutherford.

Her heart hammered against her chest. Why hadn't she

gone through the trouble of getting an envelope and sealing it, then finding a place to hide it?

"What are you doing here?" she rasped.

"What do you think? Now that I've been able to move two thousand head of cattle for my father safely into Mexico, I came for an update and Rutherford's mail."

"You... you moved that many cattle?" She blinked at him. Was there a way she could stand without seeming unnatural? Could she somehow place herself between Raul and the nightstand without arousing his suspicions?

"I did. They're being driven into a canyon that will hide any and all cattle tracks as we speak."

She grabbed her wrapper from where it hung on her bedpost and stood, but her foot slipped on that dratted loose tile, and she stumbled. Raul said nothing as she straightened herself and shoved her arms through the sleeves of her wrapper. Then she positioned herself between him and the letter.

"How did you get them past the Rangers?" Her throat felt dry as she asked the question, and only half because of the letter sitting out. If only she'd had a warning, some way of knowing that Raul was approaching the border with cattle, she could have tipped off the sheriff.

But with Raul and Felipe both gone for over three weeks, she'd had few ways to glean information.

"I used the new trail. It's too far west for the Rangers to bother keeping track of."

There was a new trail?

"What did you learn while I was gone?".

"Not much. Someone in Austin is trying to negotiate a freighting contract. It seemed like the kind of thing *Tìo* Javier would be interested in. Other than that, things have been quiet."

She turned and opened the single drawer of her nightstand, then swapped the letter atop it with the stack of mail inside.

She'd have to move it as soon as Raul left, since he thought nothing of coming into her room and helping himself to Rutherford's mail, but at least the letter was out of sight.

She handed him the stack of envelopes. "There's one from a businessman in Chihuahua you might find interesting, though I'm not sure I can decipher its meaning. It mentions your father."

"I'll see to it." He took the thin stack of mail and tapped the envelopes against his palm. "Did any more dead bodies show up on the desert while I was gone?"

She stilled. What an odd question to ask.

"No. Was one supposed to be found?" The notion caused a tremor of fear to scurry up her spine.

"No. I want you ready to leave for Mexico by the end of next week."

"Next week?" The breath in her lungs froze. "But I thought... that is, your father doesn't want me home for four more weeks, not two."

"Plans changed. I got the cattle I needed, and we've been eyeing a stretch of desert on the New Mexico border. Turns out New Mexico doesn't have any Rangers waiting for us."

"But..."

"Come on, Alejandra. It's too risky to traffic cattle through this place now that the younger Mr. Rutherford is here. Surely you can see that."

But she wasn't ready to leave for Mexico. Not without Gabriella. Not when Consuela and Gabriella could very well be somewhere between Twin Rivers and Chihuahua.

Not when it would mean permanently saying goodbye to the man she was falling in love with.

She squared her shoulders. "I thought you wanted information you could use against Harrison so he'd cooperate with you?"

It was a dumb reason to stay in Twin Rivers. The thought of

Harrison being under Raul's thumb made her want to retch. And yet, it was the only thing she could think of that might keep her here.

"Have you found anything I can use against him?" Raul took a step closer to her.

She shook her head.

"Neither did the men I hired to search his house and office in Austin." Venom dripped from his voice. "The man is too clean."

"I think it's an admirable quality." She raised her chin. "Like Daniel in the Bible."

Raul chuckled, deep and low. "I bet you do. Rooster says you've been spending plenty of time with Harrison."

"I was just doing what you said." No need to explain that her heart had gotten too attached in the process.

"Too bad you didn't turn up anything useful. I'm off to *La Colina* now, but I'm leaving Felipe here to tie up any loose ends. Be ready to leave at the end of next week."

The door closed behind Raul with a click, but all she could do was stare at it. She had until the end of next week, and she didn't have the first clue whether her sister was still in Chihuahua or with Consuela.

What was she going to do?

XXX

He was still missing something, but what? Daniel stared at the papers spread out over the dock in his office. The dusty pink light of dawn filtered through the window, but he'd already been up for over an hour, long enough to ride from his house into town and start reviewing his file.

The extra bay quarter horse that Martin had found on the desert hadn't belonged to Rutherford. He'd been able to figure that out after questioning Fordham more thoroughly.

And two nights ago, Fordham and the new guards he'd told Harrison to hire saw Rooster and five of the others leave the fort around ten at night. They hadn't returned until dawn the next morning.

Fordham had suggested he get a warrant and search Rooster's room. But Daniel didn't have anything concrete enough he could take to a judge. Leaving a trading post in the middle of the night wasn't illegal—even if it was suspicious.

Daniel took a swig of coffee. If only he had a way of placing any of the guards from Fort Ashton where the traveler's body had been found, then he could get a warrant to search—

The door burst open and Bryce, the deputy who handled most of the night shifts, burst inside.

"Sheriff, you're here. Good. Thought I was going to have to ride out to your house to get you."

Daniel stood. "What's wrong?"

"Someone tried to kill Mrs. Sherman, and the doc's not sure if she's going to live."

Mrs. Sherman? The sweet old woman was like the town grandmother. "Why would someone want to hurt Mrs. Sherman?"

"Think it was a robbery gone wrong." Bryce braced a hand on the wall and heaved in a breath as though he'd run straight here from Doc Mullins's office. "Got thunked in the back of the head with one of her own frying pans."

Daniel scratched the side of his head. "But Mrs. Sherman doesn't have anything of value to steal."

"She's got her grandmama's jewelry, brought clear over from England, remember? Wears those big fancy emeralds to church every Sunday."

He grimaced. "That's right." Other than the family heirlooms, she wasn't very wealthy, but those jewels would be worth something.

He grabbed the papers atop his desk and wrangled them into a haphazard pile, then shoved them into a desk drawer. "Let's go see if we can find any evidence at her house."

Bryce repositioned the hat on his head. "Gotta admit, I thought that crime spree we had a few months ago was done and over."

"Me too. Looks like we were both wrong."

XXX

"Come on, just a little farther." Alejandra urged the horse Harrison had let her borrow deeper into the desert, ignoring the sweat that trickled down her back and the heat from the sun beating mercilessly down on her.

Somewhere behind her, Anna Mae groaned from where she followed on her appaloosa. "Haven't we gone far enough?"

"No."

"I don't recognize where we are anymore, and with what happened to Mrs. Sherman last night, I think we should turn around. My brother won't be happy if he finds out I was this far from town with only you."

Alejandra winced. She hadn't thought about that. The entire town and fort had been abuzz that morning with news of what had happened to the poor, elderly widow, who'd still been lying unconscious in the doctor's office when they'd left. "I don't understand who would try to kill a poor woman like that."

"Someone who didn't want to be caught committing a robbery, that's who." Anna Mae's voice was sharp enough that it echoed over the desert.

The notion caused a chill to travel up her spine as she directed her horse down a narrow path that wound between two mountains. "It's all too horrible to think about. But it doesn't stop me from wanting to figure out why there was a horse roaming around out here."

"It wasn't roaming here. We passed that spot two miles back," Anna Mae whined. "And besides, I've already tried to find where that horse could have come from. There's nothing for it. It was randomly roaming without any rhyme or reason. I can't explain why it would have gone so far from a water source, but I know for a fact you won't find any reason for the horse to have been out here other than that it had gotten loose and wandered off in an unfortunate direction."

She couldn't blame Anna Mae for wanting to turn around. They'd been out here for over three hours, with few breaks and little shade from the scorching rays of the sun. "You're wrong, and I'm going to prove it."

Something about Raul's comments to her earlier that morning struck her as odd. Ever since she'd gone fishing last week, she'd been trying to work things out in her head, to figure out if the dead body that had been found in the desert had something to do with the rustlers. The body had been west of the Chihuahuan Trail, but until this morning, she hadn't known there'd been a trail west of Twin Rivers. Every trail she knew about was to the east.

When Anna Mae had shown up at the fort, claiming she had the perfect list of things planned for Alejandra's day off, Alejandra said she was going for a ride west of town, that she wanted to see the place where Martin had been caught with the "stolen" horse for herself.

And here they were three hours later, with sweat running down their backs and their canteens starting to get low.

As others had already discovered, the place where the horse had been found yielded nothing of interest. But that had only made Alejandra scan the foothills for the most likely trail the horse would have taken through the mountains—assuming it escaped from one of the rustling camps near Raul's new trail and not the paddock at Fort Ashton.

But as Alejandra surveyed the hilly terrain and mountains beyond, she was starting to lose hope. Even if the horse had belonged to one of Raul's men and wandered away from the trail, she didn't see why any beast would choose to pick its way over the steep, rocky terrain. Surely the horse would have gone to water, and there was no water where it had been found, just as there was no water where they were now.

But she hadn't run into Raul's trail yet. West, he'd said. If she headed far enough west, she'd cross it eventually.

"Alejandra, listen." A dry sort of desperation tinged Anna Mae's voice. "We're over two hours from Twin Rivers and a solid half hour from the Rio Grande. We're going to need to refill our canteens and water the horses, so unless you find a stream within the next fifteen minutes, we have to—"

"There. Do you see that?"

"What?"

Alejandra pointed to a set of stray cattle tracks, then flicked the reins of her horse. She and Anna Mae followed the tracks around the side of the foothill, only to see a set of horse tracks join it, probably from one of her cousin's men that had gone looking for the lost cow.

"These tracks are worth following. I'll give you that." Curiosity laced Anna Mae's voice. "But they're far too fresh to belong to the horse Martin found. In fact, I doubt any of those tracks will be left after this long."

"True, but these new tracks might lead us to the place where the horse Martin found escaped from."

"Wait." Anna Mae slowed her horse. "I thought the horse came from the paddock at Fort Ashton, and the only question was whether it escaped on its own and Martin found it innocently, or whether he stole it."

"What if that's the wrong question to ask? What if the horse came from somewhere else?"

"Who would be out this far into the desert with..." Anna Mae's eyes snapped to hers, and her chest drew a shuddering breath. "You think the horse came from the rustlers."

"It's just an idea. Now shush and follow me. We don't want to draw any attention."

Anna Mae nodded and clamped her lips shut, but her hand instinctively moved to the rifle she carried across the front of her saddle.

Alejandra turned forward in her saddle and dug her heels into the side of the horse. It took another twenty minutes to follow the tracks deeper into the mountains. They rounded another foothill and the base of a mountain, then crossed a small stream, which was likely the water source for both the rustlers and their cattle.

They paused to refill their own canteens and water their horses, but only for a few minutes before continuing on.

Neither of them spoke, not so much as a word. It was the quietest she'd ever seen Anna Mae, but the woman seemed to sense both the importance of what they were about to uncover and the danger their findings might put them in.

They traveled through a short canyon, then continued around the side of another mountain. And there, deep in the heart of a dusty, forgotten section of jagged mountains, was a cattle trail.

"Those are fresh!" Anna Mae whispered, her eyes scanning the thousands and thousands of hoofprints. "Where do you think they go?"

"It's not our job to find out." Alejandra whipped her horse around and dug her heels into the beast's side.

"But..."

She glanced over her shoulder to find Anna Mae with her horse still facing west, staring at the tracks. "Don't you want to follow it for at least a little way?"

"No!" she whispered as forcefully as she could without being loud enough for her voice to echo off the rock walls surrounding them. "If the rustlers find us, no one will ever learn of this trail, and another innocent man will end up framed for our murders. Now come."

Anna Mae stiffened in her saddle, then turned her horse around and kicked it into a gallop.

25

"I've told you before, that horse wasn't something that escaped out of the paddock. I found it grazing. Sure, its reins had come untethered, but it knew that stretch of desert."

Harrison blew out a breath and stared at the man behind the iron jail bars. He'd believed in Martin's account about the horse escaping from the beginning, but the trail Alejandra and Anna Mae had discovered earlier that afternoon changed everything. He now had people he could blame for the traveler's death, and a motive to go with it, both for the murder and for framing Martin.

Of course, the people to blame were a shadowy band of figures yet to be caught, but given what was known about the rustlers and the new trail, every person in West Texas now had reason to doubt Martin's guilt. That was all he needed to win in court.

"Thank you, Martin," he pushed himself off the wall where he'd been standing along with Cain. "I'll be back if I have more questions."

"Wait." The boy licked his lips. "Do you think... Is this enough to get the charges dropped?"

"Not just yet. We need to have the murderer in hand—or at least someone willing to tell us who actually murdered that man and why. But with half of Cain's men running down the cattle taken into Mexico, there's a good chance that could happen."

The boy heaved a breath, a smile creeping across his face for the first time since he'd been locked up. "Thank you, sir."

"Not a problem."

Cain followed him out of the jailhouse and into Daniel's office, where every single one of Daniel's deputies and two of Cain's Rangers stood studying a map of the desert that had been pinned to the wall.

"So the trail runs here, but the traveler was found there?" One of Daniel's deputies touched his finger to the spot on the map with a small red X. "The traveler wasn't found very far from the trail."

"Remember there wasn't any blood on the ground where we found him. He was killed somewhere else and dragged there," Abe said.

"How far are most people going to move a dead body? I'm betting he was shot somewhere near the trail, then dragged a little way off."

"It was far enough that we didn't find the trail when we searched the area," Daniel said.

"Didn't you find him a couple days after you got that tip about the rustlers and set up that ambush, Captain?" One of the Rangers turned to Cain.

"We did." Cain rubbed the side of his jaw. "Hadn't put that together before, but it could be that he spotted some rustling activity, and that's why he was killed."

The rest of the men went back to studying the map, but

Cain rested his hip on the front of Daniel's desk, then raked a hand through his long blond hair, his eyes narrowed.

"What are you thinking?" Harrison asked.

"Not sure." Cain walked around the side of Daniel's desk, pulled a key out of his pocket to unlock it, and pulled out the top right drawer. It was filled with small slips of paper with clues written on them.

Tonight, western edge of A Bar W. 10:00.

Tomorrow. East of town. 1:00 a.m.

"Are these the notes Daniel keeps getting?"

Cain nodded. "I don't see anything that would lead us to the trail that was found this afternoon, do you?"

Harrison scanned the haphazard pile of paper. There had to be at least a dozen and a half notes. "No. But speaking as a lawyer, the rustlers being responsible for the murder makes sense, especially seeing how I never had any reasonable motive for the guards at Fort Ashton to commit murder and frame Martin. But that still doesn't explain why Rooster and the other guards would have been so insistent Martin killed the man, even if they found him roaming the desert on a horse they knew wasn't his."

"Because they're involved in the rustling, you halfwit," Cain drawled.

He shook his head. "It doesn't fit. My guards don't up and disappear into Mexico when the rustlers strike. What could they possibly...?"

"Wait. What if it's the money?" Harrison sank down into the chair behind Daniel's desk.

"What money?" Daniel sauntered up to them.

But Harrison suddenly couldn't speak, couldn't move, wasn't sure he could even think.

His father had no reason to be involved with the rustlers. He had money aplenty, all of which had been acquired through legal—though not necessarily moral—means. Why go and do something illegal at this point of his life?

"Well?" Cain crossed his arms over his chest. "What money are you talking about?"

Harrison glanced at the men on the other side of the office. There were too many of them to speak, especially if this went as deep as he was starting to believe. And if he couldn't trust his father or his father's longest-working guard not to be involved, then he couldn't trust the men in the corner with tin stars pinned to their chests either.

As though sensing his thoughts, Cain barked, "Everybody out. Split up and canvas the town. See if anyone has seen any strange trails or odd movements in the desert west of town."

The men stopped talking and looked at Cain, but no one questioned him as they filed out.

The door to the office hadn't even been closed a full second before Cain slid himself onto the edge of the desk. "Talk."

Harrison had the sudden urge to run a finger around the collar of his shirt. "There's money I can't account for in my father's bank accounts."

Daniel raised an eyebrow, but Cain's face remained emotionless.

"I've spent over a month trying to make sense of it, and that includes looking through every ledger that my father has. Even with the low price he was giving the Mexicans for their goods and the high prices he was charging in Austin, it doesn't begin to account for the money that has funneled into my father's bank accounts over the last two years."

"Two years, you say?" Daniel rubbed his jaw. "That's about when the rustling started."

A sickening sensation roiled through Harrison's stomach.

"Why didn't you say something sooner?" Cain snapped.

"This is the first indication that the money might be tied to something illegal. I was convinced Father had some investments I didn't know about and was receiving irregular dividends. I mean, if my father and some of the guards are involved in the rustling, there's no evidence of it anywhere in that office. Where are the stolen cattle being sold? And while I can't track all the movements of each guard at the fort, I can tell you not a single one has been away from the fort long enough to drive cattle to a market in Mexico and sell them."

"Because it's not just your father and his guards." Cain pushed himself off the desk and started pacing, his long blond hair falling around his face like a curtain. "They've got help in Mexico. A man that everyone calls 'el jefe.'"

Harrison rubbed the palm of his hand over his chest. "*El jefe,* rustlers, murder. I just might win this case against Martin."

Daniel sauntered to the back of the office, where he poured two cups of coffee. "Didn't realize there was ever a question of whether you'd win, or I'd have sent for another lawyer."

Harrison let out a short, bitter laugh. "You think too highly of me. The last time I defended a man for murder, I lost."

"When?" Cain stopped pacing and looked up at him. "I didn't know about you and no murder trial, except for the big one that's been all over the news back in Austin."

"That's the one." Harrison looked down, the uneven wood grain of Daniel's desk suddenly fascinating. "You've been away from Austin for a while. You must not have heard that I lost."

Cain rubbed the back of his neck. "That's funny seeing how the paper that arrived at the post office for me this morning is still saying you won."

Harrison's head jerked up. "There's a paper saying I won? Is it from Austin?"

"No. It's from Japan." Cain rolled his eyes. "Of course it's from Austin."

"There must be some mistake." He picked up the coffee, then set it back down on the desk, not in the mood for the bitter brew. Had his lawyer friend won the appeal and failed to notify him? That seemed unlikely. "I assure you, a man remembers when his innocent client ends up swinging from a noose."

"I'm sure he does." Cain drew out his words, long and slow, then hooked a thumb in his gun belt. "Trouble is, Wade Tillerman never swung from a noose. Have you looked at a newspaper since you've been here?"

"No point." He'd been trying to avoid anything and everything to do with Austin.

"Daniel, show lawyer boy here that clipping I gave you."

"It's in that top desk drawer." Daniel took a swig of his coffee.

Harrison slid the drawer open and grabbed a scrap of newspaper laying on top of a few pencils and a stack of reports.

The headline and subtitle stared back at him in bold, black font.

Verdict Reversed in Wade Tillerman Case: Witness and Jury Tampering Scheme Uncovered.

"What...?" His heart pounded against his ribcage. "What happened?"

"That rich clown with the dead wife paid off the police detective and a half dozen witnesses, then decided to bribe and coerce half the jury into voting his way. Read the article for yourself if you don't believe me." Cain jutted his chin toward the clipping. "The U.S. Marshals were all over the case from the beginning, it seems. I'd wager you've got your friend, Marshal Redding, to thank for that."

"I... I didn't know." Harrison scanned the article, trying to take in everything it said.

"News broke a few days after you left Austin, starting with a parlor maid who came forward saying she overheard Franklin Crist plotting with his son Anthony to buy off some witnesses. I've got more papers back at my tent, if you want to read all the articles."

"I do." Just as soon as the news sank in.

Wade Tillerman. Freed. He wasn't buried six feet under, he was walking around the streets of Austin, and if he was smart, he was suing the police department for damages wrought by their corrupt detective...

Which would lead to him being awarded enough money to buy ten farms like the one he'd been dreaming about outside of Austin.

"I can't... I can't believe it." He dropped the clipping onto the desk, his voice trembling. "Wade's not dead. I didn't... I didn't ruin his case."

Daniel walloped him in the shoulder. "Course you didn't ruin it. You saved him."

"I thought you knew," Cain said. "Never occurred to me that you wouldn't be staying up on news from Austin, and this has been hard to miss."

"I didn't want anything to do with it. Truth is, even if I hadn't gotten that telegram from Rooster about Father suffering an apoplectic attack, I still would have come to Twin Rivers for a bit, just to get away from the messiness of everything."

But now a whole new level of corruption had been uncovered, all because Wade had been falsely declared guilty. If he would have been acquitted, the illegal activities of both the Crists and the police department could well have continued.

It looked like Alejandra had been right, and good had come of Wade being convicted.

He'd just been too blind to see it.

Too unwilling to trust that God might have a plan he couldn't see. *Dear Father, please forgive me for being so blind.*

"Now when you go back to Austin, you'll be a hero." Daniel gave his shoulder a gentler pat this time.

"A hero, right." He sank back into Daniel's chair. "Wait. If Wade was acquitted, and it's been all over the news, then maybe those letters from the senator and the judiciary aren't fake."

"What letters?" Cain picked up the coffee cup Harrison hadn't touched and took a slurp.

"The ones asking if I'm interested in becoming a federal judge. There's a vacancy in San Antonio."

"Nope," Cain drawled. "Can't say those are fake."

Harrison rubbed the back of his neck. "They commended me for my work on the Tillerman case. I assumed someone was taunting me, that it was a horrible prank, since I thought I'd lost and there was nothing commendable about Wade Tillerman's trial."

"If I were you, I'd get back to the fort and answer those letters," Cain said evenly, not so much as a hint of surprise crossing his face.

Beside him, Daniel had started frowning. "No. You can't leave Twin Rivers until either you defend Martin or I'm able to drop his charges. You're the best hope that boy has."

Harrison smiled at the both of them. "Don't worry. I won't leave Twin Rivers until Martin Owens is a free man."

Because for the first time, he didn't just hope Martin would be set free—he actually believed he had a chance of seeing it happen.

26

The rustled cattle had disappeared. Cain dug his heels into the side of his horse and flicked the reins, urging the beast to go faster as he flew over the desert. An orange ball of sunlight slanted over the far western mountains, painting the sky with soft hues of pink and orange and signaling the end of a long day.

But his day was far from over.

By the time Alejandra and Anna Mae had ridden back to Twin Rivers and reported the trail, the rustlers had moved the cattle too deep into Mexico. His men had been shot at a few times going into a narrow canyon, and then they'd never picked up the trail after that.

He was close. He could feel it.

But he was also ready to strangle someone.

He brought Maverick to a stop in the yard of the A Bar W and jumped off.

"Take him," he said to the cowhand that emerged from the barn.

He stalked inside the house, not bothering to announce himself or stop by Wes's office. Oh no. He headed straight for the kitchen. The scent of something yeasty and sweet wafted from the open door, followed by the gentle sound of humming.

"What in tarnation were you thinking?" he shouted, not quite able to help the way his words came out angrier than intended.

Anna Mae jolted at the sound of his voice, then turned around. Her dark hair was down, fanning around her shoulders in soft waves, and her cheeks were flushed from the heat of the kitchen.

She held a ball of dough in her hands as she frowned at him, but somehow the scowl did little to take away from the loveliness of her features. "What on earth are you yelling about?"

"I told you that if you went off to search the desert, you needed to take someone with you. You ignored me."

She plopped the dough on the large wooden table in the center of the kitchen and reached for the rolling pin. "I took Alejandra. It was her idea that we go in the first place."

"I meant a man, not another woman. Do you know what happened to Mrs. Sherman last night? And she was in her own house." He stalked toward her.

"I'm perfectly fine, thank you for asking. As you can see, nothing happened. No one knew we were there, and Alejandra made us leave as soon as she spotted the trail."

"At least you had the sense not to follow it," he muttered.

She winced.

He planted a hand on the table near the dough and leaned in close, his voice low. "Tell me you didn't follow it, Anna Mae, or so help me..."

"I didn't! Though you have Alejandra to thank for that, because on my own, I don't know I would have been able to resist. But now you've sent your men out there and everything is safe. Maybe I'll ride out in the morning and have a better look at things."

"No!" he bellowed, never mind he stood less than a foot from her.

She huffed. "It's not fair. I don't even know where it goes, and I'm the one who discovered it."

"You don't need to know where it goes. You need to stay away from it."

"Is everything all right in here?"

At the sound of the voice from behind him, Cain turned to find Keely standing in the doorway, wayward strands of her curly red hair creating something of a cloud around her face.

Keely's eyes moved between the two of them. "I was in the parlor trying to read when I heard shouting."

"Sorry. I'm just trying to convince Anna Mae to be a little more careful if she rides on the desert."

"He's being a brute." Anna Mae had cut the rolled-out dough into little squares and now dabbed a spoonful of raspberry jam into the center of the first square. "But he's a man, so it's to be expected."

Keely laughed. "I'll leave you two to your discussion, but if you need me, I'll be in the parlor." She gave the two of them a rather suspicious looking smile, then swept out of the kitchen.

"You need to marry," he said the second Keely was gone.

"Oh, do I?" Anna Mae flung a spoonful of jam into another square with a bit more force than before. "And tell me, what good would that do?"

"It would mean there was a man around to keep you in hand."

"And you think I need to be kept in hand?" The words dripped like acid from her tongue. But she didn't bother to look at him, just plopped more jelly into the center of the squares, each action a bit brisker and jerkier than the last.

"You were traipsing around the desert unprotected."

"I had a rifle."

"That's not what I mean." He pushed himself away from the

table before he found himself unable to resist the urge to reach out and shake her. "Hang it all, woman, why don't you just get married?"

"Are you offering?"

He jerked back toward her. "Me? Are you mad? I'm a Ranger."

"Other Rangers are married."

There was something about the way she said it, about the sudden quietness in her voice and the way she'd stopped flinging jam across the table that made him pause. "You're serious."

She kept her head down as she folded one of the doughy squares in half, forming a triangle.

"Anna Mae?"

"You asked me before if I had feelings for someone in your camp. What if..." She sighed, then swiped a strand of hair from her cheek, smearing flour across her skin in the process. "What if you're the man I have feelings for? What then?"

He stilled, every muscle in his body suddenly refusing to move. "You can't have feelings for me. We barely know each other."

"We've known each other for years." She looked up at him, and suddenly, it seemed like they stood too close, like he could almost feel her breath brush against his chin, like if he stayed there and looked deep enough into her eyes, he could read every single emotion inside her.

"Every time we talk, it turns into an argument," he croaked, unable to make himself step away from her. "I'm the reason your father lost his leg."

She rolled her eyes. "No, you're not. Stop being dramatic."

"I've never even courted you."

"And yet I've loved you for years... ever since you were a boy who needed a friend."

"No." He jumped back from her, making a slashing motion

with his hands. "You don't love me. You never have and you never will. There is nothing between us. Nothing at all. There never can be."

"I understand."

"Good." He heaved out a breath, then stilled as another thought struck him and dread filled his stomach. "Why haven't you married?"

"I told you a few weeks ago, no one's caught my fancy." She picked up a spatula and started placing the doughy triangles onto a baking sheet with brisk, efficient movements.

"Then how can you say you've loved me for years?"

"All right, let me rephrase. Once upon a time I met this boy who needed a friend. A real friend, not some other boys his age that let him tag along, but someone who actually saw him for what he was, someone who wouldn't let his prickliness push them away." She didn't spare him so much as a glance as she spoke, just kept moving the triangles.

"After a while, it became clear that this boy needed a family too, a real one that loved him and cared about him, rather than a single mother who used him to her own advantage. So I became his friend. I packed him lunches that I snuck to him every day at school and when I figured out he liked to fish at the river at all hours of the day and night, I joined him.

"But then his mother died, and he moved in with a real family, with a man and woman who didn't have children of their own but who treated him with love and kindness. He didn't need me to pack him lunches anymore, and he stopped running off to the river at odd times. But one day his true father came back for him, and so he rode off into the wide Texas sunset, never mind the family and friends he left behind in Twin Rivers."

Anna Mae slid the last turnover onto the tray, then braced her hands on the table and looked up at him. "But his friend from his youth never met anyone who compared to him, not in all the years he was gone, and so she didn't get married. When he finally came back to town, she hoped..." Her words died off, and moisture glinted in her eyes.

He drew in a breath. How did she see everything in his childhood with such clarity? She somehow took all the ugly, painful parts and made him seem redeemable, loveable.

But he wasn't.

"There can't be anything between us," he finally said.

"Then why are you here?"

He blinked at her. "What do you mean?"

"Why did you ride out here and start yelling at me for searching the desert?" She swiped a strand of hair away from her face, causing more flour to smear her cheeks. "Tell me, did you storm over to Fort Ashton all mad and huffy at Alejandra? Did you tell her she needlessly put herself in danger?"

He pushed himself away from the table. "Alejandra is Harrison's woman."

"So does you being here mean I'm your woman?"

"Confound it, that's not what I'm saying."

"Then what are you saying?"

Confound it. Why did Anna Mae have to be so all-fired infuriating? Was there even a point to her questions other than to make him mad? "Look. I don't deserve a woman like you, Anna Mae. You wouldn't be happy with me."

"How do you know?"

"Because I do." He threw up his hands, then whirled and stalked toward the door.

"Marry one of my men," he said over his shoulder. "Have your pick of them. Just... no more of this business between you and me."

XXX

Be ready to leave at the end of next week.

Raul's words from earlier that day played in her mind as Alejandra stared at the dark ceiling, watching the pattern of shadows above her makeshift pallet in Mr. Rutherford's room.

He'd be furious with her when he returned and realized she'd told the Rangers about his new trail. Not that he'd be using it again if he was headed to New Mexico, but still, she had no doubt Raul would find a way to make her pay for betraying him.

But she hadn't been able to stop herself, not once she realized she might be able to help Harrison clear Martin's name.

"Argh!" A giant shout sounded from the bed, followed by a crashing sound.

Alejandra jumped up and reached for the lamp that stood on the small table beside her pallet, but even in the shadows she could see Mr. Rutherford had already pushed himself off the bed and was stumbling forward.

"Mr. Rutherford." She rushed toward him without lighting the lamp. "What are you doing? It's nighttime. You need to get back into bed."

She gripped his shoulders and tried turning him, but he roared something unintelligible and thrust her away. He wasn't a strong man, but his strength still surprised her enough to send her stumbling into the nightstand.

Her head hit the corner of the wood, and pain sliced through her. She slumped to the floor beside the lamp that already lay broken.

But Mr. Rutherford was still up and moving, gesticulating wildly and groaning gibberish as he stumbled toward the dresser.

"Mr. Rutherford, please." She pushed herself to a sitting

position, ignoring the throbbing in her head as she stood. "You need to—"

Crash!

The pitcher and basin atop the dresser shattered against the hard tile floor, along with all his vials of medicine from the doctor.

"Mr. Rutherford!"

He let out a garbled cry and charged toward her.

She shrieked, then ducked away from the jerky, uneven fist that swung toward her face.

"Father, stop!" Harrison shouted as he rushed into the room. "Guards!"

Harrison lunged forward, capturing Mr. Rutherford's arms and dragging him away from her as two more men raced into the room.

The three men attempted to wrestle Mr. Rutherford to his bed while Alejandra scrambled away, hoping the sedative Dr. Mullins had given her somehow hadn't gotten broken, but a quick survey of the floor near the dresser told her everything had shattered.

"No, Father, you have to stay here. You can't be up and breaking things." Harrison's voice rose over the sounds of the struggle as the guards tried to hold Mr. Rutherford flat against the mattress. "Amos is going to release you, but I need you to stay in bed. Do you understand?"

Mr. Rutherford mumbled something, and the shorter of the two guards stepped back from the bed. That was all it took for Mr. Rutherford to lunge forward, gesticulating wildly as he tried to free himself from the single guard.

"Father, no!" Harrison gripped his shoulders and held him back against the mattress. "Alejandra, don't we have something to calm him?"

"The vial broke when he pushed everything off the dresser."

Mr. Rutherford let out another cry and tried to buck off the bed.

Harrison pulled back his hand and punched him. The sound of bone meeting bone resounded through the room with a sickening crack, but Mr. Rutherford slumped back on the bed, his body still.

"Ride to the doctor's and get more medicine. Now." Harrison stepped back from the bed and turned to Amos. "We'll need it for when he wakes."

"Where's the lamp?" the taller guard asked.

Alejandra turned, planning to light the one at the back of the room that hadn't been broken, but something sharp bit into the bottom of her foot, and she gasped.

Harrison was by her side in an instant. "What happened? Are you all right?"

She drew in a breath, then gripped his arm and leaned her weight against him for balance so she could lift her throbbing foot off the ground. "I just... I think I stepped on some glass."

"Peters, get the lamp."

Harrison up and swept her into his arms. Warmth and strength surrounded her, giving her the sudden urge to bury her head against his chest and listen to the steady beat of his heart.

She kept her head stiff instead. "This is unnecessary."

It was too dark to see his face clearly, but she could almost swear he lifted one of his cocky eyebrows at her. "Unnecessary to keep you from having your feet sliced to ribbons? Why would you think that?"

She swallowed and looked away just as lamplight filled the room.

He set her down on the bedroll, then crouched beside her. "Your head got injured too."

She raised a hand to the throbbing spot on the side of her

forehead, only to find it sticky with blood. "I hit my head on the nightstand when he pushed me."

A small muscle pulsed at the side of Harrison's jaw, then he looked over his shoulder at the guard. "Bring me some warm water and bandages, and do we have any carbolic acid? If not, I'll use whisky."

"Um, I believe the carbolic acid bottle broke along with the sedative." She nodded her head toward the mess of shattered vials and pooled medicine on the floor.

"Whisky will have to suffice."

"Yes, sir." Peters strode toward the door.

"And tweezers," Harrison called after him. "I'll need tweezers for the glass in her foot."

"There's tweezers in the top drawer of your father's nightstand." Alejandra jutted her chin toward the small wooden stand surrounded by a broken lamp and shattered water glass.

Harrison stood wordlessly and moved to the dresser, glass crunching under the soles of his boots.

When he returned, he knelt beside her and picked up her foot.

The gentle feeling of his bare skin against hers caused her to suck in a breath, and she jerked her foot back.

"I can do it." She held out her hand for the tweezers.

"Let me." He reached for her foot again and lay it against his bent knees, then tilted her heel toward the lamplight. "You have more than one cut."

"The one on my heel hurts the worst."

He looked down at her foot again, his eyes intent as he used the tweezers to work the biggest piece of glass from her skin. "Do you know what came over my father?"

She shook her head. "One minute he was lying there asleep, and the next he was up and shouting and trying to... well, I don't know what he was trying to do, but he ended up destroying everything on his bedside table and dresser."

"I hate that he hurt you," he whispered against the quiet of the room.

She didn't know what to say, so she watched him work, the silence stretching between them as he carefully pulled each tiny sliver of glass from her torn skin and lay the shards out on a handkerchief.

The position gave her far too much time to study him. To memorize the handsome lines of his face and small creases around his eyes, the firm set of his jaw and the dull pink color of his lips. Several thatches of dark hair had fallen over his forehead, and her fingers itched to reach out and smooth them back.

And oh, wasn't she being ridiculous? Because him treating her cuts shouldn't be romantic.

And yet, there was something about the way he studied her, or maybe about the quietness in the room, or the darkness closing in just outside the circle of lamplight, that made the moment seem entirely too intimate. Like it should be shared between a married couple, not a servant and her employer.

"I'm sorry," she whispered into the stillness.

He gave his head a small shake, his gaze still riveted to her foot. "Don't apologize. This isn't your fault."

That hadn't been why she was apologizing. In truth, she wasn't quite sure why the words had slipped out.

Because of his father's episode?

No. Because she wanted nothing more than to apologize to this man over and over and over again for everything going on at Fort Ashton that he didn't know about.

He was looking at her now, the brown orbs of his eyes soft in the flicker of the lantern. He kept her foot in his hand, and she could almost swear the warmth in her ankle from his touch spread throughout the rest of her body, clear up to her heart.

Could he feel it too? The way they couldn't help but be drawn to each other? The way his head was close enough to hers that their breaths mingled? The way he only needed to lean forward an inch or two for their lips to meet?

"Did you hear what ended up happening with the Tillerman case?" he finally asked.

She shook her head. "Only what you told me a couple weeks ago."

"Yes, about that." He drew in a breath. "Turns out Wade didn't hang after all. A witness and jury tampering scheme was uncovered shortly after I left Austin. The judgment against Wade was reversed, and the case was declared a mistrial. The U.S. Marshal's office is pressing charges against Crist and both his sons, plus the Austin Police Department."

"Harrison, that's wonderful! I'm so happy for you. I know what I told you about trusting God, but I never would have guessed the case would turn out this way."

"Me either." He smiled at her. "But God knew what He was doing all along, and now this corruption ring has been discovered in Austin. If things wouldn't have happened the way they did with Wade, other innocent people might have ended up declared guilty of crimes they never committed either."

"I want to say I'm surprised, but the truth is, you're such a good lawyer that I really shouldn't be. If you say the evidence points to a man being innocent, then he probably is."

A faint red hue crept up his neck. "Seems like my work on the Tillerman case caught the attention of some politicians. I've been offered a federal judgeship in San Antonio."

"Oh... that's... wonderful." At least she thought it was wonderful. She wasn't quite sure what a federal judgeship was, but it sounded important, even if it meant he'd be leaving town. "Good for you."

"I might not take it. I might stay here in Twin Rivers. Someone needs to run the fort."

"Here's the water and bandages, sir." Peters appeared in the doorway. "Sorry it took so long. Had to rummage around a bit in the kitchen to find the bandages, but I didn't want to wake the cook for something so small."

"You have perfect timing. I just finished with the glass." Harrison gestured to the floor beside him. "Put it here. Then you can go back to your post."

The guard came and set the tray down, then retreated without so much as a word.

Harrison lifted her foot and moved the basin beneath it, then picked up the whiskey bottle and one of the rags. "I'm afraid this is going to hurt, but it's necessary."

She squeezed her eyes shut and looked away. "Just do it."

The cool liquid felt like fire against her cuts. She clenched her hands in the top of her quilt and clamped her teeth together until the pain abated.

"There, all done. Now what were we talking about?"

"The judgeship," she gritted, peeking her eyes open.

"Ah, that's right." He picked up the bandage from the tray and began wrapping her foot. "Accepting the judgeship would be the best possible thing in terms of my career. But Twin Rivers is in need of a good lawyer, a good judge too, and a good prosecuting attorney."

He tied off her bandage and sat back. "There's not a single legal professional in the entire town. I could stay here, run the fort, and see about being elected as the prosecuting attorney."

"Whatever you decide, I'm sure you'll do well." She tried to smile at him, but her words felt wooden in her mouth.

She'd expected Harrison to leave at some point. After all, that had been the plan when he'd arrived in Twin Rivers, hadn't it? And yet, hearing him talk about the things he might do next, or worse, hearing him talk about staying in Twin Rivers with the Hardings and Owenses and Westins caused something sharp to pierce her heart.

Because she wanted to be a part of it. Wherever he ended up living, whatever job he held, she wanted to be by his side.

Did that mean she loved him? Wholly and completely? Had her feelings gone that far?

She didn't know how or why any of this had happened, not when she'd tried to see less and less of him, not when she'd been working to keep her distance.

But Harrison was so patient, so kind, so caring. She'd never in her life had a person treat her the way Harrison Rutherford did.

He might even love her even if he knew what she'd done. That she hadn't wanted to read his correspondence or spy on his father. That she felt as though she had to do all of that because of Gabriella.

She drew in a shuddering breath. Now what was she going to do? She wouldn't be able to spend her future with Harrison. She certainly couldn't marry him, and at the moment, she didn't even see how she could move to San Antonio and continue working as a maid.

She had a plan for both her and Gabriella, and it involved getting far away from both Mexico and Texas.

And yet she couldn't stop her traitorous, foolish heart from growing more attached to the man in front of her with each second they spent together.

What would it be like to stay in Twin Rivers with her friends and live the rest of her life with someone as kind and caring as Harrison Rutherford?

She wanted more than anything to find out.

But she never would, and the pain of that somehow hurt more than the throbbing in her foot.

27

Alejandra woke with a start. Something was clamped over her mouth.

She reared back and tried to scramble away, but the hand over her lips just pressed harder.

"Alejandra, stop. It's Consuela."

She blinked in the direction of the voice, her eyes searching the darkness of Mr. Rutherford's room. Sure enough, she could just make out the shadows of Consuela's round form.

She jolted upright. "Gabriella! Where's Gabriella!"

The words came out garbled against the other woman's hand.

"Hush, child, or you'll wake the house."

She didn't care who she woke. All she cared about was seeing her sister, alive and unharmed and far away from their uncle.

But Consuela shook her head as she removed her hand. "I'm sorry, dear. Your sister was too well guarded. I met with her only once, and it took me two weeks of being in Chihuahua to even arrange such a meeting. She was willing to try to escape, but one of the nuns found out about our meeting. I'm afraid Gabriella was taken back to your uncle's estate that very afternoon, and I have no means to contact her there."

"No," Alejandra whispered, her throat turning dry. "No, not there. He rules *La Colina* with an iron fist. She'll not be able to escape."

"I'm sorry." Consuela smoothed the hair away from her face. "Perhaps there'll be an opportunity for your sister to escape after she's married. Her new husband might not guard her as well as your uncle."

Alejandra shook her head. "Her betrothed lives in Mexico City. It's a far journey to the border from there."

"She wouldn't be the first person I've brought to America from so deep into Mexico."

Maybe not, but Alejandra couldn't stop the tear that slipped down her face, then another and another. Raul wanted her to leave for Mexico at the end of next week. She was out of time to formulate another plain. She either needed to return to her uncle and marry whomever he'd chosen for her or take her money and flee Twin Rivers without her sister.

But she could make herself do neither.

"I'll have to get her myself."

"It's too dangerous. Felipe will know within an hour of you leaving Twin Rivers."

"My uncle wants me back in Mexico soon. Maybe I can go back at his bidding but plan an escape with me and Gabriella."

Consuela's hand settled on her shoulder, large and warm. "If you can get away."

She sniffled. "It's risky, yes. But what if there's another option? I could always make it look like I fled to Oklahoma or New Mexico and send Felipe to the wrong place looking for me."

"With your sister still in Chihuahua? He won't believe

you've gone anywhere else. You take a day or two to think things over and let me know what you want to do next. But don't do anything rash. Promise me. Sometimes it takes many attempts to remove a woman from a bad situation. There's no cause to give up hope yet."

The words were probably supposed to reassure her, but she could tell by the flatness in Consuela's eyes, by the dull tone in her voice that she didn't believe them either—at least not when it came to stealing someone away from a man as powerful as Javier Velez.

"Before I forget, I was able to get this from the school. Gabriella left it with my name, but it's really for you." She reached into her cloak and pulled out a letter.

"Thank you." She took the letter but didn't bother to open it in the darkness.

"I best take my leave." Consuela straightened. "Dawn will be here soon. But you still haven't given me your word."

"My word?" She stared blankly down at the unopened letter.

"That you won't do anything rash."

"I won't." The words tasted like desert dust in her mouth.

"I'll come back in a few days to check on you, see if we can come up with another plan."

"*Gracias*," she said, more because it would get the other woman to leave than because she agreed to it. She wasn't even sure she'd still be here. But Consuela was right in wanting her to take a few days to think things over. Any idea she came up with today would likely get her caught in a matter of hours.

The door closed behind Consuela, and Alejandra looked over at Mr. Rutherford. He slept calmly in his bed, likely still under the effects of the sedative she'd given him after Amos had returned with more medicine. Lighting the lamp wasn't likely to disturb him.

The moment the lamp was lit, the sight of her sister's handwriting on the outside of the envelope was nearly enough to make her cry again, but she tore open the envelope before her emotions got the better of her.

Dearest Alejandra,

I'm writing this letter to you because even though the woman I visited with never mentioned your name, I know you sent her.

I hope and pray that you are well, but if you are, I bid you to flee. Uncle has designs on your future, and it's best if you escape them. Please don't worry about me. I fully intend to escape one day, and now that I have the name of the woman you sent, I will go to her to learn where you are staying.

I could never live with myself if you ended up married to a horrible man, unable to escape him, on account of me. I'm worried if you don't leave Twin Rivers soon, you'll miss your chance.

One day we will be together again. I fully believe that. And even if we don't meet again on earth, we will always have heaven. Please don't do anything that will make your life unbearable on my account.

Remember that verse Padre *used to quote?* Hope deferred maketh the heart sick. *I will hope for the best, and so will you. No matter how hard, no matter what happens, God promises to one day wipe the tears from our eyes. If nothing else, we both have that to look forward to.*

I pray you find much happiness in your new life.

Love,

Gabriella

Alejandra sniffled as one tear coursed down her cheek, then another. What was she going to do?

She was numb as she went through the motions of the morning. She couldn't get Mr. Rutherford to wake for breakfast. It was almost as though he'd gone backward after his episode, turning unresponsive once again and able to do nothing more than lie on his bed, his breathing shallow.

She gave him a sponge bath and tried to spoon him a little broth, then swept the floor again, just to make sure she'd gotten all the broken glass from the night before. She attempted to eat her own breakfast but found she had no appetite, so she sat by Mr. Rutherford's bedside, numbly embroidering handkerchiefs, even though she wouldn't be selling them at the general store anytime soon.

Somewhere around midmorning, a soft knock sounded.

"Alejandra?" The door opened a crack to reveal Harrison standing there, his brow furrowed. "Consuela sent a messenger with a note for me this morning."

She looked away. "Your father seems pretty lethargic. He hasn't woken once since his episode last night, but I tried to get a bit of broth in him at breakfast."

"I'm sorry about Gabriella." Harrison stepped into the room and closed the door behind him.

"I don't know what you're talking about," she muttered, her eyes pinned on a wrinkle in Mr. Rutherford's quilt.

"Don't do this." Harrison stopped in front of her, then reached for the handkerchief and thread in her lap. He slid them from her hands and set them on the bedside table, then took her hands and pulled her to a standing position.

She didn't resist. She was too weak to even try.

"Come here." His voice emerged soft in the otherwise silent room, and then she was in his arms, surrounded by his warmth once again.

"It's all right to cry, sweetheart," he whispered against her ear.

That was all it took for another round of tears to come, falling down her cheeks and soaking Harrison's shirt as she shook with silent, desperate sobs.

He stroked his fingers down her hair and along her back and muttered soft assurances in her ear. She only knew that she felt safe there.

And it only made her cry harder.

Because if anyone could offer her a semblance of comfort, it was Harrison Rutherford, and if she couldn't be with Gabriella, then she wanted to spend each and every day of her life with him.

But her uncle wasn't going to allow that, just as he wasn't ever going to allow her to be reunited with her sister.

"Hey, there, it's all right." He used the pad of his thumb to brush a tear away from her cheek. "Cain will come up with a plan to get Gabriella. All isn't lost just yet."

She only shook her head against his chest. "You don't know what you're saying. It's not possible to get her. She's stuck there now, and she wants me to leave Twin Rivers without her." Alejandra reached into her pocket and pulled out the letter. "See?"

He took the paper and read it, holding her with only one arm as he did so. Then he folded the letter and slid it back into her pocket. "Is that what you want? To leave Twin Rivers? I'll arrange it. Or would you rather I try to get Gabriella out of Mexico? Because I can do that too. Just let me know what you want."

She wanted to stay here with him. She wanted Raul and her uncle to disappear and Gabriella to come to Twin Rivers. But she couldn't have any of it.

"Alejandra, love, stop crying." He lifted her chin until their eyes met. Concern and worry radiated from his gaze.

"You're too good to me," she choked out.

"I'm not. You've had far too hard of a life."

She stared into his eyes for a moment, his breath feather soft against her cheek. Then she leaned toward him, and their lips touched. Just for the briefest of instants. Soft and sweet.

She drew in a breath, then blew it out to find her own breath mingled with his. Then his lips touched hers again, but this time they didn't leave. They moved tenderly against hers, coaxing her into opening her mouth, into stepping deeper into his arms, into reaching her hand up to hook around his neck and toy with the strands of hair at the base of his head.

The heat from his body radiated into her, his fingers traced soothing motions up and down her arms, and the gentleness of his mouth prodded her into tilting her head and deepening the kiss. Into sinking deeper into the feeling of him.

She drew in a breath, then wrenched herself away from him. Why was she being so foolish?

Why was she kissing a man she could never marry and letting herself wish for the impossible?

XXX

THE KISS HAD BEEN PERFECT. Utterly, completely perfect. Alejandra had all but melted into him, holding nothing back, clinging to him with an openness that only made him more determined to cherish her, to respect her, to show her how a man was supposed to treat a woman.

But now she was backing away, his body suddenly cold where she'd left his embrace. "I shouldn't have... we can't... Oh, this never should have happened!"

She turned toward the door, her muscles tense, but he darted in front of her, blocking her path before she could flee.

"I'm not sorry." He rested his hands on her shoulders, his hold light. "We're both adults, ones who are growing to... to care for each other."

Possibly even love each other. But he dare not use that word or there'd be no way to prevent her from running form him. "A kiss between us shouldn't be a problem."

"But it is." She drew in a breath, then gave her head a small shake, causing a strand of glossy black hair to catch on her shoulder. "If only you weren't so wonderful. So kind and gentle and caring. It makes me want things I can never have. And kisses between us will only lead to trouble."

She thought he was wonderful? And she wanted more with him? Like a future together? A marriage proposal? His body felt suddenly hot, but not because he was angry.

"Our kisses won't lead to trouble if I treat you honorably. And trust me, sweetheart, my intentions toward you are every bit honorable." He reached out to cup the side of her face, but she stepped away from him, her eyes dark with emotions he couldn't quite name. "What is it, Alejandra? Tell me."

She swallowed. "You're too good for me."

"That's ridiculous."

"It's not, because while *your* intentions might be honorable, *my* intentions aren't. They never have been."

"I don't understand."

"I was sent here to spy on your father." Red crept onto her cheeks. "But now that you're in charge, I'm supposed to be spying on you."

"Spy?" He refused to believe it. Alejandra was as timid as a mouse. If she was sent here to spy, then she had to be one of the worst spies to ever live. "I don't believe you."

"Well, you should." She crossed her arms over her chest, but rather than looking severe, she looked like a lost child trying in vain to hug herself. "Felipe will ask me all sorts of questions about the conversation we're having right now, and the one last night when you were helping with my cuts. He'll want to know everything you said, if you mentioned him or Raul, what your plans are for the day, if you have any love interests. He'll be furious if I take less than fifteen minutes to recount everything. And the times I end up seeing Cain and Daniel, it's worse. Raul and Felipe have only gotten more belligerent since you kicked Raul out of the fort. He's in my room almost every morning that he's in Twin Rivers, asking what—"

"He's sneaking into your room?" Harrison took a step toward her, his blood racing. "I'm going to hunt him down."

"Don't." She met his eyes, her gaze flat, right along with her voice. "It will only cause more problems. And I already have enough of them."

Harrison forced his hands to unclench, but only so that he could rake one of them through his hair. "What will you tell him about this conversation then? Will you say we kissed?"

She looked away. "He'll be happy we kissed, if you want to know. He wants me in your bed. Thinks you'll tell me your secrets then."

Alejandra's own cousin wanted her in his bed? What kind of family did that to each other?

She crossed the room and picked up the broom from where it had been leaning against the corner. "The problem is, you don't have any secrets."

He blinked. "What secrets am I supposed to have?"

"That's my point." Alejandra started sweeping, though given her stiff, quick movements, it looked more like she was using her broom to attack the tiles than collect dirt. "It would be much easier if you had some. Or if you were the kind of man who mistreated women and expected everyone to jump at your whims. Then... oh, never mind."

"Never mind what?" He threw up his hands, then glanced at his father. "Wait. What secrets does my father have?"

Did she know something that could explain the extra money in his bank account? Or something that might link him to the rustlers? "And why does your uncle care so much about them that he sent you to spy?"

"He just does." She jabbed at the crease between the wall

and floor with enough force she was sure to scatter more dust than she swept.

"Alejandra." Her name came out as a low growl.

"I've already said too much."

He wasn't sure whether to be sick or angry. It seemed like he should ask more questions, find a way to get more information from her, but the more he asked, the more lost he felt.

He should probably just get Cain. The Ranger would know how to wring every last bit of information out of her.

But no matter what Cain uncovered, it still didn't change the fact Alejandra and Gabriella needed help.

"What if I want to protect you from your uncle?" He glanced over at Alejandra, who had worked her way to the far side of the room with the broom, her movements calmer now. "How do I go about doing that?"

The broom slipped from her hands and clattered to the floor. "After everything I just told you?"

He started toward her. "I care about you, and not just a little. I care about you so much that I can see myself sharing a life with you one day. So tell me what I need to do to bring your sister here, to have you both stay. Tell me what I need to do to officially court you."

He'd meant for his words to comfort her, or maybe spark some sort of romantic confession of her own.

Instead, they only made her jaw go tight and her body stiffen. "None of that can happen. Don't you see? If Gabriella comes here, Raul will take both of us right back to my uncle. Gabriella has to come without anyone knowing, and after that, we both have to disappear to somewhere he won't be able to find us. A small town in Montana, perhaps, or Idaho. Far away from the Mexican border."

"Just how powerful is your uncle?

She raised her chin. "His name is Javier Velez. He's the former governor of Chihuahua."

"The former...? Oh."

"And lest you think my uncle will let Gabriella and me disappear easily, he won't. He intends to use both of us to procure advantageous marriages. My future happiness—Gabriella's happiness—play no role in his decision. Evidently, he's found another match for me to the owner of a silver mine, and I'm to report back at the end of next week and not mess things up this time."

"Another match? As in, you've already been married once?" He felt sick at the idea, but with the way this conversation had gone, he wasn't ruling anything out.

"No." Something hard flashed in her eyes. "I stopped that from happening, but I wish I hadn't. Now Gabriella is betrothed to marry the same man once she turns sixteen. And he's a wretched, wretched person."

"What happened?" He was almost afraid to ask, but Alejandra was finally sharing her secrets with him, and he couldn't afford to let the opportunity pass.

"At first I was going to go through with the wedding, even though I knew I wouldn't be happy with *Señor* Montrose. I assumed our house would be big enough that I could play a dutiful enough wife for dinners and parties, that I could make do because of how wealthy and distracted my husband would be. But then I found the maid..."

Her throat worked, her eyes taking on a distant look as she dredged up a memory that obviously caused her pain. "My fiancé, he'd forced her to his bed, then slapped her for crying too much, for making a racket. And I... I knew I couldn't marry a man like that. So I devised a plan. I knew *Señor* Montrose wouldn't want me if I wasn't innocent, and I knew what time he went riding every morning. So I paid a stable boy to kiss me at a time when I knew he would see, and I pretended as though we'd... done other things besides kiss."

He was going to strangle this *Señor* Montrose—right after

he tracked down and strangled Raul. It was no secret that wealthy men sometimes demanded unthinkable things from their female servants, but rape was illegal no matter how rich a man was. "Did he ever touch you, this *Señor* Montrose?"

She shook her head, her eyes dull and flat. "No. Back then I was too valuable with my innocence, though now... Let's just say I was right about the planned kiss causing the engagement to end, but I didn't anticipate the events it would unleash—or the strength of my uncle's fury."

He reached out and took her hand, using his thumb to stroke her knuckles. "What did he do?"

"He offered Gabriella in my stead, never mind that she was barely fourteen. *Señor* Montrose said he'd be willing to wait two years for her, and so the wedding is set for two months from now, shortly after she turns sixteen."

The breath rushed out of him. Gabriella was a living, breathing person, as was Alejandra. Who was this uncle who thought he had the right to control the lives of others?

But Harrison already knew the answer. He was the former governor of a Mexican state. He had to be wealthy, with ranchlands and business endeavors and numerous investments. He was the type of man who got his way. Every single time.

"My uncle fully intended to turn around and find another husband for me," Alejandra continued. "One that would still benefit him. But neither of us anticipated the role *Señor* Montrose would play. He told everyone he could think of about my indiscretion, talking about it at dinner parties and balls and business meetings to the point that I was unmarriable and my reputation in tatters. That only further incensed my uncle, and he knew he'd have to wait until the rumors died down before he could find me a new husband. Since he had some business dealings with your father, he sent me here, telling me to collect information on your father. And Gabriella was sent to a boarding school in Chihuahua, where she was to learn proper behavior for her new husband. I haven't seen her since."

Harrison pressed his eyes shut. Of all the things. He'd known her uncle wasn't a good man, but he never would have guessed the depth of his control or the carelessness he had for his nieces.

There was part of him that wanted to tell her it would be all right, that he'd go to Mexico himself and get Gabriella. That he'd give Alejandra more money than she and her sister would be able to use in a year before they left. He'd probably even check with Wes, see if he could spare a ranch hand or two to take Alejandra and Gabriella somewhere safe.

But there was another part of this that wasn't all right, and never would be.

The part where Alejandra left.

He could offer to marry her right here and right now. Her uncle wouldn't be able to marry her to another man if she was already wed, but that wouldn't save Gabriella from being wed to a cruel man, and at the age of sixteen, no less.

Dear God, what am I supposed to do? The entire situation seemed impossible.

Alejandra took a step back from him, her eyes brimming with tears. "Do you mind sitting with your father for a few minutes? I need to go... freshen up. Besides, Felipe will have noticed how long you were in here with me, and he'll have questions."

"What will you tell him?"

She shrugged. "The same as I always do. That I didn't learn anything important. I'll... I'll say that you talked to me about a woman you had feelings for, but she had to go away. That we didn't discuss the fort at all. Felipe will be mad. He'll say I should be learning more about you, but I'll tell him your heart is too broken to let me in."

"My heart isn't too broken to let you in," he croaked. "It's broken because I let you in—and I won't be able to keep you."

"I'm sorry," she said quietly. Then she turned and slipped out of the room.

And he didn't try stopping her.

28

H e was close. So close he could almost taste it.

Daniel pushed himself back from the desk in his office where he'd been studying the file on the traveler's murder. At this point, he'd read the blasted file so many times he had half the documents memorized.

But he'd read it even more, until every last pencil stroke was permanently embedded in his brain, if that's what it took to bring the actual murderer up on charges and drop the charges against Martin.

After the rustling trail had been discovered yesterday, Daniel had sent Abe over to Brewster County to get a warrant from the closest judge to Twin Rivers. Between the proof he had that several guards had lied about the quarter horse belonging to Mr. Rutherford, the discovery of the trail, and Fordham's claim that five guards had left the fort with Rooster the last time cattle had been run into Mexico, he was certain the judge would give him a warrant.

As soon as Abe returned, he'd grab his other two deputies and a couple Rangers, and they'd search the bunkhouse at Fort Ashton along with Rooster's room.

Would he find evidence that the guards had killed the traveler? Or if not that, then at least evidence linking the guards to the rustling?

Daniel rubbed his hands together, then glanced at the clock. Nine-thirty.

It would be another two hours until Abe returned, maybe longer. But if he—

The door to his office burst open, and a young Mexican woman rushed inside. She looked vaguely familiar, and not just because she wore the gray serving uniform from Fort Ashton. If he wasn't mistaken, she was one of the women he'd interviewed, and she worked with Alejandra to help care for Harrison's father.

He stood from behind his desk. *"Buenos días, señorita."*

"Buenos días." She shifted nervously from one foot to the other, eyeing him as though he might suddenly morph into a giant scorpion with a deadly sting.

"Have a seat." He gestured to the chair across from his desk.

She came forward, her eyes nervously glancing at the chair, then darting back to him.

"I... um..." She pressed her lips together, her gaze still flitting wildly about the room. Then she handed him the sack slung over her shoulder. "I found this. It was hidden under a tile at Fort Ashton."

He opened the sack, and sweat broke out on his brow. He didn't need to even pull the items out to realize just how significant they were. The missing picture frame from the murdered traveler's saddlebag, Mrs. Sherman's stolen jewelry, and several thick stacks of money. Probably enough to account for all the money that had gone missing around town over the past six months, and possibly even enough to cover the two hundred dollars that had been stolen from the bank.

No wonder the girl was nervous. Both to find it and to bring it to him.

"Where was this?" he rasped.

"I... I already said. Under a tile at Fort Ashton."

His heart thumped against his ribcage. "And where, exactly, was this tile?"

Her head suddenly dropped, and when she spoke next, her voice emerged so quiet he had to lean forward just to hear her.

"In Alejandra Loyola's room."

XXX

ALEJANDRA COULDN'T STOP the tears from coursing down her face as she raced down the stairs. Oh, why had she told Harrison she was spying on him? Why had she told him about her uncle? She'd done so well at keeping things secret, and now she'd gone and ruined everything.

And why? Because she'd been moonstruck over their kiss?

Because she was distraught over Gabriella being stuck with their uncle?

Because she'd gone and fallen in love with Harrison?

She held back a sob, ignoring the strange looks people were giving her as she dashed across the open courtyard toward the corner of the hacienda and her bedroom.

She'd gone and ruined everything now. She'd have to leave before Harrison thought to ask any more questions of her and she ended up telling him all she knew.

She wrenched open the door of her bedroom and dashed inside. Her foot slipped on that dratted loose tile, but she didn't even bother to slide it into place. Instead, she dragged her old carpetbag out from beneath her mattress and tossed her few pieces of clothing inside. Maybe if she went to Consuela, they'd be able to come up with another way to get Gabriella. She could draw a diagram of the house, maybe even go to *La Colina* with Consuela and find a way to sneak in and get her sister.

They didn't even need to go right away. Consuela could hide her for a month or two first, because *Tío* Javier would surely be looking for her. After things calmed down, she'd find a way to get Gabriella before her marriage to Montrose.

It wasn't the most ideal plan, but it was something that allowed her to slip away from her uncle and still gave her hope of getting Gabriella.

Alejandra untied the apron from about her waist and slid the scratchy fabric of her serving uniform off her body, followed by the bothersome petticoat and corset she'd been forced to wear with it. If she had her way, she'd never again don such things in her life.

She chose her shirt with the hawks to wear and slid it on over her head, then pulled on a green skirt. She still had pencil and paper atop her nightstand, and she jotted Harrison a quick note letting him know she was leaving the fort. She didn't write anything about searching her bag upstairs. He would eventually, and he'd know just how deep her secrets went. She'd tell Consuela about the rustling too, just to make sure the law understood what had happened in Twin Rivers, though she wasn't sure it would do much good since her uncle was moving Raul and his men to New Mexico.

She looked around the room a final time, drew in a deep breath, then stepped into the corridor and pulled the door shut behind her. Now she needed to head next door to the store-room to get her money.

She paused for a moment by the door and looked around, making sure no one was watching her, then slipped inside.

Voices greeted her almost instantly.

"What do you mean the money was gone?"

Alejandra stilled. She recognized the familiar sound of

Rooster's voice, but she couldn't see him given the towering stacks of crates and sacks of grain.

"Just what I said." Felipe spoke this time, another voice she had no trouble recognizing. "When I looked under the tile, it was gone. The money, the jewelry, the silver picture frame. All of it."

"That doesn't sound like my problem," Rooster said. "I'm not the one who's been robbing houses for the past few months hoping it will distract the sheriff from looking for me."

Felipe had been the one robbing houses? Alejandra sucked in a breath. Had Raul known? Or worse, maybe Raul had been party to it.

"It's your problem if you took it," Felipe snapped, his words terse against the silence of the room.

"But I didn't. If I were you, I'd—"

"If I were you, I'd start to get a little nervous. After all, you were the one who killed the traveler, and now his missing silver picture frame has just turned up where you work."

Alejandra stilled, every muscle in her body going suddenly tense. Rooster had killed the traveler? Here Martin was sitting in jail and Harrison was working day in and day out to represent him in court, and Felipe had known all along who...

"What did you expect me to do?" Rooster snarled. "The traveler found the new trail. I couldn't exactly leave him to go blab everything to the sheriff."

Alejandra's knees turned to liquid, refusing to support her body. She took a step backward, letting the wall behind her support her weight. So the murder and the rustling were connected. It was just as she'd suspected. Raul, Rooster, Felipe, the lot of them had known the details this entire time.

She had to tell the sheriff. Now.

She could come back later for her money, but she couldn't let Martin sit in jail for another moment.

Her hand shook as she reached for the doorknob. She

quietly turned it and slid outside, then listened on the other side of the door for a moment. Felipe and Rooster were still arguing, a good sign they had no idea she'd overheard them.

She hiked her carpetbag onto her shoulder, then rushed toward the back entrance of the fort and hurried down the trail that led to town. She passed countless travelers on the way, all headed toward the fort to trade. She didn't know how many of them thought it odd that she raced past them with her head down, but if anything, they seemed to step aside rather than block her path.

By the time she reached O'Reilly Street, she was running, and for the first time since arriving in Twin Rivers, she didn't care that she was going to the sheriff's office in the middle of the day for all to see. She passed a trio of wagons laden with goods, darted around a woman with four children in tow, and rushed across the street before two men on horseback trotted past.

Her chest was heaving by the time she raced up the steps and flung open the door.

"Alejandra." The sheriff was standing beside the door with one of his deputies, their hats on their heads as though they'd been ready to head out.

His eyes widened as he looked at her, though she couldn't say why. Wasn't he used to people coming into his office?

But he didn't even try to smile, let alone offer her a seat or a glass of water while she caught her breath.

"I have something to tell you," she gasped.

"I'll bet you do." He reached for his belt loop and unlocked the handcuffs hooked there, then took a step toward her. "Alejandra Loyola, you're under arrest for the robbery and attempted murder of Winifred Sherman, the robbery of several other houses around town, and accessory to murder for John Doe."

"I'm what?" She reared back, but a metal cuff locked around her wrist.

"Set the carpetbag down."

She dropped it, too shocked to do anything but obey. But the second it left her hand, Daniel yanked her other wrist in front of her and locked the second metal cuff into place.

The deputy beside him reached for her carpetbag and began pulling things out.

"What are you doing? That's mine. You can't just take it."

"I can if I have reason to suspect you've been involved in a crime."

The breath stilled in her lungs. What had he said she was being charged with? Accessory to murder? And robbing poor Mrs. Sherman?

It made no sense. He hadn't mentioned a thing to do with the rustling. "I-I don't know what's going on, but I didn't try to kill Mrs. Sherman, I promise. I'm here because I know who killed the traveler."

"I'll bet you do." Daniel's voice was as hard as iron as he jerked her forward, leading her to the door that connected the jailhouse with his office. Only then did she see the items scattered across his desk.

A silver picture frame. Jewelry. Money.

"Wait. Where... where's that from?"

"Don't pretend as though you don't know." He shoved her into the jailhouse and opened the first cell.

"But I didn't do it. I didn't do any of it. And I know who killed the traveler. It wasn't Martin."

"Isn't that convenient? A picture frame that was likely on the traveler's horse at the time of the murder shows up in your room, and you suddenly know who killed him." Daniel's face stayed firm as the metal door clanged shut behind her, locking into place. "I'll be back to take your statement after I search your room."

"My room? But—"

The door to the jailhouse slammed shut behind him.

She winced, then sank down to the floor, her mind swirling in circles to make sense of what had happened.

The tile Felipe and Rooster had been talking about, the things Felipe had said were missing from beneath it—like a silver picture frame and money.

Her foot had twisted on that dratted loose tile when she'd rushed into her room to gather her belongings. It seemed it was always twisting on that loose tile. But she'd always just slid it back into place with her foot. She'd never thought to examine the tile before or see if there was room for something beneath it.

Had Raul and Felipe cut a hole into the underflooring and hidden money and jewelry and other things they had been stealing in her room? It was just the type of thing Raul would do. Then if it was ever found, it would look like she'd been the one to steal them.

But who had found them? Who had turned her in?

She hung her head.

Did it matter? If those stolen items had truly been in her room, how was she going to prove she hadn't tried to murder Mrs. Sherman or taken money from the other houses around town?

Even if she confessed everything she knew about the rustling to the sheriff, wouldn't the fact that she'd been aware of what was going on for two years and hadn't come forward make her look guilty?

"Who killed the traveler?"

She jolted, her heart hammering against her ribcage at the sound of the voice behind her. But when she looked over her shoulder, she only saw Martin Owens.

She hadn't noticed him when Daniel had brought her into the jail, but of course he'd be there. He'd moved to the bars that separated his cell from hers and was looking at her with such hope that her chest started to ache.

"Do you really know who killed him?"

"It's... complicated."

His fists tightened around the cell bars. "Why did they do it?"

She gave a shrug, a tear choosing that moment to slip down her cheek. She couldn't tell him why without explaining everything about the rustlers, and if that was something she ended up confessing, then Daniel or Cain needed to hear it first.

"Hey now, don't be worried. You'll get out of here soon. I'm sure of it. Once Sheriff Harding searches your room at Fort Ashton, he'll realize you're innocent."

But she wasn't innocent. That was the problem. "I'm not sure anyone will believe me."

"I believe you."

The ache inside her chest turned into a gaping, open cavern. "You shouldn't."

He frowned at her, and she scooted around on the floor to better see him.

Martin Owens wasn't a difficult man to look at, even if he was younger than her. His reddish blond hair and strong shoulders made him look both masculine and handsome. His hair had grown out a bit in the weeks he'd been in jail, and his eyes held a certain maturity that had been absent from his gaze when he'd offered to escort her to the food table at the church picnic all those weeks ago.

"Why would you believe me?" she asked. "You barely know me."

"Because someone framed me for killing the traveler. So maybe that same person framed you for trying to kill Mrs. Sherman and stealing other things from around town. It would make sense."

She heaved in a breath, then let it out on a long sigh. "I hope you're not the only one that idea makes sense to."

But even though there was a good chance Martin would be out of his jail cell before nightfall, she had a feeling things wouldn't turn out quite so easy with her.

Not after she'd already admitted to spying on both Mr. Rutherford and Harrison. Not after stolen money and jewelry had shown up in her room. Not once the sheriff found the letter she wrote about the rustlers and realized just how long she'd been hiding that information from him.

29

H arrison stared at his father, whose breaths seemed to grow shallower by the minute. He'd not left his side since Alejandra had left to "freshen up" nearly an hour ago.

He could call her back to care for him, but part of him wanted to sit here. He'd spent far more time locked in his father's office than he had with his father since he'd arrived, and now that his father had taken another turn for the worse, it seemed like his place was here, at the bedside of the man who'd raised him.

Even if that man was a criminal.

"Just what secrets are you hiding?" he whispered into the silent room. "What did you do to get Velez so irate that he sent a spy to Fort Ashton?"

His father wasn't a stupid man. He should have known better than to cross the former governor of a Mexican state.

"I'm going to figure it out, you know." He tapped his fingers on the wooden arms of the chair. "I'm going to learn your secrets."

Just like he'd learned Alejandra's.

Hopefully his father's secrets wouldn't hurt as badly as hers did.

But what if they hurt worse?

He pursed his lips. He needed to tell Cain about Alejandra and have his friend question her. If anyone could wring information out of a reluctant witness, it was Cain.

And he'd go get him.

Soon.

He really would.

He just... needed a minute. Or ten. Or three thousand.

Because maybe he wasn't quite as ready to know his father's secrets as he'd thought.

Harrison swallowed and looked away from his father's still form, out the window and toward the mountains across the river. A hawk swooped in the distance, diving toward the ground and then rising a moment later with something clenched in its talons.

He drew in a breath, but the air seemed to sting his lungs. Did everything have to remind him of Alejandra?

Their kiss earlier had been wonderful. He could have held her for hours. He'd nearly been tempted to drop to one knee and ask her to marry him afterward, and he'd barely restrained himself from promising to move heaven and earth in order to get Gabriella out of Mexico.

And to think, there'd been a time when he wanted to know her secrets, to understand what troubled her. From the very beginning, he'd known she was hiding something.

And yet he'd trusted her anyway.

And even now, knowing what he did, he wasn't sure he regretted it.

Nor could he believe she'd spied on him.

There was still something harmless and vulnerable about her, even if her uncle had sent her to Twin Rivers to hurt his father.

Even if she seemed determined to dash every last hope they had of a future together.

Harrison shoved himself out of the chair and started pacing, clear down to the far side of the room where Alejandra's bedding had been rolled up and placed in the corner. *God, please, show me what comes next. Show me what You want me to do.*

There'd been times with the Tillerman case where everything had seemed hopeless, and he'd had too little faith to trust that God was working His good beyond what he could see.

Was it the same now with Alejandra? Was God at work in a way he couldn't understand?

Or was he a fool for holding out hope?

A soft knock sounded on the door, and he turned. "Alejandra?"

Daniel stepped inside, a grim look on his face.

"What's happened? Is it Martin?"

Daniel shook his head. "I'm sorry, Harrison. Truly I am. But I had to do it. I hope you understand."

The serious look in Daniel's eyes, along with the hardness in his voice, caused Harrison's heart to give a single, heavy thud against his chest. "Understand what?"

"I arrested Alejandra."

He took a step back. "You what?"

"Evidence was found in her room. A silver picture frame, Mrs. Sherman's jewelry, and money. A lot of it."

Every muscle of his body turned tight.

Could Daniel be right?

Perhaps Alejandra had been sent to Twin Rivers to spy on his father, but that didn't mean she'd steal from the townsfolk or hit Mrs. Sherman with a frying pan.

"Hermine found it under a loose tile in her room," Daniel went on. "She brought it to me about an hour ago. I know this isn't going to make you happy, but I had no choice but to lock her up. If I find something that makes it look like Alejandra was set up, I promise I'll—"

"You arrested her without saying anything to me first?"

"She showed up at my office about five minutes after Hermine left." Daniel's voice offered no apology. "It was simplest to take her into custody."

He shook his head. "I don't believe Alejandra killed that traveler any more than I think Martin did."

"Even if she had nothing to do with the traveler, there's still the jewelry and the money to account for. And at this point, all the evidence I have points to someone at Fort Ashton murdering the traveler. I'm actually waiting on Abe to return with a warrant to search the bunkhouse and Rooster's room, but given what was found in Alejandra's room, I have solid enough standing to search the entire fort without a warrant. At the very least, someone involved in the murder had access to the horses in the paddock. Alejandra fits that description a whole lot more than Martin."

Harrison looked away, out the window, only to find the hawk still soared freely through the sky. "What did she say when you arrested her? Did she admit anything? Deny it? Claim she was framed?"

Daniel crossed his arms over his chest. "That's where this gets interesting. She came to my office in a rush, her face red and chest heaving as though she'd run the whole way. She said she knew who killed the traveler before I could even open my mouth to tell her she was under arrest."

"Who does she say killed him?"

Daniel shrugged. "I told her I'd take her statement after I searched her room. I want to collect up as much information as I can on my own before I question her."

Harrison rubbed the back of his neck. From a lawman's perspective, Daniel's actions made perfect sense, but the thought of Alejandra sitting in a jail cell made his stomach churn. "What have you found?"

"Bryce is still downstairs searching. But so far... nothing except the loose tile. I came to see if there's somewhere else we should search. I don't necessarily want to tear apart the kitchen or storeroom looking for evidence, but I will if I need to."

"Alejandra was always either in her room or, well... here." He gestured to the bedroll. "She and Hermine alternate the nights that they sleep up here. This is her bag."

He walked to the far side of the room and picked up the bag by its handles, then held it out.

Daniel took it from him and began riffling through the contents.

"It looks like this belongs to her too." He reached for a half-written letter that lay atop the nightstand, but he couldn't quite stop his eyes from reading the beginning of it.

Dear Gabriella,

What if I can't? You tell me to go on and start a life without you, but what if I can't? I'd never forgive myself if...

The words trailed off, but he couldn't seem to stop staring at them. There was something familiar...

Wait.

He tilted his head to the side, studying the note as something licked at the corners of his memory.

He brought it closer, letting his eyes travel slowly over every word.

Every *word*.

That was it. The words, the writing. The size and shapes of the letters. He recognized this handwriting. He'd seen it yesterday at the sheriff's office.

On the notes Cain had shown him from Daniel's informant.

That's why something had looked familiar about them yesterday. Because he'd seen Alejandra's handwriting a time or two around the fort, like when she left a question for him on his desk in his office.

"Daniel," he rasped, his throat suddenly too thick to work properly.

Daniel had dumped the items from the bag atop the bedroll and was rummaging through them, but at the sound of his name, he stopped and looked up.

He held the letter out. "Do you recognize this handwriting?"

Daniel took the stationary. He only needed to study the words for a few seconds before his eyes snapped up. "She's... she's my informant?"

"It appears so."

"But how could she know about the rustling? She's just a maid."

Harrison rubbed the back of his neck. "If my father's been involved in it like we think, and she's had access to his office all this time... but there's more. Because now I'm wondering if her uncle in Mexico might be involved as well. If... if he could even be 'el jefe.'"

Daniel straightened, his eyes flashing with understanding as the pieces of the puzzle seemed to fall into place. "That would implicate her cousin, Raul, too."

"And Raul's men." If Alejandra's uncle was involved in the rustling, then it made sense why he would want a spy at the fort. He groaned with the obviousness of it all. "Daniel..."

"I don't understand quite how all the evidence fits together yet, but I feel like I'm close," Daniel said, glancing back down at the letter.

"I know what you mean." Harrison plopped down beside Daniel on the bedroll, his hand resting on the bag he'd seen Alejandra use countless times over the past month.

Something crinkled inside the bag, and he frowned. "I thought you emptied everything?"

"I did." Daniel tilted his head toward the haphazard pile

between them. A Spanish Bible, several pencils, stationary, a map, and a stack of handkerchiefs that Alejandra was probably hoping to sell for extra money.

"It feels like something's still in here." Harrison picked up the bag. The inside was empty, even though he could have sworn he'd heard a crinkling sound. He opened it wider, then stilled. There, on the inside of the lining, an embroidered hawk was pinned to the bag. It looked like it had been cut off one of the handkerchiefs she had made.

He lifted the bit of fabric to find the lining of the bag beneath it had been cut and stitched back shut.

Harrison didn't bother to dig through the pile of things on the bed to see if there were any scissors. He just gripped the lining on both sides and yanked.

The sound of tearing fabric filled the room, and a thick envelope fell onto his lap.

His name was scrawled across it.

30

D aniel couldn't remember the last time so many men had been packed into his office, and that didn't account for the ten men crammed into the three jail cells on the other side of the wall.

The end of Alejandra's letter had contained a list of every one of Raul's men and every guard from Fort Ashton involved in the rustling. While it appeared most of Raul's men were in Mexico, there had still been enough men to arrest at Fort Ashton that he'd sent Bryce to get Cain and a group of Rangers. He hadn't wanted to risk a single one of the men escaping while the others were being taken into custody.

As soon as the guards realized what was happening, they all started talking. The Mexican rustlers they'd captured in the past had been too scared of *el jefe* to give much information, but not Rutherford's guards. It was almost as though there was a contest over who could do the most snitching.

When Rooster and Felipe had seen Alejandra in a jail cell and realized she'd already been arrested, the three of them had started arguing, their spat giving away a whole slew of information that hadn't been included in her letter.

So he'd set up a circle of chairs in the middle of his office and handcuffed Rooster, Felipe, and Alejandra to them.

Harrison had parked himself behind his desk with a stack of papers and a pen, the legal part of his brain likely realizing everything the three of them said needed to be recorded, even though Abe was also recording things at the other desk. Every time Harrison looked at Alejandra, he sent a glare Daniel's way, but Daniel ignored it.

The rustling ring had been running roughshod over West Texas for two years. He was going to gather any and all information he could, regardless of what Harrison or Cain or anyone else thought.

Though he had to admit, Alejandra seemed like more of a victim than a criminal in this situation.

"Tell me, Felipe, was it your idea to hide the stolen jewelry and money from the bank in my room, or Raul's?" Alejandra spat, her face flushed red and she stared across the small circle at Felipe.

"Does it matter?" Felipe taunted. "You've been arrested right along with everyone else."

Alejandra sat back in her chair. "The only thing that's missing from this mess is Raul. He deserves to be sitting in a jail cell too."

"Don't worry your pretty little head, darling, I fully intend to make sure that happens." Cain sent her a wink from where he was standing just outside the circle of chairs.

"You can't touch Raul," Felipe sneered at him. "He's in Mexico with his father."

"Care to make a wager on that?" Cain's eyes narrowed into two thin slits. As soon as Felipe looked away, Cain fixed his gaze back on Alejandra. "How did your uncle come to do business with Bartholomew Rutherford?"

Alejandra looked down. "He hated that an American

controlled the trail that ran between Chihuahua and San Antonio. When Mr. Rutherford proposed an arrangement where his men would steal cattle from area ranches and run them south of the border to be sold to the slaughterhouses in Chihuahua, *Tío* Javier saw it as an opportunity to steal shipping contracts from Mr. Rutherford."

"He's been stealing shipping contracts?" Rooster shouted, the scar on the side of his face bunching into an angry fist. "That's why Mr. Rutherford was so worried about money before his apoplectic attack."

"Bartholomew Rutherford had a successful business and plenty of money." Cain cocked his head to the side. "Why would he risk losing all of it by doing something this illegal?"

Alejandra glanced at Rooster, who was trying his best to glare a hole straight through her. Then she dropped her gaze back to her shoes and blew out a long breath. "Mr. Rutherford was worried about what would happen to his shipping contracts once the railroad went through. The rustling started around the same time the railroad was supposed to open, but the laying of the track got delayed."

"And you know this how?" Daniel stepped forward. She'd written the basics of why her uncle and Rutherford had started rustling in her letter to Harrison, but he wanted to make sure he understood every detail.

"*Sí*, Alejandra, tell the sheriff how you know." A cruel smile twisted Felipe's lips.

Alejandra cast a glance Harrison's direction, then looked back down, her words soft. "Because he sent me to Twin Rivers to read Mr. Rutherford's mail and learn about his shipping partners in Mexico. I gathered enough information about his partners and the contract prices, he went to the Mexican companies and made them a better offer."

"You've been reading his mail for two years?" Rooster

leaned forward in his chair as far as his handcuffed arms would allow. "Do you know how much business you've cost my boss?"

"Do you know how many ranchers your rustling has destroyed?" Alejandra's eyes snapped up to Rooster. "Your boss is hardly a victim."

"You had no business reading his mail."

"And you had no business killing that traveler and then framing Martin."

Rooster reared back. "How do you know about that?"

"I'm not as stupid as you think."

The room was silent while the impact of their statements sank in. Rooster hadn't denied killing the traveler. A quick glance at Abe told Daniel the old deputy was busy scrawling every last bit of information down, and Harrison had started writing furiously too.

Cain stepped into the circle of chairs and positioned himself directly in front of Alejandra. "How do you know it was Rooster who killed the traveler and not Felipe or Raul?"

"Because I... I..." She looked around the room, then sighed. "I heard Rooster and Felipe talking in the storeroom earlier. It's why I came here, to tell the sheriff I knew who killed the traveler."

"So all this time, you knew who was responsible for the rustling, but you didn't know who killed the traveler?"

She licked her lips. "*Sí*. But I was hoping you would catch the rustlers. That's why I passed the sheriff notes."

"You what?" Felipe shouted.

"I'm going to strangle you," Rooster yelled at the same time.

Both men's faces contorted with rage, and they looked ready to break the wooden slats of the chairs that their hands were cuffed to.

Daniel moved behind Alejandra and rested a hand on her shoulder. "Keep talking. You're in my custody now, these men can't hurt you."

She looked up at him with round, worried eyes.

"Cooperate, Alejandra, please." Harrison said from across the room, his eyes riveted to her. "Each bit of information you give to the law makes it easier for me to get potential charges dropped against you."

"I want my charges dropped," Rooster said.

Harrison's jaw turned hard. "Sorry. The Twin Rivers County Sheriff's Department doesn't drop charges for murder."

"Why were you in the storeroom earlier?" Cain asked Alejandra, drawing her attention back to him. "You never said."

"I'd packed my bags." She glanced at Harrison, then drew in a breath. "I... I'd decided I couldn't stay in Twin Rivers anymore, and I—"

"You were going to run away?" Felipe released a cruel laugh. "Rooster's right. You're going to pay."

The color drained from her face, and she pressed her lips shut.

"The storeroom, Alejandra." Cain's voice offered no compassion. "Why were you there? And don't mind Felipe. He has no way of telling your uncle what you were about to do."

She drew in a breath, then glanced at Harrison one more time before continuing. "I'd decided to leave. There were... there were reasons. But I've been saving money, all this time I was in Twin Rivers, I saved what I earned and I tried to find ways to earn extra. I didn't trust my cousin not to search my room for it, so I hid it in the storeroom."

"You think you're smart, do you?" Felipe sneered.

"I think she's smart," Cain snapped. "I think if she would have hidden the money in her room, she would have woken one day to find it gone while that silver picture frame and stolen jewelry still remained."

Felipe sat back in his chair, a frown plastered across his face. "I'll have you know I didn't kill anyone. You might be able to blame me for rustling, but you can't blame me for anyone's death. That was all Rooster and Raul. Rooster killed the traveler because he discovered our new trail, but Raul was the one who killed Mr. Rutherford, not me."

A heavy silence fell over the room, while every eye focused on Felipe.

"What did you say?" Rooster growled, his voice dangerously low.

Felipe straightened. "You heard me. I'm not letting you blame me for either of the murders. You can take the fall for that traveler yourself."

"Mr. Rutherford isn't dead yet," Cain drawled. "Makes me awful curious to know why you're talking about his murder."

"What did he do?" Alejandra whispered, her face white. "What did my cousin do to Mr. Rutherford? Was it some kind of poison? Is that why he's in the condition he is?"

Felipe looked around the room, then swallowed. He might not have realized the full impact of what he'd said earlier, but now it appeared things were sinking in. "No. Nothing. Raul did nothing. There isn't any poison. I misspoke. English is a difficult language. Sometimes I get my words mixed up."

"*Mentiroso,* no one believes you," Alejandra seethed.

"You'd best tell us what you know, unless you want to be charged with accessory to murder on top of the rustling." Daniel came up to stand behind Felipe. "Because you seem to know an awful lot about an attempted murder you claim not to have committed."

"It was methanal," Felipe spat. "It's a type of alcohol. Like whiskey, but not. *El jefe* ordered it done. He got it from some fancy scientist down in Guadalajara who studies it. It's used to make formaldehyde. The scientist said it would cause the brain to bleed, which mimics an apoplectic attack. Raul thought the first dose a few months ago would kill him, but it didn't. So he gave Rutherford another dose before he left for Mexico yesterday morning. Said it should finish him off. But none of this had anything to do with me. I wasn't in the room when Raul gave it to him either time."

"That doesn't make you innocent," Harrison muttered.

"I'm going to kill you." Rooster tried to lunge for Felipe, but his bound hands only caused him to tip the chair forward.

Daniel stepped in and steadied it before it toppled to the floor, but Rooster's eyes were hot enough that Daniel half expected a burn to appear on Felipe's face.

Alejandra, on the other hand, stared at her lap, her shoulders caving in around her.

"Time to go back to your cells," Daniel declared.

They had enough information to ride into Mexico and arrest Javier Velez, and the longer they waited, the bigger the chance Velez would find out Felipe and Rutherford's guards had been arrested.

Daniel reached down and unlocked one wrist on Rooster's cuffs, then hauled him up. "Bryce, take him to his cell, and get Martin for me. Also, see to it Rooster and Felipe are separated."

The last thing he needed was a murder happening in his jailhouse, but after learning that Raul had tried to kill Mr. Rutherford, he had a feeling that if he locked both Rooster and Felipe together, one of them would wind up dead before tomorrow.

"He needs to sign a confession stating he killed the traveler first." Harrison tapped a paper on the desk, then held out an ink pen.

Rooster stiffened. "I ain't signing nothing."

Harrison crossed his arms over his chest. "Then I'll be sure to tell the judge you were uncooperative and don't deserve any leniency when I prosecute your case."

Daniel blinked. Harrison was going to prosecute the case against the rustlers? This was the first he'd mentioned the possibility.

"You've stolen enough cattle that I'm well within the scope

of the law to ask for a death sentence," Harrison continued, his eyes narrowed at Rooster. "And that's just based on the information I've learned in the past hour. I wonder if there are any other illegal activities you've been involved in. I'm sure some of the men sitting inside the jailhouse will be willing to tell me about them in exchange for a few years off their own sentences."

Rooster's lips twisted into a snarl, but he grabbed the paper and slapped it onto the desk. It took him a minute to read what Harrison had written, then he scrawled his name on the bottom.

"Very good." Harrison slid the paper back across the desk.

Rooster leaned forward over the scarred wood. "None of this would have happened if you hadn't come to town and messed everything up."

"I disagree," Cain said from behind him, his voice as hard as a steel beam. "Maybe the events surrounding your arrest would have been different, but your days were numbered."

A muscle ticked at the side of Rooster's jaw, but the large man turned and lumbered toward the jailhouse without another word.

"I have a confession for Felipe to sign too." Harrison scooted another paper to the far side of the desk.

"I didn't murder anyone," Felipe retorted. "Why should I sign that?"

Harrison smile tightly. "Because we need official documentation stating that you weren't the one who attempted to kill my father. Unless you want to be charged with his murder?"

"Fine." Felipe's mouth twisted into a snarl. "I'll sign it."

Daniel unlocked Felipe's handcuffs and led him to the desk.

Felipe signed the paper, then looked up at Harrison. "Your *padre*, he's still going to die. I don't know when, but the dose of methanal Raul gave him yesterday—"

"I understand." Harrison's face hardened into an emotion-less mask. "Your jail cell is waiting."

Daniel led Felipe across his office, where Bryce stood with Martin, who was looking around the room expectantly.

"Am I free now?"

Daniel smiled at him. "It might take a few minutes to draw up the paperwork, but yes."

Martin beamed, then threw his arms around Daniel. "Thank you."

Daniel gave him a pat on the back. "Don't thank me, thank Alejandra. She was the one who figured out who really killed..."

The sound of jeers erupting behind them cut off their conversation. Daniel stepped away from Martin and looked through the doorway to see that Felipe was being led down the hallway to the final jail cell.

Daniel gave his head a small shake, then moved to where Alejandra still sat handcuffed to the chair.

He unlocked the metal bands, and she stood, her eyes wide as she looked around the room.

"Thank you." Martin rushed toward her, wrapping her in a hug. "I don't know what you did or how you figured out who really killed that man, but thank you."

She offered him a small smile, then wriggled out of his hold. "You're welcome. I... I'm just sorry I didn't figure it out sooner."

"I'm just happy it's figured out. I'll never forget this. If you ever need anything, anything at all. Come to me first, all right?"

"I'm not sure I'll be needing anything, but *gracias*." She gave him another small smile, then slipped away from him and walked toward the jailhouse.

"Where are you going?" Cain stepped in front of her.

"To my cell. Unless..." She turned and looked at Harrison.

"Do you need me to sign something first? I didn't kill anyone. I didn't know Raul planned to kill anyone either, otherwise I would have told you. But I'll sign something if you need me to."

The lines around Harrison's mouth softened and his eyes turned tender.

"I have a couple things for you to sign now, and a couple more that I need to write up yet." Harrison spread several sheets of paper on the desk. "But after you sign them, you're not going into one of those cells."

"What do you mean? I knew about the rustling all this time, but I didn't tell you."

"No, you told Daniel."

She twisted her hands in her skirt. "Not everything."

"And why was that?" Harrison came around the desk toward her. "Because you liked what you were doing at the fort? Because you wanted your uncle to steal cattle?"

She shook her head. "No. I hated every minute of it. But they had Gabriella and..."

Harrison settled his hands on her shoulders, never mind that Daniel and his deputies and Cain and three of Cain's Rangers were all looking on. "That makes you a victim, love, not a criminal. There are words for what Javier and Raul did to you—blackmail and extortion. They're both illegal. And your uncle and cousin could go to prison for a long time based on those two things alone."

XXX

Alejandra stared up into Harrison's face. Was it true? Could Raul and *Tio* Javier really go to prison for the situation they'd put her in?

She swallowed. "I feel like you should hate me right now."

He gave his head a slow shake, then his arms were around her, strong and warm, pulling her against his chest. "I could never hate you, sweetheart. This only makes me love you more."

She sucked in a breath, the air so sharp it burned her lungs.

"You what?" She pushed back from him enough to stare up into his face.

"I said I love you."

"But... but you can't love me. I-I read your things, your legal papers." The words tumbled out of her before she could stop them. "In the bag you brought with you when you first came. Raul told me to. I didn't want to, but I..."

He smiled down at her. Smiled! After she'd just confessed to reading his things!

"Did the legal contracts put you to sleep?"

"*Sì, pero...*"

"Don't Alejandra. Whatever you did, whatever you felt you had to do to keep you and your sister safe, none of that is going to stop me from loving you."

"But..."

"No. I'm not convinced you did anything wrong, but even if you did, I forgive you. It's over and done, and you don't need to bring it up anymore."

Her eyes filled with tears. How many times had she wondered what Harrison would say if he found out the truth? How many times had she debated telling him about the rustlers but decided against it, not just because doing so might endanger Gabriella, but because she couldn't bear the thought of Harrison turning away from her?

But now he knew everything, the full, ugly truth of it. And he still loved her. He still wanted to help.

Dear Father God, I don't deserve a man like this.

Tears brimmed in her eyes, and then next thing she knew,

Harrison's arms were around her, warm and solid and strong. She sank into them, letting the scent of his soap fill her senses and the steadiness of his heartbeat thump beneath her ear.

"How did I let them do this to me?" She burrowed her face against Harrison's shirt. "How did it go so far? I wish I would have said something sooner or—"

"You said something. You wrote those notes."

"Those notes saved a lot of lives," Cain said from somewhere over her shoulder. "Don't make light of them. You've given me more accurate information than anyone else, and I caught a lot of men, all because of you."

She must look ridiculous, standing in Harrison's arms in the middle of the sheriff's office with half a dozen lawmen looking on, but Harrison didn't seem to mind. If anything, he only seemed more determined to hold her against him, his hand running up and down her back in a soothing motion.

"At first I thought I could keep to myself at Fort Ashton and do nothing. Or I hoped Raul would get caught, only so I wouldn't have to deal with him any longer." She turned slightly in Harrison's arms so she could glimpse Cain as she spoke. "But the longer I was here, the more I got to know the people of Twin Rivers, I realized how much my uncle and Mr. Rutherford were hurting those around them. When I learned Raul was going to try taking cattle from the Circle M last year, I couldn't sit by and do nothing. Mr. Mattherson's daughter is blind, and he needed the money from the ranch to pay for her schooling. But that didn't stop Raul from trying to steal the cattle right out from under him."

"You're the one who moved Mattherson's cattle?" Surprise flitted across Daniel's face, and he rubbed a hand over his chest. "Knowing Mattherson was on the brink of losing his ranch after that raid tore me up somethin' fierce. I still recall when we found them in that hidden valley on the A Bar W. I've never been so happy before in my life."

"It was too much for me to move that many cattle alone, so I paid some hands from Ojinaga to help me. Like I said, I couldn't let Mr. Mattherson lose his cattle when I knew it would ruin him. He came to the fort every now and then to trade, and he was always so nice. He carried a daguerreotype of his daughter and told everyone about how she was attending some special school to help her live with her blindness.

"But moving the cattle was risky. I was worried Raul would find out the whole time, and I was worried about what he would do if he discovered who any of the men I'd hired were. They had families in Ojinaga, every single one of them."

"You did well, love," Harrison pressed a kiss to her temple.

She pulled back from his embrace far enough to look up into his face. "That's when I decided to write notes and leave them at the sheriff's office. I made sure to ask more questions about the rustling runs, so I knew what to say. And it worked." She looked past the side of Harrison's arm at where Daniel stood, then sent him a small smile. "You started saving the cattle and catching some of the rustlers. I hoped you'd catch Raul, but he only got more wily. Once he learned that the cattle were most likely to be apprehended just inside the Mexican border, he stopped riding with his men into Mexico and stayed behind in Twin Rivers. Then if the cattle weren't caught, he'd catch up with his men before reaching *La Colina*."

Cain and Daniel both had questions for her, like where *La Colina* was located and if her uncle was involved in any other criminal activities besides rustling, and how many men they could expect to find at the estate. At some point she stepped away from Harrison's arms and sat in one of the chairs, but Harrison was sure to leave a hand on her shoulder or arm, always letting her know he was there.

When their questions subsided, Cain started barking orders at his Rangers while Daniel announced he'd follow the Rangers into Mexico with his own posse. The office erupted into a whirlwind of movement and voices all at once, each person rushing around to prepare for a trip into Mexico.

Harrison pulled her into the corner, his eyes latched onto hers despite the sudden chaos around them. "I'm sending you to the A Bar W. Wes has men there that can protect you while I'm in Mexico, and I want you somewhere safe."

Safe. She closed her eyes. The word sounded so nice. How long had it been since she'd truly felt safe? "Thank you for... for caring, for loving me, even after everything."

"Of course I love you. And I want you to know that while I wish you would have told me everything sooner, I understand why you didn't."

"You do?"

"I do." He tucked a strand of hair behind her ear, looking at her as though he wanted to pull her right back into his arms and not let go until tomorrow's dawn.

And she wanted to let him. "Are you sure you need to go with the posse? Couldn't you stay here and—"

"Absolutely. I told you I'd go into Mexico and get Gabriella myself if I needed to."

She reached up and pressed her palm to the side of his face. "Be careful."

He smiled. "Don't worry, Cain probably won't let me get close enough to the shooting to fire a gun, but I still want to be there when we find your sister."

"When I think of it like that, I want you to be there too." If she couldn't rescue Gabriella herself, then sending Harrison was the next best thing. "As long as you don't get hurt."

He pressed a kiss to her forehead. "I won't get hurt, but I fully plan to see your uncle answer for his crimes and bring Gabriella back here, so you and I can start a life together."

She smiled up at him. Just a few hours ago, it had seemed like both Harrison and Gabriella were lost to her forever, but if things went how Harrison said, she just might be able to have the life she'd been dreaming about ever since Harrison Rutherford had given her that thick stack of money last fall.

It almost seemed too good to believe.

31

Cain tightened the cinch on Maverick's saddle, set three canteens in his saddle bag, then double-checked to make sure he'd packed his extra ammunition.

Everything was in place, and a quick glance around the camp told him that his men were all busy getting their horses ready to hit the trail.

Good.

They would leave in a few minutes, and if they rode hard, they should be able to catch the cattle before they reached *La Colina*. That would split Javier Velez's men, and hopefully allow them to send the cattle and captured rustlers back to Twin Rivers with Daniel's posse.

That had been the main reason he'd agreed to let Daniel round up a posse and follow at their backs. He didn't have enough men to split his Rangers in two groups and take on whatever awaited them at Velez's estate.

If all went well and they captured the cattle without much trouble, they'd be able to continue on to *La Colina* before Velez learned what had happened.

The last thing the man would be expecting was a force of Rangers to show up at his home.

Cain rubbed his jaw. Hopefully he didn't get into trouble with headquarters for what he was about to do. It was one thing to cross the border into Mexico and bring back a *desperado* or two. It was another thing entirely to ride three dozen men to a former governor's estate and bring him back to the United States without having extradition papers in hand.

Trouble was, getting those extradition papers would cost him time he didn't have.

That, and sometimes it was just plumb better not to ask Austin for permission when a job needed doing.

"Five minutes," he called. "I'm not waiting for stragglers."

Each minute they lingered on the Texas side of the border increased the chances that Velez might find out they were coming.

"Cain," a female voice said from somewhere behind him.

He turned and instantly spotted a familiar mess of wavy black hair and swishing skirts hurrying toward him.

"I heard about the raid." Anna Mae rushed up to him, her chest heaving.

"You and how many others?" If word got out about where they were headed and why, they might as well pack up and head back to Austin.

She raised her hands. "No others, just Wes and Keely, which you must have expected since Alejandra was sent to the ranch and Daniel asked if some of Wes's hands could ride in the posse. And Sam knows too, of course, since Daniel released Martin and Sam's riding with you."

Cain clenched his jaw. Yes, he'd expected all those people would be told, but one of the biggest dangers about taking a posse was that news of their mission would spread. "Only the people in the posse should know what we're about. Do you understand? I don't even want the men telling their wives where they are going or why."

"I haven't told anyone, I promise."

She probably hadn't. She could yack a man's ear off with the best of them, but growing up in a lawman's home meant she'd also had to learn to keep her mouth shut when it mattered. "Good. Now what do you need?"

"I just..." she swallowed, then glanced around the camp that hummed with activity. For once, each of his Rangers found things to do without him or his lieutenant constantly barking orders. "Can I talk to you in your tent?"

"Now? We're riding out in four minutes."

"Please? It's important."

"Fine." He gave Maverick one final check, making sure the stallion was ready to saddle up the second he finished talking to Anna Mae, then stalked his tent with long, quick strides.

She had to nearly run to keep up with him.

The second the flap closed behind her, he swung around. "What is it?"

"I just..." Her jaw trembled. "It's going to be dangerous, what you're doing in Mexico."

"Comes with the job."

She took a step toward him. "But this is more dangerous than normal."

He glanced at the flap of the tent, his boot tapping impatiently. "What do you need? Out with it."

"I wanted to tell you to be careful."

His boot tapping stilled. "That's it? Be careful? You could have told me that while I was saddling Maverick."

She gulped in a breath, her chest rising and falling beneath the ruffled scoop of her neckline. Dark hair cascaded around her shoulders while her eyes shone with an emotion he wasn't going to let himself think about for too long. Her cheeks were the perfect shade of pink too, even though he knew she wouldn't have wasted a lick of time putting rouge on.

There was no question about who would haunt his dreams while he was on the trail.

"I'm worried for you," she blurted, twisting her hands together in front of her.

"And I'm leaving."

He tried to stalk past her, but suddenly she was in his arms, her lips brushing against his, tender and soft and sweet.

All it took was that one simple touch. She smelled of sunshine and wind, of sugar and yeast. And there was something else. Something subtle and feminine and intoxicating. Something he could only describe as Anna Mae.

He couldn't seem to stop himself from wrapping an arm around her back and pulling her close. From tilting her head and adjusting her face to the perfect angle for him to deepen the kiss.

A small groan erupted from her throat, and he pressed his eyes shut. Just another second, no another minute, or maybe ten, because once he released his mouth from hers, he'd never, ever be able to kiss her again.

And he wasn't quite ready to stop, not with the woman who seemed to see through his taunting smiles and careless shrugs. Not with the woman who took the time to invite him to something as boring and normal as Easter dinner—and looked genuinely disappointed when he tried to turn her down.

Not with the woman who claimed she'd loved him.

He finally pulled away, his chest heaving with the effort, though hers heaved just as hard. Her eyes were bright as she looked at him, her lips swollen and red. And somehow her hair was even wilder than before, the long, dark waves more riotous and unruly after having his hands in them.

He didn't know whether to haul her back into his arms and

kiss her again or loose a string of curses that would blister her ears for a month.

So he jabbed his finger at her, hard and fierce. "Never again. Do you understand me, Anna Mae? Don't you ever pull something like that again."

And then he stalked away, leaving her standing in the middle of his tent.

32

How did men go on cattle drives for months at a time, breathing in nothing but dust?

From where he sat atop Blaze, Daniel dragged in a breath of hot desert air, only to find his tongue once again coated in dust from the constant movement of other horses on the trail—just like it had been for the past two days since they'd left Twin Rivers.

If he ever quit being a lawman, the one thing he wouldn't become was a cowhand.

"Daniel." Sam rode toward him, his hat pulled low against the scorching rays of the sun. It was the first time Sam had sought him out on the trail. Even though he'd dropped the charges against Martin, Sam had barely looked his way once during the past two days.

Sam drew his horse to a stop beside him and stared down the dusty trail where Cain's men had disappeared several hours ago. "How you holding up?"

Was Sam referring to Martin and the rustling ring? Or the fact that they'd been sweltering on the trail for two days? "Ready to eat a piece of jerky that's not covered in trail dust. Or really, just take in a clean breath of air. Gotta be honest, it makes me wonder how you and Wes survive those cattle drives all the way to Austin."

"A few days into every drive, I start to wonder if I'm daft. Then I get a stack of banknotes at the auction, and I realize the drive was worth it." Sam jutted his chin toward where the trail continued in its southwesterly direction. "Any idea how things are going up there?"

"Last scout said the rustlers are holed up in a canyon, and there's lots of boulders to hide behind. Cain's got the high ground and more men, but it's going to take a while to flush everyone out."

They'd left Twin Rivers just before dark two days ago and had ridden all night and all day, stopped for a night, and then ridden for most of the day today in order to catch up to the slow-moving cattle. Once they'd gotten within a mile of the rustlers, Cain's men had ridden ahead to set up an ambush.

Cain had taken Wes and a few of Wes's cowhands to help drive the cattle up the trail with him, then told the rest of Daniel's posse to stay put, cutting off anyone who might try to backtrack.

That had been about four hours ago. The faint pop-pop of gunshots in the distance could be heard against the low conversations of the men ambling around the small creek where they'd stopped, but other than that, there'd been little indication of how things were going for Cain.

"There's part of me that wants to ride up there and help, even at the risk of Cain's wrath." Sam's hands tightened around his horse's reins. "I didn't come all this way to sit back and wait."

Daniel's lips twitched up into a smile. "I'm afraid that's how most of sheriffing goes. Sit around and wait until something big happens."

"I imagine it does." Sam twisted his lips and looked down at his horse. "Something big sure happened before we left town, huh?"

Daniel slanted a glance at his friend-turned-enemy, who just might want to turn back into his friend.

"Thank you for dropping the charges against Martin," he muttered. "I don't quite have the words to explain how much it means to me and Ellie."

Daniel's throat closed, and not because of the dust coating it. "Come on. I need to refill my canteen. Let's talk by the creek."

He called to two of the men, telling them to get on their horses so some of the posse was ready in case rustlers came charging down the trail, then he led his horse to one of the cottonwood trees that grew beside the stream and shucked off his boots.

Just the little bit of cool water running over his feet and ankles made him feel a little less ready to combust. Hopefully it would have a cooling effect on Sam. "Get in," he called over his shoulder. "Water feels great."

Sam tethered his horse to the tree, then pulled off his boots, rolled up his trousers, and waded in behind him.

"I never wanted to charge Martin. You understand that, right? But I didn't have a choice if I wanted to keep my job."

"Some things are worth losing a job for." Sam took the bandana from around his neck, dunked it into the water, and then straightened and rang it out over his face. Water sloshed over his skin and dampened the front of his shirt.

"I was hoping it wouldn't come to that. Seemed like I could do more good investigating on my own and handing what I found over to Cain and Harrison than letting someone else come in and investigate the murder. Because there would have had to be an investigation. The State of Texas doesn't just turn its back when a dead body shows up as evidence."

Sam straightened and looked at him. Redness rimmed his eyes, but probably not because of the dust. "Reckon you're right, but at the same time, all I could think about was losing my son."

Daniel's throat felt suddenly thick. "I know."

"Ellie too, and Leroy and Christopher and all the rest of my family." Sam plastered his wet bandana to the back of his neck. "They've already lost a mother and brother, and their father wants nothing to do with them. The possibility of losing Martin..."

"I'm not blaming you for anything, Sam." Daniel bent down and dunked his own bandana into the cool water of the creek. "Locking Martin up was the hardest thing I've ever done as sheriff, hands down. But when I look at how much harder things must have been for you, well, I can understand why you acted the way you did, even though it made the entire situation feel that much worse for me."

Sam rubbed the back of his neck. "I feel the same about you. I understand why you did what you did, even though it hurt in a way I can't rightly explain."

"So then, this is over and done? We're friends?"

Sam offered him a lopsided grin. "Not just friends. We're friends who can survive just about anything, I'd say."

Daniel drew in a breath, his heart feeling light in a way it hadn't since the day he'd searched Sam's barn. "Good. Because that's not something I want to repeat ever again."

"Me either." Sam slapped him on the back. "Now Ellie's birthday is coming up soon, and I want to plan a party to surprise her. I figured Charlotte would want to help."

"I'm sure she would." Daniel plastered his wet bandana across the back of his neck, then let the coolness from the water trickle through the rest of his body.

"Good. I'll pay a call after we get these cattle back to town and we can pick a date."

"Cattle on the trail!" A voice bellowed. "Wes is leading."

Daniel and Sam raced out of the creek and pulled on their

stockings and boots. By the time they rode their horses to where the other men had gathered, the ground shook beneath the thunderous steps of the cattle, and a massive cloud of dust rose up from the trail.

"Looks like Cain's plan worked!" Harrison rode up beside him, a smile plastered across his face. "Think I'll be able to convince Cain to let me travel on to *La Colina* while the rest of you take the cattle back?"

Sam let out a laugh. "You'll have better luck sweet talkin' a scorpion!"

Harrison shrugged. "Let's just say I've dodged Cain's sting a time or two in the past. Always survived."

Daniel smiled and looked between Sam and Harrison. They were back, joking and having fun and laughing. He still wasn't going to apologize for locking Martin up, but it was good to know his friends were the real, true kind. Like David and Jonathon in the Bible.

Even when life tried to pull them apart, their friendship was strong enough to survive.

XXX

ALEJANDRA STOOD on the balcony overlooking the mountains to her east. They rose up in a series of jagged, craggy peaks, slashing upward against a brilliantly blue sky.

It was a pretty view, but not quite pretty enough to distract her from the fact that Harrison was somewhere in Mexico trying to apprehend her uncle and cousin—and bring her sister back.

She twisted the handkerchief in her hand. Had he reached *La Colina* yet? It seemed a bit early for that. But maybe Cain and his Rangers had overtaken the cattle being driven south. Did that mean they'd captured Raul too, or had her cousin found a way to escape yet again?

Or maybe the rustlers had been warned of the Rangers coming and had set up an ambush.

Or Cain hadn't even caught up with the rustlers yet.

She dragged in a breath, then crossed to the far side of the balcony. It was all too confusing! She didn't even know which scenario she should be worrying about.

A knock sounded on the door.

"I don't feel like coming down for dinner," she called over her shoulder. "Just send a tray."

"We're not here because of dinner."

At the sound of Ellie's voice behind her, she turned. Both Ellie and Anna Mae entered the room. Anna Mae was dressed much as she was, with a ruffled shirt that revealed her collarbone and part of her shoulders, and her hair hanging free. Ellie, on the other hand, looked like a regular rancher's wife, with a green gingham dress and her red hair pulled up into a loose bun.

"I don't feel like company either."

"See?" Anna Mae nudged Ellie. "I told you."

"I can hear you. Please just leave."

Ellie set the tea service she carried on top of the dresser by the door. "You've been cooped up in here for two days, Alejandra. It's time you come out and eat a regular meal and visit with your friends."

She twisted her handkerchief. "I don't feel like eating or visiting." And she wasn't lying. There was a reason she'd kept to her room.

"Can we at least have a bath brought up for you?" Anna Mae wrinkled her nose. "You're filthy, and your hair is atrocious."

Was it? She hadn't bothered looking in the mirror today.

Yesterday she'd looked in it enough to know all she'd see was puffy, swollen eyes—which had only made her want to cry more. "I suppose."

"I understand if you don't want to talk. Truly I do." Ellie offered her a wan smile. "But will you at least let me thank you?"

She twisted the handkerchief in her hands. "For what?"

"For exonerating Martin."

She pressed a hand to her chest, which still ached anytime she thought about that poor boy being locked in a cell. "I wish I would have known sooner. I should have thought to ask Raul more questions. Martin sat in jail for weeks, and all along Rooster..." A lump rose in her throat.

"Yeah, because that's a normal question people have." Anna Mae plopped onto the bed. "Hey cousin, did you or any of your friends kill anyone this week?"

"My cousin isn't exactly normal."

Anna Mae rolled her eyes. "A bit late to announce that, don't you think?"

Ellie scowled at Anna Mae. "At least try be nice, would you?"

"It's fine," Alejandra sighed. "She's not saying anything that isn't true."

"Maybe so, but my brother is a free man because of you." Ellie came closer and wrapped her arms around her, squeezing tightly. "If you ever need anything, all you have to do is ask. My entire family owes you a debt we'll probably never be able to repay."

"You... you don't hate me?"

Ellie pulled back just far enough to frown at her. "Why would I hate you?"

"Didn't Sam almost lose his ranch to the rustlers? And here I knew what they were up to the entire time, but I didn't go to the sheriff and tell him what I knew. I just slipped bits and pieces of information to him."

"Is that what you've been in here stewing about?" Anna Mae straightened from where she still sat on the bed and crossed her arms over her chest. "And here I thought I liked you."

"Stow it, Anna Mae," Ellie growled, then she wrapped Alejandra in another hug. "Of course we don't hate you. You're the reason the rustlers were caught."

Alejandra pushed away from the warm embrace. "I still should have said something sooner."

"But you did say something. Each time you left a note for Daniel." Ellie's brow furrowed. "Don't be so hard on yourself."

If only she knew how not to be.

"Your uncle has your sister, right?" Anna Mae asked. "So the whole time you were here, you were worried about what would have happened to her if you went to my brother or Cain."

"Yes, but that doesn't excuse..."

"Oh, stop it. Was the rustling your idea? Was killing anyone your idea? From what I can see, you made the best of an impossible situation, and now, instead of being happy that the truth finally came out and your sister might be rescued, you're holed up in here worrying about all the things you think you did wrong." Anna Mae huffed. "All I can see is the things you did right."

Alejandra blinked. "Truly?"

"You remember the story of Esther in the Bible, right?" Ellie walked to the dresser, where she'd set the tea service.

"Yes."

"Well, I was reading through Esther this morning, and it seems to me like you're something of an Esther." Ellie poured an even stream of tea into the dainty-looking cup.

"Called to save the cattle instead of my people?"

Ellie turned around with the teacup, a giant smile on her

face. "Something like that, yes. Now take this tea and sit. All your fidgeting is making me antsy."

Alejandra plopped herself down in one of the chairs positioned near the bed. "The rustling was illegal, and I knew about it for two years. I can't quite stop myself from feeling guilty."

"That's ridiculous." Anna Mae sprang off the bed and headed for the tea service. "You used your knowledge to do what you could."

"But I could have done more."

"Not without risking your life or your sister's." Ellie returned with her own cup of tea, then sank down into the chair beside her.

"Does that excuse it?" She stared down into her untouched tea. "Does that make everything right?"

"I think God knows your heart." Ellie reached out and patted her leg. "And I think He worked things out so that when the time came to finally speak up, you did. In His timing, not yours."

"She's right. I mean, imagine what would have happened had you not been at the fort reporting to Daniel." Anna Mae started pacing, her cup of tea forgotten on the dresser. "First, Martin's name never would have been cleared. But what about Raul's men? How many more cattle would they have taken? Or even worse, what if they were able to figure out Cain's movements and set up an ambush for him? Had you not been at the fort passing along information, Cain and every Ranger under his command could well be dead."

The thought caused the breath to stall in her lungs. Just how much more dangerous would the rustling situation have been over the past two years without her? How many lives had she ended up saving by doing something as simple as passing notes?

"Alejandra dear, none of us are perfect. We all have sin." Ellie set her teacup down and reached for her hand. "But the

Bible says 'Let he who has no sin cast the first stone.' Now, I can't say if the decisions you made were right or wrong, but I know what I see when I look at you."

Ellie raised a finger. "First, you're a child of God, which means you're loved with an everlasting love. And second, you tried your best to do right even though every circumstance in your life was stacked against you. So yes, you sound a lot like Esther to me."

"And I don't imagine Esther had an easy time of it." Anna Mae flipped a wayward strand of hair over her shoulder. "Think about it, she was forced to marry an unbelieving king, and I'm sure there were wicked things that happened in that palace. And it's not as though her husband would have been faithful to her. He had other wives and concubines, even if Esther was his most important wife."

"Can you imagine the backbiting and lying and deceitfulness that would have gone on in that harem among his other wives?" Ellie shook her head. "I'm not sure I could have survived that palace. But then, I don't know that I could have survived two years at Fort Ashton either."

"It's not like Esther was even chosen because her husband liked her as a person or wanted to spend time with her. It was all based on how pretty she was." Anna Mae grimaced, then shook her shoulders in a little shudder. "I can't imagine being forced to marry someone who proposed to me solely because he thought I was pretty."

Alejandra couldn't help but chuckle. If anyone had been proposed to a time too many simply because men thought she was pretty, it was Anna Mae.

"The point, dear, is that Esther would have been surrounded by wicked things in that palace—a palace she had no choice about being in to begin with. She didn't try to stop everything wicked thing she saw. Instead, she waited for God's timing and she acted when He wanted her to."

"Exactly!" Anna Mae threw up her hands, her feet starting to wear a path across the tile floor as she paced. "Other people's sin isn't your fault, so stop carrying around the guilt of it and come downstairs and have dinner with us."

"You know, there was a time when I did the same thing you're doing." Ellie's voice was calm as she spoke, but her hand trembled when she reached for her tea.

"Who's sin?" Alejandra asked. "What happened?"

"Well, you see, I'm illegitimate." Ellie offered her a sad smile. "So are Martin and Leroy and, well, all of my siblings. Our father never married our mother, though we didn't know that for most of our lives. Our mother pretended as though she was wed, but our father was never around."

"Wait. Don't you have eight siblings?" Alejandra sat back in her chair. "Does that mean all of you are illegitimate—but you have the same father?"

She'd never heard of such a thing before.

"There were ten of us in all, and yes, our father was a ship captain with a wife and family of his own in Chicago. My mother was a kept woman that he visited when he was in port."

"Oh. That's... that's almost unbelievable."

"Isn't it? But the point is that I had to learn not to carry around the guilt for my parents' actions. I had to start believing that it wasn't my fault and that I had little control over it. And once I did that, I became a whole lot freer to start loving both God and my husband."

Alejandra stared down into her dark pool of tea. "I see what you're saying."

In fact, if she was able to stop stewing about Raul, stop replaying all the things that had happened over the last two years in her mind, she already knew she'd feel a good deal happier, even with Gabriella and the men still in Mexico.

"So do you think you can let your guilt go?" Ellie asked softly.

Could she? Could she take all the things she'd faced over the past two years and lay them at God's feet? Refuse to carry that burden anymore?

Could she let herself start to hope for a future once again?

Just the idea of it made her feel lighter. "I think... I think I at least need to try."

33

Harrison crouched behind a boulder, his heart hammering against his ribs as yet another series of gunshots rang out from somewhere on the hill below him.

More gunshots answered, these ones fired from one of the Rangers much closer to where he hid. He'd talked Cain into letting him accompany the Rangers while Daniel and his posse started driving the cattle back to the border. He still wasn't sure how he'd managed it, though he suspected it had something to do with Cain wanting someone to attend Gabriella on the trail home.

In fact, that had been the single bit of instruction Cain had given him before the shootout started. *Stay put, and watch for Gabriella. If you spot her, signal me.*

So here he was, hidden behind a boulder at the top of a hill and looking down into a lush green valley with a large ranch while a shootout raged below.

Trouble was, staying behind the boulder turned out to be just about the hardest thing he'd ever done. He might not know anything about positioning sharpshooters or firing pistols with both his left and right hands, but that didn't mean it was easy to sit by while good men were being shot at.

Another burst of gunshots exploded, these ones from farther down the hill.

Harrison peeked around the side of the boulder. Sure enough, the Rangers had moved closer to the ranch, and he now had a clear view of Cain and two other Rangers hiding behind boulders, plus four of Velez's men hiding around the side of what looked to be the bunkhouse.

Cain took aim around the side of the boulder where he crouched, and an instant later, one of Velez's men fell backward.

Harrison scanned the area again, keeping an eye peeled for Gabriella. Or any woman, really, since he wouldn't be able to tell a household maid from Alejandra's sister.

But he hadn't seen a single woman. Not that he should be surprised. Women weren't exactly known for racing headlong into gunfights—well, except for maybe Anna Mae.

The most likely place for Gabriella and the other women was somewhere inside the big house.

Even from a distance, he could tell the house at *La Colina* wasn't like the adobe haciendas at the A Bar W or Fort Ashton. It was a wooden monstrosity with large windows, and it must have cost thousands of dollars to build. Importing that much lumber and glass into the middle of the desert wouldn't be cheap.

Should he try going inside to look for Gabriella? If not, how did Cain intend to find her? He hadn't said, and Harrison hadn't thought to ask.

Another burst of gunshots filled the air, but this time they didn't stop after a minute or two. Instead, the sound turned unrelenting. Just as soon as one gun quieted, a different gun would fire, and he couldn't make hide nor hair over who fired what, and when.

Something pinged the boulder above his head, and he scrambled back behind the craggy rock. Had he been spotted, or was it merely a stray bullet?

It didn't matter. He was here to get Gabriella, and the best place to find her was inside the massive wooden house that loomed over the valley.

He peeked around the side of the boulder again, and when the next burst of gunfire sounded, he ran pell-mell toward another boulder farther down the hill.

Gunshots continued as he worked his way downhill. Cain and his men moved positions twice in the time it took him to reach the boulder closest to the terrace at the back of the house. That had to be a good sign Velez's men weren't able to repel the Rangers.

But what would he find when he went inside? A bevy of men with guns trained on him?

It seemed like the rustlers were firing from the barn and bunkhouse more than the wooden monstrosity in front of him, but Velez could well be holed up somewhere inside—right along with Gabriella.

Harrison drew in a breath, then waited a few minutes until there was an uptick in the shooting. He left his spot behind the rock and dashed forward, his bootsteps overly loud as he raced across the stone terrace and toward the large wooden door at the back of the house.

Dear God, please let it be unlocked.

The door swung open with nothing more than a simple twist of the knob, and Harrison found himself standing at the back of a hallway that ran along a set of elaborate stairs. Most of what he saw was wood, but large windows let in the evening sunlight at both the front and back of the house.

Now where would Gabriella be? In her room, which had to be somewhere upstairs, or below stairs with the maids and other staff?

A banging sounded from deeper inside the house, and Harrison crept forward, his pistol at the ready. The noise was coming from down the hallway, and he followed it until he stood just outside a large wooden door. Through the crack in the opening, he could make out a large, ornate desk and a fireplace on the far wall.

A fireplace with a roaring fire.

In the middle of May.

During a shootout.

He frowned. Something didn't fit.

More banging, more noise, then a low male voice muttered something in Spanish, and a man moved into view carrying a crate that looked to be filled with papers.

The man set the crate down by the fire, picked up a thick stack of papers, and shoved them into the flames.

Harrison sprang through the door, his gun trained on the man's back. "Put your hands up and turn around real slow. Don't even think about reaching for your holster."

The man stiffened, then raised his hands and looked over his shoulder. "You."

"Raul." He wasn't quite sure why he was surprised to find Alejandra's cousin staring back at him. It made perfect sense that he'd want to destroy any incriminating evidence in his father's office while the ranch was under attack. "I said turn around."

Raul did as instructed, a sneer plastered across his face. "What's the matter, Rutherford? Not man enough to join the fight outside with the others? Afraid you might get a little too much dust on your polished boots?"

"I could ask you the same thing." He approached Raul, his steps slow and even. There was an entire mess of papers on the floor that had been hidden by the desk, along with several wooden crates brimming with what looked to be ledgers.

"I suppose I have you to blame for all of this? Don't I? Just couldn't leave Alejandra alone, just couldn't stop snooping. Everything would have been fine if you would have treated her like she deserved."

"I did treat her how she deserved." Harrison inched closer, the barrel of his gun trained straight at Raul's heart. "Maybe your problem is you don't know how to treat a woman. Now keep your hands nice and high, and I just might decide to let you live."

Harrison reached out and plucked the pistol from the holster on the left side of Raul's hip, then the second pistol from the holster on his right side.

He stuffed one of the guns into his empty holster, and another against the waistband at the small of his back. Now he needed something to tie Raul up. He glanced around the office, but found nothing of use.

"What's wrong?" Raul flashed him a taunting smile. "Not sure what to do with me?"

"Oh, I know exactly what to do with you." The heavy drapes by the window were tied back with a sash. That would work. Harrison stepped sideways around the man, making sure not to take his eyes of him as he sidled closer to the curtain.

Raul's gaze narrowed. "What are you doing?"

"Getting something to tie you up with. Seems a bit nicer than shooting you, though I'm not sure you deserve any kindness."

The man made a show of yawning. "Can I at least sit down while I wait?"

Harrison scanned the rug by Raul's feet. He didn't spot anything that could be used as a weapon, and he'd seen both Cain and Daniel let criminals sit before. "As long as you sit right there. Don't get any closer to the desk."

Who knew what weapons might be hidden in those drawers.

"*Gracias.*"

It shouldn't be possible for such a polite word to sound so mean, yet somehow the venom in Raul's voice almost made it sound like he was cursing. But the man settled himself cross-legged on the rug without incident.

It took Harrison the better part of a minute to untie the sash, mainly because he was afraid to move his gun or take his eyes off Raul for more than a second.

Once he secured the sash, he made his way back to Raul.

"Put your hands behind your..."

Of a sudden, Raul grabbed a piece of kindling half sticking out of the fire grate and threw the flaming end at him. Harrison ducked, then fired a shot. It went wide, and Raul lunged toward him. Harrison dove toward the desk, landing almost on top of it and causing Raul to clip his shoulder as he went charging past. Harrison kept hold of his gun, trained it on Raul, and when the man swung back around and charged again, he pulled the trigger.

This time the man jerked, then seemed to freeze for a moment, his eyes going wide as his hands came up to clutch his chest. He fell backward with a thud, bright red blood seeping into his shirt.

Harrison looked down at the gun, then sucked in a breath, trying to find a bit of calm, but the hand holding his pistol wouldn't stop shaking.

So this was what it was like to shoot a man. His heart hammered against his ribs and sweat slicked his palms and brow. How did Cain and Daniel manage it?

He drew in another breath, then...

Wait. Was that smoke he smelled? He glanced around the office, then stilled.

The curtain where he'd untied the sash was covered in flames. The kindling Raul had thrown at him must have landed against the curtain, and the small pitcher of water on the side table wasn't going to be nearly enough to put the fire out.

Even as he watched, the flames raced across the curtain rod at the top of the window and started licking their way up the walls...

Walls that were made entirely from wood.

No adobe, no brick, no tile. Nothing but easily flammable wood.

"Gabriella!" He slid off the desk and reached for the closest crate of ledgers. "Gabriella, are you here? There's a fire. If you can hear me, get out!"

He hefted the crate and raced toward the door, then found himself skidding to a stop as it banged open.

His already too-fast heartbeat doubled as two men with guns appeared in the doorway.

Guns and star-shaped silver badges and cowboy hats.

"What's going on in here?" one of the Rangers asked.

"He was trying to burn the documents." Harrison jutted his chin towards Raul's still body, but didn't dare move more than that since neither of the men had lowered their pistols. "When I tried tying him up, he flung a piece of kindling at me and caught the curtain on fire."

The taller of the two men lowered his gun and stalked toward the desk, where Raul's head and torso were visible.

"Pretty good work for a lawyer." He holstered his gun, then picked up a crate. "Don't just stand there, Bryant, we need to get these papers out."

The other man shoved his gun into his holster and rushed forward. "Sure thing."

"Has anyone found Gabriella?" Harrison asked.

"Gabriella?" the taller Ranger asked.

Bryant elbowed him. "You know. The sister. The one we're supposed to bring back to Texas."

The man shook his head. "Haven't seen hide nor hair of no woman. The gunfight's settling down out there, and Cain sent us in here to search for Velez."

"Velez hasn't been found yet?"

"Nope."

"I'll watch for him while I look for Gabriella. You see to the papers. They're going to hold a mountain of legal evidence, and we can't afford to lose any of it."

Harrison didn't wait for a reply as he set the crate down and dashed through the door.

34

He was close. Cain could feel it in his blood as he crouched behind a wagon, his pistol trained on the door of the barn where the last of the gunshots came from. They'd had the element of surprise on their side when they'd reached *La Colina* a couple hours earlier. He'd even had a chance to set up sharpshooters without anyone on the ranch being wise to it. So while the yard was now littered with bodies, he'd only lost two Rangers.

Another pop of gunshots sounded from the barn—the barn that was completely surrounded by his men.

Cain used the mirror he kept in his breast pocket to signal two of his sharpshooters to move farther down the hill. Then he motioned at one of his men peeking around the side of the barn before looking back at the door.

"Come out with your hands up, and we won't shoot," he said in Spanish.

A bullet pinged the top of the wagon in response.

"You got two choices, either we can come in, which means our guns are firing, or we hold fire while you come out." He didn't know exactly how many men were left inside, but it couldn't be many. Four or five at the most...

And he had over thirty.

Silence was the only response from the darkened doorway. He'd take that as a good sign. If the men were intent on holing up, they'd be raining bullets down on the wagon he hid behind.

"Come out if you want to stay alive. We won't shoot." The Spanish words rolled easily off his tongue.

The door creaked farther open, and Cain motioned to his men hiding around the side of the barn to keep their guns trained on it.

Never knew when a man might decide to come out shooting rather than with his hands up.

But the first man who stepped through the door held his hands high above his head, his face white with fear. Then again, calling him a man was probably a bit generous. He looked far too young to be wielding a gun in a shootout.

"Come out, all of you. I want to see each one of you." Cain stayed crouched behind the wagon. He wasn't about to stand up when the next person who came through the door might well have a gun trained on him. He'd seen more than one Ranger killed that-a-way over the years.

Another man appeared in the doorway with his hands up. He stepped slowly into the dying sunlight, followed by another man, and another and another. Five came out in all, only three of which looked wizened enough to be caught in a gunfight. The other two were more boy than man, and it made his jaw clench.

Velez had no business drawing people that age into his criminal behavior.

If he ever got his hands on the man, it would be all he could do not to put a bullet in his heart. And truth be told, the man probably deserved worse.

But he'd seen no sign of Velez—unless he was in the house

and Rollins and Bryant had captured him. He'd have his men do a thorough search as soon as they finished with the barn, just in case the weasel had a hole somewhere inside where he was hiding.

"Is that everyone?" he asked the men standing in front of the barn.

All five of them nodded.

Cain stood from behind the wagon and motioned to two of his Rangers to start tying the prisoners up, then gave the signal for more of his men to search the barn.

Of a sudden, a magnificent black horse barreled out of the barn, carrying a large man.

Velez.

Cain didn't need to see a daguerreotype of the man to know this was *"el jefe."* Gold edged the man's coat, and the leather of the saddle was so polished it reflected the dying light.

Cain aimed his pistol at the man's chest, then dropped it to the horse and fired.

A second later, another shot rang out. Probably Simon—his best sharpshooter—making certain the horse was dead.

"Don't move or the next bullet goes in your head." Cain raced toward the man who was trying to pull his leg out from beneath where the dead horse had fallen.

Velez looked up, a sneer plastered across his face as he spoke in Spanish. "You'll never be able to prove it."

"Prove what?" It was the first time he answered in English, and he made sure to let the twang of his Texan accent ring through his voice.

The man's eyes widened. "You're Texan."

He didn't know who Velez was expecting, only that his enemies must be numerous if he'd thought someone else had brought three dozen well-trained men to a shootout. "I am, and I intend to make sure you pay for each and every cow you stole from the Texan side of the border. If that means I have to drag your sorry hide all the way back to Twin Rivers for trial, then so be it."

"Captain," someone called from behind him. "The house is on fire!"

Cain jerked his head toward the massive wooden house that towered over the valley. Smoke billowed out the windows, and the flames licking at one section of wall had almost reached the roof.

"No!" Velez wailed, trying to scramble away from the horse still pinning his leg. "Not my house! You have to put it out."

It was too far gone to be put out, especially with the entire thing being wood. "Is anyone inside?"

The man shrugged. "How should I know?"

Cain cocked his gun and pointed it directly at Velez's heart. "Think about it, because if you tell me no, and I send my men inside and they find someone you forgot to mention, I won't bother taking you to jail. I'll shoot you dead here and now."

"My son," he blurted. "My second son, Raul. He might be in my office, but that's where the fire seems the worst."

"Maybe he spotted the flames and got out." Cain wasn't about to send his men into the worst of the fire for the likes of Raul. But not all of the house had succumbed to flames yet. "Anyone else in there? Think hard."

The man swallowed. "I... ah... the maids. They're probably inside. Maybe hiding in the servants' quarters. And my niece. She'll be in there somewhere too."

"Gabriella," Cain muttered. "Handy, come tie up Velez. Keep him separate from the others."

The Ranger rushed over, unlocking the handcuffs from his belt as he ran. The second he reached Velez, Cain raced toward the burning house.

XXX

THE SMOKE WAS THICK, nearly filling the second floor of the house by the time Harrison clambered back down the stairs and started off in the direction he hoped was the kitchen.

"Gabriella," he called. "Are you in here?"

She couldn't be upstairs. He'd looked in every room and searched half the closets and still hadn't found her. By now she'd have to smell the smoke if she was anywhere on the second floor.

Which she might have done, and then ran out of the house while he'd been searching another room, never mind the fact that he'd constantly called her name.

But once he was away from the part of the house that was burning, the smoke on the first floor wasn't very thick. Someone hiding below stairs might not be able to smell it.

"Gabriella," he shouted as he passed the formal dining room and raced down a long hallway toward what he hoped was the kitchen. "Hello? Is anyone inside? The house is on fire."

The hallway seemed to go on forever, but he finally reached the kitchen, and there, in the back corner, was a staircase leading down, likely to the servant's quarters. Fortunately, the staircase was only a few feet away from a door leading outside.

An eerie crackling and groaning resonated from some-where down the hallway.

Crash! The house shook with the force of something crumbling. Harrison didn't want to think about what that might mean, so he dashed down the stairs, then skidded around the corner at the bottom of the stairway.

And there she was, standing in the hallway. She looked just like her sister, with dark hair falling in waves down her shoulders. Her face was the same shape as her sister's too, with a wider forehead that tapered into high cheekbones and a delicate jaw.

She hadn't spotted him yet. She was too busy looking up at the ceiling with a puzzled expression on her face. He'd bet his saddle she'd heard the crash and come to investigate. And he'd been right about the smoke not making its way down there yet.

"Gabriella," he croaked, his voice still rough from inhaling too much smoke on the second floor.

She startled and looked at him, then clenched her shawl tighter around her shoulders and shrank back. "Do I know you?"

He shook his head. "No, but I know your sister, Alejandra. You look just like her."

Especially her eyes. If he looked just at them, he could almost swear he was staring at Alejandra.

Gabriella scanned him from top to bottom, her back stiff. "If my sister sent you, then what are you doing in my uncle's house? I'm sure he didn't let you in."

"The gunfight. I rode down with the Rangers from Texas to deal with the rustling. But there's a fire upstairs. I need to get you out." He looked over her shoulder and down the long, empty hallway. "Is anyone else hiding down here? Everyone has to evacuate."

"The shooting was you?"

He blinked. Had she not heard that bit about the fire? "My friends. I'm a lawyer."

"And you know Alejandra?"

"Know her, love her, hope to marry her. Now let's go."

Unfortunately, his statement only seemed to root her feet to the floor. "You... you love my sister?" She searched his face with wide, vulnerable eyes—eyes that felt exactly like her sister's.

And he couldn't stop a small smile from creeping onto his face. "With all my heart. Even to the point that it hurts at times."

Crash! Another crash sounded from upstairs, causing tremors to ripple through the house.

Gabriella clutched a hand to her throat and stared back up at the ceiling. "Is that the fire?"

"Yes, now let's go."

"Wait. There are others. The maids and cook." She took off down the hallway.

Harrison would have followed, but bootsteps thundered down the stairs behind him. He pulled out his pistol and whirled around, only to find Cain rounding the corner, his gun already drawn.

They stood there for a moment, blinking at each other before Cain grinned and holstered his pistol. "Looks like you found everyone."

Cain jutted his chin down the hall, and Harrison turned to find Gabriella emerging from one of the rooms with a half dozen women.

Cain stuck his fingers in his mouth and let out a sharp whistle. "Hurry up. We don't have long before the roof collapses."

The women started to run, and he and Cain moved to the side of the hallway.

"The papers?" Harrison asked as the women rushed past. "Did Rollins and Bryant get them out?"

Cain gave a sharp nod. "Every last one."

"And the rustlers?"

"Either dead or captured, even Velez."

Dead or captured. The words took a moment to sink in. That meant there was no one to blackmail or bribe Alejandra, no one to keep her separated from Gabriella or force her to do something against her will.

No one to tell her they couldn't marry when he returned to Twin Rivers.

Cain pushed himself off the wall, but before he took a step toward the stairs, Harrison launched himself at Cain, locking his arms around his lanky friend and refusing to let go.

Cain stiffened and glared down at him. "What are you doing?"

"Saying thank you."

"You sure got a womanly way of doing it, especially with a house about to collapse on us."

"Still wanted to say thanks." Harrison gave him another tight squeeze, then he released Cain and dashed up the stairs and out the door—with a fuming Cain on his heels.

35

"Come on, Alejandra." Anna Mae gestured to the fishing poles leaning against the arch just inside the door of Wes and Keely's hacienda. "You can't just stay cooped up at the ranch day in and day out. Some fresh air will do you good."

"I can get fresh air right here." She dug her boot into the soft dirt of the courtyard. She'd been planning to tend the plants after breakfast. The Westins had the loveliest display of flowers in their courtyard, and though they required a lot of watering, in her opinion, the colorful blooms were well worth the work.

"Are we ready?" Charlotte said as she came up to where they stood.

Anna Mae rolled her eyes. "Alejandra wants to spend the day watering plants."

Keely held Madeline as she and Ellie came down the stairs, both of them dressed in lightweight, long-sleeved gowns to protect them from the sun out on the desert.

Had everyone known about the fishing trip except her?

Charlotte gently prodded the stalk of an orchid with her

shoe. "I know the plants are pretty, but surely you can use a day out? It's not doing any of us good to sit around all day wondering what's happening in Mexico."

Alejandra sighed. It had been five days since the men had left. At the very least, it seemed like someone should have returned to Twin Rivers by now with a bit of news. But here they were, with everyone from the entire Owens clan plus her and Charlotte all holed up at the A Bar W, getting antsier and antsier with each hour that passed. "I already left my room. Doesn't that count?"

"No." Ellie came up behind her. "That was only the first step."

"The creek isn't very far." Keely gave Madeline a little bounce on her hip. "And Dobbs is going to accompany us. It will be perfectly safe."

Alejandra looked around at her friends. Each one of them was smiling. Each one seemed excited to leave the ranch. And she had to admit, going for a little ride, then dipping her toes in the cool water of a stream did sound nice.

"Fine." Alejandra peeled off her gardening gloves. "But I still want to work in here when we get back."

Ellie smiled and looped their arms together. "This is going to be fun, you'll see."

She didn't doubt it would be fun. The truth was, since Ellie had coaxed her from the bedroom three days ago, she'd managed to enjoy herself. Ellie's siblings provided an endless stream of chatter and busyness. Yesterday, Keely had given her a grand tour of the house, then handed her a broom and sworn her to secrecy about sweeping some of the dusty guest rooms. Why sweeping had to be a secret, she didn't know, but she'd enjoyed visiting with the shy redhead as they'd cleaned.

After dinner each night, the lot of them had climbed the mountain behind the house to watch the sun set and wait for the stars.

And yet, she still couldn't stop herself from worrying about Harrison and Gabriella, about Cain and his Rangers, about her friends' husbands, all of whom were in Mexico.

The Rangers must have reached *La Colina* by now, but had *Tío* Javier been warned they were coming? If so, had he sent Gabriella somewhere deeper inside Mexico? Was that the delay?

"You're doing it again." Ellie jostled her arm as they walked through the wide, arched doors at the front of the hacienda.

"Doing what?"

"Worrying about things you have no control over."

"At least I'm not blaming myself for them," Alejandra muttered.

Ellie smiled. "That's a good improvement, isn't it?"

"It really is." After Anna Mae and Ellie had left her room the other day, she'd sat down on her bed and read the book of Esther—and found every word of what Ellie and Anna Mae had said was true. There must have been much about palace life that made Esther uncomfortable, but rather than blaming herself for being in a situation that didn't honor God, the young queen had found a way to serve Him anyway.

After she'd finished reading, Alejandra had gotten onto her knees and prayed.

And prayed.

And prayed some more.

She's asked God to forgive her for things she could have done better.

She'd asked God to help her move on from the past.

And she'd asked God to protect everyone in Mexico.

By the time she'd risen from the side of her bed and gone downstairs to join everyone for dinner, her heart had felt light and her spirit at peace.

Thank you, Father, for Your goodness to me. Alejandra drew in a breath of warm desert air as she stepped outside, then scanned the cloudless landscape.

She was about to walk down the steps with Ellie when she paused. "Is that a rider coming toward the house?"

Ellie narrowed her eyes at the small cloud of dust in the distance. "I think so. Keely, there's a rider," she called.

The women in front of them stopped and scanned the horizon, then turned back toward the house just as Dobbs appeared in the door of the barn.

"I need you ladies to get back in the house and bar the door," the ranch hand called.

"Of course." Ellie still kept their arms linked as they turned and headed back inside. The other women joined them while ranch hands flooded out of the barn.

One of the men followed them up the steps, then closed the doors behind them. "Bar it from the inside," he said through the thick wood. "And don't open the door unless you recognize the speaker's voice."

"The parlor has a good window." Anna Mae's face lit with excitement. "I'm going to go see who it is."

"Ah... if they want the door barred, we should probably stay back from the windows," Keely called.

But Anna Mae had already disappeared around the corner.

Alejandra dropped Ellie's arm. "I'm going too."

"Wait. It might be dangerous if you're seen," Keely protested.

"And it might be Harrison!" She whirled on her heel and raced into the parlor.

By the time she reached Anna Mae at the window, a band of five of Wes's men had appeared on horseback in the yard between the barn and the house. "Do you think it's Harrison?"

"I think it's someone in an awful hurry to get here." Anna Mae's eyes were riveted on the approaching riders. "Those horses are flying."

Alejandra looked closer, and sure enough there wasn't just one horse stirring up the cloud of dust, but three. They raced through the gateposts marking the official entrance to the ranch.

But was the rider on the third horse wearing a dress? And was that a long black braid flying out behind her?

The two men had hats pulled low on their heads, shielding their faces so they couldn't be identified. Yet there was no mistaking the long hair and dress of the third rider.

And that could only mean one thing. "Gabriella."

Alejandra left the window and raced around the corner. She dashed past Ellie, Keely, and Charlotte and lifted the heavy beam from the door, sending it clattering to the floor as she heaved one of the doors open.

"Gabriella," she shouted. It had to be her sister.

"Alejandra, wait," someone called from behind her, but she paid them no mind as she sprang down the stairs.

"Harrison and Daniel!" she yelled louder.

The horses were coming to a stop near the line of Wes's men, and she was close enough to make out all of the riders.

"Gabriella!"

Her sister's head whipped in her direction. "Alejandra?"

Gabriella slid off the horse and raced toward her.

They met in the middle of the yard, their arms wrapping around each other. Alejandra squeezed her sister, hugging her so hard she nearly forgot how to let go. Gabriella's hair was still long and silky, but it had darkened into the exact same shade as her own in their years apart. And she had grown taller and filled out too, her lithe body developing womanly curves.

Alejandra clasped her closer, burying her face in her sister's hair. "I thought I'd never see you again. But you're here and safe, so very safe. And I just..."

Tears clogged her throat, so she tightened her arms around

Gabriella even more and pressed her eyes shut. *Thank you, Father.*

All this time, she'd hoped and wondered and prayed, but she'd been too afraid to imagine what their meeting might be like, too worried that if she hoped too much, she'd only end up devastated when her sister was married off and taken to Mexico City.

"*Sí,* I'm here and safe." Gabriella's slender hands rested against her back, her touch feather soft.

"I was so worried."

Gabriella gave her a gentle pat. "Silly sister, you're always so worried about me, even when you're the one in more danger."

"I wasn't in that much danger." She closed her eyes again, drinking in every last detail about her sister. Her scent, the feel of her body, the softness of her hair, and the way she still seemed so very familiar even after two years.

"Not in that much danger?" Gabriella made a small tsking sound. "Your beau tells a different story. He says you're the reason they figured out *Tío* Javier was behind the rustling. That you worked to stop the cattle from being driven over the border most of the time you were here. Are you trying to tell me that wasn't dangerous?"

"Well, maybe I was in a bit of danger. But you were so far away, and betrothed to *Señor* Montrose—"

"And you were in Texas with Raul and Felipe." Her sister pulled back far enough to look up into her face, her brow drawn down. "I wouldn't have been able to survive it."

The words caused tears to brim in her eyes. Had it really been that difficult of a situation? She'd never stopped to question it. She'd always just squared her shoulders and tried to find a way to survive.

"Raul wouldn't give me your letters," she whispered. "I think that was the hardest part."

"What?" Shock filled Gabriella's eyes.

"He stopped letting me read them last fall, and I didn't get any of them until Harrison arrived at the fort."

Gabriella's lips twisted into a scowl, and she planted her hands on her hips. "Oh, I'm glad he's dead, and don't scold me for saying it either."

"He's dead?" Alejandra blinked at her.

"Yes," Daniel said from behind her. "You can thank Harrison for that."

Alejandra looked over her shoulder to find both Daniel and Harrison standing there. They were covered in dust, just like Gabriella, but the second she turned his direction, Harrison opened his arms.

"Come here, love."

She wasn't sure if he spoke loud enough for anyone else to hear, but she couldn't resist his arms. She stepped to him, letting him fold her in his warmth and strength while she linked her arms around his back. "Thank you for bringing her back."

"I promised you I would, didn't I?"

She gave her head a small shake. "I wasn't sure I could believe it."

"Those days are over and done now." He tucked her head beneath his chin and tightened his hold, making her entire body feel as though it was wrapped in warmth. "You don't need to be afraid to hope for the best anymore."

"Harrison here caught Raul trying to burn all of your uncle's papers and ended up saving the evidence," Daniel said from behind her.

"You did?" She searched the familiar lines and angles of Harrison's face, studying every last feature of the man she loved.

"I did, but I'm afraid I had to shoot Raul in the process. I didn't want to kill him, but I didn't have much of a choice."

She reached up and pressed a palm to the side of his face. "Don't feel guilty, Harrison, please."

"What about her uncle?" A voice said from behind her. "Is he dead too?"

Alejandra looked toward the sound of the voice, only to find that Anna Mae and the others had come into the yard. The ranch hands had all moved closer too, the lot of them standing around her and Harrison and Gabriella in a haphazard sort of circle.

"Our uncle is in jail where he belongs," Gabriella spat.

"He is?" Alejandra took a step back from Harrison and looked between her sister and Daniel.

"Yes." Harrison straightened to his full height, his voice taking on a lawyerly tone. "He's awaiting trial down in Mexico. Those papers Raul was trying to burn ended up proving your uncle was involved in a lot more than just the cattle rustling. Cain is turning everything over to the State of Chihuahua, and your uncle's going to be locked up for a long, long time—if he doesn't face the death penalty first."

"But that means..." She twisted her skirt in her hands as the implications of what Harrison said sank in. "That means... I can stay in Twin Rivers. And so can Gabriella. And we can all be together and..."

She leapt right back into his arms.

"Yes!" She couldn't help the grin that spread over her face. "We can get married now, right? My answer is yes! I want to marry you. Yes, yes, yes, yes, yes!"

Harrison chuckled, low and hearty, his arms coming up to wrap her in another hug. "I haven't asked you yet, love."

"But when you do, I'll say yes."

"Oh, don't be a dolt!" Anna Mae said from behind her. "Get down on one knee and ask her now."

Laughter erupted from around them, but Harrison looked

over her shoulder and narrowed his eyes at Anna Mae. "That's not something a man does with an audience."

Anna Mae rolled her eyes. "Everyone knows the two of you are going to get hitched. You might as well just get the asking over."

Harrison tightened his grip around her and looked down, his eyes filled with kindness and love. "I'm afraid I need a bath and a meal first, but after that, would you like to go on a stroll with me?"

Warmth unfurled in her heart, then spiraled outward until it reached the tips of her fingers and bottoms of her toes. "I would love to."

XXX

IT TOOK HALF the day to get Alejandra alone with him. They'd been eating breakfast when Wes had arrived with the cattle, which meant he'd needed to go to the sheriff's office and draw up plea agreements and a few other documents for the criminals to sign. He'd left Wes and Daniel to work out how to get the stolen cattle back to the ranches north of them, while he'd headed to Fort Ashton to figure out where he could use the two maids from *La Colina* who'd wanted to leave Mexico with Gabriella.

By the time he finally made it back to the A Bar W and invited Alejandra on a walk, it was nearing supper time, and the sun had already started tracking west against the sky.

"It's the prettiest view, isn't it?" Alejandra stared out over the valley where the Rio Grande meandered in a snake-like pattern along the border between Texas and Mexico. On the other side of the river, a wall of mountains broke free from the desert, towering so high they almost touched the sky. The waning sun cast pink and orange shadows against the rockface, making the landscape even more beautiful than it usually was.

Harrison pulled Alejandra into his arms and stared down at her. "Yes, the view is quite breathtaking. In fact, I think it's one of the most beautiful things I've ever seen."

Pink rose in her cheeks, and he took a strand of hair and tucked it behind her ear, then placed a kiss on her cheek.

"I was so worried about you in Mexico," she whispered.

"I'm here, alive and safe."

She pressed her lips together, her eyes searching his face. "Gabriella said you had a showdown with Raul, then searched the house to find her and the others while it was burning. I don't even want to think how much danger you were in."

"Then that makes two of us." He dropped his head until their foreheads touched. "Because I don't want to think about how much danger you were in the entire time you were at Fort Ashton, getting information from Raul only so that you could turn around and pass notes to Daniel. I would have stopped it in a heartbeat—if I'd known."

She pulled away from him and drew in a breath. "After you left, I was feeling guilty about not telling you everything sooner, but then Ellie and Anna Mae talked to me, and I realized I couldn't blame myself for things I had no control over."

He reached out and took her shoulders in a gentle hold, then waited for her eyes to come up and meet his. "Not one single part of it is your fault. Do you understand?"

She nodded. "I... I see that now. Though at the time..."

"That part of your life is done and over. I promise you, Alejandra, here and now, that I will give my last breath before ever allowing you to be used and manipulated by another person like your uncle."

She stepped into the fold of his arms and laid her head on his chest. "It wasn't your fault either. You realize that, right?"

"I..." He swallowed. So maybe he was a little too eager to blame himself for not figuring out what was going on. "I just hate what happened to you, and I want to make sure it never happens again. I want to stand beside you, day in and day out, every day, protecting you from anyone else who might do you harm. Will you let me do that? Will you...?"

He drew in a breath, then sank down to one knee. "Will you marry me?"

"Oh, Harrison..."

Delight filled her eyes, but only for a moment. Then her face grew serious, and she sank to the ground next to him. "You don't have to propose just because I said I'd marry you earlier. I was excited to see you home and be with Gabriella and hear that *Tío* Javier is going to prison. But I never meant to force you into doing something you don't want."

"Something I don't want?" He blinked at her. "Have you gone daft? I love you. The entire time I was in Mexico, I was planning on proposing to you the moment I returned to Twin Rivers, because I want nothing more than to spend the rest of my life with you."

But his declaration of love still didn't bring a smile to her face. Instead, she looked away from him, staring across the valley to the mountains in the distance. "You realize I won't ever make you a fancy wife, not even if I try hard. When I think of you going to San Antonio to be an important judge, I only see myself only holding you back. A Texan and *Tejano* marrying might not be so uncommon on the border, but we both know it's different in the cities. In San Antonio, you'll be invited to fancy parties and private dinners and—"

"I'm not going to San Antonio, love." He sat back on the ground then pulled her into his arms, settling her between his two open legs. "Not that I think you'd hold me back if I went, but I've decided to stay. Twin Rivers needs a prosecuting attor-ney, which means I'll be seeing to the prosecution of the lot of men currently sitting in the jailhouse. I can do that while still managing Fort Ashton. And with your cousin dead and your uncle wanted for crimes on both sides of the border, it's safe for you and Gabriella to stay here too."

He leaned down, pausing when his lips were only a breath away from hers. "Let me show you what it's like to be cherished and loved."

He didn't wait for an answer as he brushed his lips against hers, the gesture soft and tender. She sighed into the kiss, her body melting into his.

He was half inclined to gather her closer and deepen the kiss, but he pulled away instead, just far enough to peer down into the familiar depths of her eyes. "Let me make you happy, Alejandra. Live here with me on the desert and make a life with me. One that includes your sister and a passel of our own children and our friends. One that includes so much love and contentment that my heart feels full just thinking about it."

She smiled up at him. "Do you know, I remember walking to church all those weeks ago, wishing that one day I'd be able to feel like I was part of a town somewhere, that I'd have friends and family surrounding me. Wishing that one day God would give me a place I belonged. But I never expected God to let me stay here, with you and Gabriella. And now... now I never even need to leave."

"Of course you don't need to leave."

She reached up and framed his face with her hands. "Yes, Harrison, I'll marry you. I want nothing more than to build a life together with you."

Lightness filled his chest, and he grinned right back at her, then swept her into his arms, tilted her back, and kissed her the way a man was supposed to kiss the woman he intended to marry.

EPILOGUE

Harrison repositioned his hat on his head as he stared down at the marble tombstone in front of him.

Here Lies Bartholomew Rutherford.

That was all it said. Harrison hadn't been able to think of anything else to put on it. Certainly not that he was a loving father, or that he'd been respected in the community. About the only thing he could say was that his father had died rich, and that wasn't the type of thing one put on a headstone.

His father had been buried for over two months, but the headstone was still new enough the desert dust had yet to strip its shine or dull the crisp edges of the words etched into it.

Even with the doc knowing how his father had been poisoned, he'd been given too much methanal for anything to be done. His father had still been alive when Harrison had returned from Mexico, but he didn't wake once for the three days until he passed.

"I should have guessed this is where you'd be."

Harrison looked up to find Alejandra ambling up the mountain trail toward him. Behind her, at the base of the mountain, sat Fort Ashton with its endless stream of travelers.

"Most people don't make a habit of visiting another person's grave daily."

He was silent as he reached out his hand for her, and when she placed her slender palm in his, he tugged her against him. "I know."

"Are you all right, Harrison? Truly? I know you and your father weren't close, but sometimes it seems like you almost mourn him more than you would if you had been."

"I think maybe I'm mourning the parts I wanted to change, the way I wish things would have been." Indeed, there was part of him that wished he would have come to Twin Rivers several months sooner. Maybe then his father would still be alive, and the rustlers would have been caught before the end of April. But he could hardly complain about the life he had now, married to Alejandra and watching her and Gabriella grow closer every day.

He drew his wife into a deeper embrace and inhaled the scent of her, then frowned. "Aren't you back a bit early from fishing?"

Alejandra leaned back just far enough to look up into his face. "Anna Mae never showed up. She was supposed to meet us with the fishing poles, but something must have come up, because we waited at the creek for over an hour."

"She's seemed a little off lately. I think she's struggling, what with her parents in Houston."

"Call me crazy, but I think she really enjoyed baking things for the Rangers. Now that they're gone, she seems bored."

"Maybe that's it."

The Rangers had ridden out of town after the trials had wrapped up, which was almost six weeks ago now.

"If you're not fishing with Anna Mae, then it seems like you have a bit of free time." Harrison tugged Alejandra deeper into his arms. "I just might have an idea of how we can spend it."

She giggled. "Um, don't you have to be back at the trading post when lunch is over? This is Fordham's day off."

"I can get someone to fill in." He nuzzled her neck, then dropped a kiss at the gentle curve where her neck and shoulder met.

She sucked in a breath, then smacked at his arm. "You just did that last week! Remember? You said you wanted to take me on a picnic, but eating was *not* what we spent most of our time doing."

He smiled at the memory. "Maybe we should make a habit of it. At least once a week I'll take a half day off so I can spend extra time with my wife. Or maybe I should make it twice a week? Three times?"

"If you keep playing hooky to spend time with me, you're going to become known as the boss who's never at work." But in spite of her protests, a giant grin had worked its way over her face.

"And here I thought I'd become known as the man who loved his wife."

She pushed up on her tiptoes and looped her hands around his neck. "I don't suppose that would be such a bad thing, would it?"

"I certainly don't think so." He bent his head, and their lips brushed briefly before he settled his mouth on hers.

No. There was no such thing as spending too much time with Alejandra, not now that she was his wife in full.

Had someone told him six months ago that he would be happier in Twin Rivers than he'd ever been during all his years in Austin, he would have laughed.

And yet here he was, standing on a mountain with the woman he loved in his arms, looking down at the sprawling adobe fort that he owned, watching his wife make up lost time with her sister whenever possible...

And feeling the blessings of God on his life every single day.

A man couldn't ask for anything more.

A NOTE FROM NAOMI:

Wow, isn't it nice to see Harrison and Alejandra in such a happy place? Feeling the blessings of God in their lives every day? I also love how everyone is safe at Fort Ashton, even Gabriella. I don't know about you, but I'm convinced there will be a lot of bright, wonderful days ahead for both Alejandra and Harrison.

I'm also glad Alejandra's uncle, Javier, finally ended up prison where he belongs...

But how long will he stay there? Can a man as powerful as Javier Velez really be confined by a few prison bars? I have a feeling he just might make a reappearance in the next novel, and the town of Twin Rivers might not be ready to feel the full force of his wrath—especially Anna Mae and Cain.

Speaking of Cain and Anna Mae, will they the feelings growing between them ever get sorted out? Or will Cain's commitment to the Rangers and insecurities about his upbringing doom the relationship between them that Anna Mae so desperately wants?

Their story, **Tomorrow's Lasting Joy,** is coming in April, 2023. It will have Rangers and rustling and romance, family dinners and beautiful sunsets and homemade doughnuts, and so much more. I hope you'll join me for the final book in the Texas Promise Series.

Preorder *Tomorrow's Lasting Joy*!

(You can also turn the page for a sneak peek.)

TOMORROW'S LASTING JOY

Twin Rivers, Texas; July 1886She was going to die.

Anna Mae stared down at the giant wound on her ankle and tried to suck in a breath of air, but breathing only seemed to make her lungs constrict.

Calm down. You have to calm down. You won't be able to get yourself out of this mess if you panic.

But she was starting to think getting herself out of the mess she was currently in wasn't going to happen at all, regardless of whether she panicked.

She inched herself a little higher, letting the rocky wall of the outcropping where she was hiding support her back, and stared out at the mountains surrounding her.

It would normally be a pretty view, the kind she could look at for hours, taking in the majesty around her. Bald, rocky peaks jutted up toward a brilliantly blue sky, while the pinks, yellows, and grays of the mountains almost made the rocks themselves look like a gentle, streaked sunset.

But seeing how she hadn't come across a single person since she'd taken the turnoff onto the narrow mountain trail yesterday morning, the view before her only made a sad type of desperation spring up in her chest.

She was almost out of water, she couldn't walk on her ankle to search for a creek, and if she left the little outcropping where she was hiding, there was a good chance she'd be found by the wrong men.

Which meant her odds of surviving another night in the desert were nonexistent.

She gritted her teeth against the fiery wave of heat in her ankle, then leaned her head back against the warm sandstone wall behind her.

Maybe, instead of thinking about all the things that had gone wrong, she should think about what had gone right over the past week.

She should probably count it a success that she'd survived as long as she had.

And she should count it a success that the men who'd kidnapped her outside of Fort Ashton five days ago hadn't killed her right away.

She could even count it a success that after three days of her kidnappers taking her deeper and deeper into Mexico, she'd been able to steal a horse and rifle and escape.

In fact, if a woman was going to be kidnapped, everything about her situation had seemed downright successful—right up until she'd been bitten by a rattlesnake yesterday afternoon.

She crumpled her skirt in her hands, pulling it up just far enough to look down at the dirty, burning cut. After she'd been bitten, she'd hobbled to the little outcropping above the mountain trail and lain down, tucked securely out of view from anyone who might search for her. And she'd sent the horse away, since trying to keep it was more likely to lead the *desperadoes* who'd kidnapped her right back to where she was hiding.

Then she'd taken a knife to the bite, hoping to cut out the venom before her ankle swelled overmuch.

But now she wasn't sure taking a knife to her skin had ended up better than leaving the rattler venom inside her. A thin rim of white was growing around the edge of the cut, surrounded by puffy pink skin that felt tender to the touch. The inside of the cut burned as though it was on fire, and the whole thing had swelled up just as big as it would have without trying to cut the venom out.

Dear God... She slid down the sandstone wall until she lay on the single blanket she had—the one she'd taken off the horse before sending him away. *Dear Father, please...*

But the rest of the words wouldn't come.

What should she pray for? Rain?

The sky was a brilliant blue above. There'd be no rain today, and she didn't have enough water to last until tomorrow, when there was a slim chance rain might form over the mountains in the afternoon.

She couldn't pray for rescue either, not in such a remote stretch of desert.

At the time of her escape, getting far away from the large trail that ran from Chihuahua to San Antonio had seemed like a smart choice. After all, it was sure to be the first place her kidnappers looked for her.

But it was the first place her brother Daniel, the sheriff of Twin Rivers, would look for her too. And after being gone from Twin Rivers for five days, he and his friends were sure to be searching for her.

Maybe she shouldn't have done such a good job of getting away from the trail after all. It was almost as though this stretch of desert, with its wild and craggy mountains, had been forgotten about by every living person.

She pulled up her skirt a bit more, then stared down at the red lines streaking from her wound up her leg, inching ever closer to her heart. If only she had something to clean the wound with, but she couldn't afford to even dribble a few drops of water onto it, not when she needed every last bit of water for herself.

Sweat beaded on her forehead, and she slid her tongue out in an attempt to moisten her cracked lips, only to find her tongue itself was too dry for that. Her stomach was starting to feel ill too, and her head had been pounding for several hours —sure signs that the heat itself was making her sick.

She rolled onto her side, wincing at the burst of pain in her leg, but managing to shift just enough to look up at the scorching sun from beneath the shaded outcropping of rock.

Should she ask God to spare her life for another day? Or was it pointless even to try?

Preorder *Tomorrow's Lasting Joy*!

AUTHOR'S NOTE:

When South Texans returned to the border region near the Gulf of Mexico known as the Nueces Strip after the Civil War, they found the area overrun with rustlers who would run cattle south of the border, where the livestock would forever be lost to the Texan ranchers. The problem was so bad that Austin created the Texas Rangers, the first and oldest state police force in the United States to date.

There were also times when both the U.S. Army and the Rangers crossed the border without consent of the Mexican government to apprehend criminals. The Mexican government didn't have much infrastructure in place to maintain law and order in the vast, sparsely inhabited desert that ran along its northern border. Furthermore, the people who had lived in that region for years didn't think anything of crossing a river and moving between countries without much by way of customs or border security. So even though an incident like Cain's trip into Mexico would gain national attention today, in the late 1800s, if someone committed a big enough crime in Texas and crossed the border, Texas law enforcement would likely follow the criminal and bring him back to the U.S.

without anyone in either the Mexican or American govern-ments caring.

The fictional version of this situation that I created in **Tomorrow's Steadfast Prayer** put both Alejandra and Harrison in a difficult situation for most of the story. When I started this novel, I wanted to write a story about two people who did right regardless of the sacrifices they had to make. But the story grew to be more than that, because as I started writing, I realized Alejandra and Harrison also saw their problems as the things that were wrong with their lives that they needed to fix. But in reality, neither of them had the power to fix anything, because they were caught up in the messes that other people had caused.

Isn't that what life is really like? I wish difficult situations and problems only affected the people responsible for creating them, but how many children suffer because of parents' poor choices? How many parents suffer because of their grown children's poor choices?

Sometimes it's easy to see only the problems with our own situation, like health, finances, etc. But God doesn't always ask us to change those circumstances. And He doesn't always give us the ability to change them either. Instead, He asks us to try our best, to honor Him, to do right, even if we are caught up in all the bad. You see, God never tells us to live in a perfect world. He doesn't tell us to live stress-free or have the cleanest house or nicest yard on our block.

He just asks us to do right, whether the things around us are going well or whether our entire world is burning down. That's the message I tried to illustrate with Harrison and Alejandra's story. I hope you find it both encouraging and inspiring.

Tomorrow's Steadfast Prayer: © Naomi Mason 2022

Cover Design: © Clarissa Yeo 2018

Cover Photographs: Shutterstock.com

Editors: Erin Healy; Roseanna White

OTHER NOVELS BY NAOMI RAWLINGS

Texas Promise Series

Book 1—*Tomorrow's First Light* (Sam and Ellie)
Book 2—*Tomorrow's Shining Dream* (Daniel and Charlotte)
Book 3—*Tomorrow's Constant Hope* (Wes and Keely: releasing 2021)
Book 4—*Tomorrow's Steadfast Prayer* (Harrison and Alejandra)
Book 5—*Tomorrow's Lasting Joy* (Cain and Anna Mae)

Eagle Harbor Series

Book 1—*Love's Unfading Light* (Mac and Tressa)
Book 2—*Love's Every Whisper* (Elijah and Victoria)
Book 3—*Love's Sure Dawn* (Gilbert and Rebekah)
Book 4—*Love's Eternal Breath* (Seth and Lindy)
Book 5—Love's Christmas Hope (Thomas and Jessalyn)
Book 6—*Love's Bright Tomorrow* (Isaac and Aileen)
Short Story—*Love's Beginning* (Elijah, Gilbert, Mac, Victoria, Rebekah)
Prequel—*Love's Violet Sunrise* (Hiram and Mabel)

Belanger Family Saga

Book 1—*The Lady's Refuge*(Michel and Isabelle)
Book 2—*The Widow's Secret* (Jean Paul and Brigitte)
Book 3—*The Reluctant Enemy*(Gregory and Danielle)

ABOUT THE AUTHOR

USA Today bestseller Naomi Rawlings writes sweeping historical novels. She is the author of over 14 books spread across three different series. She lives with her husband and three children in Michigan's rugged Upper Peninsula, along the southern shore of Lake Superior where they get 25 feet of snow every winter, and where people still grow their own vegetables and cut down their own firewood—just like in the historical novels she writes. In each and every one of her books, she loves taking readers back to a time when things were simpler and neighbors knew each other's names.

For more information about Naomi, please visit her at www.naomirawlings.com or find her on Facebook at www.facebook.com/author.naomirawlings. If you'd like a free novella, sign up for her author newsletter.

Made in the USA
Coppell, TX
02 December 2024

41502561R00236